VICTOR HEADLEY

D1437859

X PRESS BOOKS

First published 1992 by The XPress
This edition published 2018

ISBN 978-1902934-54-9

1 3 5 7 9 8 6 4 2

A CIP catalogue record for this book is available from
the British Library

This story is livicated
to the heartical black woman;
past, present and future . . .

For some reason, people always assume that it has to be something to do with music.

'You write songs?'

I laughed and answered I didn't any more, I write books now. The official gave me a penetrating look and a nod before returning my passport. I lifted my case out towards the exit.

The last time I landed in Jamaica, less than a year ago, I remember feeling less relaxed than today. *Yardie* had just been published, the press had gone over the top and got me into an awkward position, between a rock and a hard place, as they say. Just two days before I had faced a sizeable audience at the launch of the book; I still felt the after-effects of the experience.

Over eight months have passed since *Yardie* hit the streets. I can't say I'm glad it's over because it's not. Since returning from Jamaica last year, I have resisted all requests (i.e. pressures . . . !) to give interviews. Most people think I'm wrong, especially my publisher. Yet, despite that, I still feel reluctant about getting too much media attention. What I learned from the reactions of everyday people in the community and from the questions of the audience at the book launch, is that we, as Black people, need to talk to each other more, say how we feel and try to focus on the issues which determine our quality of life.

Most people, I think, still misunderstand my story. From the questions friends often ask, I sense that the story substance – the kinda thriller feel – is their focal point. My intention in writing *Yardie* was just that; to write a story set around our community. I didn't consciously realize it might get published. When it was, I was perhaps more shocked than the other readers. I read my own book again . . . What I realized then, was how close it appeared to our everyday reality; that got more people excited, upset some . . .

Six months passed, I travelled, then settled long enough to write another book. After many long and prolonged debates with The X Press, I had agreed to write a follow-up to *Yardie*. I shelved other projects and started writing. I got kinda possessed, involved in the essence of the story, again. Four months later I presented a huge pile of half-legible sheets to my publisher. That was it . . .

But for a little editing, this second book is the product of that period of enforced retirement, meditation, huge doubt and self-confidence.

This book is both a sequel to *Yardie* and an entirely new novel at the same time. Behind the storyline, the plot, the efforts of the characters to live up to their dreams or nightmares, there is one thing which I know to be true: the lack of alternatives always brings out the worst in anyone. That really is the morality of my stories. Because of deprivation, lack of opportunity and general sense of frustration, a great proportion of Black youth is resorting to 'any means necessary' to stay alive, to be able to afford the material trappings they see all around. It doesn't really matter whether they are born in Kingston or in Clapton, this Black generation has enormous potential and riches we can't allow ourselves to waste – not a drop of it!

Victor Headley
Rosehill, 25 February 1993

FORWARD

The winter wind paralysed everyone and everything under its spell, in suspended animation. Springtime came, children too and all things gathered momentum. Away in the sun, as one more season unfolded, shifting patterns sent their shadows dancing in hearts and minds.

The leaves dropped wherever they would, unpredictable, and people came and went to and fro. Fate, which some call 'luck', brings to naught the best intentions.

Still, the dice haven't yet stopped spinning . . .

DUST TO DUST

The sun had been playing hide and seek all morning. It would appear from behind the string of clouds for a short time, only to disappear again a few minutes later. A ray of golden sunshine sparkled through the windscreen and lit Lorna's face as it bathed the car in sunlight. She closed her weary eyes until they were once again in the shadows. On both sides of the tree-lined road lay rows of graves marked by grey stone and shining marble headstones, some covered with fresh wreaths, others adorned with simple bunches of flowers.

Lorna could feel no pain inside, only a kind of numbness. She hardly noticed when they drove past the old iron gates of the cemetery where she had just buried her heart alongside Tyrone. The church service, the slow procession of cars, the burial . . . It all felt like a dream. How can a woman accept in a week, the brutality of being robbed of sixteen years of her life? She had hardly heard a word the Methodist minister said. Not until the dull sound of handfuls of dirt hitting the polished wood of the casket jolted her out of the dream-like state did she realize where she was, standing amidst dozens of people, all dressed in black, all with sorrowful countenances, looking down at the freshly dug rectangular hole. Inside the wooden box with its brass handles, was her first-born, only just out of childhood. She didn't cry. Neither did Harry. She had heard him sob the previous night, alone in his room. Since his brother's death, he had consistently refused her company and chosen to stay by himself. He had sat silent and still throughout the church ceremony, his youthful face drawn and hardened by grief.

For Lorna, Harry's face remained the morning's most enduring image. He seemed much older than his fourteen years.

Chris, Lorna's brother, weaved the car in and out of the midday traffic, avoiding the busy high street where people carried on their business, oblivious to the tragedy in their lives. No one had spoken since they left the cemetery. Chris's wife Myrtle sat in the back beside Harry, repressing her muffled sobs with a handkerchief. Lorna had done all her crying during the week since Tyrone's death. She had no more tears left, only a gaping wound inside that had swallowed her feelings. They turned off Queensbridge Road and soon reached Haggerston estate, parking in front of the old red-brick block of flats where Lorna lived.

Once upstairs, Myrtle insisted on Lorna taking it easy while she made some tea. Harry declined his mother's offer to stay with them and went up to his room.

The living room of the first-floor flat was sparsely furnished but clean and brightly decorated. Pictures of Lorna and her sons, scenes of happier times, adorned the walls amongst posters of Bob Marley and African sculpted heads. The large mirror hanging on the back wall was turned to face the wall, a tradition of mourning which Lorna didn't understand, but which her mother had insisted on respecting.

Myrtle served the tea. They sat there, eyes on the television Lorna had switched on by force of habit. Even Chris had little to say. He sipped his tea in silence, glancing at his sister from time to time.

'Do you want something to eat?' Myrtle asked.

Lorna shook her head. 'Thanks, Myrtle, I'm al'right.'

The atmosphere in the room was heavy with suppressed words and unspoken thoughts. The awkward silence prevailed for a while, for none of the three had the heart for conversation. Yet they knew that life had to go on. They needed to stay strong and they needed each other to overcome the grief. Chris looked at his sister; he could almost feel the weight of the pain dragging her down, deeper and deeper into herself. Chris was three years older than her. They and their youngest sister Ivy had grown up very close together in east London.

An educated, intelligent and conscious man in his early thirties, Chris was always at hand whenever his help was needed, even if it was only to talk and help make sense of this often confusing life. Yet today he felt so awkward, unable to find anything to say that would make sense. He had three children himself, none of them by Myrtle, and he knew he'd surely go crazy if he was to lose any of them in similar circumstances. What frightened Chris the most was the change that was slowly taking place in his sister. Three days after Tyrone's death, Lorna had suddenly stopped crying. Since then he had been unable to figure out what was going on in her head, but he wanted her to know he was still there for her.

'Lorna, let's go and see Mum tonight, she expects us,' he said softly.

'I prefer to stay on my own, Chris, I need time.'

'You can at least come and stay with us for a while,' Myrtle offered.

Lorna didn't answer. She stirred her tea mechanically and leaned back in the chair.

'At least Peter came to his son's funeral,' she said suddenly.

Chris moved towards her. He hadn't expected her to come out with that.

'He is hurt also . . .' Chris started.

5

Lorna cut in, her face changing from anguish to anger.

'I don't know why he bothered. He was never there when Tyrone was alive.'

'Come on, Lorna. There's no need for that now.'

Lorna went on, her voice louder now as she rose to her feet.

'Maybe if he had done his job as a father Tyrone would still be alive . . .'

Chris frowned from behind his glasses. He had to stop her now, before she got out of control.

'Stop that, man. You know better than that!'

'Did you see him, crying like he's got feelings now?!'

'I said enough of that, you hear?!' Chris said firmly.

Lorna fell back in her chair, head bowed. Then Myrtle started to cry.

Chris sighed. He knew he had to be strong for Lorna, for their mother and for Harry, who would need him more now. When Peter had left Lorna, the two boys were only babies. Chris had helped her survive the crisis, acting as a father for the sons over the years. He disliked Peter as much as Lorna did; he could find no excuse for a man who abandoned his wife and two young children for a white woman. He dismissed Peter as a 'confused black man', like so many others he knew. For Lorna, the passing years didn't soothe the hurt. She had nurtured a deep hatred for Peter. Any mention of him made her mad.

There was silence in the room for a few minutes.

'Look, Lorna,' Chris began, 'Tyrone is gone, we have to accept that. It makes no sense blaming anyone but those responsible for his death.' He paused. 'Tyrone's not the first youth to die at the hands of the police, and he might not be the last. That's how we live here. Black life is cheap.'

'It was no accident, they murdered him . . .' Myrtle sobbed.

'Don't you think I know that? We never really realize that these things happen all the while, until it touches us personally.' Chris smirked. 'You know what will happen?' he continued. 'They'll have an inquiry, then they'll clear everyone of the blame and that's all . . . That's all we can expect.'

The sense of powerlessness that made it all the more horrible. The young man died, but it was no one's fault. Tyrone was alive and well until police had stopped him and his friend Martin, that Sunday night on their way back from the movies in Holloway. When the officers had accused them of being the handbag snatchers they were looking for, the two boys had understandably protested vehemently. Tyrone was a quiet serious youth, but he knew his rights and he was no thief. Why did the police officers abuse the youths? Why they forcibly threw them into the van was still unclear. They were taken to Hornsey police station and locked up in separate cells. When he woke up in hospital the next day, Martin told of how they were beaten in the van and recalled that after they were locked up, he had heard shouting and other noises in the cell next to him. Tyrone was dead; he had choked on his own vomit during the night.

Chris rubbed a hand over his bearded face. He worked in a community centre and knew the kinds of things the youths faced in the street. Many of them felt unwanted, aliens in the very town they were born in. What could you tell adolescents that would help them make sense of the confusion they faced, when school deceived them, parents misunderstood them and the police hunted them without cause?

'Lorna, you're coming home with us. It's better to stick together for now.' Chris had no intention of leaving his sister alone with her thoughts. Lorna looked up at him with

7

empty eyes. She nodded slowly. Chris caught himself thinking how much she had aged over the last seven days. 'Get some things together. I'll go and talk to Harry.'

Chris went upstairs to the bedrooms. Lorna was relatively easy to deal with, Harry would be a different proposition. He was only fourteen and had just lost his only brother. Despite all his experience, Chris wondered how he was going to help the youth make sense of that.

2

DANCING IN THE STREETS

'**L**ook, Mummy, look!'

The little boy tugged at his mother's skirt, pointing to the painted face and colourful headdress of the dancer gesticulating on the platform. It wasn't the first float Marcus had seen; dozens had passed by since they arrived at the carnival that Monday afternoon. The youngster was mesmerized by the elaborately decorated vehicles, their steel bands playing full volume, and the throngs of merry revellers trailing behind them.

'Yes, it's another float, Marcus,' Charmaine said patiently. 'Come.'

She took his hand and signalled to Jenny that she was ready to move. Carrying her own son, Jenny made her way through the milling crowd. They walked on and turned right towards the main stage a hundred yards or so away. The route was too congested, however, so they turned left into a side street.

With the bright sun (an increasingly rare bonus at carnival) blazing overhead, carnival Monday had brought hundreds of thousands of people to Notting Hill. Jenny and Charmaine had decided to make the most of the weather, and made their way down to west London with the children. They had walked around for about an hour before stopping underneath the flyover to watch a procession of floats drive down Ladbroke Grove.

The children were enjoying every minute of it. Marcus literally had to be dragged away from certain spots. So much activity, so many new things and colourful-looking people excited him, as they would any two-year-old. Charmaine was having a hard time answering his many questions. For Jesse, the experience was simply puzzling. Just one month short of his first birthday, the little boy kept looking quickly around him, taking in the strange cacophony with surprise. He wasn't afraid, though; they stopped once to watch a stage show and everyone watched with laughter and encouragement as Jesse rocked to the music, his small face serious as the beat moved him.

'We can't pass through there . . .' Charmaine remarked as they reached the end of the street. At the corner, to the right, a rave was in full swing, the dancers packed tightly, jumping with careless abandon to a frenetic hard-core rhythm. They stood there for a short while and watched the thick crowd of youths bouncing up and down to the frenetic pace of the tune, arms waving in the air.

The music was deafening, a mix of screaming voices, horns, bells and sirens over a galloping drum and bass track.

Charmaine looked at Jenny, frowning.

'Follow me close,' Jenny shouted above the din.

She picked up the bemused Jesse and headed for the other side of the road, keeping to the left, away from the mass of jumping, sweating bodies. They made their way through the crowd at the back of the rave.

Holding her son tightly with her left arm, Jenny used her right hand to make a path for herself through the unending crowds of people. The little boy looked on as his mother pushed her way through, looking over her shoulder regularly to make sure Charmaine and Marcus were still in tow. On the other side, the road which led to the main stage was relatively clear until the crossroads where the worst traffic was.

'Let's check this,' Charmaine said, nodding towards the main stage to her left.

On seeing the appetizing food on display, Marcus declared that he was hungry. The portly little brown-skinned boy was always hungry, which made his mother happy. It was a sign of good health and she was rightly proud of the way her son was growing fast. She bought him some fried plantain. Jesse only wanted a drink. Jenny bought him one and got herself some chicken and dumplings as Charmaine had done. They went and sat in the small gardens to the back of the stage.

Marcus soon finished his plantains and went to work on one of his mother's dumplings.

'This child is something else.' Charmaine shook her head.

Jenny laughed, looking at her own son sipping his drink. She sometimes wished he was craven like Marcus, but he only took food as he needed it, never more.

Under the afternoon sun, people of all nationalities came and went, walking through the garden, their laughter and shouts blending into the crazy mix of musical styles. From above, the whole area probably looked like an ants' nest.

Throughout the carnival area, on every street and in every square, groups of policemen and women hung around, their faces revealing varying emotions. Carnival represented the peak of the summer season and was thus one of those occasions which had them on edge. The police never seemed comfortable when a large group of black people congregated . . .

This afternoon though, things seemed relaxed. Inevitably, a few constables were seen dancing calypso, or at least trying, and there were good-humoured exchanges with many of the revellers. Carnival was the one occasion when a black youth could draw on a spliff on the street without a police officer going out of his way to book him.

'Let's try to reach the other side,' Charmaine proposed

after they had all eaten. Marcus needed to relieve himself, so she took care of that first. The crowd by the side of the stage through to the lower side of Portobello Road was now even tighter than it had been before. Charmaine and Jenny discovered that the best way through the teeming crowd was to let yourself drift along with the flow and then slowly, gradually, edge in the right direction.

They managed to reach the fenced-off path that led to the left towards All Saints Road. There the crush lightened a little. A group of youths, maybe thirty of them, walked by at pace, going down towards the barriers. The shaved tram lines in their designer haircuts, their string vests over T-shirts, baggy patch-jeans and heavy trainers sported by all reggae youths gave the crew a kind of uniform look.

Jenny, Charmaine and the children walked up. All Saints Road on the right was packed solid. Fifty yards along, a steel band on a float that looked like a pirate ship was 'hotting up' the area, making the already tight situation even worse. Jenny pointed up the road at a gathering in front of a row of terraced houses. A set had 'strung up' on the pavement, its stack of tall black boxes spread out and pumping out hard dancehall rhythms. The two women set themselves alongside the speaker boxes, facing the control tower, Marcus and Jesse in front of them. The two boys stood there for a while, looking at the throngs of people around them, but a few minutes later they were dancing.

Charmaine didn't recognize anyone, Jenny neither. Though they listened enthusiastically to the MCs taking turn to tease the crowd of dancers, they couldn't catch the name of the set.

A group of tourists, young white men and women in shorts, stopped to take pictures of some of the dancers. They seemed quite merry, happy to mingle with the moving crowd, visibly enjoying the unique opportunity to experience some black culture first hand.

'They need some practice.' Charmaine laughed, observing two of the women as they attempted to imitate the wild contortions of some of the 'rude bwoys'. A few heads turned to watch them, but it was all good-humoured. Marcus and Jesse, now fully in the mood, were having a great time. Two men came through the crowd and stopped.

'Wha'ppen, miss!' One of them smiled, looking at Charmaine. He nodded to Jenny.

Charmaine remembered meeting him with Charlie, but couldn't quite remember his name. He was short, with a broad, open face and wore a red and black Click shorts suit. His companion, of darker complexion, had a blue bandanna around his head, wide jeans and a string vest. Each had a spliff in hand and seemed to be enjoying the carnival to the full.

'Roughneck, touch me now!' The first man held out his fist to Marcus, laughing. Marcus smiled back and interrupted his dancing just long enough to answer the greeting. Jesse didn't pay the men any attention.

'So, whe' Charlie deh?'

'I don't know. I don't think he's coming here though.'

'You know which part Radical ah play?' the man asked.

'No, this is the first reggae sound we hear.'

The man explained that the sound he sought was from south London. He was only interested in finding Radical Hi-Fi. Meanwhile, his friend had been trying to get Jenny to respond to his lines.

'So . . . Wha'ppen browning? How yuh ah gwan so stush, man?'

He couldn't be blamed for trying. With her hair tied back, her slanted eyes and smooth skin, Jenny looked very attractive.

The short man turned to him and said a few words in his ear. Immediately the man's grin disappeared. He looked at the straight-faced Jenny and then glanced briefly towards Jesse. He stepped back a little.

'No disrespect, lady, y'hear?!'

Jenny said nothing. The man turned towards the crowd and lit his spliff.

'So wha'; we gwan find de sound, seen?! Hail de don fe me. Later.'

The two men took their leave and disappeared in the crowd. At the control tower across the road, the selector lifted up the needle. The dancers paused.

'Special request to all crews. Dis one brand new . . . good for you. Coming from de champion sound. Hear dis . . .'

The MC, a burly, brown-skinned man with dark glasses and a 'cut up' Malcolm X T-shirt, was gazing down on the crowd with a grave expression. The needle touched down on the vinyl; the clatter of the drum, then a bouncing computer bass rhythm came crashing out of the speakers. Behind his desk the selector was switching, pulling and pushing controls like a wizard. The crowd, including Marcus and Jesse, were back in action.

'You see how easy you can get rid of someone quick?' Charmaine smiled at her friend.

'Did you see his face?' Jenny said thoughtfully.

'Well, he must be new.' Charmaine paused. 'All he had to do was look at . . . he would have known . . .'

Jenny was silent for a while, absent-mindedly rocking to the music. She turned to Charmaine.

'So, even if I was interested, no man would want to deal with me . . . ?'

It was more a statement than a question. Charmaine raised her eyebrows.

'Unless he's crazy or very brave . . .'

Jenny shook her head. She looked at her son, jumping

14

with unconcerned abandon a few yards away. Charmaine was right; anyone who knew his father would recognize the features instantly.

By mutual agreement, the two young women never mentioned D. Whatever Jenny's feelings were, Charmaine had made it clear that there was no point talking about it. Once, Jenny had asked about Donna. Though she didn't know her name, she was aware of the 'other woman'.

'No sense in you worrying about that,' Charmaine had said. 'Besides, I've only seen her once, there's nothing I can tell you.'

A dozen police officers came by in single file, eyes working in all directions. One of them pushed his way through the noisy crowd and went to speak with the selector. From behind his dark glasses the MC looked on, visibly resenting the interference. The selector took up the microphone.

'The police dem seh everyt'ing fe lock up by seven o'clock, seen?!'

Catcalls and whistles erupted all around. The officers stood there, some of them shifting nervously on the spot as the crowd booed them.

Over the last few years, the police had managed to reduce the size of the carnival considerably. The streets near Acklam Road where sound systems used to string up had been made 'off limits'. Similarly, they had shut down most of the shebeens where in the old days ravers would return at night, after the daytime activities were over. There was even talk of shifting the carnival from its traditional Notting Hill setting and turning it into a park event! So much for a celebration of freedom . . .

'Opa, lift it up!' the MC thundered into the mike.

'Hold on, massive . . . yuh ah hear me?'

The music stopped. The whistling and shouting grew

15

louder. The mike in one hand, a bottle of Dragon in the other, the MC was staring directly at the police officer who had dared to interrupt the dance.

'Mek me tell yuh somet'ing, mista police . . .' The voice was deep, rough and hostile, booming out of the speakers.

'Carnival is fe black people to celebrate the end of slavery, seen?! So we don't wan' no police come try disrespeck we today.'

A noisy response from the dancers greeted the MC's declaration.

'And we nuh tek back dem talk!' he added, crossing his arms over his chest.

The atmosphere was getting hotter as the hyped-up, noisy ragga crowd started to shout out their displeasure.

The police had no choice but to make an undignified exit, followed by the taunts and mocking laughter of the crowd.

'Come in again, Opa, ah we run t'ings!' The MC was back in control.

The music rolled on again, the dancers visibly re-energized by the confrontation. Everyone felt nice, boosted.

'These people have no respect, y'know,' Charmaine said.

'They're just jealous of us.' Jenny laughed.

They stayed there a little longer, taking in the last of the August sunshine, moving in time with the rest of the dancers to the pulsating rhythm line, until Charmaine suggested that they should leave early to avoid the rush. Jesse came along quietly, but Marcus was unwilling to leave the dance. Charmaine had to get tough.

'If you make any noise, I'm gonna smack you in front of everybody,' she told the stubborn little boy.

Marcus considered the threat for a while, looking up at his mother's face. In the end he decided she meant it and followed her.

Near the train station, police on horseback were keeping a watchful eye on the groups of youths, boys and girls, pushing their way through the revellers. Some of the 'rude bwoys', inebriated as much by beer as by the general euphoria, just could not resist taunting them.

'Babylon ah play cowboy!' one of them shouted before mingling into the human whirlpool.

That night, the police clashed with several hundred youths around Ladbroke Grove Underground station. There were casualties on both sides.

3

WOMAN BUSINESS

The stallholder scribbled some figures on a piece of paper and looked up.

'Anything else for you, love?' he asked the young woman.

Sweetie looked at the stack of green bananas thoughtfully. She only liked the small, thin ones which taste sweet and turn pink when boiled. The ones in front of her were not to her liking.

'No, is a'right. How much for this?'

The burly red-faced man wiped his hands on his apron and started to add up as Sweetie and her friend Pam gathered the food into their carrier bags.

'Six pounds forty, please.'

Sweetie collected the change and the two women started up towards the High Street end of the market. Ridley Road was always crowded on a Saturday morning, especially in summer. Sweetie and Pam had got there early, but so had hundreds of other shoppers. Progressing through the noisy crowd, dodging trolleys and pushchairs, they made it to the busy main road.

'I wan' buy some t'ings in deh,' Pam said, looking towards the Safeway supermarket across the street.

The light turned red, allowing the throng of shoppers to cross over. Inside the store, Pam pushed her trolley along the rows of shelves, picking up various items as she went. The place was full, with shoppers taking time to chat with friends rather than just do their shopping and leave. The store was cool and nice, a welcome relief for those who had struggled through the crowded market-place with heavy bags.

Once Pam had everything she needed, the two women joined a checkout queue behind women with trolleys stacked high as if they were stocking food for a month.

'Imagine; 'nuff ah dem woman come yah every week and buy de same amount ah t'ings,' Sweetie said.

'Ah true.' Pam laughed. 'Dem coulda feed a whole family fe a month ah Yard.'

The queue behind them was getting longer. Only three more shoppers and it would be their turn, at last.

'Me nevah see queue like this till me come up yah,' Pam remarked.

Pam had been in England for just over a year. She was a good-looking, young brown woman in her early twenties. Tall, rather big, though not a *mampy*, she wore bright US-made fashion clothes, heavy gold earrings, several bangles and rings. Pam was quite attractive. She and Sweetie with matching hair-styles stood out as 'Yard women' amongst the shoppers.

'Yuh ah come airport with me on Tuesday?' Sweetie asked. Tuesday was the day Lee was flying in. Lee was Sweetie's man, they had known each other for years but they had only really started going out after Sweetie had come to England and met him again. Lee was a record producer and, because of his work, had to travel regularly between Jamaica, New York and London. Sweetie could understand that, but she hadn't seen him for four months and was understandably impatient for his arrival.

'Yeah, man, me an' yuh go dung dere!' Pam answered. They were next at the till now. The elderly white lady in front of them packed her shopping slowly into a bag.

'Fourteen pounds sixty-five pence, please,' the young, black checkout girl said.

The old lady stopped and took the purse from her handbag. Slowly, with shaking hands, she took out a twenty-pound note and handed it to the girl. She then tried to finish packing to get out of the way as fast as she could. She turned towards Sweetie.

'Sorry, love,' she said apologetically.

Sweetie smiled at her. 'Is a'right, lady, take your time.'

The cashier handed the old woman her change. As she was still struggling with the bag, Sweetie decided to help her.

'Take your money, I'll finish dat.'

'Thank you, thank you,' the old woman said with a warm smile.

The cashier turned her attention to Pam's shopping. The old white lady thanked Sweetie again and shuffled away towards the exit.

The cashier added up while Sweetie bagged Pam's shopping.

'Nine pounds four pence, please,' she said.

'Ah who de raas yuh ah look 'pon?' Sweetie heard Pam's voice growl. Swiftly, she looked up wondering why Pam had started an argument with the cashier.

But it wasn't the cashier who was the object of Pam's wrath. She was talking to a girl in the next queue. Sweetie looked at the girl; she was dark, slim, with her hair in extensions, tied up in a pony-tail. She was wearing heavy make-up and a tight mini-dress. Sweetie didn't know the girl, but guessed that the older woman beside her was probably her mother. From the tone of her voice, Pam had no love for her.

'Yes, yuh! Yuh lickle maaga dawg yuh! Yuh know who me is?!'

The girl didn't move. Her mother looked at her, then at the big brown shouting woman in turn. Everything had stopped; the shoppers in the queues, and the cashiers looked on bewildered.

'Cool now, Pam! What happ'n?' Sweetie tried to calm her friend down.

But Pam was getting hotter by the minute, more so because of the girl's futile attempts to ignore the large shouting woman pointing her finger threateningly.

'I gwan cut up your face, gal, yuh see me?! An' you can tell your lickle bwoyfriend me will do him so too, yuh ah hear me?!' Pam was now shouting at the top of her voice, which was naturally loud anyway.

She started out towards the girl, totally unconcerned about the stunned crowd around her. The girl was getting nervous, looking everywhere except towards Pam. Her mother said something which got lost in the flow of invectives coming from the big woman. Quickly, Sweetie went after her friend, getting to her just as she was about to reach the girl.

'Pam, easy now, man! Lef' it, it nuh worth it. Come, man, come . . .' Her arm around Pam's waist, Sweetie was doing her best to pull her away. Given her small size and Pam's large structure, that was no easy job.

'Say somet'ing, now, yuh dirty bungle,' Pam was taunting the terrified girl. Sweetie was still trying to prevent Pam from getting to her, pulling her by the arm now.

'Sweetie, lef' me nuh, man!' Pam started to resist, intent on grabbing her victim.

'Look 'pon her now!' Pam stared at the girl with total contempt.

'You bettah tell your sodomite bwoyfriend fe come send some money fe him pickney before him spend it 'pon a piece ah trash like yuh!'

It was then that Sweetie understood the cause of Pam's fury. She had a young baby for a man named Bunny, a musician. Unfortunately, their relationship had been a short one and he was now living with a bed girl. Pam had found out who it was and fate had brought them together in the supermarket that morning.

Anyhow, if the girl had said anything, anything at all, violence would have already taken place. The crowd was still watching, frozen. Just as Sweetie was beginning to lose patience, and strength to hold back her friend, a voice behind her said:

'Yaow! Nuh budda wid dat!'

Sweetie turned around, Pam also; the voice was rough, commanding.

'Yuh know bettah than dat, Pam. Come!'

Norris, for that was the man's name, took Pam gently but firmly by the hand and started to pull her away from the girl.

'Mek I box her two time, nuh, man!' Pam was still prepared to vent her anger. But Norris was no man to be argued with; tall, dark, dressed in a multi-coloured vest and designer jeans, he took control of the situation. Although he wore sunglasses one could sense the strength of his gaze still, by the way his face remained expressionless. He dragged the reluctant Pam outside the store, the crowd looking on intensely. Quickly Sweetie went back to the abandoned shopping bags, paid the stunned cashier and walked out.

Outside, Norris had a frowning Pam standing against the railings, lecturing her.

'Yuh know bettah than gwan dem way deh, Pam, man. This is England; yuh don't deal with dem t'ings in public, seen?!'

Pam was still vexed, but Norris was one person she had to listen to.

'Yuh know seh ah dat deh dutty gal Bunny ah spend

him money 'pon. Me feel fe all cut her up . . .' Pam tried to justify her action.

Norris looked at her from behind his shades. He smiled slightly.

'So tell me somet'ing. Is money yuh wan' from her?'

'No, but . . .' Pam started.

'Den, leave her alone. Dat is between yuh an' Bunny, seen?!'

Pam didn't answer. Sweetie looked at her.

'Pam, hear me now: don't evah do me dat again. I don't care who de gal is; yuh don't gwan dem way deh!'

Pam saw that Sweetie was not pleased with the whole thing.

'Is a good t'ing yuh come, you know, Norris. Dat mad woman was going to beat up de girl in deh.'

Norris shook his head.

'Is pass me ah pass, you know, and me see the whole supermarket stop. When me look, nuh my girl yah ah try fe mash up de place?' He turned to Pam.

'Yuh ah hear me; go home and cool yuhself. Ah foolishness dat.'

'Me tek her home, don't worry,' Sweetie told him.

'T'anks, y'hear, sah?!'

'Cool, man. Later!'

Norris walked off. Sweetie sighed and looked at Pam.

'Come, miss, shopping done fe today.'

4

COUNTRY LIFE

'ilfred, come yah!'

The little boy took his eyes off the bird in the tall mango tree for a moment. His mother's voice had broken off his concentration and he knew he might as well not try the shot. His friend grinned and made a move to take the slingshot from him. Wilfred kissed his teeth and elbowed him out of the way.

'Move, man. Ah my shot!'

It was not wise to make his mother wait, Wilfred knew that only too well. Still, he raised the slingshot and took aim with one eye closed. The small bird was still busy picking at the fruit. Wilfred held his breath and, after a last adjustment, let the stone fly off. It hit the tree limb with a sharp sound, sending the bird into a hurried flight. Wilfred cursed and tossed the slingshot to his friend before running out towards the back of the house.

'Wilfred!'

He reached the outdoor kitchen area where his mother was preparing dinner, just as she called again.

'Yes, Mum . . .' Wilfred put on his most innocent look.

'Wha'ppen? Yuh nah hear me call yuh first time?!'

'Yes . . .'

The woman finished stirring the food in the large dutchie with a wooden spoon before turning towards the door. She took out a crumpled note from the pocket of her loose cotton dress.

'Go buy some butter up ah de shop.' She handed her

son the money. Wilfred left her and ran up the little lane that cut across the neighbour's yard to get to the road. Meanwhile, Cassie took the pot off from the coal stove and placed it on the wooden table beside it. Dinner was ready.

The big, orange sun gradually set itself behind the dome-shaped hill at the back of the house. The day's heat subsided, the cool breeze from the distant sea announcing the mellow evening.

Thomas soon come back from the farm, Cassie thought as she went for some plates inside the house. A rather large dark-skinned woman in her early thirties, she lived in the house with her husband Thomas and their four children.

She glanced into the bedroom. Vernon was sprawled across the bed still asleep. She decided she had better wake him up. Standing at the door, she called out loudly.

'Vernon!'

The man didn't move.

'Vernon!' She raised her voice some more. This time the sleeping man stirred. A third call woke him up. Cassie knew how to use her lungs well . . .

'Vernon, dinner ready.'

The man looked up and met Cassie's eyes. Rubbing a hand over his face, he propped himself up with an elbow.

'A'right . . .'

'Is how yuh so tired, man?!' Cassie laughed.

He looked at her, scratching the short stubble on his cheeks.

'Bwoy . . . me do some work over the farm with Thomas dis morning.'

Cassie shook her head, smiling.

'Thomas ah farmer from him ah yout' yuh cyan follow him,' she said. 'Come, man, yuh mus' hungry.'

She left him to gather his thoughts and went to the next room for the plates. He got up and went out of the house to the small shower area fenced by three sheets of zinc. He undressed and turned on the tap. There was nothing so sweet as the feeling of the cool water in the early evening, after the heat of the day. That morning he had sweated on the farm, digging holes for the suckers under the hot sun. Thomas had told him that the rains would start in a few days, now was the right time to plant. It took them the best part of the morning to prepare the patch where Thomas wanted to plant his crop. Thomas was a big man, over six feet tall, with large shoulders and a bearded face which exuded honesty and determination. He had spent all his life working the fields as his father had done before him. It was hard, demanding work but it was all he knew and through his toil he managed to take care of his family.

Like everywhere else in Jamaica, the soil here was rich and a man could grow anything he wanted to. There was more than enough land to work; both Thomas's mother and father came from the same area. They had raised their nine children from an early age to provide for their own needs. Thomas's siblings had all left the parish for Kingston, some had even emigrated to America. Yet Thomas had elected to remain in Harmony Vale, in the hills of St Ann where he had grown up.

D. had just finished drying himself when he heard Thomas call him from the house.

'Vernon, whe' yuh deh?!'

Thomas done work! D. thought to himself. He hung the towel on the clothes line and went inside. Thomas was on the veranda at the front of the house, still calling.

'Vernon, wake up, man!'

D. sighed; he'd been here almost six months and still couldn't get used to that name. No one had called him that since he had left Harmony Vale as a six-year-old boy to join his mother in Kingston. His maternal grandmother had given him her own father's name as a middle name and since she had raised him while he was in Harmoney Vale, it had stuck to him.

D. put on some clothes and went out on the veranda. Sitting in one of the wrought-iron chairs, his heavy 'mud-up' work boots off, Thomas was busy emptying the crocus bag he had brought back from the farm.

'Yes, iyah!' D. greeted his cousin. Thomas looked at him briefly, his bearded face lit up with a mischievous grin.

'Wait! De work mash yuh up, man.'

'No, sah.' D. sat on the low veranda wall.

A row of sweet peppers, skellions, two pumpkins, several dasheens and a bunch of callaloo adorned the concrete floor.

'Food, my youth!' Thomas announced proudly. 'The stuff of life.'

D. nodded. Finally, Thomas pulled out a folded crocus bag from the side pocket of his heavy cotton work trousers. He unfolded it slowly and took out a bunch of herb stalks. The buds were as thick as a man's finger, light green in colour with red-brown specks. Carefully, Thomas separated one of the stalks from the bunch and handed it to D. The buds had a pungent aroma, something like fresh peppermint but more biting.

'Young sensi,' D. said.

With the nail of his right thumb, Thomas extracted a few seeds from one of the buds.

'Dat green sensimilla will boil good tea,' he remarked, rubbing the herb in his palm. 'De indica plant dem soon ready too, y'know.'

Indica was of an even higher grade than what he had brought home. Beside the vast array of foodstuffs Thomas grew, he always planted a crop of prime ganja, more for his personal use than for trading. But, if necessary, he could sell a few weights of herb and make extra money to pay for the children's schooling or other expenses. Cassie usually sold the food in Claremont market. On the whole, the farm produced most of the family's food and the sales paid for the light bills and water rates. They were not rich, but they never went hungry.

Wilfred appeared at the corner of the house. He greeted his father, then proceeded to carry the food to the kitchen. Wilfred was almost twelve years old, tall for his age, with the same deep-set eyes as his father. His older sister Lisa was fifteen and living in town with some relatives. Ricky, who was nine, and Joseph six, were the two youngest boys.

'Ma ask if ouno ready fe dinner?' Wilfred asked when he returned.

'We ready, man.'

Thomas and D. went to the pipe to wash their hands. Dusk was coming over the gully with the same imposing silence that always preceded nightfall. Soon the crickets would begin their symphony.

'Me see your gal up de road,' Thomas said, handing D. the soap.

'My gal?' D. asked, seemingly puzzled.

Thomas looked at him eyes sparkling.

'Yuh t'ink seh me nah know your move, man?!'

D. laughed, shaking his head.

'Me nuh know wha' yuh ah talk . . .'

Thomas dried his hands.

'So wait; dat fit brown gal who live by de church ah nuh your t'ing?!' he asked, eyebrows raised.

D. turned the pipe off.

'Oh, dat deh gal . . .' he said, trying to sound unconcerned.

'Heh, yuh gwan like yuh smart. Nut'n is never a secret fe long; 'member dat!' Thomas was relishing his moment.

D. looked at his cousin squinting.

'Bwoy, me an' her jus' ah talk. Yuh know dem whe' deh?'

Thomas laughed.

'Dem and Cassie is family, y'know.'

D. remembered the girl mentioning that much. They went back on the veranda. The lights had been switched on, darkness had started to creep all over the valley. Wilfred and Ricky brought the dinner on trays; roast breadfruit, salt fish and callaloo, big flour dumplings and sweet potato; the food smelt and tasted delicious. D. ate heartily. He had gained weight in the past few months and that was a good sign. When he had first arrived in Harmony Vale, Cassie had taken one look at him and declared that he was 'maaga bad'. Thinking back on it now, D. realized he must have looked really thin and drawn. It had taken some time and a lot of patience and care to bring him to where he was now; fit, healthy and feeling good about himself.

'Everyt'ing a'right?' Cassie came from inside the house. Thomas nodded, chewing vigorously.

'Cassie, yuh a wicked cook, fe real. Me mus' find a woman like you,' D. said, biting into one of his dumplings.

'Enh?! I feel seh yuh start work 'pon dat already . . .' Cassie spoke matter-of-factly. D. looked at her briefly. He got back to his food. The two men ate in silence, visibly enjoying the meal. From inside the house the sound of the radio filtered through, the day was over, all was peaceful, still. Beyond the lit-up area around the veranda, the night had taken over. As usual, a pack of skinny dogs had gathered around the house, watching them eat. Every evening as the food was served, they would come and watch every moment, waiting for the scraps that would surely come their way. And every evening, D. couldn't resist throwing one small piece of dumpling in their midst to watch them fight over it. Tonight, though, by the time

29

Thomas and D. had satisfied their hunger, there wasn't much left to throw them.

The children took the plates away to the kitchen. Thomas got up and stretched.

'Yes, Vernon; yuh see how country life sweet?'

'Ah nuh lie.' D. went to the pipe to rinse out his mouth. Meanwhile, Thomas picked up the herb he had been cleaning before dinner. It was time for a good spliff. He pulled a couple of tobacco leaves from his shirt pocket.

'Hol' a pronto nah, man.' He handed one to D.

'No, sah! Dat deh t'ing too rough fe me,' D. declined, pulling out a sheet of Rizla.

Thomas laughed and rolled his spliff. He sent Wilfred for some matches. The boy would always hang around his father and circle whenever possible. He was eager to learn men's ways and watch them smoke and talk, waiting for the time when he could behave as a big man. The white smoke rose in the night air as Thomas drew on the short, fat spliff. The mix of raw tobacco and prime sensimilla was strong, too strong for the uninitiated, but Thomas had been smoking nothing else for years. D. had tried the mix once, when he first arrived, but the first pull had raked his throat, sending him into a coughing fit for several minutes.

'Yuh ah town man, yuh nah ready fe dis,' Thomas had teased him about it for days afterwards. The two men smoked in silence for a while, enjoying the aroma of the herb. Once in a while someone would pass the gate and call out a greeting. Thomas would answer. A group of youths walked by talking and laughing. The sound of their voices faded as they walked down towards the village square.

'Yuh goin' to the wake?' Thomas asked after a time.

D. blew out some smoke, pondering his answer.

'Is best to go out an' pay respect, y'know,' Thomas remarked.

Miss Winnie, one of the oldest people in the community, had passed away two nights before. Like most people living in the area, she was also a relation. She was well beloved by all and had lived to be almost a hundred years old. Some older folks insisted that she was in fact a hundred and two! As in all small rural communities a death was always occasion for a social gathering. Old and young congregated round the deceased person's yard, bringing food and drinks and generally 'celebrating'. It was rarely a sad occasion, especially if the death was a 'natural' one. Should anyone die in suspicious circumstances, however, the old folks in the village would gather and talk amongst themselves in hushed voices of 'obeah', the dreaded witchcraft, and discuss what measures should be taken to avoid retribution from the deceased's duppy. Such things were part of life as death is, and time and progress had no effect on the vitality of these African traditions.

'I gwan pass dung dere later,' D. said finally. He remembered Miss Winnie from when he was a boy, a tall dark black woman with laughing eyes. I will go and pay respect, yes, he thought to himself.

Like all Jamaicans, no matter how removed they were from their rural background, D. was superstitious. There was no reason to disrespect the dead and risk incurring the wrath of their spirit. He disliked funerals and his face hardened as he recalled his mother's several years before. She never recovered from the death of Jerry, D.'s older brother. She weakened gradually, complaining of pains in the stomach, spending her days lying down or sitting in a chair staring aimlessly. She had been a staunch Christian, but stopped attending services at her local church in Greenwich Town. She passed away within two years of Jerry's death. As she requested, her family arranged for her to be buried in Harmony Vale near her parents and relatives. That was the last time D. had visited the Village before now. A cold sensation crept over him. He lit up his spliff and drew deeply.

Thomas got up, yawning. 'I gwan hol' a fresh,' he said.

D. remained there alone, his back against the rugged plaster of the wall, retracing his steps since his mother's death. A stream of images unfolded in his head, each one with its own particular flavour. There he was again in the streets of Kingston, making a name, working his way up from the posse, earning respect. Then the big day at the airport, his flight, leaving Jamaica like a bird fleeing the fowler's snare. Then London, the famed city . . . From then on the pictures had a different quality. More hazy colouring. He saw himself driving his gleaming machine through the dark cold streets of London. He remembered the smoky places, the faces of friends and foes juxtaposed like in a child's collage. The film rolled on in D.'s head, but now the images were more defined, individualized. There was Donna's face, sad, fearful, then the long corridors, the cells, the bleak life in the bounded world of a foreign jail house. For almost five months he was locked up awaiting his trial date; during that time the police had visited him often asking him countless questions, offering him deals – all to no avail. D. knew very well that their only chance of having him convicted depended on one particular witness testifying against him. Although his situation was precarious he wasn't really worried. Doing time in England, where his reputation alone could get him almost anything he wanted, the months had gone by fast. Then the trial date was set. Although he didn't have much contact with his people outside, he felt confident on the day and went in front of the female judge looking relaxed. Sure enough, the prosecution witness didn't show up. The police were fuming. D. smiled at them. He wasn't really surprised when his lawyer told him they were checking his immigration status and eventually he was served with a deportation order. So one sunny spring morning, D. was put on a flight back to Jamaica accompanied by two detectives. Under the circumstances, D. wasn't too happy to find himself back home, but it was better than being locked up for murder, he reflected. On his arrival at Kingston, the Jamaican police took him in and locked him up again. The conditions there were radically different, overcrowded, squalid and brutal. He met a few former friends, but also many enemies. Another unwelcome change was the drug situation. While in prison in England, D. continued to use cocaine. For a don like him, getting it in was no problem. Where he was now was a totally different scene. Soon he started to feel the changes in his body and mind. At night sweat drenched his body and he'd wake up choking and aching. Most of the time he was in a sombre mood, brooding and quick to get angry. The conditions in the jail and the uncertainty about his future only made things worse. That was probably D.'s darkest hour.

The solution came unexpectedly one afternoon. D. was in the prison yard, killing time, waiting for another day to tick by when one of the wardens called him in.

'Yuh had a visit,' the man said unsmiling.

D. frowned, his mind racing. Mus' police again. More bad news, he thought. The guard led him into a small room and locked the door behind him. Sitting on the wooden table inside was a big man dressed in well-cut slacks and a ganzee. He was clean-shaven, sporting a pair of dark shades, looking straight at D., his head slightly tilted to the right.

D. felt many things go through his mind in those few seconds of silence. Surprise was one of them.

'How yuh doin', missa D.?' There was no anger in

Skeets's voice, there never was. To anyone who didn't know the two men, the greeting sounded almost cordial. D. nodded slowly.

'A'right, y'know,' he said unconvincingly.

Skeets was still staring at him. He took in D.'s unshaven, sallow face, the torn vest, the crumpled trousers and shook his head sighing,

'Yuh used to look sharp, man,' he said almost sadly. 'Wha'ppen to yah?'

D. felt really uncomfortable for once, but not because of his appearance. All along he had known the day would come when he had to face Skeets, and now here he was.

'Sit down, man, sit down . . .' Skeets pointed to a bench against the wall.

D. complied, looking up at Skeets as he sat. He couldn't see the man's eyes, but even that would be no great help to guess what was in his mind. Skeets was the most unpredictable man D. had ever known. It was one of the main reasons that he was so respected and feared. Somehow he managed to out-think his opponents, to outwit them. Right now D. was on the receiving end and he didn't enjoy that at all. He'd rather Skeets cursed him and told him what he had to say. But the man was in no hurry. He got up and walked up to the small window which overlooked the prison yard.

'I didn't expect fe see yuh back here fe now, y'know. I hear seh yuh was doin' a'right. . . ?' Skeets said, looking outside.

Why de man cyan stop playing games? D. wondered to himself. He was getting increasingly edgy.

'Certain t'ings happ'n,' he let out evasively.

Skeets spun around to look at him, his hands in his pockets.

'Certain t'ings?!' Skeets smirked, emphasizing the words. 'Yuh reach ah foreign and turn fool . . .' D. noticed that the voice had turned colder now. Skeets walked back towards the table. He sat back. 'All dese years I show yuh how fe run t'ings, I try to teach yuh how fe survive.' He paused. 'Tell me somet'ing; yuh evah see police hold me?' Skeets was looking down at D. from behind his shades. 'Rape . . . murder . . .?! Yuh is jus' a lickle common criminal!'

D. said nothing, he was looking towards the window, waiting. Skeets had taken off his glasses and placed them on the table. He got back up and walked to the bench. He stood over D.

'Stand up, man!'

D. got up. Despite himself, he had to look into Skeets's face. The eyes were deep, still.

'Yuh know why your life mash up so?' Skeets asked softly. 'I tell yuh why; yuh lick too much shit and fuck up yuh head.' The voice had grown louder. D. tried to avoid the eyes boring into his. Skeets was right in front of him, too close for comfort, towering over him.

'Ah nuh dat. Somebody try fe kill me,' D. said, looking straight at the man now.

He didn't see it coming. Without warning, Skeets slapped him across the face with the back of his right hand, hard. D. lost his balance and went crashing down on the bench, hitting the back of his head against the brick wall in the process. He tasted blood in his mouth. Still dazed by the blow from the big man, D. felt a large hand, gripping him on the throat, pulling him upright. Skeets had him against the wall, holding him by the neck, D.'s face right up against his own. There was no anger in his voice when he spoke.

'Listen an' listen good; if I did want yuh dead, yuh would dead long time. Right now 'nuff ah yuh enemies dem wan' dun yuh, an' since yuh deh ah jail it's ah easy job.'

Skeets paused and sighed, taking his eyes off D. for a

brief moment, seemingly thoughtful. His hands were still pressed against D.'s throat, holding him up. He continued. 'Why yuh disrespect me, I don't really know.' He held up his hand as D. was attempting to speak. 'I wan' yuh fe 'member somet'ing. Yuh might be a big man out dere an' nuff people 'fraid ah yuh, but me grow yuh an' I know seh yuh no bad enough fe me yet.' Skeets kept his eyes deep into D.'s own for a few seconds after he stopped talking. Finally, he let him go.

D. slumped on the hard bench and coughed, wiped off some blood from his lower lip where Skeets's ring had cut into the flesh. Skeets looked down at him, shaking his head. As calm as ever he pulled a packet of cigarettes from his pocket, lit one and handed it to D. before lighting one for himself and sitting back on the table. Slowly D. placed the cigarette in the left corner of his mouth and pulled. He felt numb, his head empty. The conditions he was living under, the lack of food and the withdrawal symptoms had weakened him. Just now, he had come as close to fear as he had ever felt. He tried to steady his breath, keeping his eyes down to avoid Skeets's stare. The men sat in silence for several minutes.

'Ah gwan give yuh a chance . . .' Skeets said firmly. 'Yuh know why? Because yuh mudda was a good woman, God rest her soul.'

D. didn't really want to hear anything about his mother. He pulled nervously on his cigarette.

'Everybody can make a mistake and I believe yuh have potential.' His voice went slightly colder as he spoke. 'But hear me now, anyhow I hear seh yuh start use drugs again, I will kill yuh myself, yuh understan' dat part . . . ?'

D. looked up at Skeets; he believed him.

'Yes, sah!' he said meekly.

'A'right, now listen; I can get yuh out ah here, but yuh cyan stay in town, even I cyan protect yuh from Lancey . . .'

D. frowned. He had totally forgotten about that one . . .
For the first time Skeets let out a short, hollow laugh.

'Yes, man, Lancey ah Detective Inspector now, an' him know whe' yuh deh too. I surprise him nevah visit yuh yet.'

D. pulled on the cigarette, aware that he was in more danger than he had thought. Skeets got up holding his glasses.

'I'll get yuh out in a few days, I want yuh to go ah country and stay dere until I saw out t'ings fe yuh, seen?!'

D. nodded and stood up. He took the packet of cigarettes Skeets handed him and hid it in his shorts. Skeets took a few steps towards the door, then stopped and turned.

'Tell me somet'ing: yuh know seh yuh ha'fe repay what yuh owe, don't?!'

'Yes, sah, dat ah nuh no problem. I will call my people dem ah foreign.'

'Good, I will see yuh soon. Take it easy nuh.'

Skeets put on his shades and banged on the door with his open palm. The guard unlocked the door for him and he stepped out the room.

'Yuh know, Vernon, the herb have yuh away.' Thomas laughed.

D. hadn't noticed his cousin coming and his voice shook him out of his trance. He looked around and realized he was still in the cool, safe haven of his native village. He stood up.

'No, man, I jus' meditating 'pon certain t'ings.'

'So wha', mek we go dung at de wake now?'

'A'right.'

They left the house and walked down towards the centre of the village under the moonlit sky. The area around Miss Winnie's house was crowded. Groups of young people stood in the semi-darkness, talking around the gate, while in the yard proper relatives, adults and older people were seated around the small thatched hut where the coffin was lain. Miss Winnie's daughters and granddaughter were busy greeting new arrivals and serving food and drinks. D. followed Thomas into the yard to pay their respects. Cassie was already there helping with the food. The whole affair felt rather like a happy occasion. Everyone talked and drank, greeting friends and acquaintances. Children ran around – happy to be allowed to stay up late. The only crying came from a big brown-skinned woman seated at the foot of the coffin, a glass in her hand, tears streaming down her face. She wore a flowing white dress with a red waistband and a white knitted head-tie. Oblivious to the activity around the yard, she kept quoting passages from the Bible and stood up at regular intervals to 'salute' the departed sister, glass in hand. From time to time, she would use the large white kerchief in her hand to wipe away her tears. Everyone else, including Miss Winnie's daughters, seemed composed about the way things were taking shape. Once the guests had eaten and drunk their fill, the elders in the yard started a singsong, joined by all who knew those old-time rhymes. The youngest ones were pleased to hum along, swaying to the rhythm patterns woven by the warm voices. D. had politely declined the offer of a glass of rum from one of the women serving and he had settled for a hot beer. As the second song started, he slowly walked out of the yard and into the road. As he exchanged a few words with a local youth, he heard a call from behind.

'Vernon . . . ?!' D. stopped, turning and looking in the direction of the voice which came from the low stone wall that bordered Miss Winnie's house. He took leave of the youth and walked down, peering into the darkness.

Maas Zack was sitting alone, his hands resting on his knees, surveying the courtyard from his vantage point.

'Good evening, Maas Zack,' D. greeted the old man.

'Good night, me son!' The old man smiled. D. sat beside him.

'So, how yuh nuh dung dere wid de people, sah?' he asked.

'De place full a'ready, man. Right yah is a good spot,' Maas Zack said. He spoke with a nasal sound and one had to pay close attention at times to understand everything he said. People said Maas Zack was over ninety years old. He had grown up in the village and had left it only once to tour the world – for thirty years! He'd been to England and America and also Panama and other places he would sometimes mention. Sometimes when he was in a talkative mood, he would recall the days when he had lived in Harlem, in the days when the 'great black redeemer' Marcus Garvey was organizing his people for the 'promised land'. By all accounts, Maas Zack had lived an eventful life and he was one of the most respected elders in the community. Another reason for this was his uncanny ability to 'reach' and heal people. He was a very private person, though, and lived alone in his hilltop house on the outskirts of the village. Yet when all else failed anyone with a serious health or 'mind' problem could come to Maas Zack. It was Zack who, at Thomas's request, attended to D. when he arrived from town gaunt and sick. The old man had known both Thomas and D.'s fathers and their grandfathers. D. had stayed at Maas Zack's house, a rare privilege, for three weeks. There the old man had fed him a diet of fruit and vegetable soup and health drinks, tirelessly tending to him during the long sleepless nights when D., bathed in sweat, had purged himself of the poison. He was forced to drink bitter potions and went through 'hell and back'. After three weeks he gradually began to feel stronger. The nausea disappeared, and he slowly started to put on weight. He practically owed his life to Maas Zack and he knew it.

'So how yuh feel, man?' the old man asked after a moment.

'Good yuh know, sah. I feel 'trong, now.'

'Nice . . . nice.' Maaz Zack laughed. They both listened as a new song started in the yard. Some people were standing rocking on their feet, arms moving, while others still sat raising their glasses occasionally in response to certain verses of the song.

'A nice funeral dis . . .' D. heard Maas Zack mutter as if talking to himself. He had to admit that it was, as everyone seemed to be enjoying it. 'Miss Winnie will be please, yes, sah!' the old man continued.

D. was quiet for a while; despite himself he felt almost hypnotized by the chorus of voices rising in the night. He could feel vibrations flowing through his body like a soft breeze, caressing his neck and his arms. Almost despite himself he heard himself say:

'An' fe her dawtas, dem look pleased too.'

Maas Zack turned towards him, his eyes sparkling in the dark.

'Dem have cause fe be pleased, dem mudda was a respectable woman.' Maas Zack paused. D. waited. 'De children ah de livin' testimony . . . but the good works, the memory, the good name she left behind – dat is de testimony before God.' The old man cleared his throat, and suddenly D. felt his hand lightly but firmly on his arm. 'Yuh see dis,' Maas Zack said, his eyes firmly on the coffin laying neatly inside the little hut. 'No matter who yuh is, when de time comes an' yuh life force fly away, dem res' yuh dung same so . . .'

Maas Zack drew back his hand, but D. didn't feel it. His eyes were set on the circle of light, the cloth-covered box and the chanting people around it. Only when the echo of the last verse of the song had died down was he able to take his eyes away and turned to his right, but Maas Zack wasn't there any more. D. squinted; a little distance away the frail silhouette was melting into the depth of the darkness.

5

ROUGHNECK LOVE

'Now, dis is . . . a special . . .'

A tentative drum roll and two bars of music filled the smoky space, then stopped abruptly.

'Dis . . . is de wicked, rugged and dangerous Firefly, exclusively on Radical Hi-Powah. Selector!'

After a little more teasing from Max, the selector, Radical Hi-Powah let off the 'special', loud and heavy through the set of boxes covering the relatively small club. There was an enthusiastic response, especially from the dressed-up pretty girls in the audience. Firefly was the ladies' favourite at the moment. The special sounded criss too. Firefly's potent high-pitched voice carried the lyrics on the gliding bass line. For the past three months, Radical Hi-Powah had consistently packed out Rocco's on Thursday nights. The place got so hot, tight and smoky by three o'clock in the morning that ravers often had to be carried outside.

Yet, that was nothing compared to the masses of people that found their way to Radical's dances on Saturday nights, or rather early Sunday mornings. Only High Noon, the long-established reigning sound, could claim to match Radical for attendance. And even this was the subject of much debate. Certain people would swear that Radical now ruled the area. It was always unwise to disagree with them.

Though Rocco's was only a small, nicely decorated club, as many people would pack the place as would fit into a large four- or five-roomed house for a blues dance on a Sunday morning. As a result, nights like tonight were for the fittest of the fit. Pressed from all sides by moving, sweaty bodies, Linton's height enabled him to see where he was going. Standing at six feet plus, he stretched his neck, squinted through the smoke and located the man he was looking for on the other side of the bar. Linton gently pushed a big, pretty girl out of his way, shoved a little harder past two men, kissed his teeth a couple of times and let out a few loud curses before he finally made it.

'Gimme two hot Guinness.'

The girl behind the bar had a sleepy look. She took out the bottles, opened them and took the money from Linton. He, meanwhile, had spun around looking through the crowd, trying to locate Puggy. He couldn't see him anywhere.

Linton took the change from the barmaid. Holding the bottle high up, he pushed on alongside the bar, disturbing a tightly embraced couple, rocking by the concrete pillar. Frowning, the man looked up, thrown off beat, but quickly decided he had better concentrate on his dancing. Linton got through and found his friend in a darkened corner.

'Yaow, Supa!'

The girl let go of her partner reluctantly.

'Yes! Respeck, my yout'.' Sticks thanked Linton and took his Guinness, his left arm still around the girl's shoulder. She stood in front of him, hoping that Linton's intrusion would be brief.

'Which part Puggy deh?' Linton asked.

Sticks shrugged. 'I t'ink seh him deh wid yuh. Him come ask me fe de car key lickle while ago.'

Linton took a sip from his bottle, looking around. 'I gone!' he announced eventually.

'Look, if yuh see Puggy, seen . . . ?!' Sticks began. 'I don't want him fe cause no problem again.'

Linton nodded and left.

The tunes kept coming hard and fast. Max was throw-

ing down dancehall fillers by Capleton, Ninjaman, Zebra
. . . Mixing non-stop, 'lifting up' regularly as he teased the
dancers.

'Radical the roughneck sound! Ah we rule . . . Special
request to the south London crew. Hol' dis . . .'

Sticks looked at the girl. She was short, but as he
explained to Linton, 'very fit'. He felt good, sipping his
Guinness, back to the wall, in the packed club. He and his
crew usually came down to Radical Hi-Powah most Thursday nights. He wiped some sweat from his brow with his
rag. He felt wet through to his vest, even though he had
unbuttoned his white silk shirt much earlier. The girl was
taking in the music, dancing close in front of him. They had
talked little. Sticks wasn't really in a talking mood tonight.
Still, he was dancing and had decided he would go home
with her tonight. Linton could take care of things.

Sticks wondered where Puggy was. He searched
around the crowded, misty club but couldn't see him. The
girl looked up, wanting to speak in Sticks's ear. She only
reached to his shoulders. He bent down.

'What's your name?' she asked.

'Michael,' Sticks answered, sizing her up and down.

Dressed as she was in a black sequinned, sleeveless
short dress with high heels and make-up, it wasn't easy
figuring out how old she was. However, her large eyes were
clearly trying to elicit some information about the man she
had been dancing with for the last hour.

'Why d'you wear sunglasses?' she asked.

'Why, yuh don't like me glass?!'

'Are you hiding from someone?'

Sticks played along with her without giving much
away, amused by it all. Girls always tried at some point or
other to find things out about him. He would usually just
give them some story they might believe and everything
would be sweet. He felt nice tonight, but lazy. For the first

time in about a year, business was going smooth with no problems at hand. Though he still scanned the room regularly by force of habit, since the treaty with Chin's people, things had been quiet.

He took a long sip of warm stout. He didn't feel like staying at the club.

Me an' dis gal bettah leave soon, he thought to himself, dipping into his trouser pocket and pulling out some money. He handed the girl a note.

'Go an' buy a drink. I soon come.'

She looked at him, took the ten-pound note and nodded.

'Don't talk to nobody!' he whispered in her ear before disappearing into the crowd. He headed for the stairs all the way across the packed room. People were pushing in all directions; some trying to escape the heat, others wanting to join the mass of dancers in the crowded space towards the back. A man of Sticks's status couldn't imagine not getting through by priority. He edged his way forward, pushing, easing off, squeezing past dozens of less important clubbers. He finally managed to reach the stairs, climbing up past the cloakroom and out the main entrance. The night air felt nice and fresh after the sweat bath downstairs. For September, the weather was good. The cold wind would be back within a few weeks though . . .

Sticks located two friends sitting on the bonnet of a car. He walked down.

'It col' out deh, eh, man?!'

'Wha'? So wha' yuh ah seh, don?'

'Cool, y'know.' Sticks grinned at the two men. They lived in west London, but the club attracted people from all over. One of the men, Johnson, handed Sticks a printed card.

'Yuh mus' come check me, Supa!'

44

Sticks examined the card. It advertised a Caribbean take-away food shop.

'Wait, ah yuh dat?!'

'Yes, mon! We jus' open las' week.'

'Yeah, mon! Me check it out.' Sticks tucked the card in his back pocket. Linton was coming down the road behind the line of parked cars, with Puggy a little way behind, a girl at his side. Sticks finished his Guinness and dropped the bottle.

'Wha'ppen?!'

Linton laughed, turning back towards Puggy and the girl coming after.

'Me find de yout' an' a gal ina de car! Right by de roadside, y'know.'

Linton found it real funny. Johnson and his companion also. Sticks simply glared at Puggy and his tall, slim, Lycra-dressed girlfriend. Puggy casually adjusted the red Kangol hat on his head.

'Star whe' yuh a deal wid?' Sticks asked sternly. The girl slipped past them and into the club, fast. 'Wha' ah gwan?'

Short and dark with a genial smile, Puggy didn't seem to know what Sticks meant. He was only fifteen years old and had arrived in England from Jamaica with a visiting sound two weeks before. Puggy was a singer. He had had several records released over the past months. Two had made the charts and he was consequently engaged on a promotion tour. He had already performed a handful of shows in and around London. Apart from recording 'specials' for various sets and some PAs in clubs such as Rocco's, he spent most of his time making trouble . . .

Unfortunately for Sticks they were related, which meant he had to try his best to keep the youth safe until he returned to Jamaica. In the last week alone, Puggy had caused a fight in a record shop by refusing to pay for some forty-fives and then had to be rescued from an irate local hustler whose girlfriend he had tried to molest. Sticks shook his head.

'Dis in Inglan', yuh know. You cyan do dem t'ings soh.'

'Bwoy, de girl ready fe me, mon . . .' Puggy protested, still smiling.

'An' hear me now; don't use my car fe dem t'ings, seen?!' Sticks said sternly.

They all laughed except Sticks. Puggy was hard to keep up with. Sticks *bigged up* Johnson and departed, following Linton and Puggy back inside the club. On his way down the stairs he saw his girl (he didn't know her name) at the bar, engaged in a loud argument with a curly-haired, broad-shouldered man. A small crowd of onlookers watched bemused as the girl tried to ignore the shouting man.

'Hey, dat's my gal!' Sticks shouted above the music. Puggy beside him was suddenly interested.

The girl turned to the barmaid and collected some change. At that moment, the man poked her in the back, unwilling to cease hostilities. She turned immediately and said something, looking him straight in the eyes. Though he couldn't hear the words from where he was standing, Sticks could read on her face that they had to be coarse. The music was still pumping, but more and more people were gathering around the bar to watch the encounter. As the girl turned her back the man poked her again, this time harder, and shouted something. It happened so fast, no one anticipated it, least of all the angry, curly-haired man. One moment, the bottle of white Canei wine was on the counter, the next the girl had snatched it, turned and raised it and smashed it down on her attacker's head with all her strength.

Sticks saw it all as if in slow motion. The man was so

stunned, he probably didn't even feel the impact of the blow immediately. He just stood there for a few seconds as people watched in disbelief. Then thick blood started gushing out of the large gash above his left eyebrow, down his face and on to his shirt. Meanwhile, the girl had slipped by him, pushed her way through the crowd towards the stairs and the exit. Once he realized what had happened, the man flew into a rage and attempted to pursue her, his blood now dripping on the floor. A few women screamed as he staggered in their direction, others ducked out of the way. A couple of men rushed after him, pulling him back as he tried furiously to grab the girl a few yards away in the crowd. He tried to shake them off, but the two men had him firmly. Sticks meanwhile had come across, followed by Linton and Puggy. The girl saw him and came his way, ducking safely behind him as the crowd parted around them. The music had stopped.

'Yaow! Ouno gwan go fight outside!' Max commanded in the microphone. 'Don't come ah Radical, distress the vibes.'

It now took several men to hold back the wild, cursing, bloody man. Safely behind Sticks a few yards away, the short 'glamour' girl sneered at him unsympathetically.

'I told him to leave me alone,' she explained.

'Just cool, mon,' Sticks assured her.

The man was still cursing, but he had now lost a lot of blood and seemed to be weakening.

'Let me go! Let me go . . . I'll kill her!' he hollered.

'Take him out, mon!' Puggy ordered loudly. 'Yuh nuh see seh de man ah blood-up de place?'

'Carry him go ah hospital, him done rave fe tonight,' Sticks quipped. He seemed to enjoy the incident.

People debated the incident throughout the club as the man was marched up the stairs and out. The atmosphere had relaxed following the sudden explosion of violence. Serious fights were common at Rocco's. On a couple of occasions guns had even been fired inside the premises.

'So wait, I leave you five minutes an' yuh have a fight wid man!' Sticks grinned at the girl. She looked at him, but didn't answer. There was no fear or remorse in her eyes, only defiance. 'Me love a girl weh defend herself, still,' Sticks said.

The crowd had resumed what they came to do; dance to the sounds of Radical Hi-Powah. Sticks led his little group to the bar and bought some drinks.

'Hol' dis.' He handed the girl a Canei. 'An' don't hit nobody wid it, seen?!' He laughed.

Puggy drank his Guinness. Linton took his and left to go and dance at the back.

Sticks had found the girl nice-looking but a bit dull earlier on. Now he looked at her differently; the way she handled the disturbance had increased his interest in her. Puggy pushed his hand past him pointing at the girl.

'So wha'ppen? Yuh find any friend?'

Sticks looked at him.

'Just cool nuh, man! Buil' a spliff.' He handed Puggy a Rizla and continued talking to the girl.

'Yuh nuh tell me your name yet . . .' he whispered in her ear.

'Soni,' the girl answered.

'Seh wha'?'

'Soni! It's short for Sonia.'

'Oh . . . So wha'? Dat bwoy yuh kuff 'pon de head is your boyfriend?'

'I used to go out with him last year . . .'

Sticks took a swig of his Guinness. He passed Puggy a bag of herb, then turned his attentions back to the girl.

'Is wha' him want wid yuh?'

Soni shrugged.

'He's always after me, trying to get me back.'

'De way yuh kuff him head t'night, he mus' come back fe yuh . . .' Sticks warned her. The girl kissed her teeth defiantly.

'Let him come! You think I'm scared of him?!'

Sticks laughed. He continued talking for a while.

'Do remember; next week Thursday, same place, same time . . . Sound called Radical Hi-Powah, with crucial Firefly and PA by Puggy out of JA.' Radical Hi-Powah was in the last hour of the Thursday-night session, mixing dancehall tracks back to back. On the floor, it was the best time; early morning shakedown to tease the ravers just before they went home. For Sticks, in tune with his new conquest, it felt like time to leave. He sent Puggy to locate Linton.

'Which part you live again?'

'Holloway.'

The girl seemed more relaxed and had been laughing at Sticks's jokes. He sauntered over to the bar and bought her a brandy and Babycham and another Guinness for himself.

They stood close together, not really dancing. Sticks caressed the girl's bare shoulders with his fingertips while whispering sweet nothings in her ear. By the time Radical had spun the next record, he had no doubt in his mind that they were going home together.

Linton and Puggy came back. They waited until most of the crowd had gone before making their way upstairs towards the exit. Outside, dawn was breaking. The ravers returned to their cars, taking leave of friends, sharing a last joke before going home. In front of the club small groups still congregated, talking and finishing their drinks. Sticks leant against a car, his arms around Soni. Glancing to her left, he noticed someone sneaking stealthily behind, anxious to avoid being seen. Sticks let go of Soni and spun around, his face suddenly hardened.

49

'Linton!' he called, tracking the disappearing man from behind his glasses. 'Deal wid dat bwoy fe me!'

The man stopped in his tracks, realizing that he had no chance of escaping.

'Wha'ppen, Supa. I was going to check you, y'know . . .' he began unsteadily.

Sticks threw him a scornful look and turned back to Soni without a word. In a flash, Linton had pounced on the man, holding him down by his shirt collar, pinning him firmly against the car.

'Yuh look like yuh hiding, man . . .'

'No, man! How me fe hide?!' The man tried to laugh off Linton's accusations.

'Listen good; if yuh don't pay what you owe today, it's your head me ah come for? Yuh understan'?'

'Yeah, man! Today? No problem.'

The man was visibly scared, though he tried to stay composed. Sticks paid no attention to what was happening on the other side of the car. He knew Linton would make the debtor see his point. A handful of bystanders looked on. No one laughed or commented, Sticks was known as a cantankerous character with a short fuse. Only a fool would risk getting involved in something that didn't concern him.

Linton let go of his victim who disappeared hastily. Sticks decided it was time to go. Still holding Soni he walked down the street in the misty morning, Linton and Puggy following him.

'That's your car?!' Soni asked as they stopped in front of the gleaming black Saab convertible.

'Yeah, man, yuh like it?' Sticks smiled. He was really proud of the beautiful machine he had bought only three weeks before. Linton got into the driving seat, Puggy beside him, whilst Sticks continued sweeting-up Soni in the back.

They dropped Puggy off first in Stamford Hill, where he was staying, and made their way down to Leyton, where

Sticks and Linton had moved when Hackney had become too 'hot' for them after the upsurge of police activities that followed D.'s arrest. In the space of a few months the police had cracked down on everybody, taking pictures on the front line, filming people's cars and generally making it impossible to operate safely. Everything had to be reorganized and most of D.'s crew had relocated to new addresses. Since then Sticks had been in charge of their operations, controlling things on the street, dealing with supplies, collection and security. Charlie was content with keeping a low profile by 'administrating' the business from his new base in Camden Town.

'That's not the way to Holloway,' Soni remarked. After the excitement of the night she had begun to sober up.

'We gwan drop off my bredrin first. Relax!' Sticks assured her.

A bright, early morning sun had risen above the rooftops as they drove through the quiet town. Linton drove through some narrow back streets before parking in front of a two-storey house, with plants and shrubs neatly lined along the tiled garden path. Sticks stepped out of the car. Soni followed him.

'Take me home, Michael . . .' she begged sleepily.

'Come inside and check out my house.'

'I can't. My daughter is going to wake up soon.'

'Wha'?! Yuh have baby already?!' Sticks exclaimed.

'Yeah, my mum's keeping her.'

'Well, dat cool then. Come nuh, man!' Sticks pushed her gently but firmly towards the front door of the house.

'I have to get home, seriously.' Soni tried to convince him to drive her home, but Sticks had other plans. He cajoled the girl, pulling her, joking, teasing . . . He eventually managed to overcome her feeble resistance and got her inside the house.

'Hear dis; stay a lickle while then I'll drive yuh home.

It's still early, yuh know,' Sticks said, locking the door behind him.

The music carried through the living-room speaker boxes. Linton was in the kitchen, looking after his breakfast.

'Sit down, mon. You wanna drink or somet'ing?' Sticks tried to make Soni comfortable. She looked around the nicely decorated room and sat down gingerly on the leather settee. Sticks popped into the kitchen and returned, switching on the TV. He noticed Soni sitting upright, her eyes opened wide.

'Wha'ppen t'yuh?' Sticks followed her eyes. On a shelf between a potted plant and the stack of cassettes lay a silver automatic handgun.

'Oh . . . ah dat yuh ah look 'pon? Ah nuh nut'n. Ah nuh nut'n . . .' Sticks insisted, sitting beside Soni and running a finger over her neck and earlobe playfully. But the girl's eyes kept on staring at the weapon.

'Is it a real gun?' she asked somberly.

'Nuh, man; a toy dis!' Sticks laughed.

Soni didn't buy that.

'It is a real gun . . .' she said as if convincing herself. 'What you doing wid dat?'

'It's my bredrin piece, man. Him keep it for protection.'

Soni turned to him as he lay on the comfortable settee.

'You have one too, ain't it?'

It wasn't really a question. For the first time, Sticks took off his dark glasses. He smiled at the girl.

'Relax, mon; yuh safe . . .'

Clearly Soni didn't feel safe. Linton brought in some hot drinks, fried plantain and fried egg sandwiches. The two men ate but Soni only sipped some tea then watched TV for a while. Linton decided he needed some sleep. On his way out he nonchalantly picked up the gun from the shelf.

'Take me home, now,' Soni demanded.

'How yuh a gwan so, baby?! We soon drive out.' Sticks got up, walked over to the wall unit and turned over the cassette.

'Yuh smoke?' he asked Soni.

'No, I don't.'

Pulling out some Rizla, Sticks built himself a cocktail spliff while moving to the beat, observing the girl. He lit up and pulled on the spliff before sitting down again.

'Listen, man, me really like yuh, y'know?' he told Soni in a soft tone of voice. 'Me an' yuh can spar . . . But hear wha'; me is a man who run certain business, seen?! So I wan' know seh yuh is the right kind of girl fe me. 'Nuff gal try but nuh ready. I feel seh, me an' yuh coulda get on.'

Sticks observed Soni's reaction closely as he spoke.

'From yuh is my bonafide yuh get anyt'ing yuh want . . .'

Something told her to resist, get up and leave, yet she stayed, listening as he conquered her resistance with flattering words and promises as he massaged her neck and shoulders. He soon took her to the point where she could not say no. A little more teasing, a little more squeezing and rubbing and she forgot all about the daughter her mother had babysat.

When the kiss was over, Soni's sequinned dress lay on the floor, and the murmur of the television blended in with their breathless noises.

6

REBEL SOUL

A few pupils were still hanging around the hall chatting and laughing. Lorna knocked lightly on the glass of the small office at the left of the entrance. Inside she could see two women talking, one of them sitting over a typewriter. Apparently, neither had heard anything. Lorna knocked harder, this time both women looked up. One of them came over and opened the glass window. 'Can I help you?' she asked smiling.

'I have an appointment with Mrs Nichols.'

'Your name is . . . ?'

'Thomas,' Lorna said.

'Please have a seat, I'll let Mrs Nichols know you're here.' The woman closed the window and picked up the phone. Lorna walked to the row of plastic chairs against the opposite wall and sat down. Chris was busy reading from the large notice-board across the hall. Lorna had called him at work earlier that day and asked him to accompany her to Harry's school. She sounded confused and angry on the phone; all he could ascertain was that Harry had been suspended and the head teacher wanted to see her. It wasn't the first time such a problem had occurred; Lorna always called him to help her with the children's schooling. Chris didn't mind. Lorna was his younger sister and he knew she couldn't really take care of everything by herself. Since the children's father left home, she had relied on him increasingly to discipline the boys and generally supervise their education. From the start, Harry had been the one causing problems. Somehow, he always found himself in trouble, whether in school, or on the street. Chris had always taken care of the boy, talking to him, helping him occasionally and punishing him if it was called for. Twice already during his school years, Harry had been suspended for fighting, but this time it seemed more serious. He was now at secondary school and should have grown out of this behaviour. Besides, he was barely one month into his first term there . . .

Chris sat down beside Lorna.

'Remember; hear what they have to say first. And keep calm, OK?' he said. He knew his sister only too well; she was as nice a person as could be, but tended to lose her temper easily when pushed. She was aware of that and therefore always asked Chris to accompany her to these types of meetings. The first time Harry had been in trouble at school, only Chris's swift intervention had saved an insensitive teacher from being beaten up.

The woman who had spoken to Lorna came out of the office.

'Mrs Nichols will see you now. If you would please follow me . . .'

They got up and walked down the long corridor to the headmistress's office and knocked. She opened the door and showed Lorna and Chris in.

It was a rather small office, with bookshelves, framed official documents and a painting of a stern-looking white-haired man on the wall. A middle-aged woman with glasses stood up from behind her polished desk and introduced herself.

'Mr and Mrs Thomas? I'm Mrs Nichols, headmistress. Please have a seat. Her voice was rather high-pitched, snobbish. She definitely wasn't from east London . . . She held out her hand, giving Chris and Lorna a limp handshake before sitting down again. Chris and Lorna also sat. Mrs

Nichols shifted some of the papers on the desk in front of her, cleared her throat and looked up.

'I see that your son is not with you . . .' she started.

'No, he didn't want to come,' Lorna said.

'I see . . . Well, I'm sorry to have to meet you in these circumstances, we're dealing with a rather serious matter.'

Lorna was trying her best not to dislike the woman on first impressions, but her affected tone and the way her eyes kept shifting up and down made that difficult.

'What exactly has Harry done?' she asked calmly.

Mrs Nichols peered down at her papers. Chris watched her silently, the woman looked at him briefly, then at Lorna.

'Your son threatened a member of staff and consequently I had no choice but to suspend him.'

'What d'you mean "threatened" a member of staff?' Lorna asked.

Mrs Nichols shifted in her seat.

'Well, he was very abusive towards one of his teachers and actually threatened to . . . assault him. I'm afraid we cannot tolerate this kind of behaviour in our establishment.'

Lorna stared at the headmistress hard, making her more uncomfortable.

'Look, I know my son is sometimes hot-tempered, but if he did what you say he did, there must be a reason.'

His hands crossed over his lap, Chris listened, intent on allowing Lorna to handle the problem as long as she kept calm. Mrs Nichols cleared her throat once again.

'Mrs Thomas, I can assure you that . . .'

'Miss, actually . . .' Lorna cut in.

'Right . . . Well, Miss Thomas, I've spoken to the teacher about the incident and he's quite shocked by your son's behaviour.'

Lorna sighed loudly, she gazed towards the window briefly. Chris was watching her, wondering how much longer she would contain the anger he could see rising inside. Mrs Nichols started again; 'Your son objected in . . . well, strong terms to certain topics on the curriculum. He also used very abusive language towards the teacher. I think it's very important you should talk to him and make him understand that he needs to respect other people's point of view—'

Lorna didn't let her finish. Straightening up in her seat she said, 'Let me tell you something: first, I don't have a clue what you're talking about so you better tell me straight. Second, I don't need to make my son understand nothing. He's almost fourteen and he can make up his own mind about things. Now, if you have a problem . . .' Lorna stopped, feeling Chris's hand upon hers.

'I think what we have here is a misunderstanding,' Chris said amiably, looking at Mrs Nichols. 'Tell me,' he looked at the woman smiling, 'what is the whole story?'

The headmistress seemed relieved by the timely intervention. She ventured to ask:

'You are . . . ?'

'I am Harry's uncle. I "stand in" for his father.'

Chris's manner was still cordial, though he stressed 'stand in' to drive home his point. He added politely: 'You see, contrary to certain beliefs that all black people are one-parent families . . .'

Mrs Nichols was visibly disturbed by the reference, but Chris continued.

'As I was saying, I raised Harry and I know that he can be difficult at times, but I'm surprised that he should have to be suspended.'

'Well, sir, as part of the new curriculum we teach pupils to respect other people's cultures and lifestyles.' Mrs Nichols paused. 'The incident happened during a class discussion on sexuality. Apparently your, erm . . . Harry disrupted the class and used abusive language towards the teacher who happened to be of a minority group.' Mrs

Nichols paused, waiting for Chris's reaction. Lorna stared at her intensely, but the woman resolutely avoided her eyes. Chris remembered Harry mentioning something earlier on about not going back to a 'batty man school'. He waited a little.

'You mean the teacher in question is a homosexual?' he asked. Mrs Nichols took off her glasses.

'He's gay, yes.'

Chris looked at the headmistress; she looked flushed, uneasy.

'I know that we can't change the curriculum in your school,' he began. 'I also know all about this idea of a multi-cultural society and the so-called "equal opportunity" policies you're talking about, believe me. But I want you to understand something. The majority of black parents don't really want their children to learn about practices they don't agree with. Because of these . . . topics you teach here, my nephew is refusing to come back to school. As a result, you have another fourteen-year-old black pupil who is likely to lose interest in education and find himself running the streets. Don't you think it's disturbing?'

Chris stopped, letting the question hang in the air. The headmistress searched for an answer. She hadn't expected an articulate black man, one who would put the problem in a perspective she had never bothered to consider. She tried to find something intelligent to say, but there was nothing she could think of.

'I think we have covered everything here,' Chris said matter-of-factly. He signalled to Lorna. They got up and walked out, leaving a confused Mrs Nichols still sitting behind her desk.

Back in the car, Chris changed the cassette on the stereo. They drove home through the drizzle, neither speaking more than the odd word, lost in their own thoughts.

'I want you to talk to Harry,' Lorna said as they entered the estate.

'And tell him what?' Chris sighed.

'He still has to go to school.'

Chris parked the car. They went up to the flat. Inside, music filtered down from upstairs. Lorna went in the kitchen and made some tea, while Chris sat in front of the TV, thoughtful.

'Harry left his dinner . . .' he heard his sister say. She came into the living room and placed a steaming cup in front of Chris and sat down.

'He's never hungry lately,' Lorna said dejectedly.

'Don't worry so much; he'll eat when he's ready.' Chris had noticed how Lorna had started fussing and worrying about Harry more than usual since Tyrone's death. Harry was the youngest and she always treated him like a baby.

Yet as she had tried to get even more motherly towards him, to get closer to the only child she had left, Harry had become more distant and even more prone to silence than before. He would come home late most nights, then shun his mother's company, preferring to lock himself up in his bedroom with music. Chris sipped his tea as he watched the daily catalogue of disasters, crime and gloom on the news.

'Chris, you're not listening to me . . .'

He turned towards his sister.

'What did you say?'

'I'm worried about Harry, he doesn't speak to me, he stays out late all the time, I can't get through to him.'

'You've got to give him time. You know how much he misses Tyrone. You'll have to deal with it somehow.' Chris tried to allay his sister's fears. The tragedy had affected all of them.

'D'you hear this?' Lorna pointed upstairs. 'That's all he

does, every day; playing records and deejaying over them. That's all he's interested in. It's driving me crazy.'

Chris shrugged. 'They all do it, believe me. Right now, these kids take music seriously. Too seriously sometimes. Harry needs to release his anger, his frustration. Anyway, at least he's got something to relate to. Don't worry too much, OK?'

'I thought we would be even closer because of that, but Harry just refuses to talk about it . . .'

'Come on, Lorna, he's just fourteen. Boys change at that age. They turn man. To lose his brother now is just too much for him. But he will learn to cope, he just needs time, y'understand?'

Though he tried his best to put things into perspective, Chris could see that he really didn't reassure his sister. Just then they heard the bedroom door open and footsteps on the stairs. Harry came down followed by Rodney, his closest friend. Rodney was a tubby, good-natured fifteen-year-old boy who lived on the estate. He and Harry had known each other since primary school.

'Good evening,' Rodney said smiling. Chris and Lorna answered him. Harry went to the kitchen while his friend stood in the middle of the room hesitating.

'Sit down, Rodney,' Lorna offered. The boy sat on the settee beside Chris. Harry came back with a carton of juice and two tall glasses. He sat down opposite his mother.

'You left your dinner again,' Lorna stated.

'I'm not hungry . . .' Harry poured some juice in each glass and handed one to Rodney.

'You need to eat, look at you. I'm sure you've lost weight . . .'

Chris looked at his sister.

'Harry can't get fat like Rodney,' he said jokingly, trying to ease the atmosphere. Harry said nothing. 'We went to the school,' Chris said finally.

'Yeah?' Harry didn't seem interested.

'So what you thinking of doing now?'

Harry's face was hard, he looked at his uncle.

'I'm not going back.'

Chris tried not to sound too pushy.

'You can't leave school yet. We've got to work out something.'

Lorna held her knees with both hands, watching her son. Harry was in no mood to talk about school, especially now, but he liked Chris and respected him. He turned to his uncle.

'Look, Chris, I can't take their schools, they're all the same, anyway. They're racists.'

'Come on, man; you still need some for the things they teach you there.' Chris wanted to keep Harry talking, expressing himself. 'What do you think, Rod?'

The chubby youngster grinned; he would have preferred not to have been asked. Harry was his friend and he couldn't really come out against him.

'Well, it's hard to keep on going sometimes,' he said quickly. 'Some of the stuff is interesting, but they still treat us like kids.'

Lorna kept quiet, unwilling to stem the flow of the discussion.

'How's that?' Chris asked.

Rodney was warming up slowly.

'I mean we know the streets, right?! We know the world is not what they teach us, but most of the times we can't express ourselves. Any time we disagree, they say we're . . . what's the word . . . disruptive. They don't respect us.'

Chris looked at the two boys, nodding despite himself. He found it hard to disagree with them. He had the same problem at the youth club where he worked. How do you give youngsters who have already been victimized faith in the system? He tried to compromise.

'You're right; I know they don't teach you reality, but black people got to get an education, otherwise we'll always be down.'

Harry looked at Chris thoughtfully, then he spoke, his voice calm but clearly bitter.

'Tyrone was one of the best pupils in the whole school, but even that couldn't help him . . .'

Lorna's eyes met Harry's for a brief moment. This was the first time he'd mentioned his brother's death since the funeral. Reminded of the sorrow, she felt tears welling up in her eyes. Rodney shifted uncomfortably in his seat. Chris couldn't think of anything sensible to say in reply. Harry got up.

'We're going out, see you later.' He motioned to his friend.

'Goodbye.' Rodney followed him.

Lorna and Chris heard the door closing behind the two boys. They remained there silent, Harry's words echoing in the room.

7

THE RETURN OF A DON

I t all looked the same; the busy streets with people walking by fast and the impatient roar of car engines in the midday rush hour.

A bus ground to a halt, a flow of passengers poured out on to the pavement, some boldly dodging the slow-moving traffic to cross the road. One of a dozen bicycle couriers darting in and out between the cars narrowly missed a woman as she emerged from behind a van. She cursed the rider.

A group of schoolchildren in dark-grey uniforms filed past the car, some eating chips out of greasy paper cones.

The shrill sound of a siren suddenly erupted a few yards behind, cutting through the noise of the street. The police car managed to squeeze its way through, the insistent wailing sending vehicles into the bus lane. As the siren faded in the distance, Charlie edged the Mazda back into the re-forming line of traffic and turned to his passenger:

'. . . Always busy,' he quipped.

D. smiled but said nothing. Charlie had picked him up from Gatwick Airport a little while earlier. They were now reaching the outskirts of London on this breezy, grey September afternoon.

D. had remained quiet throughout the car journey, though he had clearly been glad to see Charlie waiting by the barriers in the airport lounge. Charlie guessed that D. had a lot on his mind.

Charlie had received D.'s call from Jamaica early one morning six months earlier. He was happy to hear that his friend was out of jail, and had no problem fulfilling D.'s request to settle his 'obligation'. But that was business. They hadn't really had time to talk. Then nothing. Charlie didn't hear any more from Jamaica until a week ago when D. called to announce his arrival, charging Charlie not to let anyone else know. And now, here he was, seemingly absorbed by the sights of London town, or the bounce of the ragga beat from the speakers . . .

It had been a long trip. Now, back in the familiar greyness of England, D.'s mind drifted, focused on nothing and everything.

All through the flight from Montego Bay, he had been similarly occupied, backtracking lazily through the last few months, people, places and moves . . . and himself; still alive, still free, and about to get a second break . . .

D. had eased up from talking business in the car. He had asked Charlie only about Charmaine and Marcus, then mostly answered his partner's queries about Jamaica. Charlie could see that the time out in Jamaica had done D. some good; he looked bigger and fitter in his designer denim outfit. D. told him briefly about the country life he had enjoyed back-a-yard. He was even briefer on Skeets.

'We soon reach now,' Charlie said.

D. looked around, remembering that Charlie had mentioned moving to Camden Town.

'So, how dis area stay?' he asked.

'Nice, it's kinda quiet, y'know.' Charlie took his eyes off the road for a few seconds. 'Since last year, a lot of t'ings happen,' he started. 'Ev'rybody had to shift.'

'Yeah?'

D. was listening, his head against the seat top.

Charlie took time to explain the changes that had taken place since D.'s arrest the previous year; the police crackdown on the street scene, the raids, the turf disputes with Chin's people, the emergence of local gangs flexing in on the trade . . .

D. smiled faintly.

"Nuff t'ings happ'n, fe real!' he remarked.

'Yeah, business has changed, man.' Charlie paused. 'I tried to reorganize, but it's not as easy as before.'

'So yuh have problems?' D. asked.

Charlie took a right turn before answering.

'Since the front-line mash-up everything's scattered, everybody's dealing all over the place.'

For a moment only the music floating inside the car disturbed the men's thoughts.

'Wha'ppen to Chin?'

D.'s voice was totally relaxed, as if it was a normal question.

Charlie let out a short laugh.

'We had some problems with them at first. That got the police even more excited. Right now, we've got an arrangement, a kind of treaty.'

D. said nothing. He was quietly studying his companion.

Charlie slowed the car down and edged to the left, parking alongside a two-storey house near the end of a dead-end street. He switched off the ignition.

'Check this out,' he continued. 'Chin left for New York a couple of months ago, so his people are really quiet, you know what I mean?!' Charlie's lips curled in a half-smile. Then the smile vanished as he looked straight at D.

'Don't worry about Chin, D. I've got him covered, trust me . . .'

Charlie opened his door and got out of the car. D. joined him on the pavement as he took the small suitcase from the boot. Charlie had explained that the neat little white car was Charmaine's. He had bought it for her, but drove it while she was practising for her driving test. Using less conspicuous vehicles was one of the necessary adjustments to the current climate. 'Low profile,' Charlie had said. He slammed down the boot.

'Come on, let's get in.'

D. followed him up the tiled front area and inside the house. Charlie closed the door behind him.

'You like the style?' he asked as D. spun around to admire the fully mirrored wall.

'Yeah, man. Looks pretty.'

'Charlie?' Charmaine's voice called out from upstairs.

'Yaow, come down, baby!'

As he called her, Charlie waved D. inside the kitchen, motioning him to keep quiet. Charmaine came down the stairs.

'Where are you?'

'Right here.'

Charmaine pushed the kitchen door, her eyes fell on Charlie's smiling face. Then she caught sight of the figure to his right . . . It took her a few seconds to regain her voice.

'What?! D.! Hi, how are you . . . ?'

She rushed him with a big hug. Charlie laughed; Charmaine was certainly surprised! D. enjoyed the shock on her face.

'Why didn't you tell me?' she scolded Charlie gently.

'It was a secret, man!'

Then she started firing questions at D.

'You look bigger . . .'

D. laughed.

'Give the man a break, he's just landed!' Charlie interrupted.

'Yeah?! Sit down, you're staying for dinner?'

'Well, I'm not saying no; I couldn't touch the plane food . . .'

Charlie led the way out to the living room. D. sat on one of the large two-seater chairs. Beyond the television he could see a spacious garden with a few trees and a pond.

The walls of the living room were covered with striped,

velvet-look paper, and paintings – one of a fully attired bejewelled African queen – completed the tasty impression. At the centre of the room stood a nest of black and white marble-topped tables, above which hung a set of golden wrought chandeliers. Several waist-high sculpted wooden figures gave the place a baroque yet 'cultural' feel. Charlie programmed the music centre atop a high shelf above the brick fireplace.

'Here you are, D., have some juice.'

Charmaine walked in and placed a tray on the table. She smiled at D. again, clearly delighted to see him, then left the two men alone. D. took one of the two glasses and emptied it. The juice was sweet and cool.

'I don't know how you feel about it,' Charlie said, sitting himself down, 'but I was thinking you could stay with us, for a while at least.'

'Yeah!' D. answered thoughtfully.

Charlie sipped his drink. He paused, looking for the words.

'I think you should keep low at first and try to "feel" how things go.'

'It's true . . .' D. put down his glass.

'Apart from anything else, things have been rough since you left, but we still manage to turn over, you know?! I've got your cut set aside . . .'

D. appreciated the gesture; a man like Charlie was hard to come by. Many would have taken advantage of the situation; after all he had no way of knowing whether D. would make it back.

'Respect, Charlie, man. Me love how yuh ah gwan!'

Charlie smiled.

'It's OK, man. You'd do the same for me, right?!'

'Charlie, me an' yuh ah breddah.'

D.'s eye caught the clock on the wall in front of him. He'd been back in England just about three hours and he wasn't too sure how he was feeling. At least he still had Charlie by his side. That was good to know.

'So how de team stay?' D. asked. Charlie had gotten up to switch on the television.

'We still have the same people except Blacka, who's gone to America to produce music, and Slinga . . .'

'Wha'ppen to him?'

'He got locked up shortly after they sent you out; he got caught after a shootout in south London.'

D. shook his head.

'I heard t'ings did bad out deh . . .'

'You're right about that; we had to get rough with Chin's people, they were everywhere.' Charlie sighed as he told D. about the 'war' after his arrest. 'I had to reprogramme everything. Mickey took most of the heat out there in the streets. He did a good job.'

Sticks . . ., D. thought. He had often wondered how his 'lieutenant' had coped after his departure.

'Chin was hard to find and well-protected as you can imagine,' Charlie continued.

'What happen to the witness?' D. asked, a sudden interest in his voice.

'Oh, nothing happened to her.' Charlie grinned.

'How yuh mean? She nevah came to court . . .'

'No, she changed her mind.' Charlie laughed, enjoying the joke. 'Chin had a good plan, but we figured out his play. We just sent a message to the girl about her son . . .'

D. was interested; he had never really known how they managed to achieve that trick.

'She got scared?!' he asked, grinning also.

Charlie nodded.

'She realized Chin couldn't protect her for ever.'

'Tell me, who got through to her?'

'Sweetie,' Charlie said.

'Sweetie?!' D. repeated appreciatively.

'Anyway, once you beat the rap and they realized we had the strength to resist them, they called a truce.'

'Enh?'

'Believe it, man, it's still working more or less.' Charlie laughed. 'We've got problems with some local guys . . .'

'What local guys?' D. asked curious.

'I told you things have changed; gangs of youths from some estates we used to control have set up their own network.'

D. was listening with interest; that was new . . .

'They getting their own supplies now and know how to cut it, too. In the last few months we've had a few clashes with them.'

'Dem get brave!' D. said.

'Yeah, they've got guns too . . .' Charlie added. He picked up his glass and took a sip. He sighed. 'Look, D., I don't know what your plans are. You had some time out; so you had time to think, but I'm telling you, the scene is getting ugly out there.'

Charmaine came in, carrying a tray with two plates of dinner; they left the discussion to concentrate on the food.

'I'm going to get Marcus,' Charmaine said.

'OK; remember it's still a secret . . .' Charlie told her, glancing at D. She nodded and left for the nursery.

D. ate heartily; the long trip had given him an appetite.

'Charmaine can cook, enh, man!' he told Charlie between two bites.

'Yeah, man, she's good.'

While they were on the subject, Charlie asked about the girls back home, whether D. had been well looked after. D. laughed, explaining that his stay in Jamaica had been a 'rest' mostly.

'Still I have a girl ah country weh "powder" me all de while.'

'I know that; anywhere you go, there's got to be some action, man.'

The men finished their dinner, exchanging jokes and anecdotes about women. Charlie took the empty plates to the kitchen and returned with a couple of bottles of Guinness stout.

'Wanna smoke?'

It was a casual question, but Charlie noticed the slight pause before D. answered.

'Bwoy, I kinda ease up from dat, y'know.'

Standing by the wall unit, Charlie observed his friend.

'Serious?' he asked, unconvinced.

'Yeah, man.' D. nodded.

Charlie seemed surprised. He certainly hadn't expected that much change in his friend.

'So what about some sensi?'

'Sensi? Bring it come, man!' D. grinned.

'A'right.' Charlie went out and came back with a sizeable plastic bag full of dark-green herb.

'Wait, yuh ah run ganja now?!'

Charlie shrugged and sat down.

'Not really, but I've got connections,' he said. 'Plus, you know I always use herb to mix . . .'

They built a spliff each. The ganja was prime-quality stuff, still fresh with very few seeds. Charlie watched D. as he inspected the herb.

'We still get a nice draw. Most people don't bother with it no more. There's not enough money in it nowadays,' he explained.

D. lit up his spliff and took a long pull.

'True . . .' He looked at Charlie through the smoke.

'Yuh know somet'ing; I nevah seen yuh use rock yet . . .'

After all this time, D. had only just considered that Charlie, though he was one of the top men in the trade, didn't do crack at all. Charlie let out a short laugh. He took time to smoke, not answering D.'s question immediately.

'I'm surprised you didn't notice that before,' he said finally. 'I use shit, yeah, but I don't base and I don't touch rock, that's me . . .' He could see his friend wanted to know more. Charlie drank some stout and took a couple more pulls on the spliff.

'It might sound funny, 'cause I make my money from that stuff,' he said, 'but crack is the worst drug that was ever made by man, believe me.' The statement hung in the air for a few seconds. His mind eased up by the sweet, mellow herb, D. was waiting to hear more. He and Charlie had dealt in crack for a relatively long period, yet they had never really discussed it. Money had seemed a good enough motive to dispense with any reasoning about that. Charlie talked on.

'I grew up in New York, D. That's a town where drugs have been part of life since the beginning. I've seen guys hooked on all kinds of shit. Acid, speed, heroin, coke, PCP, opium even . . . But when crack came on the scene in the late seventies, everything changed for the worse.'

'What about cocaine? Dat wicked too, though!'

Charlie pushed the lighter across the table for D. to use.

'Yeah, cocaine's wicked, you're right. But I know people who use cocaine for years, snorting, you know, and they're still around. The thing that fucks you up is freebase, that's bad, man, you've got to have a lot of money to afford it. Even snorting or a cocktail can mess you up if you abuse it.'

Charlie paused, took another sip from the bottle of stout and continued. 'You see, crack now; crack is perfect . . . Check it out: crack is stronger, more purified than base cocaine, it's easier to handle because it's solid and it's cheap. The day that came on the market, everything went BOOM!' Charlie gestured his two hands in the air, mimicking an

explosion. D. looked at him reflectively. He'd never both-·
ered to research anything about it.

'So wha' yuh used to take it?' he asked.

Charlie let out a short, hollow laugh. His eyes hardened
briefly, as if bad memories had bumrushed his thoughts.

'Let me tell you, D.; what I know about drugs is not
something I studied. I grew up in the streets and like
everyone else I had to pay dues. You know what I mean?'

D. nodded, he knew. There was a short silence.

'I used to be married, you know.'

The statement surprised D. at first. He wondered why
Charlie had switched subjects. He listened, intrigued.

'You look surprised. Yeah, I got married at eighteen.'

D. saw the twist of bitterness and cynicism on his
friend's face. Charlie was usually secretive about his background. This was the first time he had even mentioned his
marriage.

'You see, at that time I had everything I wanted.
Imagine; eighteen . . . I had a big car, clothes, jewellery,
money – don't mention it. I was one of the most successful
hustlers in my neighbourhood. But I married a girl, man,
you should have seen this girl . . . Every man in town
wanted that girl, I'm not lying . . .' Charlie paused, a pained
smile on his lips as he recalled his wife.

'I mean; I had guys twice my age working for me. I
even opened up a restaurant with one of my spar . . .
Anyway, Gina, my wife, was doing stuff with me. We used
to take coke to keep going. I had to stay on top, you know
how it goes. Some of my guys came down one day with this
new thing, "rock" they called it. They got it from some
Latino gangsters we used to know. The "new product" they
said. I was a little suspicious at first, but they said they'd
tried it and it was "magic".'

The flame of the lighter flickered as Charlie lit up his
spliff and got up to play a new cassette. He turned to D.

'It was magic, al'right . . . Over the next few months, that shit took over the market, everywhere it was just rock, rock and more rock. Obviously, I had to try it before I got involved with selling it.' Charlie looked at D. as he sat back down. 'You know crack as well as me . . .' He smiled. 'In fact, you almost got fucked up for good, you must know that . . .'

It was a simple statement of fact. D. knew it to be the truth. He didn't answer. Charlie went on talking, as much to himself as to D.

'Take one lick and the hit you get inside your head is like nothing else. It don't last long and that's the trap at first. You need to get more and more to get the same effect, to stay on the same level. I mean, that shit will mess up your body and your brain faster than anything else in the world. The worst is what it does to people around you.'

'So what about your wife?' D. cut in. He wanted to know the rest of the story.

'Yeah, I'm getting there. As I say, when you're high from crack, you can do anything, that's the way you feel . . . So Gina started to use it too. She got more hyped, more "digital", y'know?! After a few weeks I could see she changed a little, but remember I was getting into it too. I used to go and do business and leave her with my supplies. Imagine that! She'd stay home and get really bombed up with her friends, but I was so busy and so in love with the girl I just let things happen.'

Charlie took a sip from his glass. He seemed to need to go on with the story and relive the pain of it.

'So one day I left her to go out of town with some people. She and her friends got so hyped up they got into a car and went straight to a club operated by a Puerto Rican gang to "fix" somebody. From what I learned after, one of the girls from the gang had "dissed" her in some way. So five of them picked up themselves and went there. Imagine five against a house full of *them*! They got into a shootout, one of them died on the spot. Then they tried to escape, but by this time the police had arrived on the scene, they chased them for miles across the city. Gina was driving. Finally they got cornered, but instead of surrendering, Gina shot one of the officers. The police massacred the four of them in the street. Gina was just seventeen . . .'

D. couldn't find anything to say. He observed Charlie slouched in his chair, eyes half-closed.

'I've always blamed myself for her death, you know, D.,' he heard Charlie say softly.

The sound of the key in the door broke the vibe.

'Daddy! Daddy!' Footsteps running in the corridor announced Marcus's entrance. He leapt into his father's lap, throwing his little arms around his neck.

'Look what I done . . .' Marcus proudly handed Charlie a rolled-up sheet of cardboard.

He stopped suddenly, noticing D. in the chair.

'Marcus, come yah, rude boy!'

Marcus looked at his father then at D. again, clearly surprised to see him after such a long time.

'Come nah, man . . . wha'ppen? We nuh friend again?!'

Marcus left his father, forgetting all about his drawing and stepped to D., his little face tight with concentration as he recalled his long-time friend.

D. grabbed the child and held him up in the air.

'Yuh get big, enh, man?'

Marcus had grown up fast; he no longer looked like a baby with his hair cut short and in his nice corduroy 'ragamuffin suit'. D. poked him gently in the belly, teasing him and shaking him until the little boy started to giggle and fight back. From the doorway, Charmaine was looking on smiling.

'Wait 'til you see yours . . .'

D. only glanced at her briefly; he had known all along

that she was dying to bring up the subject. Charmaine looked at Charlie. He only smiled and shook his head. After all, this was none of his business.

'I will go dung dere, man, but right now I wan' yuh to hol' it down until I ready, seen?!'

'I won't say a word, promise,' Charmaine said, holding up her right hand in a mock oath. 'Come on, Marcus, dinner-time.'

Marcus quit playing with D. and followed his mother to the kitchen.

'Jenny comes here all the while, you know,' Charlie said. 'Your boy looks exactly like you . . .'

D. didn't answer, but Charlie thought he saw a fleeting smile of pride flash across his face.

Two more stouts and a few spliffs later, the two men were feeling nice as they watched some music videos. Outside, a breezy night had fallen over old London town.

Marcus had hung around for as long as he was allowed to and then been sent to bed. The phone rang.

'Yeah . . . ? Yes, my youth . . . hmmm . . . Who? Al'right, take care of that . . . OK . . . tomorrow.' Charlie put down the receiver and looked at D.

'Mickey . . . It's best not to tell him yet if you want to cool off for a while.'

D. nodded. He'd need a few days to chill out and decide on his next move.

'So, you wanna go for a ride?' Charlie asked.

'Yeah, man.'

Charlie went upstairs to see Charmaine, then they left.

'Cold a'ready!' D. remembered as the wind hit him outside.

Charlie laughed.

'You just come, man; you're going to feel it even more . . .'

They got in the car and drove out, cruising around the

near-empty streets. They passed through his old stomping ground; D. sat and observed the few men and women outside the pubs, cafés and clubs of Clapton and Stoke Newington, from behind the car window. He recognized a few faces but no one noticed him. Charlie headed for Shoreditch, listening to D. relate a few stories about his stay in Jamaica. He'd warmed up a little by now, slowly reverting back to the D. Charlie had known before the edgy latter days. Charlie hit a right turn, then drove round a small cluster of newly built houses at the back of a tower block.

'You might want to visit some people in here . . .' he said enigmatically, stopping in front of a black wrought-iron gate. D. looked at him, eyebrows raised. Charlie left him hanging on for a little while, enjoying the puzzled look on D.'s face.

'Donna moved, you know.'

D. frowned, looked at Charlie then towards the gate. Was he ready for this now? He was undecided.

'You don't have to, Supa,' Charlie said.

'Sooner or later anyway.' D. sighed. 'Come.'

They left the car and walked across the courtyard. Charlie rang the bell. A light came on behind the glass panel. The door opened on Cindy's doll-like features. As she looked up, her eyes opened wide, her mouth also.

'Mummy! Mummy!' she shouted.

D. looked at Charlie and stepped in. Cindy jumped up ecstatic and grabbed him around the neck.

'Lord have mercy!'

D. heard the shout before he could even see Donna bent over the upstairs banisters.

8

DISSIN' TIME

'Skipper, talk to me nuh!'

Leroy stopped in mid-sentence and looked at the man calling from the far end of the counter.

'I soon come,' he told Lee before stepping off his stool and making his way down. He knew exactly what the Squeeze was going to say. A large pile of records, mostly twelve-inches, were stacked up in front of him.

'My boss, hear wha', mek I check yuh Monday about dis . . .' Squeezy smiled engagingly. Leroy didn't smile back. Squeezy, one of Radical Hi-Powah's operators, always did the same thing; he'd take a few dozen records from Leroy and ask for credit until the following week. Leroy had to admit he was usually true to his word and paid up. But all the same it was hard times for everyone and cash was badly needed.

'Cho, Squeeze, man. Let off somet'ing nuh!' Leroy tried to pressure the sound man into paying for some of the tunes at least.

'Bwoy, yuh know seh we have a big dance Saturday. Me check yuh first thing Monday. Fe real.' Squeeze was still smiling, trying to soften Leroy up.

'Business bad, y'know, Supa. All de while ouno sound man wan' credit. Me cyan buy records, if ouno don't pay me. Y'understand?'

'Me know dat, Skipper. But wha'! Me always pay on time, nuh true?'

Leroy agreed, shaking his head.

'Look, man, mek de yout' check dat out and write it

down. But mek sure yuh settle first thing Monday morning. Yuh hear?!'

'Monday morning. God knows. Respeck my boss!' Squeeze grinned.

On his way back to Lee, Leroy said a few words in Gary's ear. The youth nodded, changed a record on the turntable and went to attend to the Squeeze. Gary was Leroy's nephew, recently arrived from Canada where his mother lived. He was a quiet, slim sixteen-year-old who enjoyed nothing better than running the ship for his uncle. Gary's ambition was to own his own sound system one day, but in the meanwhile he was content to earn a wage by helping Leroy. Besides, he knew everything about reggae music and that was a big bonus. Leroy trusted him and could now find time for his other business interests.

'Dem sound man, yuh see . . .' Leroy said as he sat back down to the conversation with his friend.

'Ah so business run, papa!' Lee smiled. Lee had arrived from New York a few weeks earlier. He and Leroy were long-time brethren and whenever he was in London Lee would spend a lot of time at the shop. He had a string of artists signed up to his own label based in New York City and had produced several hit records over the past few months. Leroy had expressed some interest in getting involved in producing, hinting that Lee might want to get involved in a joint venture.

'Skipper, me gone. Mek sure yuh check the dance Saturday!' Squeeze shouted above the music.

'A'right, later,' Leroy answered from his corner.

Gary resumed spinning tunes one after the other, a rapid selection of hits and dancehall 'killers'.

There were less than a dozen customers in Leroy's record store on this cold Wednesday afternoon: a few music addicts buying for their personal collections, a couple of sound men and three girls, regulars who loved nothing better than to hang around and take in the vibe in anticipation of the next weekend's session. The busy time was really from Thursday to Saturday, when the serious crowd would pile up in the small shop, talking, dancing while they chatted up girls and bought the latest releases. Not far from where Leroy sat, a young man with a serious face under his black leather baseball cap kept signalling to Gary after almost every record with a flash of the gold rings that adorned every finger of his right hand. Obliging, Gary placed a copy of the tune he had just played on top of the already high stack in front of the man motioning. The man picked up each record in turn, pulling it out of its sleeve and briefly inspecting both sides of the vinyl. Satisfied, he would slot the record back inside its jacket and on top of the pile. Leroy had seen him in the shop several times before, but didn't know his name.

'Yuh hear 'bout Baby Wayne?!' Lee said.

Leroy shook his head disapprovingly.

'Pure foolishness, man. The yout' mek a good record.'

Lee explained how the youth's first record 'Moma' had hit the charts, but failed to find approval with some of the 'bad bwoys' in Jamaica who felt that it was an insult to them.

'De yout' talk the truth, man,' Leroy said. ''Nuff man quick fe kill somebody, but when dem get sentence, it's then dem start realize it nuh wort' it.'

Lee agreed, adding that 'Nobody like prison.'

'Ah so reggae music stay nowadays, you know; people don't want no intelligent lyrics,' Lee bemoaned.

'True. Right now me ah tell yuh, it's slackness music I sell the most,' Leroy remarked.

'Well, 'nuff people like slackness and I don't really fight against it. As a producer I know seh every artist ha fe eat still, so if it's slackness dem want ah dat dem ah get!'

'Awright, Opa, me ready fe you,' the man with the

black cap called to Gary. He counted the records on the counter rapidly and waited for Gary to check out his bill.

'Eighty-seven pounds, seventy-five pence,' Gary said.

The man slowly peeled off a few twenty-pound notes from the fat wad he had taken out of his pocket. From the corner of his eye, Gary couldn't help noticing the money, it looked like a lot of cash.

'Supa, it nuh look like recession reach yuh yet!' Leroy joked, smiling at the youth.

The youth looked at Leroy from beneath the peak of his cap while picking up the bags of records from Gary. His features relaxed a little with a flash of a gold tooth . . .

'Recession?' he chuckled. 'Dat cyan affect my business, y'know . . .' The man glanced at Lee briefly then back to Leroy. 'Later . . .'

'Yes, man. Respeck.'

Lee lit up a cigarette, while paying attention to the record Gary had just put on. It was one of the countless versions of the 'Bam Bam' rhythm, but made to sound different somehow. The pace was slower, the high-pitched nasal voice of the MC weaving in and out of the beat gave it an uncanny, almost eerie feeling.

'Is what tune dis?' Lee asked, intrigued.

'England mix, man. Yuh like it?' Leroy signalled to Gary to touch back the record. One of the girls, interrupted in mid-bogling by the sudden 'rewind', looked towards the counter. Gary sent it forward again, only bringing up the bass after several bars of the tune.

'It sound different, don't it?' Leroy said.

Lee nodded. It was a peculiar cut to the popular rhythm, but it grew on you after a while. He couldn't quite tell what did it. Whether it was the foghorn-like sound dispersed within the bass and drum track or the MC's shrill tone of voice, or maybe the unorthodox blend of the tune . . .

'Who's de yout'?' Lee asked.

'A local yout' named Firefly. One ah de Radical sound man produced de tune. Sell good too!'

Lee was impressed.

'I looking fe some new artists.'

'Yeah? But you have 'nuff top MC a'ready.'

'True. But I lose few ah dem still. Some jus' waste themselves.'

Producing business was getting more difficult now, Lee told Leroy. It wasn't just the competition; Jamaica had a wealth of artists who only needed a good producer to burst on the scene. Unfortunately, as Lee discovered to his expense, it often happened that a producer would bring out a youngster from Jamaica, set him up, coach him and spend money on him, only to see him 'turn fool' in the jungle of New York.

'Me bring up a yout' from Yard about six months ago, seen?! I look after him good, mon. Spend "x" amount ah dollars 'pon him; the yout' mek one record fe me. The tune hits . . . Hear dis: nex' t'ing I know, him gone go do a tune fe a nex' producer!? So me get vex now and show him seh t'ings cyan go so. Anyway, I write a lyrics, get a new rhythm fe him. Guess wha'ppen: de bwoy nuh go get involved ina de drugs business! Before I could even get him fe voice de tune, him shoot one guy ina club dead. Right now, dem have him ah Rikers Island.'

Leroy listened to the tale of woe from his friend, shaking his head; the music business wasn't as simple as it used to be.

'Me hear seh Shabba mash up Japan last month.'

'Shabba big, man,' Lee agreed. 'Dat you' yah mix wid de biggest movie star dem ina America, y'know.'

'Reggae music ah run t'ings now.' Leroy got up to go answer a call from someone. Right about the same time, one of the girls who had been eyeing Lee for some time, slid alongside the counter neatly.

'Excuse me.' She flashed a toothy grin. 'My friend says you're a producer?'

Lee looked the girl over; short skirt with small features framed by large earrings. He sighed.

'Sometimes . . . right now I doing some different business, y'know.' Careful not to encourage the girl to press on, he put on a 'screw', and touched his brow as if concentrating on the music.

'I can sing, I need someone to coach me.' Undeterred the girl asked a couple more questions, which Lee answered *his* way. He wasn't interested, but there was no point being unkind. The last three weeks since he arrived from New York had been quiet. He had committed himself to a strict programme of exercise, good food and care. He needed it after the hectic pace of life in the Big Apple. He had managed to get three of his records in the top ten in three months; that made him one of the hottest producers of the moment. It also meant a host of MCs and singers were only too eager to work with him, which meant he usually ended up working round the clock. All he wanted to do now was relax. Sweetie made sure he was properly looked after.

Lee fended off the girl's persistent enquiries absent-mindedly. He had suddenly become aware of someone watching him. A few yards away across the room, a tall man was flicking through the LPs in the large wall box slowly, one by one. His eyes, though, were focused directly on Lee. He had a rather long face with a prominent jaw, his eyes hidden behind small, round, dark glasses. Somehow, it seemed as if he should be bigger, heavier, for his height, but the leather jacket he wore only accentuated his angular frame. Lee glanced at the girl beside him and then his eyes snaked back towards the man standing by the record boxes; the dark glasses were still on him. His brain scanned through countless faces automatically, searching for a name to match the man, who obviously knew him. It was the voice that made him connect.

'Lee, big timer! Wha' ah gwan?' There was no warmth in the greeting and no smile in the long gaunt face.

'Wha'ppen, Killer?' Lee wasn't exactly pleased to meet the man who had recorded one tune for him the previous year amidst much acrimony, due to the fact that Killer refused obstinantly to be directed in his work. Lee had tried to explain that his job was to produce, which meant to bring out the best in the artist, but Killer thought he knew everything better than him . . .

'Ah yuh me ah look fe, y'know; me hear seh my tune a sell,' Killer said drily.

Lee frowned.

'Weh yuh ah talk 'bout?'

'Yeah, my bredrin up ah New York seh de tune ah play 'pon de radio 'nuff!' The words carried loudly over the music. Killer had made no move forward. The girl next to Lee had moved back slightly, watching and waiting.

'Killer, hear me; me jus' come from New York, you know? An' I don't hear dat tune yah from last year. It nevah sell much anyway,' Lee said patiently. He could feel Killer's vibe was not friendly, but he decided to be easy. Killer, though, wasn't lightening up.

'Yeah, ah dat me ah talk 'bout; me know seh de tune sell, man.'

Lee straightened up on his stool slowly.

'So wait, tell me somet'ing; yuh check de record shop dem?' He paused. 'I ah tell yuh seh de tune wasn't a hit, seen?! Sell a few hundred. Now, if yuh t'ink ah lie, yuh bes' check de shop dem? Y'understand?'

Being easy was one thing, being called a liar was another.

'No, Lee, man. Me wan' de res' ah my money.' Killer kissed his teeth.

Lee was not prepared to be distressed by the arrogant man any longer. He had to be crazy coming against him like this, and in public too.

'Hey, star, me wan' yuh listen an' listen good: your tune nevah sell an' what it sell, me done pay yuh a'ready. Yuh know dat, so gwan whe' yuh ah go, OK?!'

By that time twelve pairs of eyes were on the two men. The music hadn't stopped, but no one was dancing any more. Leroy had slid back closer to Lee.

'Pay me a'ready?!' Killer erupted. 'Me seh gimme me money, man. Yuh t'ink any producer can rob me?'

Lee slid off his stool. The guy had to be crazy. In New York, his people wouldn't even have let him say that much. Killer wasn't even a recognized MC.

'Boss, yuh wan' leave now . . . ?' Lee's voice was low and threatening. He took one step forward slowly, watching Killer's right hand which had not left his jacket pocket. 'Yuh t'ink seh me 'fraid ah yuh?'

'Me we shot your bloodclat! Any bwoy mess wid Killer dead . . .'

For all his threats and shouting, Killer was still standing on the same spot. The record came to an abrupt end. Gary didn't replay it.

'Yaow! Me nuh want no bad bwoy business ina my place, yuh see me!' Leroy's voice thundered through the tension.

Killer looked at Leroy then at Lee, who was now ready to jump on his opponent.

'Lee, cool, man . . . Mek him gwan!' Leroy called out.

'Hey, bwoy, yuh done!' Lee said pointing.

'Oooh, oh yuh see me, me we shot yuh!'

'Do it nuh, do it!' Lee went forward, challenging.

'Leave de place, man!' Leroy shouted.

Lee was now three yards away from Killer, arms outstretched, in front of the incredulous small crowd. He taunted the tall and ragged-looking Killer.

'Yuh ah bad bwoy?! Shoot me nuh!'

Rigid, as if in a trance, Killer looked around him. His eyes rested on Leroy for a fraction of a second, then on Lee still standing there. He suddenly turned and ran out, his right hand still checked inside his pocket.

For a few seconds, the only noise was the hissing of the speakers, then Leroy turned to Gary; the youngster strapped a twelve-inch vinyl on the turntable and re-established normality. Lee returned to his seat amidst the buzzing of voices of the others in the shop as the bystanders conferred in whispered tones about the incident.

'Dat bwoy deh ah madman, fe real.' Leroy shook his head. Lee didn't say anything right away. He was clearly well wrecked.

'De bloodclat tune nevah sell, fe real,' Lee muttered later. 'Me know, man . . . Even if him did right . . . no weh a bwoy can come talk to you dem way deh!' Lee kissed his teeth. He left the shop about half an hour later; he couldn't get back in the vibe to reason with Leroy. He said he would call later.

Outside, the early October night was not as cold as it could have been. In the car, then through the back streets across Newington Green, Lee headed for Sweetie's house. The more he replayed the encounter in his mind, the more he was bitter about one fact: no way Killer would have left the shop alive if Lee had been amongst his usual partners. He was supposed to be on vacation and now this fool had got him all wound up.

By the time he pushed his key into the door of the flat, he was in a cold anger of the kind that makes your brain empty and your eyes fixed. Lee walked through the corridor and into the living room where Sweetie was chatting to the next-door neighbour, a fat baby-faced girl who worked in a shoe shop. She and Sweetie had several businesses going, so she would spend a few hours hanging around the flat every so often. Lee had talked to her a couple of times, yet tonight, by the way she saw him march in and sink himself into one of the deep chairs without even a glance, the poor girl didn't dare risk a hello. Sweetie took in the situation; she motioned the girl discreetly out of the room. She closed the front door behind her and came to sit right beside Lee. She waited at least a minute, watching him, his eyes focused on the TV screen.

'Yuh want dinner?'

Lee threw a cold darting eye her way. She knew him as a usually even-tempered man, hard to get angry, but Sweetie could read the deep seething rage within him.

'It's best you eat first, before yuh tell me 'bout it,' Sweetie said again in a normal tone of voice. Despite his anger, Lee knew that Sweetie was not going to be deterred by silence. She was a very hard woman to ignore. He would have to tell her sometime anyway so he told her there and then about the incident at the shop, getting more incensed with the thought of it again.

'So wha' ah gwan happen now?' she asked.

Lee looked at her as if puzzled by the question's effect. 'How yuh mean?'

Sweetie raised her eyebrows. She was serious.

'I want to know wha' yuh gwan do now . . .'

'So wait, yuh nuh hear seh de bwoy diss me in public. Wha'ppen to yuh?'

Sweetie didn't back down. She stayed calm.

'Take off your jacket, man,' she said.

As if despite himself Lee got up and let Sweetie take his jacket off. He sat down again. She went to hang the jacket and came back to sit on the arm of the chair.

'A'right, Lee, de bwoy diss yuh an' yuh know seh yuh nevah teef him, right?!' Sweetie reasoned. 'By right him fe dead. But yuh is a big man with work fe do an' 'nuff people need yuh still.'

Lee was still tense, his jaws clenched but listening.

'So leave it, man. Somebody else will deal with him.'

'Sweetie, I cyan mek ah bwoy tes' me dem way deh. Me ha fe do him somet'ing.'

Sweetie's hand was at the back of his neck. She knew it would take a while to get her man out of his vexation. She alone could cool him down.

'Easy nuh, easy. Hear me, Lee, it's not every dawg whe' bark yuh ha fe kick, y'know.'

Lee turned to her and smiled.

'Yuh see why me ha'fe carry me t'ing now?' he said accusingly. Sweetie had insisted that London was not like New York and that he should not carry a gun. She looked at him.

'So tell me somet'ing Lee; anyhow you have a gun, dung dere you would ah shoot the bwoy, nah true?'

Lee didn't answer, he went back to watching the TV. Sweetie left the question hanging in the air. After a little coaxing she got him to eat some dinner and built him a spliff. They sat to watch the video and later on when all was a little lighter, they talked and joked like they usually did. Still later, when she wasn't expecting it, Lee stopped and smiled at her.

'Yuh know yuh different?!' he said.

'Den yuh nevah see dat yet?' She laughed.

'No serious. Yuh know somet'ing? I nevah see yuh get vexed yet. Not really vexed.'

Sweetie looked at him seriously.

'Is when yuh get vex, yuh make the biggest mistakes,' she said simply. She pointed at him with a half-smile.

'And I don't want fe lose yuh because dem t'ings, y'hear me?' Playfully, Lee gently slapped her finger.

'Have manners!' he laughed.

9

PUPPY LOVE

With the music blaring out of the bedroom's stereo and his concentration totally on the mirror where he was putting the finishing touch to his outfit, Harry didn't hear the bell right away. Then the track finished and the insistent buzz reverberated in the otherwise silent flat. He ran down the stairs, opened the door and saw Rodney's frowning face.

'What's happening, man, you getting deaf?'

Harry let him in and closed the door.

'I was jus' getting ready.'

'I could hear the music from downstairs,' Rodney said as they climbed up to Harry's bedroom. 'Your mother's gone out?'

'Yeah, it's bingo night!' Harry laughed.

No way could he have played the stereo so loud unless Lorna had gone out. She went with her friends to play bingo religiously on Friday nights.

The music started again. Harry turned it down just a touch.

'So, you gonna model tonight!' Rodney grinned, admiring his friend's brand new red and black Click suit.

He looked fine himself, in a pair of patched-up, and artistically cut up, rolled-up jeans and checkered shirt. Harry was busy choosing from the half a dozen baseball caps lined up on top of his wardrobe. He decided on a black one with a big X printed in white on it. Carefully, he adjusted the cap on his head, the peak at a thirty-degree angle to the left. He cast a last critical glance in the tall mirror, propped up on the wall. Satisfied, he turned to Rodney.

'Yeah, Marcia's supposed to come down tonight.'

Rodney raised his eyebrows.

'Marcia? She doesn't go out, man.'

'She promised she'd come tonight,' Harry insisted, slipping on a pair of high-top black Nike trainers.

Every other Friday night, there was a disco at the nearby youth club, and the two boys usually attended it. Tonight, Harry was especially eager, because Marcia had assured him she would get her mother to let her go. Marcia was a fourteen-year-old pretty local girl, who Harry had been trying to 'conquer' for the last six months. She was the youngest of a family of five and her mother, a regular church-goer, was very strict. As a rule, she never went out after nightfall, and Harry had mainly made his moves at school. Since he had not been back after the row with the teacher six weeks earlier, it had been difficult to see her. It was a known fact that she was very much in demand, but kept every boy 'off limits'. From his few conversations with her, Harry was sure that she liked him. He hoped for confirmation of that belief and tonight could be the right time . . .

'I'm ready, let's go!' Harry announced finally. He switched off the stereo and the lights. The two boys descended the stairs and out of the flat they went. As they turned the corner of the block, they noticed someone standing in the darkness of the shed, housing the tall metal garbage bins. It was the incandescent red light of a cigarette that caught their eyes. The shape moved forward.

'Harry, what's happening?'

They stopped, waiting for Bob to come across. He stubbed out the cigarette and shuffled towards them. Bob was a white youth who lived on the estate. He had grown up with them and, as many other white kids of these inner-city areas, dressed, talked and walked like most black teenagers.

'Bob, what you doing?' Harry asked.

'I was waiting to see you. You going to the disco?'

'Yeah, man, come on.'

The three started out, cutting across the dark expanse of lawn between the blocks of flats, on to the alleyway leading to the high street.

'Let's get some drinks,' Bob suggested as they passed a row of shops.

Bob, who was now sixteen, had dropped out of school and was now helping his older brother who owned a garage near Bethnal Green. He was learning the mechanic trade which, he reflected, was a good 'earner' and was certainly better than hanging around a classroom, bored and broke. Since then, Bob always seemed to have money, which was fine with Harry and Rodney, as he regularly treated them. Bob went in the off-licence and came out shortly after with three Dragon stouts. Although he was under age, he never had too much trouble persuading the Asian shopkeepers to let him buy drinks. The three boys walked down, sipping from their bottles and talking.

Friday nights were always busy, for everybody. It was the best time of the week in fact when, after five days spent studying or working, everyone felt able to 'release' and enjoy themselves. Cars zoomed past on the busy high street. People inside the take-away shops and the crowded pubs were having a good time on this early November night. It was cold, but not really that much for the season, and besides, the weather never stopped anyone going out. They passed a clearly inebriated middle-aged man, holding on to the street railing with one hand while clutching a can of beer with the other. He made an attempt to straighten up and walk, but had to retreat to the safety of the railing after two steps, conscious not to appear drunk. The three boys stopped and watched him for a few minutes, laughing at his efforts to maintain an upright stance.

'Oi, mate, buy us a drink then!' Bob teased him, imitating the man's drunken walk. The man didn't even seem to notice him.

'Come on, man, leave him alone,' Harry said.

They left him there and walked on, turning left into a dark, narrow road, boarded on one side with tall sheets of zinc. Finally, they emerged on the lit-up area in front of the disused church, used as a youth club. A dozen or so youths of both sexes were huddled in small groups around the entrance, chatting in the cold night air. Several of them hailed Harry as he passed. He was something of a celebrity with the youths of the area, known to be a rough but fair ragga, especially so since he had débuted in the music arena the year before. He had recently won the latest deejay contests held regularly on disco nights and that had enhanced his status with everyone.

'Hi, Harry . . .' a tall girl with a curly hair-style called out. Harry looked at her as she smiled invitingly. Her two friends giggled, looking at him sideways. He flashed a knowing smile.

'Althea, wha'ppen?' Harry knew very well that Althea liked him. She lived in Stoke Newington, but visited Tisha her best friend, who lived across from him, quite regularly. She also usually attended the youth club. In the past few weeks Harry had noticed her smiling warmly at him several times. In fact, Tisha had spoken to him about her. Or rather, she had made some hardly veiled hints . . . In any case, Harry knew, but he had played it cool so far. Althea was attractive and actively 'hunted' by quite a few boys who had made it clear that they loved the tall 'browning', yet the girl kept every one of them at bay, everyone except Harry that is. It wasn't that Harry didn't like Althea, on the contrary.

They had talked several times and even danced together, yet Harry felt for Marcia more.

He left the three grinning girls and led the way inside. The entrance to the disco was a nominal three pounds, that was no problem. As he dug into his pockets, Harry heard Ian's voice.

'You can't come in with the drinks, Harry, you know that.'

Ian was a white youth worker, part of the team operating the club. Harry stopped and looked at the man sitting behind the table. He knew the rules, but somehow resented the remark. After all, he was a 'celebrity' and considered himself beyond such petty rules.

'It soon finish, Ian, man, jus' cool.'

But Ian was serious about the drinks. Rodney and Bob looked at him.

'Come on, man . . .' Bob argued.

A few other youths looked on. They knew Harry wasn't about to take any 'chat' from nobody.

'Look, you know the rules, right?! No drinks inside and that goes for everybody.'

Straight-faced, Harry looked at Ian.

'I told you I'm going to finish it. Don't distress me, seen?!'

The white youth worker remained seated behind the table, unwilling to antagonize Harry with whom he usually got on well, but still, he had to enforce the rules. A queue had started to form behind Rodney and Bob.

'Harry, you go outside and finish your drink, then you can come in.'

Harry kissed his teeth contemptuously.

'You're trying to disrespect me, man?!' he spat, stubborn.

Ian said nothing. Behind, everyone was watching the confrontation. Harry looked down at the man, defiant.

'Cho, you're a fool . . .'

Slowly, he put the bottle to his mouth and emptied it. In the same movement, he slammed the empty bottle down on the table, dropped three pound coins in front of Ian and walked past him without a look. Rodney and Bob drank the rest of their drinks, paid the fee and followed him. Sneers and derisive laughs rose from the small crowd behind. Harry wasn't to be meddled with, that was obvious.

Inside the large, half-full hall, it was dark and things hadn't warmed up yet. Harry went straight to the right where a small set was rigged up. He nodded to the selector and the rest of the crew and stopped by the tiny stage, peering around through the crowd of dancers. Some hip-hop acid track was playing, a rough mix of bass, drums, and other samples of screaming voices that had at least thirty or so youths gesticulating wildly in the middle of the hall. Rodney and Bob stood to one side watching. One of the youths from the set came to talk to Harry. They had to shout in each other's ear to cover the din of the music. Meanwhile, Harry scanned the room in vain; no sign of Marcia.

After a while he decided to go back outside; it wasn't really his kind of music. Rodney followed. On the way, he turned right before the door to reach the foyer, where, in the daytime, classes and workshops were held. Tonight, though, the area was lit only by a dim neon lamp. Purposefully, it seemed, as several 'rude boys' and their girlfriends hung around in there talking and flirting. Marcia wasn't in the foyer either. She probably didn't get to come, Harry reflected; might as well forget it. He and Rodney walked out past Ian, and through a crowd of youths waiting to enter.

'Let's check over there!' Harry said, heading for the parking lot to the left of the church. That was usually the spot where the ragga youths hung around when the set played excessively long soul selections. It was darker there, out of reach of the light that illuminated the front of the church. Only shadows, voices and the incandescent red tips of cigarettes.

'Yaow, my yout'! Come in, rude boy!' someone called on the right. Harry walked down towards the sound of the voice.

'Yes . . . !' he greeted the thickly built youth who called out. Rodney muttered a greeting.

'What happenin', Buster?'

Buster was one of Harry's friends who lived in Tottenham, out of the area. He was also a deejay and a good one too. They had gotten talking one evening at the club during a contest and since then often exchanged lyrics and other news related to their mutual field of interest.

'Everyt'ing cool. You go inside a'ready?'

'Yeah, nothing too hot so far . . .' Harry answered.

Beside Buster stood Raymond, his cousin, also big-built with a woolly hat pulled low over his forehead. The two were about the same age, around fifteen, and looked alike in many ways. Raymond was born and bred in north London, whereas Buster had only come in from his native Jamaica around five years earlier.

'I hear you mash up the place last week . . . ?' Buster remarked.

'Fe real, man; some bad lyrics!' Raymond nodded, pulling on the spliff he was holding.

Harry laughed modestly.

'You should have been there, man.'

'I was busy; important runnins,' Buster explained.

'You want a draw?' Raymond handed Harry the spliff.

'What you've got?' Harry asked him.

'Just 'ash, man, no good weed around,' Raymond said. He knew Harry preferred herb. Harry took the spliff and drew. A pungent, aromatic smell rose up as the end burned red in the dark.

'I'll be inside,' Rodney told Harry, heading back towards the church. He didn't smoke, and moreover usually preferred to stay clear of some of Harry's friends.

'So what about dem new lyrics you supposed to record?' Harry asked Buster.

'I'm going to the studio next week . . .'

They talked 'business' for a while, passing the spliff around, shuffling on the spot under the fresh winter breeze. From around them, muffled voices sounded in the night from small groups of youths similarly occupied.

'Your tune doing well!' Buster complimented Harry, referring to Harry's recent début recording.

For an inspiring young and ambitious MC, getting a first break, someone to believe in you enough to get you into the studio was the vital thing. There was so much talent around, so many 'homeboys' whose only dream was to make it on vinyl and into the charts, that producers had more than enough choice. Buster had started to deejay early back home and ever since coming over, he had been around sound systems non-stop, practising his craft. He had already made a name for himself in his area. He liked Harry, who, he claimed, had a natural talent to 'ride' riddim. They talked until the echo of sounds coming from the church during the darkness changed subtly and the syncopated beat of a raggamuffin record reached them.

'Yes,' Buster smiled, 'them ah get ready now!'

The three youths headed for the church, so did everyone else in the car park. They all pressed in, Buster and Raymond managing to flash past the beleaguered Ian undetected. Inside the hall, the atmosphere had changed. It was full house. In front of the set, in the centre and all around the walls, dozens of similarly dressed youths were getting into the heavy 'bogle' rhythm. Harry, Buster and Raymond took position a few yards in front of the control tower and joined in. Besides being a better than average deejay, or maybe because of it, Harry could really dance. The bogle dance, a new craze all over the London scene now, suited him perfectly. There was scope to improvise within the rhythm, a thousand and one ways to 'design' one's particular style depending on the theme of the tune, the mood of the dancer and the degree to which one was willing to show off to the rest of the crowd. Arms in the air, legs bent just enough to rock back and forth, his head cocked up at a suitable angle, Harry 'bogled out' confidently.

Rodney appeared to his right and did his thing too. There were quite a lot of girls in the centre, most of them wearing jeans and corduroys like the boys but a few in Lycra dresses, sacrificing warmth for style in this cold winter climate. Each youth improvised their own dance patterns as the tune progressed, rivalling for the attention of the circle of admirers around them. Before the last bars of the record, the selector switched, neatly blending in the next record. The dancers tuned in without missing a step. Harry enjoyed himself, relaxed, in perfect synchronization with the bass and drum pattern.

He didn't notice Althea until she was standing right in front of him. The brown girl, her two friends still flanking her, had made her way through the mass of rocking bodies until she found herself facing Harry. He returned her smile. They fell in time naturally; she, body arched back, feet spaced out enough to allow for her low style, the index finger of each hand elegantly pointed upwards. He, straighter, one shoulder slightly forward, head leaning right, rude-boy fashion . . . Harry and Althea blended out of the record and into the following one. Meanwhile, Rodney moved closer to Nadine, one of Althea's friends. He liked her, but being less bold than Harry, had until then maintained his discretion. He admired the way his friend could just walk up to a girl, any girl, and start a conversation. Harry seemed even more direct since coming back from Jamaica the previous year; more than the ability to deejay, that was one skill Rodney had been eager to develop! He was quite close to Nadine now, and she, though carrying on as if she hadn't noticed him, had read the move right away. She flashed him a little teasing smile as their eyes met, but no more. Althea had gotten even closer to Harry; they danced, matching move for move, step for step, while around them the crowd bogled as one to the bass lines bouncing against the old brick walls. Harry threw casual glances around him, checking for known faces in between concentrating on his style. To his left, behind a couple of big girls in similar outfits, he saw Bob doing his version of bogle dance. A little behind him, he saw Buster and a girl similarly occupied. Althea looked him in the eye, still in time with the beat, following him close. It was the fourth or maybe fifth record they had danced and things seemed to get nicer with each tune. The operator maintained a minimum of talking in the mike, preferring to enjoy the rhythm, like everyone else. As Harry leant his body to the left, shifting into what he thought was a particularly wicked move, he saw her, five yards away, her head just about visible behind a group of bouncing youths. Marcia's eyes were fixed on Harry's. Despite the shock, Harry managed not to miss a step and smiled, aware of the precarious position he was in. He sighed to himself, and attempted to distance himself from Althea, but to no avail. The record ended and, thankfully for Harry, the operator changed the style, branching into a much faster, more urgent ragga-funk style. Harry eased up from Althea's semi-embrace neatly and turned to Rodney.

'Why you nevah tell me Marcia was here, man?' he shouted in his ear. Rodney shrugged.

'I haven't seen her!'

Harry looked around. Marcia had disappeared. He pushed his way across the mass of bodies towards the door. Before going out, he checked the foyer just in case. In the half-light of the corridor, he saw her, against the wall, talking to a friend. Harry composed himself and walked over. Marcia had her back to him. She didn't turn around despite warning, no more than a furtive glance her friend threw over her shoulder. She waited until he came to face her. Even out here, the music was too loud for a conversation. Harry ignored the friend's knowing smile. He leant over.

'I've been looking for you.'

Her squinted eyes told him, she doubted that. Marcia looked at her friend, giggling stupidly behind Harry's back. He decided they needed to talk somewhere he could get his point across without shouting over the music, and without the friend.

'Come; let's get out of here,' Harry gently urged in her ear as he pulled her out. Marcia shrugged off his hand, but followed him, not without a last conspiratorial glance at her friend. Harry led the way out towards the car park.

'Where are you going?' the girl asked behind him.

He turned around.

'Come on, just over there!'

She walked on reluctantly, gathering her jacket collar about her neck.

Harry stopped by a van, from where he could see the entrance of the church without being seen. Marcia joined him in the semi-darkness, but standing at arm's length.

'You jus' come?' he asked.

Hands in her pockets, Marcia simply looked at him.

'I've been here a while,' she answered in a detached tone of voice.

'I looked around, couldn't see you . . .'

'Oh yeah?!'

Harry could feel her coldness. It was probably something to do with the girl she had seen him dancing with. He tried softening her.

'Come over here.'

She shook her head.

'Come on, what's the matter with you?'

'Nothing . . .' She paused. 'Who's your girlfriend?'

There it was. Marcia was jealous, but trying not to let it show. A good sign . . .

'Girlfriend? No, man; she just came to dance, that's all.'

Harry explained that he had nothing to do with the girl.

'Marcia, I've been waiting for you, serious . . .'

Harry looked at the girl; her back against the van, shadows playing across her profile, he could just about make out her features. Somehow, he felt a strong attraction for Marcia, the kind that pinches inside the chest at close quarters.

'Come here . . .' he said quietly.

'No.'

Harry laughed. She was looking away from him, seemingly disinterested. Lightly stepping to the beat he could hear drifting from the club he slid towards her slowly. She didn't move, neither did she turn her head his way. Harry stopped just short of touching her, upright, hands behind his back. He edged his face a little closer, almost touching her ear.

'Listen, Marcia; I've been waiting a long time, just to talk to you . . .'

Marcia stood still, the back of her head against the side of the van. He went on, speaking softly, so close he could smell a discreet touch of perfume.

'You know I check for you . . . But you've got to let me know . . .'

She remained silent, so Harry decided to force the play.

'I know a lot of guys are trying to get to you, maybe that's why you jus' leave me hanging on.'

Sure enough, it worked.

Marcia's head made a quarter turn.

'I don't know what you're talking about. And I don't leave you hanging on!' she said, stressing the words.

OK, Harry thought, she's talking to me now. He sighed.

'Maybe not, but you know I can't see you that often. I've wanted to talk to you all week.' Harry's mind was clear, completely focused on Marcia and the way she made him feel. He had no need to make up 'lyrics' as he would have for other girls. At that precise moment, Marcia was all that mattered. She didn't answer, she looked away once more. Harry brought his arm across her shoulders, brushing the back of her hair as he gently pulled her face towards his. Marcia didn't resist. She almost touched him. His gaze floated, admiring her neat, darkly shaped features, and then it stopped, locked in her eyes.

'I've got to know that me an' you have the same vibe,' Harry said, almost whispering. Marcia's hands were still tucked in her jacket pockets. She looked at him, half-smiling at last.

'Al'right . . .' she said. 'But, Harry; you're a musician, that means there's a lot of girls looking for you . . .'

Harry's right hand caressed her face, real slow. His forefinger slid across her temple, feeling the softness of her hair. He brought his face closer to hers.

'Maybe . . . but they're not pretty, not like you.' Marcia's eyes were still for a few seconds, locked into his, seeing if he really meant it. She didn't move when his lips touched hers, lightly, more a caress than a kiss. Marcia's hands fell around Harry's waist. They stayed there for what seemed like a long time. They whispered in the dark, the glow of their emotions defined the fresh winter night. Lost and satisfied, Harry had forgotten everything else – the club, the music, his friends . . . They talked, sharing words, laughs and thoughts that they had meant to share for some time. A few other courting couples strolled by them, also seeking the dark, private world of the car park. Not even the compulsive pulse of the ragga beat floating out from the club could draw Harry from the sweetness of the embrace. Time though, whizzing by, has a primary order compulsion.

'I've got to go soon,' Marcia whispered in Harry's ear, her eyes closed.

'Yeah?'

'My sister's coming for me. What time is it?'

Harry released her reluctantly to check his watch. It was too dark to see, so he dug into his trouser pocket for the lighter he kept. The flame lit up both their faces, briefly.

'Five past twelve,' he said.

'So, you smoke now?' Marcia asked.

'No, man . . .' He didn't elaborate. 'What time she's coming?'

'She said twelve; if it wasn't for her, my mother wouldn't let me go out.'

Harry had a silent, grateful thought for the sister then took hold of Marcia again.

'When you gonna go back to school?' she asked, touching on a thorny subject.

Harry sighed.

'Soon, my mother's sorting out another place,' he mumbled, trying to avoid the subject.

'You coming to see me after school next week?' Marcia asked.

'Yeah, you know I'll come,' he answered, slowly unzipping her jacket and wrapping his hand around her waist.

'Which day?' she asked, pulling out his hand and zipping up the jacket.

'Any day, seen?' Harry said, stealing a kiss.

'Come on Tuesday.' Marcia straightened the peak of his baseball cap.

'I'll be there.' Harry switched the cap back sideways. Marcia laughed.

'Why you wear it like that for?'

'Me ah roughneck, seen?!' he said with a heavy accent.

Raising her eyebrows, Marcia grabbed his collar with both hands, gently pulling him to her. She kissed him.

'Not with me, you're not!'

Harry laughed.

'Come, let's go inside until my sister gets here,' Marcia said.

They walked slowly towards the church, feeling light, through the little groups of youths hanging out by the entrance and inside the hall. The set was playing a heavy, techno-funk groove, strictly for aficionados. They slipped back into the foyer, keeping close to each other, away from the crowded areas. They couldn't hide for long, however . . .

Buster walked past, a girl in tow.

'Wait, ev'rybody ah look fe yuh! Yuh nuh chat tonight?' he asked.

'No, man; I'm busy . . .'

Buster glanced at Marcia, gave Harry a knowing smile and walked on.

Marcia's friend came rushing in before they settled down.

'Marcia, your sister's outside for you!'

Harry looked at her; she shrugged, taking his hand. He followed her out. Chris was talking to a couple of boys just outside the entrance. He usually passed through the club on Fridays to make sure everything was going fine. There had been a few fights, though nothing serious, but it was a safe precaution in case a police patrol happened to pass by at any time.

'Harry, I wanna talk to you . . . !' Chris called out. Marcia had gone out to talk to her sister who had parked her car a little way down the road.

'I soon come,' Harry said as he walked on. Turning to him, Marcia smiled.

'See you Tuesday, OK?!'

'Yeah, take care.' Harry nodded.

Marcia's sister gave him a brief look, she said something to Marcia and smiled. Harry watched them get inside the car before walking back. Chris was waiting.

'What's happening?'

'Nothing.' Harry shrugged.

'So what's this story about you and Ian?'

Harry sighed, he had a feeling that was what Chris wanted to see him about.

'Come on; what's your problem?' Chris insisted.

'I ain't got a problem. The guy distressed me, that's all.'

Chris shook his head.

'Distressed you? That's not what he said.'

'I don't care what he said.' Harry frowned. He wished Chris would drop it; it was over and he had other things on his mind. But Chris was intent on finding out more.

'Hey, man, it's me you're talking to!'

'Al'right, al'right; I had a bottle and he didn't want me to go in with it, that's all.'

'Was he right?' Chris asked.

Harry looked at him sideways, shuffling on the spot. He felt the cold now. Chris asked again.

'Was he right?'

'Yeah, yeah, he was right . . .'

Chris sighed.

'Look, man; you know better than that, OK? I don't

want to hear that again.' Then he switched subject. 'You know you've got to go check a school with your mother on Monday?'

'Yeah, I know,' Harry answered.

Chris could see he was less than eager.

'I know you think you don't need to go no more, but you're wrong. By the way, how come you don't come to the black history classes any more?'

Chris organized classes for the local youths, black history was one of the most successful. Harry had attended them at first, but had been conspicuously absent in the last few weeks.

'I've been busy . . .' he mumbled, shivering in the cold night.

'OK, I know you've got other interests.' Chris lightened up a little. 'Still, listen; music is not everything, y'know. Sure, you can make money, but money won't help if you don't know yourself. So, you think about that. I'll see you later.'

Chris left Harry there and went inside. The club was closing soon and the crowd had started heading out. Harry went back inside the hall to look for Rodney. He felt moody now. Chris had succeeded in pulling him down from the height he had climbed to with Marcia. He found Rodney talking with some friends.

'You ready?' he asked.

'Yeah, OK.' They left the church and walked home, hardly talking.

'Chris was looking for you,' Rodney said. Harry kissed his teeth.

'Yeah, I know.' Everything was quiet on the estate. Only a few windows were still lit. Harry slipped into the flat quietly. By the time he got into bed, he had managed to switch his mind back to Marcia; the echo of her voice and the image of her smile rocked him gently to sleep.

10

NIGHT SHIFT

The little girl was still for about a minute, no more, then began inching forward over the edge of the settee, bending over slowly to see the toy she had just thrown down. She kept on repeating a particular sound which, as she was still too young to speak, could be taken as signalling a desire to get her toy back. The hand of the man sitting to her right gently pulled her backwards once more, then the man returned to the draughts match he was involved in. Sitting up, the child looked at the man, then at the table where she could see the attractively contrasting black and white shapes. The other man sitting across the table seemed as absorbed in the game as the man sitting beside her. She simply sat there, staring for a while, as if to analyse the situation before grabbing for the arm of the man beside her. Forcefully, she pulled herself upwards and stood erect, holding on to the man's shoulder. The little girl grinned as he turned away from his game to look at her.

'Oh, it's you again!' He laughed. The little girl uttered a sound; once again she meant something specific.

'A'right then, gwan!' Gently, D. held up the small child and placed her on the floor where she could reach her toy. Then he went back to the disputed game he and Leroy were having. D. had already lost two games. Strangely enough, he had won the first one, but since then Leroy had destroyed him with disconcerting ease. There was no way he was going to let him have this one too! D. watched closely as Leroy's hand descended on the board. His face was totally blank, his eyes immobile, reading the play carefully before he made his move. His hovered over one of the pieces, covering low, not quite touching it. D. knew that if Leroy managed to get through with that particular move, he was finished. He had always seen himself as a wicked draughts player; he had spent enough hours as a youth in the back yards of his old area to be good . . . But until he played Leroy, he never really knew what it was to doubt in a game. Leroy had a way of advancing, a planned strategy which completely puzzled D. but which paid every time. D. watched as Leroy's large hand slowly, almost delicately, pushed a black piece, not the one it had been shadowing, forward. Then, with a big sigh (whether of relief, resignation or satisfaction), he sat back in his chair, smiling. D. looked at him briefly before returning to the board. He didn't like that smile; kind of amused, knowing.

D. checked every single possibility resulting from Leroy's play mentally. Then he felt a sharp tug on the left leg of his trousers. He tried to ignore it, resolutely at first, keeping his mind on the game opening in front of him, but the tugging continued harder, and the baby's shrill cry made concentration on the game impossible. Leroy laughed as D. bent down and picked up the little girl.

'Wha'ppen now?' he asked, looking her in the eyes.

She answered something, a couple of syllables, pointing at him with her fingers. D. had to smile at the pretty little face.

'You gwan mek me lose the game, y'know!' he said, poking her softly in the belly. The little girl laughed and tried to get away from her father's accusing finger. He persisted until she eventually fell giggling on the settee.

'Hey, nuh budda try blame her, boss; yuh get mash up!' Leroy told D.

'Mash up? Me nuh mash up yet! Ah my play, true?' But the child was coming back for him. He took her in his arms, patiently explaining to her, as if she cared, that he was about to lose the game.

'Awright,' D. said, holding up the child. 'You take her then, so me can play.'

Leroy reached out and seized her, pulling her to his face.

'Avril, come here!' He pressed his nose against her, blowing in her face, teasing her. She pulled his beard and grabbed his chin in her tiny hands. Leroy laughed; he was very proud of his little niece and since she had been born, he would come regularly and spend a little time with her whenever he could. Meanwhile, D. had read the play, or so he thought, and was about to push one of his few remaining pieces forward. After a last check, he made a move. With Avril sitting on his lap, Leroy looked at the board; he knew he was on his way to winning this game also.

'So, my play now?' he said thoughtfully. He pushed one piece forward. D. frowned, wondering where the trap was. Yet, he could do nothing but what Leroy had 'programmed' him to do, so he took the piece offered him. Doing so, he realized what was going to happen, but it was too late. Leroy switched Avril from his right hand to his left, then calmly jumped three of D.'s pieces. None of them said anything for a few seconds. D. looked up and met Leroy's unnerving smile; he knew it was the end. He crowned one piece. After that, it was over very quickly.

'Another game?' Leroy asked. D. kissed his teeth, shaking his head dejectedly.

'Nuh, man; is al'right . . .'

Leroy put Avril down, standing her up against the low table where she could play with the game as she had wanted to do from earlier on. D. went to the kitchen and brought back some fruit juice. He had been babysitting all morning while Donna was out taking Cindy to school, shopping and running some errands. By now, he was eager to get out. Especially after the frustrating experience he had suffered at the hands of Leroy.

D. had been back about six weeks. Most of his time had been spent either by Donna or at Sticks's place. He had relaxed mostly, only going to a couple of dances, content with leaving Sticks to continue running the business as he had been doing. Donna was overjoyed to have him back of course. As for Cindy, she spent every moment he was in around him. The little girl had a deep affection for D., a feeling which not even her natural father could claim to enjoy. Donna had told D. that her daughter's father had come by once, several months before, on his release from prison, yet Cindy had not shown much interest. Since that day, he had not returned. For his part, D. had been happy to see his five-month-old daughter. She was so little and pretty, yet so strong in personality and restless. Donna had left her with him in bed that morning and, sure enough, she had not allowed him a moment's peace. He didn't mind though, he felt surprisingly good looking after her. He was virtually a family man now, and Donna did everything she could to make him feel that way. She was herself pleasantly surprised by D.'s new attitude and the way he spent most of his time at home. Still, though he enjoyed that part, he often felt the urge to do something more concrete with his time. So far, he had stayed cool, thinking of what Charlie had told him about going 'legit'. He could see the point. D. knew now that life on the street, hustling and operating the kind of business they were into, could not last for ever. 'There's only three ways out in that line of work,' Charlie had said, 'dead, locked up, or cracked up.' He had tried to think otherwise, but his partner was usually right. Charlie himself had started getting involved in other things. He had gotten into music; promoting shows and dances, also managing a few artists and distributing music videos which some of his contacts sent him from America. D. wasn't in a hurry to get something up. At least not financially. True to his word, Charlie had given him his share of the business, more than enough to lay low for a while, until he decided on which play to make. On the other hand, Sticks and the rest of the soldiers had been more than happy about D.'s return. If he had listened to them, he would have been back on the streets immediately, taking over the whole town. But, as D. told them, he had to be careful. After all, he still had to keep out of sight from the police for one . . .

Avril watched as D. poured out two glasses of juice. Sure enough, as he started to sip his drink, she let go of the table and dropped to the floor, crawling hurriedly in his direction. He allowed her to have some. It was early afternoon, a cold day under a dull, grey sky outside. Leroy had dropped by earlier, as he sometimes did on his way to the record shop, to bring D. some recent session cassettes. He was glad to see D. back in England. Though he asked very few questions concerning the events of the past year, D. had told him a little about his stay in Jamaica. Leroy explained that he planned to set up something back home soon; he found life in England cold and boring and wanted to return to Jamaica to live with his family. 'When you get to a certain stage in your life,' he told D., 'if you don't move, then you never will.'

Leroy was still only in his mid-thirties, but he longed for the place where he had grown up.

'So how the business go?' D. asked.

'Bwoy, not so good, y'know. I jus' about manage.'

'Yeah?'

'It's recession time, so dem seh . . .' Leroy remarked. 'Right now, I gwan try to get into another side of the business.'

'Like wha'?' D. asked, interested.

'I wan' start to do some producing; I have a bredrin

whe' gwan line up some t'ings fe me . . . Yuh know Lee, nuh true?'

'Yeah, man, Lee big ina dat!' D. paused. 'I t'inkin' about settin' up some business too.'

'Wha'; ina de music too?' Leroy asked.

'Maybe, yuh know . . . I still meditating about it.'

Leroy nodded; he clearly approved of D.'s intention.

'Yes, man; yuh have 'nuff potential, somet'ing mus' work out.'

They reasoned some more about the possibilities, D. paying attention to Leroy's ideas. He trusted his judgement and had always admired the way he had cooled down from his former bad-bwoy days and set out to make a living the straight way. Meanwhile, Avril, after having drunk D.'s juice, set out after Leroy's glass.

While the two men talked, the front door opened and slammed shut. Donna appeared in the room. Avril immediately forgot about everything else and crawled hastily towards her mother, greeting her with a chorus of shrill cries.

'Come here, baby.' Donna lifted her up and kissed her. 'So, Daddy look after you?'

'She a'right, man,' D. said confidently.

'But yuh nuh change her?!' Donna looked at him accusingly.

D. frowned; he knew he'd forgotten something. Leroy laughed.

'Yes, Daddy!' Leroy teased as he got up and stretched, looking at his watch. 'I got to reach the shop now.'

'Yuh nuh want somet'ing to eat?' Donna asked.

'No, man, me a'right.' Leroy declined his sister's offer. 'So wha'; later, D., seen?'

Leroy took his leave.

'Yes, man, respeck. Me come check yuh soon.'

'A'right. Anytime you want your revenge . . .' Leroy couldn't resist a last reference to the draughts game.

'Cho, you gwan!' D. laughed.

Leroy left. D. went to slot one of the new cassettes in the stereo.

'Yuh hungry?' Donna returned from changing Avril.

'Not really; I get somet'ing earlier.'

Donna prepared some food for herself and her ever hungry daughter. They sat in front of the television, relaxing, watching a movie for a while. Avril soon fell asleep, so Donna put her to bed. She came back and handed D. a plastic carrier bag.

'I got somet'ing fe yuh.'

D. took the bag, eyeing her suspiciously.

'Is wha'?'

'Look at it nuh!'

He opened the bag and took out the shirt she had bought for him. It was a nice black and gold silk garment, expensive-looking.

'Yuh like it?' Donna asked expectantly.

She knew D. was fussy when it came to clothes, but he seemed pleasantly surprised.

'Yeah, man, it pretty.'

Donna smiled. D. folded back the shirt carefully and placed it on one of the chairs.

'It's not my birt'day yet,' he said, teasing his woman.

'I know dat; so wha' I cyan buy yuh presents?!'

'How yuh mean?!' D. put his arm around her shoulders. Donna glanced at him briefly, saying nothing.

'Me like how yuh deal wid me, y'know,' he told her.

'Dat's because yuh good now . . .' she said.

'So wait, I wasn't good before?'

'Yeah, man, but yuh bettah now,' Donna stated simply.

D. decided against asking further questions. He had an

111

idea of what she meant and, anyway, why rock the boat when everything was smooth? As long as she was happy, that was cool with him. Donna and he went back a long way; she was a sweet woman and very loyal to him, but he knew she could be difficult if she wanted to be. They watched television, talking and joking, enjoying each other's company. Then the phone rang. D. let Donna answer it; it was for him.

'Yeah? Wha' ah gwan, me breddah?'

It was Charlie. They talked briefly. As he replaced the receiver, D. noticed Donna looking at him sideways, enquiringly. He simply kept his eyes on the TV screen, saying nothing.

'You going out?' she asked after a while.

D. laughed.

'So wha'; yuh don't wan' me to go nowhere?'

'I cyan stop yuh.'

'True. Still, it comin' like yuh wan' keep me fe yuhself alone!'

D. stretched. Charlie had said he would meet him by Sticks's in an hour's time. He didn't say much on the phone. Sticks would come to pick him up shortly. So far, D. had not found it necessary to buy a car. He was taken everywhere he needed to go and Charlie, cautious as always, insisted that he should always have someone with him. That was cool for now. D. left Donna and went to get ready.

'Yuh comin' back fe dinner?' Donna asked when he later returned to the living room.

'Mmnh, I soon come . . .' The bell rang, D. went to open the door.

'Yes, Don!' Sticks greeted him. He followed D. inside the flat, waiting as he picked up his keys and slipped on a jacket.

'Hi, sis,' Sticks said, smiling at Donna.

'Awright, sah,' she answered less than enthusiastically.

112

Somehow, Donna had never taken to Sticks. Not that she could claim he had any bad influence on D., she simply distrusted the tall, self-assured youth who was so devoted to her man. Sticks didn't notice her reserve; he was in a good mood, nodding appreciatively to the sound of the Yard cassette coming out of the speakers. D. was ready.

'Soon come, y'hear?' he told Donna as he stepped out. D. got into Sticks's gleaming Saab, closing the door against the winter weather. Sticks spun the car around and they drove up through the narrow back streets until they emerged on to Kingsland Road. The night before, they had gone to attend a Radical Hi-Powah session. D. liked the sound; he still checked for High Noon, but thought the new sound had an edge, an authentic Yard feel. He had met the sound owner and even talked about holding a dance one of these days . . . The sounds inside the plush car was pumping loud and heavy, the way Sticks liked it. As they breezed through Clapton, heading for Leyton, a beeping sound rang out, faintly audible against the thumping beat of the car stereo. Sticks turned the car hi-fi down and took the cell phone out of his jacket inside pocket.

'Yes . . . Who? Wait, wha'ppen, baby.' He spent a few minutes sweet-talking the girl at the other end of the line. He assured her he'd come to see her later, then switched off. Grinning, he looked at D.

'Me cyan even 'member what de gal look like, y'know.'

D. laughed. Sticks's mobile phone was strictly for his personal use. Everyone knew they were now easy to tap and not safe to talk business on any more. They reached the street where Sticks lived. He parked his car behind Charlie's Mazda and walked to the house. Inside, Charlie sat stretched out in a chair, punching data into his personal organizer, while Linton, who had apparently just woken up, was busy building a spliff. They greeted D. warmly. In one corner, near the television set, Puggy was involved in a lengthy and gratifying telephone conversation. He held up his fist, hailing D.

'How yuh ah gwan so; yuh know seh me love yuh, twenty-four seven,' D. heard him tell whoever he had on the line. He sat across from Charlie, waiting for him to finish what he was doing. Sticks returned from the kitchen with some bottles of stout and beer.

'Hey, lovah bwoy, leggo de phone, nuh?!' he called out to Puggy. The youth signalled he had almost finished.

'Telephone love . . .' Linton laughed, lighting up his smoke.

'Yes, D., everyt'ing cool?' Charlie asked.

'Yeah, mon, copacetic!' The drinks went around.

'Wha'ppen, Linton?' D. asked the tall, heavy-set man. 'How yuh look so mash-up, man?'

The man scratched his head; he was just about recovering from the previous night. He and Sticks had dropped D. off and then driven home with the two girls they had left the dance with. It was obvious that Linton had not gone to bed right away . . .

'Yuh wan' see; dat gal nevah let me res' at all, Don!'

D. laughed. 'Den me nevah tell yuh seh she too wil' fe yuh?' He had warned Linton about the woman they had met at the dance. D. remembered her from before; she was one of those heavy ravers and heavy drinkers with a reputation for being 'over-sexed'. Furthermore, by the time they had left the dance, she and her friend had smoked enough stuff to stone an elephant.

'Ah nuh lie; me all ha'fe stone it up, y'know!' Everybody laughed.

Puggy was now off the phone. Officially, he had been due to leave the country the previous week, his tour now completed. But, as he saw it, he'd been wanting to travel for a long time, and life with his cousin Sticks and the team was much too exciting to leave now. Also, he had too many girls to cater for at the present moment to go away. So he decided to indefinitely extend his stay. He could make his money cutting records, doing PAs and he had also convinced Sticks to bring him in to run some business.

'I've got news for you,' Charlie said looking at D.

'What kinda news?'

'Well; our friend Chin got arrested in New York . . .'

D. took in the information, waiting for Charlie to explain. The others were listening too. Charlie seemed satisfied with the effect he was having. He paused, grinning, before going on.

'Yeah, he was in a hotel sorting out a deal with some guys, when all on a sudden the place was full of cops. Apparently, he'd been set up; the guys he was doing business with were undercover drugs enforcement agents. Can you believe it?'

There was something in Charlie's sarcastic tone of voice. D. looked at him, eyebrows raised.

'So, what happen to him?'

Charlie took a sip of beer, shook his head in mock sadness.

'Man, they got him with two cases full of shit, a "hot" shotgun in his car, plus some "immigration" problems.' Charlie laughed. 'I think it was just bad luck.'

D. nodded, thoughtful.

'Yeah, bad luck . . .'

'How long him get?' Sticks asked.

'Well, it's hard to tell fe now. But since it's DEA business . . . plus the shotgun got traced to at least two murders; it's gonna be heavy.' Charlie paused, maximizing the effect of his speech.

'He didn't make bail . . .' he finally added, smirking.

D. leant back in a chair, taking the news in. He would have preferred to deal with Chin personally; he was still bitter about the way the man had tried to set him up. Yet, he was now out of the way, for a while at least, and that was cool.

In his corner, Sticks had also been busy thinking the news over.

'Dem done nuh!' he said coldly.

'Chin's done for now, but there ain't gonna be no war,' Charlie pointed out.

Sticks couldn't see the finer points of the situation.

'How yuh mean? We jus' kill dem an' done!' he insisted, looking at D. for approval, but D. was absorbed in thoughts of his own.

'That's not the way we operate; that thing with Chin is personal, but we still have a business arrangement with his people.'

Sticks was indignant.

'Wha'? Ah nuh nut'n dat; we run dem outta town and tek over everyt'ing, man!'

Charlie sighed.

'So, tell me, you wanna take on the whole posse?' he asked.

'Den yuh nuh 'member seh, dem was out to close we down?!' Sticks looked at Linton. 'Hey, Linton, tell 'im what happened ah Stonebridge!'

Six months earlier at the height of the war, Sticks, Linton and two other soldiers had had a chance encounter with their opponents at a dance on the Stonebridge estate. In the ensuing shootout, Linton had received a bullet in the shoulder and only an undignified flight had saved all of them from certain death. Sticks was still smarting from it. Linton drew on his spliff and said nothing.

'I know what happened, Mikey. And that was why we had to have a truce.'

Sticks couldn't see that at all.

'Yeah, dat was den, but now Chin's gone; so mek we wipe dem out!'

D. had listened to the exchange in silence. He could see Sticks's point and he would have probably said the same thing before, but there were more important considerations now. He could feel Charlie's eyes on him, waiting for him to intervene. He picked up the bottle of stout and drank some.

'A'right; hear dis . . . Dem did want me outta de way, fe two reasons. First, because I took from dem, den because dem did wan' to control everyt'ing, seen?' D. paused. 'De firs' business get sort out when I get back ah Yard, an' dat was before Chin. The nex' t'ing is dat Chin set me up, I was in his way. Everyt'ing dat happen after dat come from him.' Everyone listened attentively, knowing that, in the last instance, D.'s ruling would prevail. He looked around the room and continued.

'Charlie was right to call a truce, 'cause we cyan mek money if war ah gwan. De way t'ings ah run now, we making al'right, true?' D. looked at Sticks.

'True,' the soldier answered sternly.

'An' dat is what we all want. Anyhow, we start war again, we gwan lose money. An' also, dis t'ing don't stop here, y'know; if dem man dere cyan operate, dem will have no choice but come after we. There is enough fe ev'rybody.'

Charlie nodded, satisfied with D.'s wise decision. He was impressed by the fact that his partner was so level-headed. Much more now than before. Sticks reflected on D.'s words, then tried to appeal.

'Me respeck wha' yuh ah seh, Don. But some ah Chin's people, diss we out deh. I feel seh we bettah dus' fe him bodyguard dem, at least.'

D. looked at his lieutenant, not unsympathetically.

'I know whe' yuh ah talk 'bout, Sticks, man. But hear wha'; it's best to hol' it down fe now. Time will come.'

Sticks accepted the logic of the argument reluctantly. He still thought he should have been allowed to settle accounts with his enemies. But D.'s word was final. As he said, time will come . . .

Linton got up and went to play a cassette on the system. The radio was tuned to a reggae station, but the deejay had spoiled the vibe by talking all through while the records played. Live sounds from a session cassette changed the mood.

'I've got an idea . . .' Charlie announced. When he saw he had everyone's attention, he spelt it out.

'As we agreed, we stick to the arrangement with the Spicers . . . But that don't include Chin's own business.'

D. listened. Even Sticks seemed intrigued. Charlie smiled mischievously, looking at D.

'Chin's no fool, y'know, D.? He knows you can't just run drugs alone. After you were gone, he started setting up some legit or semi-legit operations around town. Some, we can't touch, because it's not strictly his own . . . But I know one we should be able to take over.'

'What yuh mean?' D. asked.

'Mikey, you know the gambling house, round the back of Finsbury Park, near where Sweetie's friend live?'

'Yeah, I know it,' Sticks answered interested.

'It's a basement place; they've got a set in there, a bar and a small food shop inside,' Charlie explained for D.'s benefit. And then he continued.

'Well, I found out that Chin paid off the old guy who used to run it and took it over. They're turning good money in there. I think we should take it over now, for free . . .'

There was a short silence as the idea sank in . . . Then Sticks let out a short laugh, while D. smiled, looking at Charlie.

'It's clean, Chin's own joint. No one can object to that,' the brown man added.

'Charlie, yuh is a genius,' D. said. Even Linton enjoyed the irony of the play.

'It's best we look after Chin's investment,' he said seriously. They all laughed, appreciating the joke. D. seemed happy with the idea. That way, he thought, he would start running his own thing, and if it wasn't fully legal, at least it was safe and profitable. That was definitely a brilliant idea.

Sticks went for more drinks. Some Rizla paper appeared, and some spliff building started. Charlie handed D. a small bag full of strong-smelling ganja. Sticks had noticed that D. didn't touch coke any more. He had heard him mention vaguely that he was temporarily 'cooling out' from the stuff. He himself was rarely without it, having increased his use of crack in particular. As he had told D. when he'd given him the low-down on the events since he'd been gone, 'You gotta be sharp out deh.'

Puggy, the youth with the golden voice, had listened carefully to the various arguments. He was new to it all, but very eager to emulate his older cousin, who was now a big-timer in England. He was also, through Sticks, related to Charlie though from another branch of their extended family. Puggy's aims were clear: he wanted to stay on top as a singer, get the most girls and, last but not least, be like Sticks, respected, smart-looking and never short of money. As far as drugs were concerned, he'd smoke herb and the odd pull from a cocktail spliff, but had so far kept away from crack. They were all relaxed now that business had been taken care of. The music pumped through the living room, the discussion had drifted to more pleasant topics.

'Hey, Puggy!' D. called out to the youth. 'Is how yuh love fat gal so?!' D. was referring to the 'mampy' he had seen the ambitious youth man stuck against for most of the dance the previous night. Everyone laughed.

'T'rough me ah celebrity, Don; all type ah gal ah rush me, y'know?'

'Dat t'ing almost kill yuh, man. Yuh couldn't even sing

119

good after she done press yuh 'gainst the wall,' Sticks teased him. Puggy disagreed, boasting.

'Ah whe' yuh ah seh?! Me can handle anyt'ing.'

Everyone liked the young singer, loving his verve and natural fearless disposition. In turn, his newly found friends and the 'prestige' lifestyle he now enjoyed with them, only made Puggy all the more boisterous. That he was immensely talented, no one could deny. At barely sixteen years of age, Puggy had exploded on the reggae scene in Jamaica as an accomplished artist. Having spent most of his time from the age of seven dreaming of being a singer, tirelessly listening to and imitating anything that he could hear on the radio and at local sound systems, he had a natural flair for riding any type of riddim and a voice to match. His fame had already spread to America and Canada. England had been the last leg of his first tour abroad, and there also he had set dances alight, as much by his visual antics on stage as by his singing. He had already cut a few demos with two local producers and, as a youth full of ambition, was now planning his next career move. As another singer he'd met on the circuit had advised, the first thing he needed was a good manager, and Puggy already had an idea about that.

'Watch the bike back!' Sticks exclaimed from his corner, commenting on a couple of girls on the TV screen winding low to the beat. One of the two live dancehall video cassettes Charlie obtained recently was showing. Every pair of eyes in the room turned to admire the two fit girls, each clad in a diminutive batty rider and leggings, demonstrating one of the popular dancehall styles with application. Puggy threw a couple of salacious remarks that went down well in the general macho mood. In his chair, D. was halfway through his second Guinness stout, laughing at one of the jokes. He looked at Charlie, also checking the action on the video. Something which he had wanted to ask came across his mind. He leaned towards his partner across the table.

'Show me somet'ing; how a old veteran like Chin coulda slip up so, man?'

Charlie read the real question in D.'s squint, he pulled a falsely affected face.

'He must have gotten careless . . .'

D. pressed on, still squinting.

'Or maybe . . . him get set up?'

'It's possible . . . these things happen?' Charlie shrugged. D. looked away, thinking. He heard Charlie say, matter-of-factly, 'One thing I like about the States; you can buy anything . . . anybody.' The two men's eyes met briefly then D. leaned back in his chair.

'Nice work,' he said simply. Nothing else was mentioned, but D. knew now. It was totally in character with Charlie's style to have masterminded such a plan. He had never forgiven the way D. had been set up and, sure enough, in his usual quiet and efficient way, had made sure the guilty got repaid in kind. Apparently, he still had some good friends back in America . . .

Through the window, the night had descended on the street. Puggy walked across the room to Charlie.

'Supa, I wan' to talk to yuh about some business matters.' He stood there waiting to see if Charlie was open for the discussion he had planned to have with him.

'Yeah? What kind of business?' Charlie asked, slightly intrigued. The youth squatted beside him and revealed his idea, straight to the point.

'Hear wha'ppen: I need a manager, seen?! I feel seh, the man coulda deal wid me right.'

'You want me to manage you?' Charlie asked.

'Yeah, man. Me have potential, y'know, but I want somebody to deal wid de business side fe me, somebody I can trust.'

Charlie listened as Puggy explained how he planned on capitalizing on his current success to build his career on a solid basis. He didn't want to end up like so many other talented singers before him, burnt out within a few years, unable to match the ever-rising competition because they had peaked too early. It was a well-known fact in the music business that a young artist unprepared for the temptation of the 'glamour life' as a performer, usually had a short shelf-life, so to speak. Puggy rightly considered that he was meant to become something more durable, who would still rule in his category in years to come. He told Charlie, who already acted as a kind of agent for a couple of artists, that he was serious about it. He looked sincere enough.

'I don't know, Puggy, man; maybe it could work. Let's talk about it a little later, OK? Right now I'm gonna reach home.' Charlie left the option open. 'Maybe you're right. Check me in a few days.'

'A'right, serious t'ing.' Puggy held out his fist for Charlie to touch, heartically. Charlie got up to leave, saying that he had a couple of people to check.

'When you planning on making this move on the gambling house?' he asked D.

'Tonight, man!'

'Tonight?' Charlie repeated, surprised.

D. was confident.

'Yeah, man. Yuh know how long I wait fe dem runnins deh?!'

Charlie reflected that tonight was Thursday; the place would be busy, a profitable night . . . Once Charlie had gone, D. began questioning Sticks about the club, how it was situated, who usually managed it and so on . . . He wanted to get an idea of what he was facing, but Sticks, confident as usual, assured him that everything would be easy. D. knew that Sticks was all the more eager to make the move because he had a personal grudge against Chin's top lieutenant. Puggy, meanwhile, had disappeared into the kitchen to cook a pot. Another of his skills was cooking.

Everyone who had tasted it agreed that Puggy was a wicked cook. The youth himself usually gave credit to his grandmother who had taught him from an early age back in the countryside in Jamaica. Sticks ordered Linton to call Pablo, he was sure four of them was enough. They finished eating but it was still too early to go anywhere; early morning would be best. A game of Ludo started, noisy and good-humoured; the four friends drank more beer and stout, with a good few spliffs to burn. True to his habit, Sticks made himself a pipe on top of all that, so did Linton. Later on, after they had all lost and won games, Puggy stretched.

'So, what time we ah move?'

Sticks turned to him, cigarette at the corner of his mouth: 'We?! Yuh nah come!'

'How you mean, me mus' come . . .' Puggy protested, offended. D. looked on, amused by the youthman's insistence on being part of the squad. Puggy had the kind of fearless disposition and bare-faced feistiness he had at the same age; he could relate to that.

'Yuh cyan come dis time, star,' D. told him sympathetically after the argument had gone on a little. 'Yuh have a skill, yuh know; ah dat yuh mus' work on. Jus' concentrate on music, man.'

Puggy resigned himself.

'Ouno drop me off at Stamford Hill, den,' he demanded, checking his watch.

Sticks laughed; he knew where his cousin was going.

'A'right,' he said. 'Bwoy, it comin' like yuh live over dere.'

Shortly after, Pablo showed up, explaining that he just came from a party in south London where a big fight had taken place. Apparently, as he told D. and the others, the man giving the party had unknowingly invited his two baby mothers. Arguments had rapidly degenerated into a fight, with supporters in both camps. By the time Pablo left, around two o'clock, the domestic problem had spilled into the street, with police already on the scene. They laughed at his graphic descriptions of the scuffles.

'Yuh know where we ah go?' D. asked him a little after. Pablo shrugged. 'Not really.'

Briefly, D. explained the operation. Pablo simply nodded.

'Yes, Don. Long time we due fe tek over!'

'A'right, I wan' this t'ing done neatly, seen?' D. pointed out, as much for Sticks as for the other two. 'We work our way in and control the place without too much damage; we ah go run it.'

Everybody understood. They got ready. D. watched Sticks as he carefully tucked a gun in his belt, under his jumper.

'Yuh ah carry some big t'ing, my yout', mek me see it nuh?'

He took the piece from Sticks, a large automatic with a steely blue finish.

'Forty-five; dem corn deh big, man,' he said appreciatively, looking at the fat bullets on top of the clip he pulled out.

'Me have somet'ing fe yuh, don't worry yuhself.'

Sticks sent Linton to pick up something. He came back and handed D. a plastic carrier bag. D. took out the pretty-looking gun, grey-steel framed with blue polished slide.

'Executive style, Don,' Sticks said. 'Is a present fe yuh.' He explained that he got the weapon from a contact of his, as a bonus for delivering quality stuff.

'Defender, .40 Smith and Wesson 'munition. Big holes!!'

The gun looked neat, to D., powerful. It was a nice surprise. They called Puggy, who had disappeared inside the bedroom, and left.

A breezy, biting night greeted them. English winter at

its best. They had agreed to use Pablo's large Ford Granada, as Sticks's car was too well-known. They dropped Puggy off as agreed and drove on through the quiet night until Pablo finally eased the car into a dark, narrow back street. Lights off, they watched for a while, eyes on the alley between the two houses leading to the basement gambling place. Half an hour passed. One man went in with two girls, another man came out. A car pulled over and stopped for a few minutes. Someone ran in and out again . . . It was busy all right. D. kept quiet, sitting in the back beside Sticks, checking the surroundings. The cassette in the stereo played low, the bass bouncing regularly out of the loudspeakers. Linton and Pablo, in the front, talked and watched, waiting for D. to give the signal. As if despite himself, D.'s eyes followed the long silhouette of a man, wrapped in a sheepskin coat, who had just emerged from the alley. Frowning, he tried to dismiss the feeling that the look and the walk were familiar to him. In vain, he had to check it out.

The man passed the car on the opposite pavement.

'I wan' talk to dat man.' D. tapped Linton on the shoulder.

Linton opened his door and stepped out without questioning the command. He called out to the man as he walked across the street. The tall man was suspicious. D. saw him hesitate as Linton pointed to the car. But he had no choice but to follow the soldier. D. unlocked his door and pushed it open, sliding along to allow the man to enter. Linton closed the door behind him. The man looked around the car slowly, his eyes finally resting on D.'s face. He was in his late thirties, wearing a flat leather cap, of dark complexion, with staring eyes, hollowed cheeks and a stubble of beard. D. said nothing at first, watching the man's eyes change as he slowly tried to figure out if he knew him.

125

'Wha'ppen, boss?' he asked in a worried voice.

D. waited a little more, then he said, 'Wha' yuh ah seh, Pips?'

This time the man's eyes opened wide; his brain working overtime. D. clearly knew him, but the man just couldn't make him. It took another minute before he exclaimed:

'D.? Ah you, man?'

D. smiled.

'Jah Pips, is wha' happen to yuh, man?'

The tall man couldn't believe it.

'Wha'? Lord, man; wha' ah gwan?'

Pips, or Jah Pips as D. knew him then, was one of Jerry's close brethren. He was in fact slightly older than him and had been one of the men instrumental in bringing Jerry the rasta philosophy. At the time, Jah Pips lived literally down the road from D.'s house in Denham Town. He and Jerry used to reason for hours and make moves; they would cool and eat at Pips's house and congregate with the other local dreads for long smoking and meditating sessions. But Pips had changed a lot. It was only his peculiar, slightly limping walk that had D. convinced it was him. His full head of bushy locks had gone and he seemed thinner and older . . .

'Wha' yuh ah do 'round yah, man?'

D. explained vaguely that he had some business to take care of.

'Tell me; how in deh stay?' D. asked the man.

Pressing him nicely into describing the place, D. found out what he wanted to know. There were two guys behind the door, then a flight of stairs downstairs, where there were two rooms; one for dancers, the other one with gambling tables and a bar. With a little more questioning, Pips told D. there was a door behind, through the bar, leading to the 'office', from where the people in charge operated.

Apparently Pips was a regular at the club.

'So, is wha'ppen to yuh, Jah Pips, man?' D. asked him.

'Me deh yah, man; I come 'bout two years now.'

Pips said he'd been running a business for some people, trying to get money together. D. could see he was a long way from the proud, calm and self-assured rastaman he used to be. Pips didn't just look older, something in the man wasn't there any more.

'So, wha'ppen to Selassie I and t'ings . . . ?' D. asked him.

The man's eyes flickered once, as if surprised by the question.

'I leggo dat, man; is money me ah look . . .'

D. nodded. 'Seen . . . !'

He let Pips go, saying he was on a mission right now, and telling him to take care of himself. They waited ten more minutes then set out.

As they filed down the alley, D. told Sticks, ''Member: no shooting in deh!'

Sticks assured him he understood. They went down the few concrete steps leading to a heavy wooden door. It had been agreed that Pablo, who had been at the club a couple of times before, would act as decoy in case the bouncers knew the others for who they were. He knocked on the rectangular glass trap. A panel slid open, two eyes appeared briefly, just missing Pablo's grinning face. D. and his two soldiers were out of sight, pressed flat against the brick wall to the left-hand side. The sound of heavy locks, then the door opened and a ray of light illuminated Pablo's silhouette.

'From de cold!' D. heard Pablo say, good-humoured as he stepped in. Sticks was in front of him, waiting. As the panel swung back to shut again, they pounced. The large man behind the door felt the door's full weight as it shoved

127

him backwards, his back smashing against the concrete behind him. Meanwhile, Pablo had taken care of the other one, who was now staring at the muzzle of a gun, wide-eyed. Linton carefully locked the door behind them.

'Keep quiet; maybe we give yuh a chance . . .' Sticks told the big bouncer with the glasses as he searched him. It had clearly been a surprise; neither of the two men had time to make a move. Pablo retrieved a gun from the short man he was frisking, a Yard man, judging by his clothes and the way he was keeping cool under pressure. The big guy was of a more serious disposition, hands up in the air, unsteady on his feet.

'Don't shoot, man, take what you want,' he begged, swallowing nervously.

Sticks put the man's fear to good use.

'Weh your boss deh?'

D. watched, hands in his pocket. He looked down the flight of stairs. He could see another door opened, from beyond which music came floating out.

'In the office,' the big man answered.

The short man looked at D., straight-faced, the barrel of Pablo's gun against his throat.

'Yuh know me?' D. asked calmly.

The man nodded. D. looked at the leather pouch Pablo had taken from the man's waist.

'Who dung deh?' he asked, looking into the man's eyes.

'Ongo Judge, and Willie, a nex' yout'.'

'Yuh keep de cash fe dem?' D. pressed on.

The pressure of Pablo's gun muzzle against his throat precluded any hesitation.

'I bring de money dung ev'ry hour . . .'

D. turned to Pablo.

'Yuh an' Linton control yah so. Search ev'rybody, but mek dem let people in.'

128

'Put your hand dem down,' Linton growled at the big, seated bouncer.

Sticks started down the stairs, his right hand inside his jacket pocket. Before he followed him, D. asked the short man:

'Weh yuh name, star?'

'Costa . . .' he said simply.

D. nodded, giving him a last stare before stepping down.

'Keep cool an' yuh might still have a job tomorrow.'

D. joined Sticks in the darkness and smoke at the bottom of the stairs. The room was half-full with dancers, gesticulating to the bouncing beat. Sticks in front, they walked straight through, slowly, looking around until they got to the back room. There, groups of men were busy gambling, cursing and shouting, drinking and calling on luck . . . This second room was lit up, but no one paid attention to D. and Sticks as they walked towards the small bar at the end of the room. Two girls passed them, carrying drinks and giving them the eye. Sticks smiled at one of them, attractive, medium height, dressed in a short skirt and see-through top. Behind the bar, a light-skinned youth with a baseball cap and a fat, smiling woman were attending to the customers. D. spotted the door leading to the office, to the right side of the counter, at the back.

'Two hot Guinness,' Sticks ordered as the fat woman came to him.

The red youth was busy chatting up a girl at the far corner.

'Three pounds,' the woman said.

Smiling, Sticks took his hand out of his pocket, placed the gun butt on the counter.

'Keep smiling,' he told the bewildered fat woman.

Coolly, D. took the drinks and went to the corner of the bar, lifted up the counter panel and walked behind, carefully watching for any sudden move amongst the gamblers.

Sticks followed him, appearing behind the youth with the baseball cap and pulling him away from his girlfriend.

'We have some personal business in deh,' he warned in his ear, the gun low against the youth's side. 'Do wha' yuh ah do; no sense yuh get hurt.'

The two bartenders watched as D. knocked on the door, Sticks covering him, still smiling.

'Who dat!' a voice called out from inside the office.

'Costa,' D. answered, checking behind him quickly. Sticks was ready. A key turned in the lock, a man's face appeared briefly then retreated at the sight of D.'s automatic. Sticks following quickly, closed the door and covered the man D. had first faced. Meanwhile, D. had walked on straight to the desk, where a thickset man with dark shades and a thin moustache sat. His right hand disappeared under the desk for a second, then came back up, joining his left hand in the air as he realized he'd never be fast enough. D. shook his head, standing on the other side of the desk, his gun held low, horizontal, almost casually. A slim, dark woman with heavy make-up, wearing black leggings and a green jumper, sat in an armchair to the man's right. She froze, eyeing the figure in front of her with total bemusement. Sticks searched the soldier and had him face against the wall in the standard US police style position.

'D., I heard you was back in town,' the man said casually. He was the same man who had 'invited' D. to see Chin that night at the Reggae Awards.

'Get up, man,' D. ordered. The man complied, and obeyed D.'s instruction to stand against the wall. The woman still hadn't moved. Sticks roughly pushed the soldier he was covering forward until the two men stood together. D. came around the desk, opened the top drawer and took out a mean-looking, loaded black handgun. He stuck the weapon in his waistband. Sticks searched the owner, just in case.

'Judge, judgement day come fe yuh!' He smirked, looking at the man with a vicious smile.

'Bring him,' D. ordered.

Prodding Judge with his gun barrel, Sticks pushed him forward until he stood to attention in front of D. Sticks would have clearly preferred to give vent to his intense dislike of Judge; he had been waiting to deal with him for some time . . .

'Listen good now,' D. told the man without animosity. 'I taking over dis place. I don't really have nothin' against yuh, so you stay alive, seen?!'

The man stood there, observing D. from behind his shades. He knew it was not the time for bargaining. 'We 'ave an agreement, man,' he said nevertheless.

D. laughed.

'Yeah, man, dat still stands, else you'll be dead a'ready.'

'You lucky bwoy; if ah me, I'd a kill yuh right now,' Sticks commented, throwing Judge a scornful look. D. left the man standing there and picked up the briefcase standing against the desk. He opened it. Several wads of banknotes and a couple of plastic bags filled with smaller bags containing white rocks fell out.

'I have to confiscate dat.' D. chuckled.

'We comin' like de tax man,' Sticks added. They both laughed. Cold, mirthless laughter.

'Said speed; dat confiscate too.' Sticks tapped the large rolled gold chain and pendant Judge was wearing with the tip of his gun's nozzle, motioning the man to take it off. He didn't have much choice so did as he was told. Sticks looked at the heavy piece of jewellery then at the man.

'Dis is your lucky day; my boss don't like too much killing,' he told him coldly. Then he turned towards the petrified woman, her hands folded in her lap, watching the whole scene with obvious fear. Sticks walked over to her, squatted down beside the chair, his face close to hers.

'Me 'member yuh, y'know. Ah yuh did deh wid dat ugly bwoy down at de show las' year.' He was right. She remembered him too, but didn't acknowledge it.

'Hey, Judge!' Sticks called out. 'It look like yuh tek way your boss woman!'

D. laughed. The other soldier was still against the wall where Sticks had left him, anxious to stay alive.

'A'right, hear dis; I run dis place now, same business, new management,' D. told Judge. 'Until your boss come back,' he added as an afterthought.

The clock on the otherwise bare wall said four-thirty. When asked, the soldier said they usually closed by 5 a.m.

'Gwan, man, go home,' D. told Judge. The man picked up his jacket and started towards the door, followed by his soldier. The girl made as if to get up. Sticks motioned her back in the chair.

'Not you, lady; yuh is my bonus.' He smiled. Judge looked at Sticks briefly, then at the girl.

'Yuh can leave your staff here, they're safe,' D. said as Judge went out. He signalled to Sticks to follow him upstairs. The girl stared at him with a mixture of fear and expectation. She wasn't really pretty, but seemed well-proportioned, tall and shapely. D. himself didn't like women with make-up; Sticks could have her . . .

Once Judge had gone, they stayed in the office. They talked with the girl until closing time. She said her name was Mona. Apparently, Judge had taken her over from Chin when he left for the US. She told D. she had never liked him anyway.

The people started to leave. The staff, supervised by Sticks, closed the place down. He explained to them about the new management and offered to let them keep their jobs, if they wanted to. They all elected to stay, except the fat barmaid, who told him she was related to Judge. She was allowed to leave in peace. Then D. and his crew left, with Mona in tow. On the whole, it had been an easy take-over, D. reflected as he drove home, the briefcase tucked between Mona and himself. At last, things were starting to get interesting. Pablo dropped him off near Donna's house.

11

FIRE AND ICE

't's a'right, drop me off here.' D. opened the door and stepped out of the car.

'Tomorrow, y'hear? Easy!' he told Charlie. The Mazda drove off, leaving him on the pavement, closing his coat. A cold drizzle had started to fall earlier that afternoon, a tediously continuous light rain that turned the streets into glistening mirrors. Then with the approaching nightfall, a chill had started to settle. It looked like it could even snow this year before Christmas. D. wanted to get a newspaper, that's why he had preferred Charlie to drop him by the row of shops. He only had to cut across the flats to get to Donna's after that. He went inside the newsagents and picked up a paper, getting one of the box of chocolates behind the counter also. D. felt like buying Cindy something and he knew how much she loved chocolates. The previous day, she had proudly shown him the excellent results she got in the maths test at school. D. congratulated her and watched the little girl beam with pride. Cindy was bright, and very keen to learn. D. remembered Donna mentioning that the teacher told her the child was 'exceptionally advanced for her age'. Donna was very pleased with her daughter's ability. Avril had begun to show that she could be similarly precocious. D. was proud of her, too. She might even taste some chocolate, he mused to himself.

He had spent most of the day at Charlie's, talking business and reviewing the progress of their operations. For the past two weeks, D. had operated the gambling club in Finsbury Park, or rather, supervised it, having given Sticks and Linton full responsibility for the place. He passed over there late every night to ensure all was well. So far, everything was running sweet. Most of the regulars had noticed the subtle switch that had occurred on management level. Most people knew the story behind it. It was no business of anyone but the two men concerned; runnins had to run . . . ! Besides, D. was apparently in favour with everyone. He had put in appearances at various places throughout town since his return. He was welcome everywhere it seemed. In fact his status had increased. The more he kept low, as now, the more he appreciated the rare appearances at a dance or a show. Today, he had attended to the promotion of his own dance to take place the following month. D. felt it was the right time for him to start keeping dances and stage shows. He had told Charlie about his intention to get into promoting and hopefully to get into it on a big scale after a while. Music, he felt, was something he had to get into. Since Charlie himself was now quite involved with producing and managing the few artists he controlled, that was a good connection right there. So, for a start, D. had gone to both High Noon and Radical Hi-Powah's owners and told them he intended to keep a big sound clash with them for the coming Christmas holiday. Both owners, one after the other, respectfully pointed out that they had bookings as it were, right through the holiday period, dates that were arranged with various people long in advance. But D. wasn't interested in that line of thinking; as he told the two sound owners, he had just come back and he wanted to set up a big dance to celebrate his return. The fact that it was holiday was even nicer! So, as he told them, the dance would take place on 19 December, the week before Christmas. Since Charlie was supposed to meet a man about the venue later that day, he'd let them know about that soon. And that's the way it went. Anyway, everything had to be right. D. felt a tremendous urge to do something, to get involved in various enterprises . . . It was as if the enforced rest he'd enjoyed in Jamaica and since returning, was beginning to have an effect on him. After the 'capture' of the club he had been out every night and that's the way he liked it. Though he felt good about his new baby daughter and also appreciated Donna's company, too much of anything never feels good. That was just D.'s nature. He needed to be busy!

He came out of the shop and under the drizzle walked across to the estate to get to the front where Donna lived. He checked his watch; after five. He'd had some food by Charlie's. Maybe he would rest until later when Sticks was supposed to pick him up. D. considered buying himself a car, but wasn't quite sure which kind yet. It would be wiser to avoid the type of vehicles he really liked, BMW or Mercedes, for reasons of security. He was still considering as he pushed his key into the lock. The rain seemed to get heavier as the day got darker. He shook himself and hung his coat up. As he was about to climb the stairs, he heard Avril's high-pitched voice from the bedroom. He caught a glimpse of a pair of feet and trouser-legs in the living room . . . Someone was seated on the settee watching the television. Frowning, D. left his newspaper and the box of chocolates on the steps, walked into the living room and stopped. A man sat comfortably, eyes on the screen, a glass in his right hand. He looked older than D., unshaven, with an old-fashioned semi-afro hair-style. He didn't notice D. right away. When he did, D. was coming at him, right hand in his trousers pocket, looking rather unfriendly. The man looked up, surprised. D. stopped just short of reaching him.

'Who is yuh?' he asked hostile. The man felt the negative vibrations. He straightened up instinctively in the chair.

'I'm Cindy's father . . .' The voice was deep, hoarse.

D. stood motionless for a few seconds, glaring down at the startled man. Then he turned and went upstairs, where Donna was changing Avril.

'Wha'ppen, D.?' she greeted him.

D. walked up slowly to the bedroom window, glanced outside then turned to Donna.

'Wha'ppen?! Ah dat me wan' ask yuh . . .'

Donna picked up Avril from the bed. The little girl smiled at her father, but he hardly noticed. Donna saw from his expression that something was wrong; she could guess what it was.

'Is wha' yuh vex about now?'

'Whe' dis ugly bwoy ah do downstairs?' he asked drily.

Donna looked at him, innocently.

'Ah Cindy fadder, him ah wait fe her . . .'

'Well, hear dis; me nuh know de bwoy, an' I don't care who him is.' He paused. 'If him wan' see his daughter, mek him tek her out. I don't want him in here,' D. told her.

Donna couldn't see why he was upset.

'How yuh ah gwan so?'

D. looked away towards the window, then back at Donna. Calmly, too calmly, he asked:

'Yuh nuh hear wha' me ah seh . . . ?!'

Donna left him there and went to the bathroom, without answering. She had known D. long enough to know he was short-tempered and didn't like to be contradicted. Still, she couldn't see what the harm was. She came out of the bathroom; D. hadn't moved.

'Look, D., don't make no trouble. The man jus' come see fe him pickney.'

D. nodded slowly. Then he asked, pointing to Avril in Donna's arms: 'Is who fe pickney dat one deh?'

Frowning Donna shook her head, sighed heavily. She didn't like the way the argument was turning.

'What kind ah question is dat, man?'

D. threw her a cold stare, then walked past her, kissing his teeth.

'Mek me lef' dis place, y'hear?'

D. jumped down the stairs, grabbing his coat on his way out of the house, back in the rainy night. He turned the corner and crossed the estate. The incident had put him in a bad mood. He regretted not having already bought a car. He swore, gathering his collar about his neck, and headed for the phone booth near the shops. Inside, he picked up the receiver, but stopped himself from dialling. He didn't really feel like calling Sticks and he'd spent the day with Charlie. Something crossed his mind, and, gradually, the frown eased up his features. Through the glass of the phone booth, he looked up at the dark sky, the downpour and the few people hurrying past towards the warmth of their homes. He replaced the receiver and stepped outside, walked up the street until he reached the traffic lights. Crossing over, he headed for the neon sign above a shack-like shop front and walked in.

'Boss, I need a drive,' he told the sleepy-looking, middle-aged white woman behind the counter.

'Where you going?'

He told her and she shouted a number. Soon, a young black man came out of the room to the right. He wore a checkered jacket and a baseball cap, with a pair of horn-rimmed glasses on his smiling African features. He greeted D. and they walked outside under the rain to a blue Datsun. D. sat beside the driver, gave him the address and they started out. The young cabbie switched on his stereo; D. was surprised to hear a reggae beat float out with the latest ragga music. He turned to the driver.

'So yuh like reggae music?'

The African youth smiled broadly.

'Oh yes, it's great.'

138

D. smiled to himself. Slowly, he started to relax, making conversation with the driver.

'Tell me, yuh understand the lyrics?'

'Most of it.' The youth shrugged, laughing. 'It is still a form of English.'

In his melodious accent, he explained that Africans, too, spoke a kind of pidgin English that had some similarities to the Jamaican patois. D. nodded. The youth seemed open, friendly, manoeuvring his car skilfully through the rush-hour traffic.

'Which part you're from?' D. asked. 'What country?'

'Nigeria,' the youth answered. D. thought as much; most of the Africans he'd met in London seemed to come from there.

'Yuh going back there?' D. asked again.

'Oh yes, I'm just studying here. I do some cabbing to make a living, you know. When I finish, I'm going back straight home.' The driver laughed. He told D. that England was too cold and wet. He missed his country, but he knew he was only here for a time. They talked further, D. told the man that he was doing some business. He'd also recently arrived.

'Yuh smoke?' D. asked him after a while.

The youth looked at him, briefly taking his eyes off the road.

'Yes, I smoke.'

As he suspected, D. found out that the student-cabbie enjoyed a good spliff. The youth told him he had gotten some really 'heavy' ganja from back home the previous month. Unfortunately, it was now all finished. They talked a little more until D. saw the street he was looking for. The driver pulled up by the kerb. D. paid the fare, then pulled out the rolled-up plastic bag he carried in his shirt pocket.

'Hol' a spliff, man, good Jamaican herb,' he told the cabbie.

The youth appreciated the gift. He tore up a piece of newspaper and wrapped up the ganja D. handed him. Before he left the car, D. wrote down Donna's phone number and gave it to the driver.

'Anyhow, you get any good herb, yuh call me. But only quality stuff, seen?!' he told the driver.

The driver assured him he'd call as soon as anything came through. He thanked D. again, waved and drove off.

D. got out of the rain, walked inside the hall of the low block of flats. Mentally, he anticipated the surprise he was likely to cause tonight. He climbed the two flights of stairs and stopped in front of the brown, varnished door of one of the flats.

D. rang the bell once. He waited a full minute; nothing. Another sharp finger jab on the button, this time he thought he heard the shuffling of feet coming towards the door. Presumably, someone inside was looking through the peephole, but since he had drawn himself sideways they couldn't see anyone. Finally, the door was unlocked and opened. D. stepped slowly into full view. Unsure of the kind of welcome he would get, he put on a half-smile.

'Special guest . . .' he said simply.

Holding the door half-opened, Jenny stood there, unsmiling, looking at the man. They remained like that for what seemed like a long time to D., standing on either side of the door, he maintaining his cautious half-smile, she staring at him with that indefinable expression. D. thought it better to wait for a reaction. Just as he was about to give up on waiting, Jenny moved back and opened the door wider.

'Come in,' she said in a quiet voice. Still unsure about what was on her mind, D. stepped inside the flat. He waited for her to lock the door behind her, then followed her into the living room. The place looked different; the furnishings had changed, the curtains also. Only the small coffee table and the long wall unit were the same as before, though they had been moved around. D. sat in one of the large cloth chairs. Jenny went to the kitchen, came back and sat across from him, a finely carved wooden table with matching ornaments between them. The television was on to the right, dwarfed by a huge luxuriant cheese plant that occupied a whole corner of the room.

'In yah look pretty, man,' D. remarked admiringly.

Sitting cross-legged in front of him, Jenny continued to stare with that same expression, making D. feel unsettled. He wasn't too sure what to say or where to start. He would have preferred her to react more angrily, but she simply stared with those slanted, impenetrable eyes. It was all the more weird because he used to live in this flat.

'Do you want a drink?' Jenny asked.

The question took D. by surprise. That was just too nice.

'No, I'm a'right,' he answered. Then, since she still kept cool, he asked, 'So wha'ppen?'

Jenny waited a few seconds, the question hanging in the air.

'I don't know, D., you tell me.'

She still didn't sound vexed. That kind of vibe was too unsettling for D. It was the same out on the streets; by character, he didn't like ambiguous situations. He always preferred action to the kind of stand-off he was facing now. He shrugged.

'Bwoy, 'nuff t'ings happen, yuh known, Jenny!'

Jenny got up, came around the table towards him.

'Give me your coat,' she said.

D. got up, took off his coat and gave it to her. She went to hang it up in the corridor and returned to her seat. Is wha' ah gwan!? D. wondered to himself. He couldn't tell if she meant something by that, or maybe she was concerned about the wet garment ruining her chair . . . D. decided to initiate the dialogue.

'I come back lickle while now . . .' he said, watching for a reaction.

'Yes, I know.' Then, with a kind of smile, she added, 'Don't worry, it wasn't Charmaine.'

She had gathered that Charmaine, her best friend, had been asked not to say anything. But she felt no way about it.

'Who tell you?' D. asked curious.

'You're a big man out there, D.; that kind of thing can't stay a secret for long,' she told him. D. knew she was right. He went on, changing strategy.

'Yuh want to know why I nevah come look fe yuh before?'

'You're going to tell me?' she asked.

In truth, D. wasn't too sure why.

'To tell yuh the truth, I nevah know how yuh would react.'

Jenny threw him a sideways glance.

'Why, you're afraid of me?'

D. laughed, but didn't answer directly. Then Jenny took it further.

'Well . . . I'm glad you didn't forget the address.' Since he didn't know how to take the remark, D. sidestepped.

'So yuh working still?' he asked.

'Yeah, I went back a couple of months ago.'

The way Jenny answered, D. knew they were getting to the crucial point. She was smart, he had never doubted that. He wondered if she was playing, or if she had changed that much to be so calm, so unemotional.

'Yuh look a'right, though . . .' he said appreciatively. This time, Jenny smiled, looked down then back at him.

'Did you think I was going to break down?' she asked.

'No, man, me know seh yuh tuff a'ready.'

D. meant that as a compliment. He meant it, too, in fact he was finding it difficult not to compliment her further. Jenny looked even better now, more womanly perhaps; her brown, shiny skin and dark eyes, the luscious black hair pulled back from her face and her full, finely shaped lips.

'So, you've solved your problems now?' It was impossible to know what exactly she was referring to. D. took it to mean his business problems.

'T'ings bettah now, fe real,' he told her, unwilling to discuss that now. There was silence for a time as both looked at each other and stood their respective gazes for the first time since D. had arrived. D. was surprised to find that in that short exchange he could read more than in their superficial conversation. He remembered, and maybe she did right then also, how they had had this strange ability to communicate without talking so much, back when things were easy between them. He broke the silence.

'Look, Jenny; I know yuh cyan understan' how t'ings happened last year. To tell yuh the truth, I don't really know neither.' He paused, she didn't interrupt. Jenny simply looked on as D. tried to explain.

'Yuh mus' have heard certain t'ings at the time. Same time the pressure buil' up between me an' you . . . Well, the past done happen already, an' I don't come to apologize, but ah so a man life go sometime.' He stopped, aware that it wasn't much of an explanation, but at least she knew that he was aware of the situation.

'Funny enough, I don't hate you, y'know, D.,' she said. 'I don't think you yourself knew what was going on.'

D. reflected that she was probably right. But why did she take it so cool now?

'So how yuh nuh cuss me, though?' he asked her.

Jenny sighed and shook her head.

'All these things changed me, D., you changed me . . .'

143

She stopped. D. knew better than to say anything; she had not finished yet. 'You know, I sat in that hospital last year, holding your son, and I was so angry . . .' She laughed, a funny-sounding laugh. 'So mad, because all the other women were getting flowers and gifts and cards. I got some too; from my family and my friends, they all came and were so happy.' Jenny paused again, her eyes somewhere inside her memory as she cast her mind back through time.

'But I didn't really care about all that. I wanted you to come and see that baby I just had for you, your son. For the five days I stayed at the hospital, I still kept on hoping you'd show up, I don't know why. Even after I came back home, at least for the first few months, I still hoped you would walk in . . . But you didn't . . .' Jenny stopped. She didn't sound sad, D. couldn't hear any pain as she spoke about that time in her life. For all his toughness, all the imperviousness to feelings he'd learned to build up long ago, at that precise moment, D. felt uncomfortable. Listening to the woman recounting her experience to him, the father of her son, he didn't quite know what to say, if anything at all. He waited. She looked at him.

'That's why I don't feel angry towards you, not any more; you taught me something, you made me tough.'

D. shifted in his seat.

'So whe' de yout' deh?' he asked.

'Carol picks him up from the child-minder for me.' She looked at her watch. 'They should be here soon.'

After waiting so long to show his face, D. was now impatient to see his son. Since returning to England, he had postponed the moment as long as he could. He now knew why. He just hadn't been sure how he would face Jenny. Now, sitting there in the flat which used to be his home, he felt like he'd never left. But he had, and so much had taken place in a short year.

'So how is yuh mudda?' D. asked. He had met Jenny's

mother only once, when she arrived unexpectantly one evening. D. couldn't quite remember what he had said but she seemed highly suspicious of him, though not hostile, as far as he could recollect.

'She's al'right,' Jenny said, adding, 'you can just imagine the kind of remarks she came up with when Jesse was born. All about single mother and all that.'

'How yuh name de yout'?' D. asked, picking up on what she just said.

'I called him Jesse. You like that?'

D. thought about it for a moment, he smiled.

'Yeah, man. It sound a'right. A Bible name still.'

They talked a little more, a friendly atmosphere between them, watching each other like cat and mouse. Then the bell rang. Jenny got up to open the door. D. heard the sound of hushed voices coming from the corridor, then a little boy dressed in jeans and a thick anorak walked inside the room. He stopped as he saw the man in the armchair. D. and the son he'd never seen stared at each other, as surprised one as the other. Even the child realized how much they looked alike. He stood there, unsmiling, his eyes fixed on his father's face, arms by his side. D. was as shocked as the child; it was his face, his features exactly, a smaller version of himself. The only difference was Jesse's copper-coloured complexion which he owed to his mother. Jenny came in, followed by Carol, and found them still staring at each other. D. couldn't help the grin on his face, a broad, proud one that spoke a whole range of feelings inside him.

'Good evening, sir,' Carol said, mockingly polite. She and D. had had a strange relationship from the start. Whereas most people, especially women, watched how they talked to D., Carol had always been straightforward with him. She was never rude or anything, but she spoke her mind and, in a way, D. respected her for that. She had made her feelings plain about drugs without getting too personal and at the time, D. had simply ignored her remarks. She knew D. as a 'bad man' and probably thought he was not right for her younger sister, yet she made a point of staying out of the story as it unfolded. D. recalled the last occasion Carol had seen him, on that day when he had to get rough with Jenny . . . He looked up at her.

'Hi, sis, wha'ppen?'

'Al'right, so you finally came?!' She looked at Jenny briefly, smiling.

'Yeah, man, me deh 'bout!'

Carol seemed pleasantly surprised to find D. in a good mood. As far as she remembered, he was usually difficult to talk to. At the moment he was busy getting acquainted with his son. The little boy couldn't help looking back at him as his mother took off his outdoor coat.

'You see your daddy now?' Jenny laughed at her son's surprised expression.

Carol sat down. She picked up Jesse from the child-minders every day as it was near her workplace. She was a social worker, an educated, intelligent woman in her early thirties who had two children of her own. Her son Damien was twelve, while his sister Venetta was almost ten. Carol had been separated from their father for several years, but had managed to raise them in a straight and narrow way, working hard to pay for their school and upbringing, staying close to them to give the two youth the strength she knew they would need. Though Carol and Jenny looked alike in features, Carol was slightly taller and also bigger in size. Jenny used to tell D. jokes about their schooldays when Carol was known for beating up boys her own age and bigger. She had retained the same fearless disposition, though she was more restrained nowadays. ·

'So, how is life, D.?' Carol asked, inquisitive as ever.

'Bwoy, t'ings ruff, but me nah give up still,' D. answered. Carol laughed.

'I know that.' Then she pressed on, as he knew she would. 'So where have you been?'

'I did travel, y'know; go ah Yard and come back,' D. said. He knew that Carol knew what everybody knew.

'So how Jamaica stay?' she asked.

'It nice, but money short, y'know.'

Carol knew that too. She'd been there a couple of times to visit her mother's family and had enjoyed the experience to the full. In fact, she planned to take her children on holiday there, as soon as she could afford it, she told D.

'Dem will love dat, man,' he remarked. 'Yard bettah dan yahso fe raise children.' In a sense, he was right. As a social worker, Carol was only too aware of the problems black youth faced growing up in England, many of which had to do with the missing family structure that still existed in Jamaica. She had noticed when she went there how well-mannered children were, how polite and behaved most youngsters were. That was exactly how she had managed to raise her own two, determined they would never become like the numerous rude and uncouth types she too often saw on the streets of London.

'When you gonna take your son out there?' Carol asked, aware of the insidious nature of the question.

D. gave her a little smile and looked briefly at Jenny, sitting across with Jesse on her lap.

'Maybe soon, y'know,' he said evasively.

Carol laughed. Meanwhile, Jesse was still looking at D.

'Go say hello to your daddy then,' Jenny urged him. But the child wasn't ready yet. He was content to simply stare. He was clearly fascinated by that bigger version of himself.

'He'll get there, just give him time,' Carol said.

She got up to leave. Her children were making their own dinner, whatever that might be. They laughed as Carol told of some of the 'menus' they invented. She kissed Jesse goodbye.

'Nice to see you, D. I hope you'll stick around,' Carol said with a mischievous smile in her sister's direction.

'Yeah, man, me see yuh again,' D. said.

When she had seen her sister out, Jenny asked Jesse if he was hungry. He nodded, so she went into the kitchen to fix his dinner. She asked D. if he wanted anything, but he told her he was all right.

While his mother was away, Jesse walked across to the table of his own accord and stopped there, looking at his father. D. smiled at him and called him over. Jesse returned the smile, but didn't move. So D. decided to use some psychology on him.

'Yuh shoes look nice, eeh man! Who buy dem fe yuh?' he said, pointing at the child's new boots.

Jesse looked down at his shoes, then back at D.

'Let me see dem?' D. asked, motioning to the child to come over. 'Let me see the boots, man.'

The child jumped up gingerly and stood in front of his father. D. reached out and touched one of the leather ankle boots.

'Wha', dem nice!'

Jesse beamed. He allowed D. to take hold of him and pull him closer. He was tall for his fourteen months of age, slim but strong. D. looked at his son, holding him for the first time. He felt proud of him, all the more because of their uncanny likeness. He started to talk to him, gradually coaxing Jesse along. The child was still reserved, but they were getting on fine. When Jenny's voice came through the kitchen calling her son to dinner, D. held him back. He smiled at the little boy, motioning to him to keep quiet. Jenny finally walked in to find Jesse comfortably settled on his father's lap and looking quite contented. D. saw the look in her eyes; he knew she was happy to see them together at last.

'Oh, you know your dad now? He made you wait long enough,' she jibed, picking Jesse up.

D. didn't say anything, he felt nice. Things had turned out better than he had anticipated. He relaxed, watching the news on the television. Sometimes, times like now, he really felt he could have enjoyed the quiet life: spending time with his children, learning to live a more 'normal' existence, but he knew very well that the feeling would only last for a while. Lurking at the back of his mind, ever present, was the call of the streets, the limelight and the status he had out there. There was money to be made and that was the bottom line in everything. In his new state of lucidity, after his spell back to the place of his birth, D. now knew more about himself. He had had time to retrace his steps, all the way back. Deep inside, he believed in some kind of destiny, like a road more or less preset, maybe which he had followed up to now. And all the way, it had been money, or rather the lack of it, the need to never be without it, that had shaped everything. His thoughts drifted, memory slowly unwinding as the rain outside tapped its winter dance on the window pane. Then Jesse came running back in with that infectious smile of his, his father's smile. He was no longer shy and played with D. for a long time, mock fighting, full of youthful energy, laughing and giggling. From her corner, Jenny watched the two of them, smiling to herself, keeping her thoughts secret. She had waited long for this day. Seeing now how happy her son was, how easily he had taken to the father he had never seen before, it was worth it. She put a reggae CD in the stereo. Jesse gave a demonstration of his dancing skills. D. laughed heartily as he watched the tiny boy imitate the moves he had picked up here and there. Jenny explained that his cousins, Carol's children, had trained him well. He definitely had an attitude for dancing.

Jesse tired later and retreated into his mother's arms, drifting into a deep sleep. D. checked his watch; it was coming up to nine o'clock. He had nothing pressing to attend to. Sticks would probably come for him later, around 2 a.m. As tonight was Friday night, the club would certainly be busy. D. was in no hurry to get back to Donna's . . .

Jenny went to put her sleeping child to bed.

'So yuh don't rave again?' D. asked when she returned.

'Not really. I only go to parties sometimes when my mum or Carol babysit.' Then she asked, 'Where are you going tonight?'

'I run a lickle club, y'know. I'll probably pass down there later.'

Jenny looked at him.

'You run a club?'

'It's only a gambling place,' D. said. 'A shebeen.'

'Well, you move fast,' Jenny remarked. D. shrugged modestly.

'I took it over recently . . .'

They watched TV for a while, Jenny asking him only those questions she knew he would answer. He told her about his stay in the hills in Jamaica, a little about the people there. Jenny realized she had not really known much about him. She had quickly learned when they first met and started living together not to ask too many questions, especially about D.'s background. Tonight, for the first time, he seemed relaxed, more inclined to talk. Apparently, he had also changed.

'When you're going back?' she asked.

'I'm not ready yet,' D. said. 'Certain t'ings have to be right first. Money ha'fe turn.' Then he added, 'Yuh know seh las' year I was forced to leave, it wasn't my choice . . . ?'

Jenny smiled, confirming that she knew it.

150

'You don't really have nobody out there, do you? I mean, like family?'

At first, D. thought she was talking about women, something like that. Then he realized what Jenny was saying; he had never really thought about it in that way. Sure enough, she was right, he reflected, he didn't have any close family in Jamaica any more. Sure, he had left three children there, two of which he hardly knew. He had met their mother when he was himself quite young, and despite giving her two boys had not taken the time to live with them. While in St Ann's, he had not even bothered to cross into nearby Clarendon to visit them. His other child, a girl, lived in Town and he had passed there when he got released. She was a pretty, vivacious four-year-old. She remembered him but he had not been able to go back there after that.

'No, not really,' he answered Jenny quietly. She could see her question had touched him somewhere inside. She changed the subject.

'You know Charlie helped me after Jesse was born. I mean, he sent money through Charmaine a few times.'

D. didn't know that.

'Yeah?'

'I didn't want to take it. I wasn't really desperate, but it helps sometimes. He didn't tell you?' Jenny asked.

'No, man, I nevah know.'

Jenny smiled. D. had a thought for his partner. Men like Charlie were hard to come by.

'Me an' Charlie heartical,' he said simply.

'You sure you don't want a drink?' Jenny asked.

Thinking about it, D. could have done with a stout. After all, it was Friday night, and a special Friday night at that. Seeing his son had put him in a good mood.

'A'right. I get a drink fe yuh. What d'you want?' he asked. But Jenny had a better idea.

'No, I'll get it for you, you stay here.'

He couldn't refuse. He took a twenty-pound note out of his pocket, but Jenny refused that also.

'It's al'right, I've got money, I won't be long.'

She left him there, wondering why he had left her in the first place. But then again, those were troubled times.

He took hold of the remote control and switched between channels until he found something interesting. Then he got up and went to insert another CD from the pile near the stereo. To be really comfortable, D. proceeded to build himself a nice, big spliff. These days you had to have serious contacts to get good herb in London, but so far Charlie had managed to arrange that. The rest of the crew had found it strange that D. no longer used the hard stuff, and to be truthful, D. had to admit to himself that he was often tempted to get a 'touch'. He remembered only too well the boost coke gave, the extra energy and the feeling of invincibility. Yet so far, he had managed successfully without it. He lit up, drew deeply on the spliff of prime sensi, lay back in the chair and waited for Jenny to return. She was treating him real nice, much nicer than he had expected. Soothed by the strong and sweet ganja and the hypnotic music, D. recalled the niceness they had shared in their early days.

Jenny returned soon enough. She handed him his Guinness, put her own drink on the table, glanced at the spliff in the ashtray. D. saw the question in her eyes.

'Ganja, man. Yuh wan' some?' Jenny used to take the odd pull before.

'No thanks, I stopped smoke, y'know.'

'Yeah?'

Jenny explained that she'd given up cigarettes as soon as she discovered she was pregnant. Just like that. D. was impressed. They sat, talking and drinking as time passed by. Around midnight, as they watched a video, D. decided to make a call before his soldiers started looking for him. He used the telephone and got to Charlie as Sticks couldn't be reached at the club and explained the situation. D. asked his friend to go to the club and tell Sticks to take care of business for the night since he was otherwise engaged. Charlie laughed, assuring him not to worry. He understood. D. put down the receiver and looked at Jenny. He knew she had listened keenly.

'Dem can handle t'ings,' he said.

Jenny put down the drink she was sipping.

'You're sure?' she asked mischievously. Then, switching in her characteristic way, she asked, 'Where do you live now?'

D. gave her a penetrating look; he knew she'd ask sooner or later.

'I stay by my soldier, down in Leyton,' he lied. From Jenny's expression, D. couldn't tell whether she believed him or not.

He said, 'I don't drive, yuh know.'

'No?' Jenny opened her eyes wide in mock amazement.

'Dat mean I have to stay here till morning . . .' D. added.

She didn't comment on that. They remained seated side by side, comfortable. D. realized early on that he had no intention to leave and Jenny seemed happy enough having him there. A little later, Jenny got up to change the video cassette, then she came back to sit down and he felt her slide up against him, like a cat curling in search of warmth. He wrapped his arm around her shoulders. The lights were off, they both felt good in the relative silence of the room. Neither of them said much for a long time, until, after the show was over, they finally found their way into the bedroom. Much later, when the intensity of their embrace had spent itself, after they had proven to one another the enduring memory of each other's touch, Jenny whispered:

'I always knew you'd come back.'

D. sighed, his fingers lightly brushing her hair.

'So yuh did wait fe me?'

'I had no choice,' Jenny said.

'Why?'

'Everybody knows I'm your woman; even if I wanted to, I probably couldn't get nobody.'

D. thought about it for a moment and laughed.

'Oh, ah so it go? An' I did t'ink seh yuh really check fe me.'

Jenny pinched him in the side playfully.

'Stop it, yuh know bettah dan dat.'

'I have your son already,' he heard her say softly. 'With you here, I've got everything I want.'

D. heard Jesse's regular breathing in the other bedroom. He held Jenny close until they both drifted to sleep with the approaching dawn.

12

REAL LIFE

A s soon as he walked through the narrow door and out into the dark alley, Kevin knew he had made a mistake. He should have known better than to believe that Philip guy. He stopped, as Philip walked on towards the end of the alley; there was no exit that way. Kevin looked over his shoulder at the street lights fifty yards or so away behind him, and noticed that three silhouettes had just emerged from the warehouse, now standing between him and the exit.

It was a foolish move; as if the guy with whom he already had a brush-up a couple of weeks earlier could be trusted! 'Just want to talk,' Philip had said. Instead of alerting Hopper, who was busy dancing, Kevin had naively followed Philip out of the club.

Under his heavy army-style parka, Kevin felt a sharp chill through his body. He took a deep breath and stepped towards Philip, both hands in his pockets and keeping an eye on the men to the side.

'What d'you want to talk about, man?' he asked.

'You know what I want to talk about!'

There was undisguised hostility in the voice. Kevin noticed Philip's right hand hanging by his side, half-hidden. He waited.

'I told you before; stay away from my sister!'

'And I told you, it's nothing to do with you, right?'

Kevin could just see his opponent's face.

'Yeah?' he heard the hate-filled voice. 'You asked for it, you black bastard!'

Though he expected the attack, Kevin was surprised by the sudden move. As he spat the insult, Philip lunged forward. His right hand rose above his head and slashed downwards. The long blade cut across, right where its intended target was standing a split second earlier; only Kevin's desperate, backward dodge saved him from getting badly cut. He hardly noticed the sharp jab of pain as the metal sliced through his left sleeve, grazing the skin. At the same time, his own right hand appeared, holding a knife in ready anticipation. He jabbed forward as Philip came towards him. The tip of the blade hit something, but not deeply. Meanwhile, Philip's three accomplices came running at him, fast. Everything happened so rapidly there wasn't time to be afraid. Kevin had been in several fights before, but tonight's seemed like a really desperate situation. He backed towards the brick wall of the building to his right. I'm taking somebody with me, he caught himself thinking, breathing hard and fast. His boot hit something with a sharp sound as he backed off. Kevin bent down quickly and picked up the bottle. With it in his left hand and the blade in his right he got ready to go down fighting. To his left, the three white guys were watching, ready, waiting for a chance to pounce on him. Kevin saw at least two gleaming blades in the faint light from the warehouse entrance behind him. To his right, cursing as much to frighten his opponent as to give himself courage, Philip was approaching.

'I'm gonna slice you good and proper, nigger!'

Kevin surprised himself by letting out a sarcastic laugh.

'Come on then, one of you ain't gonna make it.'

The biggest of the men to his left came forward, the large blade in his hand intended for the black youth's chest. Kevin deflected the hit with a powerful downward slice of the bottle. He heard the guy swear and groan as the glass shattered on his hand. The knife fell to the ground, halfway

156

between them. Before Kevin could make a dash for the weapon, Philip rushed him, slashing at his head. Kevin kicked out ferociously, striking his attacker in the stomach. Philip recoiled, winded. But Kevin knew he couldn't keep them away for ever. At four against one the seconds were ticking in their favour . . . At the end of the alley he saw the street lights, the open, his escape route. He was still unsure of his chances of going for the big knife, temptingly lying on the ground in front of him, when help arrived unexpectedly.

'What the fuck's going on?'

Hopper's voice! He heard it before he saw his friend running out of the club into the alley. Hopper didn't waste time; he took in the situation and reacted, no messing about. Kevin saw the short, wiry youth grab a large metal bin standing at the entrance to the warehouse. Lifting it up above his head, Hopper flung it at the group of men threatening his friend. They were still too surprised by his sudden appearance to avoid the projectile in time. One of the guys took the full force on his head. He fell back, garbage scattered all around. The other two hesitated for a few seconds. Too long . . . Hopper rushed them, his arms and legs flailing like a windmill. He picked up the knife from the ground and faced the men as they tried to stand up to him. Kevin had his opportunity with Philip now. The white guy seemed less bold, unsettled to find himself on a one to one basis.

'What was you sayin'? Slice me? Come on then!' Kevin smirked. He circled his opponent, knife horizontal at the ready, his free hand forward for balance, feet lightly treading the ground beneath him. Philip swore and slashed; he missed. Kevin jabbed his blade forward fast and caught Philip's left arm, slicing through his biceps. Swearing, Philip kicked in desperation, slashing wildly. Kevin now had him backed against a wall, under pressure.

'You and me now, come on, boy.'

Philip's contorted face was a mask of hate and fear.

'I'll kill you, you cunt!' He jabbed at Kevin's face, expecting him to back off, but the black youth stood his ground and managed to grab Philip by the wrist before he could draw it back. He stabbed his opponent quickly, plunging his blade deep into Philip's left side. The white youth cried out with fear as he felt the cold steel enter his flesh. Kevin stood and watched as Philip weakened and slumped against the wall behind him.

'You fucker, you. Take this!' Kevin slashed him swiftly across the face, cutting into his left cheek. Then he turned to see how his friend was doing. Hopper had cut one of the other guys, who now knelt on the ground, holding his face. The other guy had run away. As he made his way towards Hopper, Kevin saw a group of men approaching, shouting. They were only a few yards away. Still holding his knife, he started running. Hopper had seen them too.

'Come on, Kev, let's move!' he called out.

Kevin raced on, Hopper in front of him. Behind them, their pursuers were running and gaining ground. Hopper made it to the street, Kevin saw him stop, waiting for him.

'Come on, man, come on!' Hopper shouted. Kevin ran as fast as he could, breathing heavily, still tired by the fight. He glanced behind him; two big white guys were catching up on him.

I've got to make it to the lights! he thought. At the end of the alley, Hopper had picked up some stones which he flung at Kevin's pursuers. A shout of pain as a missile found its mark. Kevin glanced over his shoulder again. Behind him only one man remained, ahead of the pack and catching up. Kevin slowed down and turned, surprising the unexpecting man. He was big, taller than Kevin, with a reddish puffed-up face. Kevin kept the knife low until the big guy was almost on top of him, unable to stop. He made a grab for Kevin's coat, ready to hit him. That's when he felt the blade of the knife rip through his rib-cage; a sharp swift upward cut that sliced with ease through his jumper and into his stomach. He stopped and looked down at the blood oozing out of his clothes and started to holler. The whole incident only took a few seconds. Then Kevin turned and ran. The crowd behind was coming up fast, their shouts grew louder as they watched the big man fall to the ground holding his stomach. At the top of the alley, Hopper waited until Kevin was clear before high-stepping it down the road to his right. Kevin couldn't risk going the same way. He was out of breath, but pushed on down the deserted street, the heavily vocal pack behind him. Kevin turned left into a small street, breathing hard, his lungs hurting and blood pumping through his head. Then right, into a side passage leading into a back garden. He scaled a fence to another garden. Still holding the knife, he ran on. A small parking lot presented the possibility for transport, but there was no time to get inside any of the cars, let alone hotwire one. Kevin ran on alongside the stretch of railings bordering the back of a large supermarket. He stopped; he couldn't hear anything behind him, but he wasn't prepared to take any chances. Besides, this was East Ham, the wrong place to get into problems with white guys. If they caught up with him he was a dead man. Quickly, he scaled the railing and slipped inside the yard, making for three huge metal bins by the loading bays. With the last of his strength, he climbed up and dropped inside one of them. Fortunately, there was only a few flattened cardboard boxes inside. Not that he was too fussy. Kevin sat up inside the bin, listening, trying to catch his breath silently. His body was wet with sweat, his heart pounded so hard he feared the sound would echo through the empty yard.

He stayed there for a long time, ears cocked for the slightest sound, throat dry, knife still in his hands ready.

He pulled his hood over his head, feeling the cold creep in, there was nothing to do but wait and reflect on the recent events. He was angry about the whole thing, all the more because he hadn't wanted to come in the first place. But Hopper had insisted that it was a cool rave and, after all, it was Friday night and they had a little money between them. Kevin had gone along with it, and here he was now, early morning, cold, hungry and on the run from a crowd of white guys who wanted his blood! He was seriously vexed. He wondered how Hopper had done. His friend had practically saved his life back there, but Kevin wasn't too concerned about him. Hopper always survived. They had been through some hot spots together, always backing each other and trusting their luck. But tonight's fight was a stupid and unnecessary one. Now, he had to get back home alive. He stood up and looked out over the edge. He couldn't see any sign of life. There was no noise either. He took a deep breath and hoisted himself out, and dropped silently to the ground, scanned the darkness around the yard, and tiptoed towards the gate, listening, every muscle tense. The sound of a car engine roared in his direction. Kevin waited, squatting low, watching. The car roared past. Kevin took one last look from behind a pallet and ran across the yard to the gates, scaled the railing once again and found himself back on the street. He couldn't take a chance on the high road, it would have to be strictly back streets.

He ran down a dark alley bordered on one side by garden fences, on the other by an expanse of thick brush demarcating the railway embankment. At the other end of the alley, Kevin turned into a deserted road, keeping nevertheless well away from the kerb. He finally managed to hitch a lift and found himself on Katherine Road; at least he knew where he was now. He half-walked, half-jogged. He ran across Romford Road, disappearing swiftly from view into another side street. It made no sense trying to get a cab; much too risky. Kevin knew the white people around these parts well enough to know that they would be scouting around for him. One way or another, he would make it back to Hackney.

Running through the back streets, Kevin finally reached Stratford, from where he made his way along the long stretch of road that he knew led back to the Eastway. It took him two hours of dodging and dribbling to make it safely home to Homerton at 5 a.m. Kevin felt tired and dirty. He longed for a bath and bed. His bed was only a few hundred yards further, but he couldn't go home! It had dawned on him in the last few miles of his long march. That was the first place the police and Philip's friends would look for him. After all, he had cut two of them, they weren't going to let it go. Kevin knew that Philip's sister, Tracey, would give them his address. He cursed the day he got the foolish notion to get involved with her. The worst part of it, he reminisced bitterly, was that he didn't even want the girl. He never usually went out with white girls. He had them as friends yes, to talk to, but never anything more. But he had been weak enough to take it when offered to him; temptation . . . And now it had all gone sour. He had been trying to explain to the same Tracey, only last week, that he wasn't really interested in seeing her again, that it would be better if they parted and so on. He had had a little problem with her brother, who had accosted him on the street the week before. He didn't even know the guy but their encounter ended with threats and ugly behaviour. Kevin realized then that he'd made a mistake. It wasn't worth it.

Dawn was breaking. Kevin took in a gulp of cold air as he passed the block of flats where he lived, then carried on towards Victoria Park. From there, he turned the corner by the pub where he had waited for Sophia so many times and ducked into the fenced-in pathway. Sophia's house was the fifth one. He doubted if anyone would be awake so early on a Saturday morning. That was just as well; Sophia's mother didn't mind Kevin, but her father, well, that was another story. It just wouldn't be a good idea to wake him up.

As quietly as he could, Kevin unlatched the garden door and slipped inside. Fortunately, Sophia's window was the one above the patio, he had always liked that. He picked up a small pebble from the flower bed and threw it gently at the window. The second stone was on target and tapped the glass with a sharp sound before falling to the ground. Sophia's sleepy eyes looked down from behind the curtains briefly. Within minutes she had descended and opened the patio door, motioning him to keep quiet. Exhausted, Kevin threw himself unceremoniously into one of the plastic garden chairs.

'What's the matter with you, where you coming from?' she asked. He looked a state.

'I had some problems, I had to walk all the way back from east London,' he answered drily. Sophia sat down beside him. She was a shortish, open-faced sixteen-year-old. Though her hair was tied inside a scarf, she still had the baby look that had drawn Kevin to her in the first place. They had met around eighteen months earlier at an ice rink in east London and had been seeing each other ever since. Kevin would sometimes go several weeks without visiting her. But, on the whole, he checked her as his regular. At seventeen, he didn't feel like settling down to one girl yet. But he trusted Sophia. She had always been good and loyal to him.

'What happened?' she asked, concerned.

Kevin kissed his teeth, slid the hood off his head and rubbed his face wearily.

'I had a fight with some white guys.'

'What?! Why?'

Kevin shook his head, averting Sophia's inquisitive gaze.

'It's a long story, they attacked me.'

The girl was clearly shaken by the news. She got even more distressed when Kevin explained that he had stabbed them and police would surely be looking for him by now. He neatly avoided any reference to the initial cause of the fight.

'I even lost Hopper in the action, man.'

Sophia didn't know what to say. She knew Kevin wasn't really bad, despite her father's opinion, but he somehow always found himself in trouble.

Kevin felt like laying down on the patio floor tiles and sleeping for a day and a night, forgetting all about the night's events. He could feel his body relaxing, his muscles aching and the fatigue in his legs. The sharp burn on his left arm reminded him for the first time that he had been cut also. But he couldn't stop, not now.

'So what are you gonna do, Kevin?'

Sophia's concerned tone forced him back to the sad reality.

'I don't know.'

He really didn't. Forcing his mind to work, he explored his possibilities; they weren't many. Maybe one.

'Can I use the phone?' he asked.

'You're crazy? My dad would hear you. He'd kill me . . .'

Sophia was adamant. Kevin sighed, got up and stretched, fighting back the feeling of desperation. There had to be a way out.

'Look, I've gotta go, OK? I'll call you.'

'Where are you gonna go now?' Sophia would have done anything to help Kevin, but what could she do?

'I'm gonna sort myself out, Sophia, man. Don't worry too much.'

'What d'you mean, don't worry? This is serious, y'know?'

Kevin smiled at his girlfriend, so pretty, so caring. He bent and gave her a light kiss on the lips.

'I'll call you, go back to bed,' he said.

She unlocked the patio door and watched as Kevin slipped back out of the garden. Then he was gone, once more, back to the cold hostile street. In her heart she prayed he would be back, soon and safe. Sophia went back up to her bed, but not back to sleep . . .

The first thing to do, Kevin reflected as he hurried down the high street, was to find refuge until things cooled down. He decided to make a couple of calls, but first he had to check on Hopper. As he reached the bottom of the street he started to jog, his hood pulled well over his head. He ran, cutting a left into Kingsmead, then right through to where Hopper lived with his mother. Kevin slowed down, walked across the entrance hall and climbed the stairs to the second floor. He'd just turned the corner out on the open landing when his eyes caught a glimpse of a dark-blue Cavalier in the residents' car park below. His mind was ticking over fast. He noticed the recent registration, the two aerials. He backed up, making his way down the stairs with one stride for every flight. Outside, he ran to the far side of the park, taking position behind the old Ford van that was always parked there. Alert to everything around him, he waited. He could be wrong, but he had a vibe. In less than ten minutes, the vibe justified itself. Two white men, both in leather jackets, appeared on the landing, Hopper's diminutive stature bobbing between them. Kevin watched from his vantage point, he had been right all the way. The bitch grassed us up, he thought to himself angrily. There was nothing he could do for Hopper. The first thing to do was to get away. The Vauxhall with the two policemen and his friend drove quickly past his hiding place. Then Kevin started in the opposite direction.

He went straight around the back of the flats where he

knew there was a phone booth. Luckily it hadn't been smashed. He dropped a twenty-pence coin in and dialled a number from memory. The phone rang on. Kevin finally reflected that Simon was out. That was a let-down; he was sure that if anybody could help him, Simon could. He released his finger from the 'follow on' button and dialled again, also from memory. This time he only needed to wait for four rings before a sleepy female voice answered.

'Hello?'

Kevin cleared his throat.

'Excuse me to disturb you, but could I speak to Chris, please.'

'Well, he's still asleep,' the woman stalled.

'It's very important,' Kevin cut in, as politely as he could. 'I need to speak to him urgently.'

Convinced by the boy's tone, Myrtle told him to hang on.

'Who is this?'

'Chris, it's me, Kevin . . . Yeah, Kevin. Listen, man, I'm in some serious problems . . . I need to see you . . . OK, I'll be there.'

Realizing it had to be serious, Chris agreed to meet Kevin. Despite the early hour on this cold winter Saturday, after having had a late night, Chris was as dependable as always. He was used to having to take time, besides the hours at the youth club for which he wasn't even properly paid, to take care of the various troubles youths like Kevin regularly got themselves into. In fact, it wasn't the first time that he had been called on to rescue Kevin. The previous year he'd been caught driving an unlicensed, uninsured car, apparently under the influence of alcohol. There were two other inebriated youths in the car. Chris had a hard time getting them released and then followed them to court and tried to get them jobs. But his efforts were all in vain. Kevin was a typical case, as Chris had found out. There was no doubt that he was bright and good at college where he was supposed to be preparing for an exam. But the other side of the coin was his restlessness. He rejected authority and devised the craziest schemes, just for fun. Like many of those youths Chris had seen grow up on the estates, Kevin had little faith in the system he was born into. After his course, if he completed it, he would probably give up looking for a job after a year or so of rejections. Some didn't even get that far . . .

Adolescents will always go a little wild. As Chris saw it, the vital thing was to give them a chance to overcome that first mistake. Even Harry had to be rescued from Stoke Newington police station one evening a few months earlier. According to him, and Chris had chosen to believe it, he did not know the car he was travelling in was stolen.

Chris got dressed, picked up his keys, told a sleeping Myrtle he would be back later and left the flat. The Datsun took a little persuading to kick up, but Chris finally got it going. He pulled down his wool hat over his ears and slipped a new cassette into the stereo and waited a few minutes for the engine to warm up.

There wasn't much traffic on the road, but with six days to go before Christmas, people would be out on the streets in a couple of hours, spending like there's no tomorrow. Chris drove down New North Road, then right and straight across until he reached London Fields. Checking his rear-view mirror, just in case, he got to the college gates and slowed down. From the corner of the council building next door, a hooded figure crossed the road and opened the door of the Datsun and climbed in.

'Thanks, man,' Kevin said.

'Al'right, so what happened to you now?'

Kevin explained everything as they drove towards Bethnal Green and beyond. Chris listened solemnly.

'They've got Hopper, I saw him get taken away,' Kevin concluded.

Chris sighed, weighing up the seriousness of the situation. It looked pretty bad.

'I heard you're spending a lot of time with Simon and his friends . . .' he said, turning to Kevin. 'Anything you wanna tell me?'

'No, we're friends that's all.' Kevin could see what Chris was asking.

'Friends?' Chris repeated, then he paused. 'Are you doing stuff, Kevin?' he asked quietly.

'No, Chris, man. You know me better than that,' Kevin protested.

'Yeah, I know you . . . I also know what friendship can lead to. These guys are into shit, in a big way. You wanna keep better company, Kevin,' Chris said.

Kevin knew what he meant. He didn't resent Chris talking to him that way, though like any other youth his age, he wouldn't take talk from adults just because they were adults. He respected Chris. He knew that the man he had once again called upon in his hour of need was just like him. Chris was also from the ghetto, had grown up on the same turf, and been through the same experience of alienation, like you want to escape from yourself sometimes. Chris always stuck up for the youths, even against the police, everybody knew that.

'Maybe you're right, but I don't take nothing,' Kevin said, trying to sound as truthful as he could.

'So how come you always end up in these fucked-up situations, man?'

Kevin shook his head, sighing.

'I don't know, man. I'm just unlucky maybe.'

'Luck's got nothing to do with it, Kevin, man, you've got to make your own luck. You've got to feel lucky as long as you're alive, if that's what you believe in,' Chris said. He wanted to shake the youth out of his fatalistic outlook on life, but relented and lightened up a little.

'Look, I know sometimes people do things that feel OK at the time, then it all gets out of hand, but you need to start thinking positive.' Chris could see Kevin was listening intensely, trying to see further than his present problems.

'If you go on this way, you're gonna kill somebody, then you'll really be out of luck.' He let a few seconds pass before asking, 'So what are you planning to do now?'

'I don't really know.' Kevin looked at him blankly.

Chris thought for a moment; there weren't many options.

'You've got two choices, if you can call them that. You can go to the police station now and face the rap . . . Hold on, let me finish,' he said as Kevin protested.

'. . . Or you can run away and hide, for a while, but you know it can't last for ever. They'll catch up with you, sooner or later.'

Chris waited. He could almost hear Kevin's mind ticking away, almost feel the strain inside the youngster.

'I'm not giving myself up, man, no way,' Kevin said after a while.

'You didn't kill that guy, did you?' Chris asked.

'Nah, man,' Kevin said, trying to sound certain.

'So just go down there, I'll go with you. Explain what happened. It's better to face it now.'

Kevin couldn't buy that.

'Tell me something, Chris; I cut two white guys, right? On top of that the whole thing happened over a white girl, who do you think the police going to listen to? Do you think it's going to make any difference because they started the fight? I ain't going down there!'

Chris couldn't really fault his reasoning, Kevin was no

fool. The way things looked, he wouldn't stand much of a chance in front of a judge, no matter how lenient.

'I know you're right, Kevin, but sooner or later you'll have to deal with it.'

Kevin thought some more:

'Man, you know this police station is bad news,' he said. ''Nuff black people dying there. I ain't going.'

Chris nodded.

'So what's your plan?'

'I've got to leave town first thing. I've got a cousin in the country, I think I'll go there and chill out for a while.'

It didn't sound like much of a plan, Kevin knew that. But Chris understood how he felt; his main concern was to get out of reach of the police, let things die down and have time to think things over.

'You're sure about that?'

'Yeah, that's what I'm going to do.'

Kevin's mind was made up. He was tired, hungry and scared. No use telling him about 'he who fights and runs away . . .' Now wasn't the time to worry about that 'other day'.

Chris drove Kevin to the train station. He gave him all the money he had in his pockets, about twenty-five pounds, and insisted that he call him every couple of days.

'I appreciate what you do for me, Chris. I'll see you, OK?'

Chris shook his head, looking into his eyes.

'Take care of yourself, Kev,' he said, and stood watching as the youth ran into the station and disappeared from view.

He drove back on to the main road and headed towards Hackney. Kevin's story kept spinning in his head. It was hard to see how the boy could have done anything wrong that would lead to such a disaster.

On either side of the road, and in the adjacent stores, the rush had now started. Every year at this time, people would get up really early to go shopping, hoping to avoid the main rush. However, since they all tried the same trick, there would be crowds from around 8.30 a.m., solid, busy spending big. Chris slowed down to allow a group of people across the pedestrian crossing. The carnival-type atmosphere seemed somehow strange to him, out of place. Christmas, whatever that might really mean, was a 'time-out', a short period of outings, eating, drinking and dancing, a kind of collective release of the pressures and frustrations of the whole year, but under the circumstances it seemed inappropriate. He turned left into a side street beside the police station and parked behind a large van. Chris walked into the foyer and down to the desk as he had done so many times before.

'Good morning, I'd like to see a young black man that you brought in a couple of hours ago.'

The duty officer eyed him with an interested look.

'What would his name be, sir?'

'Walters, Hopeton Walters.'

'Oh, I see who you mean. And who are you? His lawyer?' the policeman asked.

Chris looked at the PC, his hands spread flat across the counter; he wasn't one of the officers he knew.

'No, I'm not, but I work with these youngsters and he's therefore my responsibility.'

The officer listened as Chris spoke his formal English.

'Oh, that's what you call them,' the officer said with a heavy hint of irony. '"Youngsters". That youngster in there,' he pointed over his shoulder, 'nearly stabbed somebody to death. We're still looking for his mate!'

Chris didn't care to get into the details of the story. Besides, he really wasn't supposed to know much.

'You wouldn't happen to know where he is, by any chance?' the policeman asked.

Chris wasn't surprised by the question.

'Look, I'd like to speak to him just for a few minutes.'

'And I'm telling you, as I've just told his own mother, that you can't see him. He's in here and he stays in here.'

The tone was vindictive-like, as if the officer was taking the whole thing personally. Chris picked up on the tip.

'So where is his mother?'

The officer told him she was with the 'arresting officer, sir'. She'd be out soon. Chris waited, hands in his pockets, gazing around. Hopper's mother and sister came out of a side door.

'Mrs Walters, how're you doing?' Chris greeted them.

'Lawd, Chris, imagine what de bwoy go do?!'

As a church woman, whose utmost concern was never to be at fault in regard to the law of the land, Mrs Walters was visibly shaken. She explained that she had talked to the arresting officer, one of those who had come to the house earlier, but he had not allowed her to see her son. She was upset, and Chris did his best to comfort her. Diana, Hopper's sister, was equally upset.

'I've called a lawyer, he should be here soon,' she told Chris.

He stayed with the shaken mother for a little while, then she agreed to let him drop her home. Diana elected to wait for the lawyer, and promised she'd call Chris later.

Mrs Walters remained passive all the way home. She seemed like she was in a trance, as if unable to believe in the enormity of her son's offence. She shook her head sadly before turning to Chris, speaking for the first time since they left the station.

'My son a criminal now, Chris.'

She was deeply affected. Chris shook his head.

'No, Mrs Walters, you can't say that! He's young, everybody makes mistakes,' he told her, patting her on the arm. She was quiet for a few minutes.

'Dem a look fe Kevin, y'know?' She sounded as concerned for Kevin as she was for her son. 'I can't believe it, Chris,' she said again.

Chris tried to be as helpful as he could with the old lady. He assured her that Hopeton would surely get bail. That nobody had died and that everything would turn out all right. But she was too shaken to comprehend how her younger son could have 'turned bad'. Her two other sons both lived in south London; she didn't see much of them but they were both doing well. Diana lived in the area but had her own family, her own busy life. Hopeton lived at home, he was a good son and her pride. Chris knew that Hopper, as his friends called him, was not a troublesome youth. His talent was dancing; he'd won most of the competitions at the centre. Apart from that, he checked girls same as the others. He had never been in any kind of trouble with the police, that was why Mrs Walters was so shocked by it all. By the time Chris helped her up to her flat on the estate, she was nearer accepting the situation but still felt powerless to deal with it. Chris held the front door open for her to step in. Her posture told of her grief to anyone who cared to listen. Chris sat her down and patiently made her a hot drink and switched on the television. He reassured her once again and promised he would deal with the situation and call later.

Back in the car, Chris couldn't help but feel let down about the whole thing. Unfortunately, he'd seen the same scenario all too often. For him there was no immunity from that kind of business. He had worked with the youths in the borough for ten years, doing his job as best he could. He allowed his work to encroach on his domestic life –

giving help, time and, though it didn't seem as if he was getting anywhere, he still had hope. Even in his lowest ebb, the flame of hope flickered precariously. So many times throughout the years he'd watched helplessly as a proportion of each group of youths would fall by the wayside and get wasted. And once they'd received custody for that crucial first mistake, there was no turning back. As if by compulsion, the youths would replay the patterns that would send them right back to the prison world, as if they really belonged there.

Chris manoeuvred the car into a parking space not too far from his door. He glanced at his watch, it was almost one. He entered his house feeling weary, defeated, cynical and hungry. There were voices in the kitchen.

'Aaah, you find your home?' Chris frowned at his mother sitting at the kitchen table with Myrtle, Lorna and Colette around her. 'What're you doing here?'

Even as he spoke Chris remembered they had agreed that she would come for the weekend, as she did every year for the Christmas season. The slender woman laughed, taking her son's outstretched hand in hers.

'Ohhh, so you don't want me in here no more?' She frowned, looking him in the eyes. 'Is what happened to you? How you look so tired?'

Chris explained that he hadn't had enough sleep lately, due to work and other things. Though he was now over thirty, Mrs Thomas always fussed about her son as if he were still a child. In her eyes, of course, he was. She had been protective since bringing him and Lorna from her native Jamaica. Chris was close to his mother, more than ever now, because, as an adult, he better understood the struggle she had gone through. Their mother loved Lorna, of course, but theirs was the love between women, mother to daughter, a sisterly kind of love. With her son Chris, she had a different kind of affection. Chris substituted the son she had had before him who died in infancy. As a child born after and who survived, Chris was special to her.

'How did it go?' asked Myrtle from the cooker.

'Not so good,' Chris answered vaguely. There was no need for her to ask any more for now. Chris usually told her all the stories that kept him up late or dragged him out of his bed so often.

Chris sat at the table beside his daughter Coleen.

'Dad, you forgot about this morning!' she chastised.

Chris threw his twelve-year-old a puzzled glance.

'This morning? Oh yes!'

He had promised to take her to the market to buy some clothes. Another promise unfulfilled. He apologized, stroking her hair. Coleen smiled mischievously.

'That's al'right,' she said, 'you can take me to Petticoat Lane tomorrow morning, it's better there anyway.'

Chris couldn't believe it. His mother and Myrtle laughed.

'That's just like her,' Myrtle said.

Coleen was known to be a 'cunning little rascal' and her mother was always wary of her. Chris, however, always fell for it. He actually loved her resourcefulness. Yet Petticoat Lane on the Sunday before Christmas, it had to be madness.

'OK, let's talk about it later,' he proposed. Coleen smiled and agreed.

By the stove, Myrtle was working several pots at the same time. The aroma of some good old home-style cooking filled the kitchen and tortured Chris's empty stomach. When his mother heard he had left the house at 6 a.m., before breakfast, she got up.

'It's al'right, Myrtle, I'll fix him something.'

While Mrs Thomas sorted out some food for him, Coleen slipped quietly out of the kitchen.

'Where's Stevie?' Chris asked his wife.

'Where do you think?'

Whatever free time he had Stevie spent in front of a monitor screen playing video games. At almost ten years of age, his life revolved around school, football and Nintendo. At least he didn't cause any problems. He was a quiet, polite boy. His mother's friends often marvelled at him, wishing their own male offspring were as nice.

Chris got up and went downstairs, took off his coat and shoes, washed his hands and face and stretched to shake the fatigue off his body. He returned to the kitchen to find a steaming plate of food waiting for him. He took a sip of boiling-hot mint tea. Under his mother's watchful gaze, he went through the salt fish, roasted sweet potato and hard dough bread effortlessly. He felt a lot better for it.

'So, Mum, you don't go to church today?' Chris asked, sipping his tea.

'Today is not Sunday.'

'Oh no, of course not.' Chris felt a day older, everything considered.

'I'm going to church too tomorrow,' Myrtle said, staring at her husband.

'Hmmm . . .' Chris didn't comment. They had had several discussions about this church business, without agreeing on much, but if Myrtle wanted to go to church, that was her business. She had taken to accompanying his mother once in a while, which pleased Mrs Thomas enormously.

Church was nothing new for Myrtle. She came from a family of Methodists, but since marrying Chris eleven years earlier, she hadn't bothered with it. It wasn't really Chris's doing. Growing up in a church family, Myrtle had never really questioned anything. When she left home, she simply stopped going to church, though she would still read her Bible. All the pressure from Chris's mother over the years had not got him back to church, despite his mother's ceaseless badgering. By the time he was sixteen he had begun to rebel against it for the sake of rebelling. He later went back to the Scriptures, however, studying everything he could find about Christianity in particular, digging and probing. He often sat down with his mother, patiently showing her why he couldn't accept the validity of most of the points of her religion. It had all been in vain of course. Chris didn't mind that, as long as everyone was free to do whatever they wished. Problems only occurred when Mrs Thomas tried to enforce her religion surreptitiously, like when she arranged a 'shotgun christening' for Coleen. Despite understanding the truth of Chris's point, Myrtle was easily won over by Mrs Thomas. But Chris didn't flinch, declaring that he wouldn't submit his child to a practice he didn't recognize. His mother and the church people insisted. Chris told them politely but firmly to mind their business and leave his child alone. Myrtle's family didn't get too involved, though Myrtle's mother, a staunch Christian before her arrival in England from Barbados, never really forgave Chris. They had to settle for a family blessing, a very nice reunion which went quite nicely, despite the vibes. The same happened with Stevie a few years later . . .

'Al'right,' Myrtle said, switching one burner off and turning the others low, 'let's go and relax now.'

They all went downstairs and sat in the living room, watching the television; Coleen was already there.

'Where's Harry?' Mrs Thomas asked after a while.

Good question, Lorna thought to herself.

'He promised he would come for dinner, Mum,' she said, trying to sound sure.

Chris sat in his chair going through the morning's events in his mind. With his family's voices chattering around him, he thought about Hopper, locked up; about Kevin, on the run; Mrs Walters, aggrieved, lonely . . .

176

Stevie came in from his bedroom, attracted by the noise. His grandmother grabbed him, pulling him to her and stroking his hair. Stevie endured the 'powdering' with good grace. After an hour or so, Myrtle declared that dinner was ready to be served. Just then, the bell rang upstairs. Stevie and Coleen jostled to get upstairs first.

'Stop it!' their mother called out, following them on her way to the kitchen. Lorna went to help her. Chris sat there, listening to his mother as she gave him news of her friends, church sisters and the like, many of whom he only knew vaguely. He smiled as she told stories, and laughed at the vivacity and mischievous wit that belied her usual religious outlook on things. In between stories, she mentioned that their father had phoned from Jamaica earlier that week. Chris's father had decided to return to his native home when he retired from British Rail. His decision had caused his wife much anguish. She didn't think life in England was perfect either, but at least it was more or less secure. She had tried to understand his point of view. Having visited Jamaica two years before, for the first time since she came to Britain in the fifties, she felt she couldn't live there any more. Things had changed, she was older, many of the people she had left behind were no more. She felt like a foreigner in her own land. In London her life was ordered, quiet and relatively comfortable.

Her husband saw it differently. He had never really felt at home in his new country. Sure he had a family, friends. Sure he earned a wage and relaxed at weekends, having a drink and playing dominoes. But deep inside, he had always missed Jamaica; its climate, freedom he couldn't feel in England and the beautiful sea. He returned to England in a dreamy state after his first trip back home in ten years. He would sit his son Chris down and tell him how much he had enjoyed his stay, his old friends, and the sea from which his family out there still made a living. Chris understood; he'd been back too and felt the same, though he left as a child. When the time came for his father to return, he knew his mother would be hurt. Yet as a man he couldn't blame his father for refusing to grow old and die in a land he had never loved as much as his home. He left, his wife stayed and now her life centred around the church and her children . . .

Stevie came running down the stairs excitedly, ahead of Harry.

'Hi, Grandma.' Harry kissed her.

'Harry, me son. Look 'pon you!' she said admiringly. Then she turned to the pretty, shy girl beside him.

'So you don't introduce me?' she chided him gently.

'Yes, this is Marcia.'

Smiling, Marcia held out her hand. Mrs Thomas took it in hers.

'But, Harry, she's your girlfriend? She's pretty! How are you, my dear?' Harry grinned as Marcia tried not to be shy, her hands still trapped.

'Hello, I'm fine, thank you.' She was now free but forced to sit beside the old lady. Harry meanwhile took a place next to his uncle.

'Al'right Chris?'

'What's happening?'

Harry explained that he had gone to see some friends, then decided on inviting Marcia to dinner. Chris said it was a good idea. Then, as Mrs Thomas busied herself quizzing Marcia, he told Harry in hushed tones about Kevin and Hopper.

'Really?' Harry couldn't believe it. The two boys were older than him, but he knew them. They always supported him, encouraged him to deejay and helped him, whenever.

'What's gonna happen to Hopper?' Harry asked.

Chris shook his head sadly.

'I don't think he'll get bail, especially because they ain't got Kevin.'

Harry felt bad hearing that. The two boys were not really bad like some youths who looked for trouble. They were just prepared to stand up for themselves. He wondered what Kevin would do.

Lorna came down, balancing two trays which she handed to her mother, who insisted on tormenting the shy Marcia with stories about Harry as a toddler. Marcia looked helplessly at Harry. He simply smiled, enjoying her suffering.

Myrtle brought more trays. Chris got one, Harry the other. They sat down to eat, but not before Mrs Thomas's obligatory, though brief, blessing. The television was on, but only Stevie paid much attention to it. The food was excellent and despite his late breakfast Chris enjoyed every bit of it. Coleen and Lorna cleared up after and produced tall glasses of Guinness punch for everyone. The atmosphere switched from mellow to warm, even Marcia loosened up. In the middle of the jollities, Mrs Thomas, who never missed a thing, brought her son's attention to the framed picture on the wall behind him.

'Chris, what's this?'

Glancing up, Chris smiled. He had bought the picture in a bookshop the previous week. It was a drawing of the Last Supper, set exactly as it is in traditional Christian pictures, only all the characters, including the central one, were depicted as black and bearded.

'So, Mum, you don't recognize it? Why do you ask me?' Chris asked, amused. He knew what she meant.

'Yes, I know, but why dem look like dat?'

Chris laughed to himself.

'Mum, leave it alone, al'right. It's my house, it's my picture. I like it, OK?'

'I'm only asking a question. Can't I ask a question?' Mrs Thomas responded innocently.

Lorna and Myrtle frowned, they knew only too well where this was going.

'Don't start, man, leave him with his picture,' Lorna said, turning to Chris with a 'please don't start her off' look.

Harry laughed. His grandma hadn't given up on trying to get him to church. Chris and his mother managed nevertheless to have a brief but lively debate about the picture. Mrs Thomas satisfied her curiosity. Chris assured her that it was likely that his drawing was a truer representation of Jesus and his disciples than the ones she was used to seeing. He sometimes suspected his mother of knowing the truth but clinging to her conformist beliefs by force of habit.

'So, Mum, you're black but you don't want Christ to be black?' He laughed.

Myrtle bravely tried to step in.

'But you don't know that for sure?'

'You don't know if he wasn't for sure either, do you?' Chris retorted.

Harry smiled, listening as Chris switched to a more basic topic of discussion. The bearded men in the picture looked on, forgotten for now, as the family went about their festivities in the comfort of the living room. Coleen switched on the lights.

'You going out later?' Chris asked Harry. He had seen his nephew check his watch several times.

'Yeah, I've got to check a dance tonight.'

'You be careful out there, you hear?' Chris said.

'Yeah, don't worry.'

A little later, Harry announced his intention of walking Marcia home. Harry deflected his grandmother's query by saying he'd be back soon. The young lovers left the happy atmosphere of the family reunion and stepped into the cold darkness outside. They walked to the bus stop but Harry decided that they'd better catch a cab. After all, it was holiday time . . .

13

THE BIG CLASH

'**H**ear dis, man,' Sticks said as he pushed up the volume of the car stereo for Linton to get the fullness of the lyrics. He'd just gotten the cassette earlier that day from a girl who had returned from Jamaica. The bass pumped through the big speaker set at the back of the Saab. Sticks's head bobbed back and forth to the pulse. A grinning Linton listened as the MC unfolded a string of tightly woven lyrics to the rhythm, and let out a shout as the punch line hit home. The crowd on the cassette reacted in the same way, thousands of miles away and thousands of times louder, cutting the MC short and forcing the selector to spin the record again.

'Wicked my yout' yuh mus get a run offa it!'

'Yeah, man,' Sticks answered. The two had been in the car for an hour. Inside the hall, the dance was in progress, warming up fast, though it was only after two in the morning. Sticks had co-ordinated the whole thing on D.'s instructions, making sure the two sets stringed up on time, supervising the setting up of the bar, organizing the gate. By the time D. got to the hall, everything was rolling, the crowd had started to arrive in droves and he had nothing to worry about. The much-publicized clash between long-time champion High Noon and the aggressive up and coming Radical Hi-Powah was definitely happening! Not only that, but the fact that it was billed as D.'s personal dance had added to the attraction. Judging by the crowd jostling outside the doors of the community hall in the cold, inside was probably quite full by now. Also, because it was holiday, less than a week before Christmas, this was one of the busiest Saturday nights of the year. The way he had promoted it, D. expected people from all over London and even outside. The hall was big, which was just as well, with a stage at one end and a high ceiling. Such venues were usually hard to get, especially at short notice; D. had cunningly programmed a girl he knew to book it for her 'birthday party'. A large booking fee, passed as a contribution to the centre, had convinced the manager to overlook the usual time restrictions. The way things were going, the dance was likely to run well into the Sunday morning. From where Sticks had parked the car, just outside the pub facing the hall, he could see the continuous flow of cars coming from Tottenham turning off the one-way system into the congested side street. There were no more parking spaces, already the road was lined up on both sides and arriving vehicles had started filling the other side roads to the left.

'Ah dem kinda dance me love.' Sticks smiled. 'I gwan keep one nex' month, y'know.' Linton nodded, still enthralled by the fresh cassette on the stereo. After making sure everything was running smoothly, seeing that D. had arrived, the two had retreated to the car to burn a couple of rocks. They felt nice now. In a little while they would be on the dancefloor letting off some energy.

'Watch dis now,' Linton called his friend's attention to a group of girls coming from the other side of the road on their way to the hall. The four of them were dressed up, sequinned short dresses, low-cut, hurrying through the cold December night. Sticks looked on, his head against the headrest, as they passed the car.

'Bumper!' he muttered, watching the wide hips of the last girl in the group. Linton passed a remark about women's shape in general, then Sticks came up with a story;

they laughed. The cassette auto-reversed churning out more exclusive lyrics. The way the crowd sounded through the speakers, it felt almost as if it was happening right there.

'Still, nut'n nuh nice like de dance dem ah Yard,' Sticks declared emphatically.

'Fe real, sometimes me well feel fe fly out, y'know, Supa?'

Sticks agreed. England was hard to bear for him too, especially in winter. No matter how much comfort, they still missed Jamaica and that feeling of liveliness, the special mix of tension and exhilaration found in downtown Kingston on dance nights. True, before arriving in England, Sticks had lived a pauper's life, hustling since he was but a child to make a living. In those days, he'd wake up hungry and sometimes went to bed hungry too. He grew up without anything much, wearing the same patched pants, the same torn shirt and battered old shoes day after day. Now Sticks took pride in his appearance. He remembered his grand-mother used to tell him, 'Only the best is good enough for you.' That was long ago, but he'd never forgotten those words. So when he finally escaped the hungry streets of his childhood it had become a kind of motto for him. He'd been here over two years now and he'd done good. Sticks opened his window, cleared his throat and spat.

Linton lit up a cigarette. 'Hey, yuh see dem bwoy down at the estate, them fuck themselves now, y'know,' he said, referring to a little problem they had had in the week. Apparently some local guys had decided to start dealing for their own selves, refusing to be controlled by Sticks's people. Sticks had personally gone to check it out a few days before, but it looked as if some action was going to be necessary. Sticks wound the window back up, picked up his beer bottle from the dashboard and took a sip.

'Don't worry, man, we gwan deal wid' dem proper.' Right now, Sticks couldn't bother about that, he felt nice and the night was young. Next week he would take care of the problem. He looked at Linton, adding:

'Any bwoy come between me an' my business – dead, y'know dat.'

Linton agreed. They had driven through the estate and held up one youth, who, despite an earlier warning, was doing business on their patch. Linton had been for shooting him there and then but Sticks held him back. He got a beating. But that was all. Sticks had explained afterwards that it wasn't worth it; he wanted the top guy, the one who supplied the youth, the one who was 'dissin' the programme.

'Yuh see me,' Sticks said defiantly, 'me nuh respeck nobody, seen?!'

Linton pulled on his cigarette.

Sticks went on. 'No man gwan stop me from making some pounds. Nuh care wha' de man ah seh; it's drugs the people dem want an' is we run dem t'ings deh.'

'Yes, my yout',' Linton agreed.

Sticks was quiet for a moment, thinking, then, as if switching topic, he told his partner, 'My father was a handcart man, y'know.' He went on: 'Yeah, man, it's country my father come from, come ah town try fe mek a living.' Sticks stopped. He seemed to be concentrating on some deeply buried memories. 'When him get sick, the man get maaga, y'know, Linton. T'in bad, man. Dem time deh, me is jus' a lickle pickney. My mudda, she look after him, but she couldn't even buy no medicine, or send him to hospital.' Sticks nodded slowly, his eyes staring through the windscreen, as if momentarily hypnotized by the bounce of the bass and the reminiscences.

'Yuh see when him dead; ah jus' skin and bones, y'know,' he said softly. Then he shook himself out of it. Turning to Linton he said resolutely:

'Dat nah happ'n t' me, God know!'

'Y'nuh know, rude bwoy.' Linton felt the same way.

'Yuh see dis.' Sticks patted the bulge in his waist. 'Dat ah me backative; I mus' get my share.' They continued on that vibe, debating the wretched condition they had escaped from, vowing they would never suffer and beg as their elders had had to. In the middle of their rhetoric Linton's eyes spotted something across the road that caught his attention.

'Check over dere, nah your t'ing dat?' Outside the hall, Sticks recognized the three girls as they crossed the road coming towards the car.

'Yeah, man.'

He watched as Soni and her two friends walked down.

'I feel like hol' down one ah dem gal tonight,' Linton said. Sticks laughed.

'The one ina de tights?'

'No, man,' Linton replied. 'Me cyan tek de bony business. Ah de udda one me ah talk.' The girl he was talking about was short, fat, with strong legs hardly covered by her tight mini dress.

Sticks kissed his teeth.

'Nuh budda wid dat, man, some wicked girls ina dis dance. Dem deh t'ing will give yuh a shine fe a stone.'

Linton grinned, considering the possibility.

'I know what de girl want, y'know?' Sticks lowered down his window as Soni came up.

'What you doing, you're not coming in?' she asked.

'Yeah, man. We ah chill out yah so first.'

The three girls shuffled on the spot, their clothes hardly protecting against the cold wind.

'Can I have a rock?' Soni asked.

Sticks laughed, glancing at Linton.

'A'right, ouno come in.'

Soni opened the door and the three girls hurried into the car shivering.

'Grill dem now, Linton,' Sticks said to his partner.

Linton prepared a pipe and passed in on at the back. Soni lit it and passed it to her friends. The smell filled the car. There was some coughing at the back, then Linton set up another one. They stayed in the car for a while, talking, until Sticks decided the time was about right to get back inside.

'How in dere stay?' he asked.

'It's rammed, man, no space,' Soni replied.

'Space deh-deh fe me.' Sticks laughed opening his door. The five of them stepped out and headed for the hall, Linton slightly behind, negotiating something with the fat girl he'd been watching. The front of the hall was packed with people still wanting to get in. This seemed to be the main dance tonight, and many ravers who had attended parties in and out of the area were only now arriving. Linton cleared a path for them through the milling crowd, shoving people as he went. A visibly inebriated young man in a suit protested as he was pushed out of the way. A cold stare from the tall and fierce-looking Linton cooled him down. As they entered, Sticks stopped to check with Riley, one of his gate men who was involved in a discussion with two others who were holding up the queue.

'Wha' ah gwan, man?'

Riley pointed disdainfully at the two men.

'Dem man dere nah wan' pay de rate.'

Sticks turned to the closest one, big-built with a short beard and a golden star in his left ear.

'Is wha' happ'n, sah? You nuh see seh yuh ah hold up the queue?' The man looked at him, standing his ground.

'Me ah entertainer, I don't pay to come a dance, seen?' he stated stubbornly.

Sticks glanced at Riley, then back at the man.

'Tell me somet'ing,' he asked drily, 'yuh ah chat 'pon any udda set dem tonight?'

The man hesitated a second, Sticks didn't give him any more time. 'Den yuh mus' pay, man, or jus' leave de place, seen?'

Behind the men, the front of the crowd watched the challenge. The man stood there a little too long for Sticks.

'Yuh ah hear me; ah the Don's personal dance, dis. Me nuh even gwan budda wid yuh. Mek him deal wid' yuh himself.' The man dipped his hand in his pocket under Sticks's watchful eye, and looked at him for at least a second before he placed a twenty-pound note on the table. Him and his friend walked by Riley and Sticks, stony-faced, visibly upset but unwilling to carry it any further. Sticks said a few words in Riley's ear then walked inside. The place was full, people lined up in the corridor, massed against the bar with the bulk of the crowd, pressed all over the length of the hall. Sticks squinted in the smoky darkness. High Noon had set up right against the near wall, and had just entered the bar. The mixer and the amp were raised up on a platform. It was their turn to play and they were making full use of it. Beetle, their star selector, was visible intermittently, his head bobbing above the wall of dancers standing around the control tower. He was short of stature but rather big, with a moustache and glasses. He was a feisty fireplug, always ready to cuss any sound who dared contest High Noon's crown. Tonight, Beetle seemed in great shape, literally jumping in the air as he exhorted his sound's faithful followers. Cheers, whistles and shouts rose from the crowd all around as he shouted into the microphone. Sticks stopped for a short while against the stack to the right of the entrance and watched the action. Beetle let the needle of the turntable fly on to the record for a few seconds then, responding to the crowd's heated roar, he lifted up – looking all around him with a studied frown.

'High Noon massive – I wan' ouno listen to the lyrics

. . . No sound can tes' we. Only High Noon alone can play dem type ah special. Come again!'

The needle went down, the drums rattled and rolled briefly across the packed room. Then, without any music, the deep voice of one of Jamaica's top singers of the moment floated through the speakers, praising High Noon. The record ran for a minute at the most before Beetle started it all over again. In his corner, Sticks was taking in the beat. He liked High Noon, they had managed to run the whole of north London uncontested for years now. Sticks enjoyed the way they sounded, always amused by the charismatic Beetle and his tricks. Yet since last year, Radical Hi-Powah had made a serious bid for the crown. The new sound had busted upon the reggae scene with a fresh talented crew and had rallied a lot of the regular ravers around them. Radical received a good response everywhere they played and always managed to come up with fresh 'specials'. Also, because of the owners' extensive contacts, most of the visiting artists from Jamaica turned up to do PAs at their sessions. Tonight was a hot night, in all senses of the word. A clash to the finish, with both crews hyped up to the maximum to make their respective sounds come out on top. Sticks looked around, recognized a few faces. He knew most of his people were gathered at the other end of the hall, around the stage where Radical was stringed up. He braced himself up and started pushing through the bodies towards the end of the room. It was no easy task, even for a determined man like him who didn't worry about mashing a few toes. When he finally got there, Linton was already leaning against the back wall, Soni's fat friend pressed against him. He stepped up on to the stage and went to speak with Max, Radical's selector. They had a wicked crew tonight, Max told him. Every MC in town had wanted a spot on the mike for the big clash.

'Where Puggy deh?' Sticks asked. Max didn't know.

'Him bettah mek sure him show up though . . .' Max added. Puggy, the latest singing sensation, was scheduled to tear the place down later on. Knowing his tendency to get involved in schemes, Sticks wondered where he could be. He hailed a few soldiers and artists he knew, then made his way towards the door to the right of the stage. He knocked. The door opened from inside and Pablo's face appeared. He drew back to allow Sticks in. In the small room, a dozen men were sitting or leaning against the walls. Sticks hailed Indian, Lee, Norris, Leroy and a couple of artists he knew, amongst them Davey, Radical's resident MC.

'Me ah look fe yuh all night, man. Wha'ppen?' Davey asked.

'Me deh yah, man, I did go outside fe a touch.'

Davey grinned.

'Me can see dat. Touch me nuh!'

'I soon talk t'yuh mek I check de Don first.' Sticks walked down to the corner where Charlie and D. were busy talking.

'Me t'ink seh yuh gone home,' D. said.

'No, man, how me fe go home an' de dance jus' start? Everyt'ing awright?'

D. nodded. 'Yeah, man, everyt'ing curry.'

As long as D. was happy with the way things were going, everything was fine.

'De place full, yuh know? All outside, people still ah queue,' Sticks said.

'We've gotta set up some boxes outside,' Charlie joked. D. laughed.

D. called out to Davey standing nearby.

'Yaow, my yout' comin' like High Noon ah mash up de place.'

From outside, the noise was coming right through the

doors, a deafening commotion coming as much from the crowd as from the music itself. Beetle was whipping up his audience to a frenzy.

'Ah nuh nut'n, Don,' Davey said dismissively. 'Radical gwan rul t'night. Me have lyrics fe slaughter dem!'

Sticks went over and dealt with Davey. Charlie got out a Rizla and built himself a spliff. D. also. He spread out some herb, Charlie topped up his with some white powder. He held up the small foil paper. D. hesitated for maybe just a few seconds, then he declined, rolling up his spliff as it was. The blend of various substances filled the little room with smoke. From outside, a short silence was followed by a loud uproar, punctuated by three high-pitched notes out of the synthesizer box: Radical was tuning in.

On the corner where he was busy burning with Sticks, Davey looked up with a satisfied smile. He stretched.

'Ah my time now!' he declared.

He stepped outside, exalted by all present in the room. Everyone soon followed him. The dance was about to kick up. Up to now, the two sounds had played various tracks, warming up as the venue filled to capacity. The last half-hour had belonged to High Noon and the tone had grown notably more aggressive, with Beetle working up a sweat, taunting his opponent, teasing the dancers. Things were about to get more serious, everybody could feel that. Most of D.'s crew were around Radical's set, waiting expectantly, watching as Max set his mixer right.

'Before we start . . .' he said calmly into the mike. 'Before we start, I want to say somet'ing.' Radical's crowd were raring to go, but Max went on.

'When de Don call me fe come play at dis clash, I laughed . . .' he declared, looking straight ahead of him across the hall. A few laughs erupted in the crowd below Radical's set.

'Yuh know why, I tell ouno why I laugh; from a longer

time I hear High Noon ah talk all kinda t'ings 'bout Radical. Dem seh dis an' dem seh dat. Now, we nevah answer dem, yuh know why?' Max was working up his audience, his voice clear through the powerful set of speakers.

'I seh dis without malice; Radical don't need to cuss other sounds, seen? We is de original criss, international, invincible export sound, seen?' The crowd erupted in approval. Davey looked at Max and smiled.

'Anyway, talking done now. I wan' de people dem fe listen to Radical and judge fe demselves. Radical Massive?!' A deafening roar rose up around the set. Without any further warning, Max dropped the needle on the record that had been spinning for a while, waiting. The tune exploded through the hall, Max holding back the bass for a full minute before he let fly the control. The voices almost covered the music as the popular riddim bounced against the walls, filling the atmosphere with an electric quality. Up on the stage, the forest of raised arms testified to the hot reception Radical's tunes were getting. Max had to wait a little to make himself heard.

'High Noon!' he called out when the roar subsided. 'Ouno hear dis. Well, I don't need to talk anyt'ing against any sound; this is all that I need, music.' The crowd cheered, Max touched back the record. For the next half an hour there was sheer delight on the dancefloor as Radical Hi-Powah played record after record, with matching 'specials' by all the big names in past and present reggae music. D. and his people were as ecstatic as the crowd below and around them. The crates of drinks stacked on one side of the stage for them and Radical's crew were being emptied fast. When Davey seized the microphone halfway through the set, he didn't disappoint. Relentlessly, with faultless phrasing and inventiveness, he rode every rhythm Max threw down, responding to the crowd's spontaneous calls for more.

'Yuh see, we,' Davey shouted in between restarts, 'we nuh need a whole heap ah MC like certain sounds.' Shouts rose from the audience, along with simulated gunshots.

'Yuh know seh me ah de resident and I rule, seen?! Later, Radical Hi-Powah is going to bring on stage live and direc' – pause – 'Puggy fe real.' More shouts of approbation.

'An' also, Firefly, new MC fe de year.' Roars of delight.

'But fe now, hol' dis!' With that, Max sent down the record to bring down the house, loud, crisp, hard-hitting. At the back of the stage, with a spliff in one hand and a Guinness stout in the other, D. rocked gently to the sounds. He looked particularly sharp in a black and green matching shirt and pants with gold trimmings. Jewellery gleamed around his neck and fingers. He had spent the day relaxing, letting Sticks run the show while he went to the barber and spent most of the day at Jenny's. In the last month, he had been there quite regularly, getting to know his son and rekindling the vibe he had before with Jenny. She was really nice to him, visibly eager to keep him there as much as possible. She didn't ask about Donna, though D. could guess she knew about the 'competition'. Rather she was being so sweet as to win him over completely. As for Donna, she had of course passed a few stinging remarks about his change of attitude. Though he still looked after her and spent time with Avril, D. was much busier now, and he could see Donna feared he had gone back to his old self. But he couldn't be too bothered about living up to a woman's expectations; after all, he had things to take care of. As for the two women competing, that was their problem. Right now, he was where he wanted to be; at his own dance, safe amongst his people and having a good time. Neither of his women was here tonight, which was just as well. Earlier in the week, he had taken Jenny out for her birthday, wined and dined her and given her a really nice and expensive present. Of course, she was overwhelmed by

that and thought the world of him. So tonight, D. felt totally
at ease with himself. He fleetingly recalled how he had been
last Christmas, when he was in jail . . . D. took a good sip
from his Guinness, as Max announced his last record before
he gave High Noon back the floor. To his right, Charlie was
talking with a slim, tastily dressed girl. D. smiled to him
and crossed the stage to speak to Pablo. He heard Max
sending him a dedication, acknowledged it. Down on the
floor, a video crew was busy filming the proceedings.

High Noon started their set, Beetle as cantankerous as
ever, more so now because of the hot reception the crowd
had given the other sound. First, after declaring that 'No
sound could ever test High Noon, them coulda come from
de moon,' he flung down a hot 'special' – the ever popular
'Burial' of old-time Wailers fame. After starting it out twice
more, in a crash of cymbals and various electronic sounds,
he let the rhythm run. Then, on a version of the same
rhythm, Beetle introduced one of their long-time MCs who,
as he put it himself, had been on a 'vacation'. Everybody in
the know laughed, as the vacation Beetle mentioned was in
fact a spell in HM prison.

'Yes, Pecos!' Beetle laughed. 'Fresh from "vacation",
come an' kill dem, my yout'!'

Pecos took up the mike, looked around at the crowd,
sent a few dedications, then stated, 'Watch me now; ouno
know why me dress up ina black t'night? Ouno don't
know?' Various responses from the crowd.

'A'right, dress up ina black t'night cause I come fe bury
a sound . . . Ouno nuh hear de riddim High Noon just
play?' This time High Noon's crowd let off several simulated
gunshots, anxious to break the vibe Radical had built up.
Then Beetle let the record run and Pecos got busy flashing
out his lyrics. Apparently, his vacation had not dulled his
DJ skills and the crowd's shouts of 'Ease!' 'Seize!' and
'Forward!' proved it. High Noon went on spinning their

plates. A bigger crowd had gathered around their set as the video crew had started filming around the control tower. At the other end of the hall the little private room was once again busy. Much talking, drinking, laughing and smoking was taking place.

'Rude bwoy, respeck due!' D. called out to Davey. Davey acknowledged the praise, adding that he wasn't finished with High Noon yet. Charlie was visibly enjoying himself, smiling widely as he listened to Indian talking to him. Sticks walked in, looking satisfied.

'Me ah watch yuh, yuh know,' Davey called to him. 'Yuh know seh de girl yuh a rub down is a man woman?'

'Me nuh response pappa; the bwoy mus' get a bun!' Davey laughed. Sticks went to sit by D.

'Roadblock outside, yuh know, Don!' D. seemed happy about it, his dance was definitely a big success. They talked for a little while, until Pablo caught D.'s attention from the door. Someone was asking to see him. D. told Pablo to let him in. He was surprised to see his old friend Sammy enter the room. Sammy came up and D. greeted him.

'Sammy, wait, wha' ah gwan, me breddah?'

'Yes, D., me jus' reach, y'know. Love, man!' The two friends shook hands, D. happy and surprised by the unexpected visit. Sammy sat beside him. D. asked for a drink to be brought to his friend. He had only seen Sammy once, in Brixton what seemed a long time ago, before he got busted. Even then, D. was so 'spaced out' that time and so busy that they had not really had the opportunity to talk much. Sammy operated a garage, was married with children and lived outside the hustling scene. D. had promised then to check him again, but things had caught up with him. They settled down drinking. Sammy explained that he had heard about the dance in south London and had made the point of checking his bredrin. D. told him he'd only recently been back, and summed up his adventures since they had last

195

seen each other. It was a really nice feeling to see Sammy again, especially tonight when the atmosphere was perfect. Both had travelled a long way since their schooldays in West Kingston. They were men now.

'But you look fat, enh, man?' D. laughed, looking at his friend's protruding stomach. Sammy patted his belly.

'Married life.' He asked D. about his status, and D. joked that he was still too young to get married. He told Sammy about his two recently born offspring. Sammy built the sensi spliff D. offered him and they had a good time drawing back on memories of their early days. Sammy told D. he was supposed to take his family to Jamaica for a holiday in the spring. It would be the first time his mother would see her grandchildren.

Meanwhile, Sticks had left the room. He still had not seen Puggy. No one had. Sticks finished his beer and made his way towards the exit. In the corridor, the dancing was as heavy as in the hall itself. Some serious bogling was taking place. High Noon had the crowd well in hand, spinning all the popular favourites of the moment, including several versions of the 'Batty Rider' riddim. Sticks was about to step outside, past the gates, when he saw something that froze him in his tracks. Against the wall, behind a row of dancers, some guy in a double-breasted suit was talking into Soni's ear. Sticks had had no idea where she was. He'd been busy for the last half an hour or so, and he assumed she had been with her friends. Instantly vexed, Sticks pushed through the dancers and stopped right in front of Soni. The guy saw him first; he realized something was wrong, took one look at Sticks's malevolent face and wisely stepped away. Soni stood there, a glass in her hand, surprised. Sticks said nothing. As people watched, he grabbed the front of the girl's dress and dragged her out and through the gates, her feet hardly touching the ground. She let go of the glass. Riley said something as Sticks passed

196

him, but didn't get an answer. Sticks was angry. Still holding Soni, who had started shouting and protesting, he emerged outside and flung her forward, sending her crashing against the railings. He watched her regain her balance. She was cursing and trying to fix her clothing. Smirking, pointing at Soni, Sticks spat out:

'Hey, gal, is did yuh wan' dis me?'

Soni was trying to regain her composure. A few people were watching as she answered back insolently:

'So what?! You was busy with some girl?!' Then she added defiantly, 'I can talk to who I want to!' It was the wrong answer. Probably because she was high, she misunderstood Sticks's grin.

'Yeah? So yuh get bad now?!' The box was as sudden as it was powerful. The blow sent Soni back against the railings, her head rocking, but she didn't drop. It was the backhand that followed, slapping her hard across the face, that threw her on to the ground. She didn't even make a sound. He stood over her as she tried to push herself up. Soni was a small woman, the blows had shaken her and the fact that she had also drunk quite a lot made it all worse. But Sticks was still angry. He was about to kick her when Linton appeared with Soni's friend in tow.

'Yush!' he called out, running towards Sticks. 'Hold on, man!' Linton came just in time. Sticks was cursing his already half-unconscious woman. 'No, man, leave it . . . let it go, star!'

Patiently, Linton pulled his friend away, talking to him. Apart from D. and Charlie, only Linton could have done that. Anyone else would have put their life on the line. But Linton managed to get him away and calm him down a little. Meanwhile, Soni's friend helped her back to her feet. Her face was already looking bad, quickly swelling where the blows had connected. The friend wiped the blood dripping on to Soni's chin. Sticks was still cussing. Linton was doing his best to prevent his friend from getting back closer to Soni.

'Me tek her home, man, jus' cool,' he said once he was sure Sticks wouldn't go any nearer, Linton took the car keys from him and helped Soni across the road. He got her into the car and, with her friend tending to her at the back, drove out. Sticks stayed outside for a short while, cooling down. No one looked at him when he walked back inside, his face contorted. He pushed through the crowd, cursing those who didn't make way fast enough. By now he had even forgotten about Puggy. Back in the room, he got into a corner and made himself a pipe. Slowly, the vexation subsided as he reasoned with Indian. From the hall, High Noon selection was pumping. Beetle came on the mike, stirred up the sweating crowd a little, then he called up his ace. After a few minutes of shouting, exhortations to 'forward' from the ravers and other noises, a woman's voice came through the speakers.

'High Noon massive, respeck, seen?!' Whistles, cheers and fake gunshots greeted Babsy Ranks. A regular MC on the High Noon set, Babsy had originally arrived from Canada the year before. She was one of the few female deejays on the circuit and quite popular with the crowds. Despite her often abrasive style and 'raw' lyrics, Babsy Ranks could actually hold her own in the competitive world of live reggae entertainment. She had recorded a couple of tunes since coming over, one of which had made the charts. A tall, black-skinned young woman with attractive features, Babsy always cut a fine figure behind the microphone. Tonight, dressed in a low-cut purple dress with a short wig and large gold earrings, the fearless MC got a loud reception. Her voice, which sounded more bassy when she talked than when she deejayed, floated through the hall.

'Well, first of all, big request to the promoter D.,

maximum respeck! Also all donettes, hol' tight!' More shouts of 'Let off!' and 'Gwan!'.

'I deyah from early, seen?! All me hear is pure man ah get reques'; it's like no woman nuh deh ina de dance.' Laughs from the crowd around High Noon's set. The video camera was focused on Babsy Ranks.

'Now me come fe big up de woman dem. Debbie, Pam . . . ouno safe! Sweetie? Anyway, yuh deh . . .' Babsy made a few faces and paused for the camera, then shouted out: 'My selector, time fe release! Watch me . . .'

Beetle 'released' as requested, and Babsy got to work. Even the crew who had gathered around Radical's set shouted for the lyrics to start again. Babsy was in great shape tonight, in every sense of the word. Maybe for the first time tonight, there were as many men around High Noon as women. On the floor, hundreds of versions of the bogle dance were being demonstrated. Early morning, like now, was the best time, the finest hour for a session, especially a clash like this one. At the end of Babsy's second tune, Beetle's big loud voice came through.

'Yuh see High Noon, ah so we play any day of the year, no sound can tes', seen?!' He threw a few more jibes, obviously aimed at Radical Hi-Powah, then Babsy's hit tune rolled on. Not for long; it had to be restarted no less than three times to satisfy the rowdy crowd.

'Hear dis!' Babsy Ranks held up her hand as Beetle was about to let fly. 'Some people ah talk 'bout me too slack, but ouno mus' understand, slackness ah deal wid woman more time. So yuh see me, as a woman, I call fe deal wid slackness my way, seen?!' Babsy had everyone's attention. 'All man, take me in . . . Nuh feel no way.' Shrill women's voices rose from the audience, shouting in support, and with this the rhythm crashed through the boxes and Babsy Ranks unleashed a string of strongly worded no-nonsense lyrics which, for all the apparent vulgarity, still made a point. Of course she had to chat it more than once.

At the other end of the hall, around the stage, Max was calmly getting ready. By the time Babsy Ranks finished her set and Beetle had made a few more sarcastic remarks, the crowd was restless. By now, the whole place was in a state of collective euphoria, the bar was constantly packed and big clouds of smoke were drifting upwards above the dancers. Max took a sip from his plastic cup, lit his spliff and cleared his throat.

'Radical Hi-Powah deh 'pon de frequency.' The dancers greeted the return of the sound. Max had something to say.

'Before I fling de selection, hear dis; I respeck all sounds, fe real. We work fe entertain de people dem, so me nuh ina no bad vibes with nobody. An' me nuh carry feelings neither.' Max's left hand touched the synthesizer and a horn sound came through.

'High Noon play some wicked music tonight,' he assured Radical's followers. 'Yuh mus' give credit where it is due. Dem fling some special weh amaze me, but for everyt'ing High Noon play, Radical counter-attack, ah lie?!'

The sound supporters agreed noisily. Max listed every artist High Noon had played from the start. The crowd cheered his feat of memory. Max laughed. 'Me nevah know seh me have computer brain. Dat is why dem call me Max Superfax!' Everyone laughed, urging him on.

'Now High Noon bring in some wicked MCs, fe real. Pecos, Babsy Ranks, me love ounu! But dis is the time when Radical bring in the answer.' The crowd was impatient, calling for the 'answer'.

'Lickle more, I gwan bring in, not one but two dangerous yout's. Wha' dem name again?' Max teased the crowd.

'Awright, Puggy, live and direc', an' Firefly, wicked and dangerous.' Around the hall, it all sounded as if a riot was about to erupt. 'But first, massive . . . Cho me nuh even gwan introduce de record. Radical run t'ings.' There was a hiss, a whistling sound, drum roll and then . . . fever, general, epidemic, incurable FEVER. From the first bar of the 'Fever' rhythm, one of the most popular old-time dancehall killers, it was chaos. The original version by the late, great Tenor Saw, nearly tore off the roof. As he started it again, Mac called out, 'Puggy, you're wanted, now!' A fever that no doctor could have cured had now taken hold of the crowd. Threatening, punchy, atmospheric, the bass line of the tune was shaking even those too tired to dance. The cameraman, who knew a crucial shot when he saw one, was right in the middle of the floor, his lights man doing his best to follow, as he crouched low to take an upward angle of the dozens of pretty girls winding with abandon. The stage around Radical's set was full, crowded with celebrities, musicians, and D. and his full crew. Sticks had forgotten about the incident earlier on and was stepping wildly, smiling, so was Linton. Charlie and the girl he'd spent most of the night with were keeping close. Indian, an enormous spliff in hand, was also visibly enjoying himself. Beside D., Sammy was also rocking, a bottle held high as he followed the bass pattern. Leroy, who came up from the corner where he'd spent his time with Lee, Norris and their girls, was there too, shaking up. To the left of Max, impassive as ever, Pablo had his open arms resting on two girls' shoulders, while Davey was shouting above the music, feeling sweet.

'Puggy, las' call!' Max called out again.

The singing yout' man was still nowhere to be seen. Two more deadly records had everyone bouncing and shocking, drinks were flowing freely, the bar had definitely been bought up. As he turned to say something to Charlie, D. noticed the girl in front of the stage who had been staring at him. He mentally checked whether he knew her, but her face didn't seem familiar. The video crew had set up at the left corner of the stage now. The cameraman exchanged a few words with Max, who nodded and returned to his desk. Then Sticks came up to the mike; right as the tune ended, he growled.

'Puggy, dis is Sticks speaking, yuh ah diss de programme, seen?! Las' warning; let go offa dat big t'ing yuh under and reach, right now!' There were laughters and jeers as the missing singer was admonished. Max stressed the point.

'Puggy, whe' yuh dealing-dealing? Come in, fast!' Then he played for time. 'Massive an' crew, all bandeleros, gundeleros, sexeleros.' He laughed. 'Radical is proud to announce the highlight of the night. All girls, don't worry yuhselves.' Suddenly, there was movement in the mass of people packed around the stage. Max looked down, the microphone held up, waiting to find out the reason for the commotion. As if by magic the sea of ravers parted for a bobbing green Kangol hat, which made its way up the steps to reveal Puggy, all smiles, bouncing up on the stage. Looking relaxed, dressed in an all-white silk suit with green epaulettes, the yout' man ignored the recriminations and shouts and came up to the mike. Max shook his head, said something in his ear and gave him the spot.

'A'right,' Puggy said, pausing as he saw the camera moving in.

'Video, man, take me in!' Laughter around the stage. 'Big reques' to all de girls dem, me hear seh some gals ah cry, t'rough dem t'ink seh me nuh come again.' More laughter, jeers and whistles. Puggy, self-assured, looked around at the sea of faces in the bright glare of the video light. 'First, special reques' to the promoter: D., me come fe big yuh up; fe real. Sticks, me an' yuh ah family, seen?! Yuh know seh me cyan diss the programme. Charlie T., ah yuh rule.' With his cockiness and wit, it took Puggy less than five minutes to send his dedications and win over the crowd. He looked at Max. 'My selector, come in wid de business. Massive, Puggy live 'pon Radical Hi-Powah!' Max obliged and neatly, easily, Puggy's voice took over the rhythm. The dozens of pretty girls in front of the stage screamed as Puggy cut into a rendition of a popular soul tune. The delivery was faultless, as ever, his thin melodious voice weaving around the bass line perfectly. He had taken some time to show up, but the crowd loved Puggy and hardly let him finish the first couple of verses of each song before they cut in. Max lifted up the needle and changed the record. Puggy quipped, 'Now I want all girls to sing dis wid me, 'cause dis is a special tune. Tonight I gwan sing, till some ouno ha fe feint in yah.' Then, laughing, he added, 'Hold on, I don't want no man faint fe me still, it's strictly girls me a deal wid, y'hear.' The crowd laughed. Max took the mike, pointing out before he gave it back to Puggy, 'Yeah, we don't cater fe batty man, seen?!' Puggy, without any music, started singing his hit tune, the one that had been making the rounds of every dancehall in the last months and was still topping the charts. After less than a minute, the screams of the women in the front rows had him stopping and starting. The cameraman was working hard on his angles. Then Max gave him the track, and Puggy was rolling. By the end of the song, even the roughest roughnecks in the audience were smiling appreciatively. Puggy drank some beer from the bottle Sticks had handed him, then, after scanning around him, he declared, 'I wan' tell ouno somet'ing; since I come here from Yard, me nuh see no dance sweeter dan dis dance yah tonight, fe real.' The statement sparked a massive spontaneous cheer from the crowd. Puggy smiled, waiting for the noise to subside before continuing.

'Hear wha': yuh see tonight!? Me hear sound man ah cuss sound man, and MC ah tes' MC seen?! Nex' t'ing me hear a man ah talk 'bout him come fe bury sound.' The

203

crowd was with Puggy all the way. They cooled down and let him go on. 'Last t'ing me hear, a woman ah trace man . . . Ah nuh nut'n still, dancehall business. But hear dis; me ah go get personal now.' Expecting a scathing attack, Radical's crowd shouted and screamed, 'Prram pramm!' But Puggy had something else in mind. 'No, don't get me wrong, weh me seh? Me ah go get personal an' show ouno seh it's love me ah deal wid.' Everyone waited, watching Puggy as he took another sip and adjusted his Kangol.

'Dis nex' song, I want to reques' to Babsy Ranks.' No one knew yet what to make of it. A woman shouted something . . .

'Babsy, anywhe' yuh deh, hear me now, me nevah know ah so yuh stay. God know right now, Babsy Ranks, me ah go big yuh up, fe real! Me love how yuh ah gwan, same way me love how yuh look . . .' Then, as everyone was still trying to work it out, Puggy signalled to Max, listened to the first few bars of the rhythm and proceeded to sing for the woman MC. With his usual skill, Puggy, with lyrics he was making up as he went, sang a melody which soon had the startled crowd bawling out for more. It was unheard of for a singer to boost an MC from a rival sound system in a clash. But then Puggy was no ordinary singer. He finished the song and passed the microphone to Max as the whole dance erupted to praise him. Puggy was definitely not only a brilliant singer but also a personality, no doubt about that.

'Radical Hi-Powah; we do it diff'rent.' Max grinned into the mike.

But the audience, especially the girls, were noisily calling Puggy back. He was being congratulated by the crew as Max played a version, cleverly plotting the follow-up. Sure enough it worked. Puggy nodded to something D. was saying in his ear, then leapt forward. Max watched him as he held up his hand and took up the mike.

'Seize, selector! Yuh cyan play dem tune an' de artist deyah ina de dance,' Puggy cried out in a tone of voice as if he was offended.

'Massive an' crew, I want to bring on now the original artist fe dis record.' A name started to circulate amongst the ravers. 'Big t'ings ah gwan t'night!' Puggy shouted. 'All girls, me nuh come alone, seen?!' He paused. 'Al'right, selector, I wan' yuh start up the tune low, low . . .' Finally, Puggy looked around at the crowd below him. 'Radical Hi-Powah exclusively bring up on stage tonight, live and direck, the roughest MC fe de year . . . FIREFLY!' he shouted. The name was repeated around the hall as every neck stretched to see what was happening. 'FIREFLY!' Puggy repeated. 'Step up, my yout', fast!' The crowd was on edge now, waiting for the attraction the posters had promised. From the right corner of the room, below the stage where he had been raving with his friends for several hours, Harry walked slowly to the steps. Serious, he stepped up and approached the control tower, warmly encouraged by the crew. When he got to the mike, the yout' cast a glance at the jumping mass of people below him. Puggy tapped Harry on the shoulder, this was definitely the biggest dance he'd ever attended, let alone deejayed for. Still, he was not the nervous type, especially after a good herb spliff and a couple of beers. Max stopped the record. Puggy said, 'Firefly, see dem ah bawl out fe yuh?! Seh somet'ing, yout'!'

The crowd grew a little quieter, looking at the young MC dressed in a black and gold shirt and pants, with a black bandanna around his head. Firefly took up the microphone.

'Dancehall massive, big respeck!' This time the noise was just deafening. For many ravers, this was the first time they'd ever seen the young local MC in the flesh. His first release had taken the town by storm, making him an instant celebrity. Those in the music circuit who had gotten to know Firefly all agreed that, at fourteen years of age, he had a great career in front of him. His uncanny ability to make up lyrics and his versatility amazed many older and established MCs. Also, because he remained seemingly unaffected by his sudden success, Firefly was a favourite anywhere. The girls had a weakness for his youthful dreamy face and high-pitched voice. Firefly continued once the noise had died down sufficiently . . .

'Puggy, you're right, fe real; dis dance sweet.' The statement only caused more pandemonium. Max restored order so that the MC could continue.

'First of all, big respeck to D., the promoter, also Charlie T, my manager. Yeah, Yard man massive, big up. New York crew, respeck. Inglan' crew, love ouno! Request to my bredrin Buster, also Raymond, Ricky, not forgetting all the sexy girls dem.' The last part of the dedication had the front rows screaming in response as the said sexy girls held up their hands towards him. Then Max ran the rhythm and Firefly went to work. The hit tune was crisp. He ran through a couple more records, riding neatly and intelligently, building up the crowd's response. Behind him the crew were dancing along, boosting him up while Puggy remained by his side throughout. Finally, Max took up the mike.

'Wha' ouno ah seh?' he teased.

'More!' was the general consensus, loudly expressed by hundreds of voices. Puggy took up the mike confidently.

'Al'right, hear dis now; yuh see like how ev'rybody hot now, Firefly and Puggy gonna deal wid ouno right. Combination style,' he thundered. 'Selector I wan; yuh gimme a piece ah de "Punnany" riddim, seen?! Firefly, me an' yuh. Watch me.' As the celebrated rhythm pumped through the speakers, Puggy started to sing and got the crowd rocking, then passed on the microphone to his sidekick. True to himself, Firefly gave them entirely new lyrics which they didn't even let him finish. In similar fashion, Puggy and Firefly ran a few more tunes and set fire to the hall with their powerful combination of showmanship and inventiveness. It was the sweetest part of the dance, and the video crew made no mistake about it. They had set up below the stage and were totally focused on the two sensations. Feeling totally in tune now, Firefly decided he had something more to give his audience.

'Before we done, I want to talk a new lyrics.' At that moment, Beetle decided to intervene from his corner. Switching on, he declared through the mike, 'Radical, yuh ah diss now; it's High Noon time fe play!'

Instantly, cursing and jeers rose from the crowd directed at the impertinent selector. He tried to insist.

'No disrespeck, Radical, yuh time done.' It took no less than D.'s intervention to calm down the situation.

'Hol' on, dis is D. speaking: Beetle, wid respeck, de yout' seh him wan' chat one las' lyrics, seen?! Wha' yuh ah seh?' Beetle had more sense than to refuse D.'s request.

To cheers from the crowd, Firefly took up the microphone. 'Hol' it,' he asked Max. 'People, yuh know dat police kill my bigga bruddah fe no reason. But yuh see me; dem cyan tek me down so. Shot ha'fe fire!' In the present state of things, nothing could have provoked more response, could have gone down with so much force than that simply stated fact. This was also history, exclusive; no one who knew Firefly had ever heard such a thing from the young MC. Then, oblivious to the noise, the shouts, the gunshots, Firefly simply looked at Max, who put down the needle. As the rhythm ran, Firefly gave the crowd what was surely the most spontaneous, tightly delivered and intelligent lyrics of the whole night, a scathing denunciation of police brutality towards black people with a reference to the Scriptures. He ran it only twice, then retreated to the back of the stage where he received a hero's welcome. Graciously, Max gave the floor to High Noon, knowing full well that no matter what happened, Radical Hi-Powah had won the clash. He was sure of that! High Noon wisely started with a selection of Studio One tunes, to the delight of the crowd who were just about ready for that smoother vibe.

D. and the crew retreated once again to the back room, taking Firefly and Puggy along, inside it was drinks all around, spliffs and congratulations, and an unmistakable feeling of victory and power. D. took Firefly aside.

'Yuh have talent, yout', God know. Me nuh hear lyrics like dat fe years.' He touched fists with the young MC.

'It's reality,' Harry said simply, sipping from his bottle.

Charlie came in, smiling.

'Man, I'm your manager and I didn't even know you was dat bad!' He laughed.

'Yuh fe get de Grammy nex'!' Sticks declared.

Puggy felt good too. Everything had gone down perfectly. He built himself a spliff; he deserved it. Buster and Raymond worked their way in to congratulate their friend. They were proud of him like everyone else. Even the usually reserved Max was enthusiastic about the youth's performance.

'Bonafide respeck!' he told him, beaming.

On the other side, out there on the floor, early morning and Studio One were the perfect mix. Everywhere couples were busy swaying to the raw groove of the eternal Coxsone riddim 'Rocking Time'.

A crew came into the hall and everyone got busy, most of them getting hold of a girl and finding a suitable corner. Near the wall to the right of the entrance Lee, Norris and Leroy were having a nice time. Sweet revival riddims were flying off High Noon's turntables. Sweetie and Pam had just gone back to the bar for more supplies, Leroy was building himself a spliff and listening to Lee explaining something to him. Meanwhile, Norris had made a sly move backwards and caught up with the brown, good-looking girl he'd spotted earlier on. He had convinced her to dance and was well into the groove with his conquest. Lee didn't see them at first, it was Leroy who, sharp as ever, noticed what was going on. Standing opposite them, three men were watching, one of them looking directly at Lee. Alerted, Lee stopped talking and checked it out. He had noticed Killer and his two friends earlier on when they had walked in. Apart from casting him an evil look, Killer had gone about his business somewhere at the other end of the room near the High Noon set. But he was now only a few yards across, watching Lee. Leroy finished building his spliff but didn't light it. He was slipping it into his shirt pocket when he saw one of the guys behind Killer say something in his ear. The rest happened fast, so fast that nothing could have prepared Lee for it. All at once, he saw Killer walk towards him, pushing people out of the way. He couldn't see his hands. Close behind, the two henchmen followed. The crowd was still thick behind them. In this dark part of the hall, the dancers were tightly moving against each other. That was probably what caused Killer's downfall. All of a sudden, Lee saw him raise his right hand, at the same time he heard the boom of a gun as a bullet hit the ceiling. In a flash there was empty space between Lee and Leroy on one side and Killer and the two other guys as people screamed and scattered. Norris froze for half a second, let go of his girl and made to go forward. Lee could see the gunman's face frozen, his eyes set on him. Then, as the gun started to level at him, something happened that no one expected, least of all Killer. From his right side, a full bottle came crashing heavily against the side of his head. The blow stunned him and he momentarily lost balance, still holding the gun. But that gave Leroy time to leap forward, closely followed by Norris, knife in hand. The ensuing scene was total mayhem, screams, shouts, curses and a mad scramble that progressed quickly towards the door as Killer's two friends tried to save him. Killer ended up on the floor in the corridor, blood pouring from his chest. One of his friends had a big gash in the middle of his head, while the other, who had realized how desperate the situation was, managed to push his way through the door in the confusion.

Charlie, who had made it to the scene first, was all that stood between Killer and his friend and instant death. Leroy had gotten hold of the gun and wisely hidden it out of sight. Norris, his blade still red, had to be stopped from finishing them off. Only those involved were in the corridor now. The crowd had either retreated in panic far inside the hall or fled outside. On the mike, D.'s voice came out, loud and threatening.

'Any bwoy diss my dance, mus' dead t'night.'

Then he came down quickly to check it out for himself. Killer's friend, the only one still conscious despite his gaping head wound, pleaded for his life. There was no way of telling whether the gunman was dead or alive. D. rapidly took charge of things and the two men were carried to their car and abandoned in a deserted spot by two of D.'s soldiers. That was the best thing to do. Lee had to be dissuaded by D. from taking revenge there and then. D. explained that the last thing he wanted was for the police to barge in. Things got back to a kind of order but the vibe wasn't there any more as most people were now too shaken to resume their enjoyment. As it was well after seven by now, the dance folded up. On his way back to the room to check Charlie, D. stopped by Lee. He looked at him as Sweetie held him tight in her arms.

'Yuh have a good woman,' he told him, 'look after her.' Then he went on. Lee knew that only too well; his woman had just saved his life. He couldn't really say anything much to her, but she knew what he meant. They left with Pam, Norris and Leroy. D. decided to leave Pablo in charge; it had been a long night. He called Sticks and asked him to pay the sounds and see to it that everyone got home. As he turned to walk back across the hall, he found himself face-to-face with the girl, the same one whom he had seen staring at him earlier on. He had watched as she danced to the music but kept her eyes on him most of the time. She stood there. D.'s mind was still on the incident.

'Hi, Tony,' she said. D. paused, looking her over. She was young, maybe sixteen or seventeen, with a dark complexion, short hair-style and a pleasant, open smile. Dressed in a silver all-in-one body-suit with a large black belt around her slim waist, the girl was enjoying D.'s puzzlement.

'I know yuh?' D. asked, trying not to sound too hostile. It was early morning, he started to feel like going home, and the fight had sort of spoiled his mood.

'You don't remember me, do you?' the girl asked.

He would have liked to.

The hall was almost empty now, but for the sound-system crew packing up the equipment and a few hangers-on.

'Come, me an' yuh talk,' D. said. The girl followed him outside, on the way he said a few words to Beetle, who was supervising the loading of the boxes into a big van. D. had left the car he'd recently bought in a street behind a pub. He walked down with the girl on this cold grey Sunday morning. No matter how he had tried, he couldn't place the girl.

'What's your name?' he asked as they approached his car.

'Sherry,' she answered.

'Sherry?' D. repeated, looking at her. The girl laughed. Then D. hit on something, he stopped.

'Why yuh call me Tony a while ago?'

'When we met, you told me that was your name.' She shrugged.

'Yeah?' D. muttered. That was quite possible, but then he often used the name, at least until he got too well-known to fool anyone. He walked on, the girl followed. Just as something was starting to click in his mind, she said:

'I met you the first time you came over, in Clapton.'

Clapton? D. thought, digging in his memory. Yes, that was it! He stopped again. He squinted as he looked her over once again.

'Wha'? Yuh mean, is yuh direct me dat day, from de bus?' The girl laughed again. D. couldn't believe it! She looked different, but now that she had told him he could recall the features. What had fooled him was that she had looked like a schoolgirl then. Now it was a young woman he was seeing, a nice one at that.

'You grow up fast!' he exclaimed, smiling.

'That was over two years ago,' Sherry pointed out.

D. stopped by the shiny black Audi he'd been driving for the last two weeks and unlocked the doors. Sherry got in the passenger seat. D. switched on the engine and the music. He turned to Sherry. She smiled and told him she had recognized him while he was on the stage. D. said he'd noticed her, but that he couldn't place her at the time. Besides, he pointed out, a lot of girls always tried to draw his attention. D. usually didn't respond. Sherry agreed that, since he was quite famous, it was understandable.

'What was the shooting about?' Sherry asked.

'Jus' some guy going on bad, foolishness,' D. answered dismissively. The girl explained that she had come to the dance with her auntie but had lost track of her in the panic after the gunshot. She didn't seem too distressed by that.

'So yuh still live in the same area?' D. asked her.

'Yeah. You remember the road?' D. recalled the girl telling him the name of the road at the time, but that was long ago. He said he'd drop her at home and they drove off. They talked on the way as D. took his time along the quiet and near-empty streets. Sherry told him she'd been to Jamaica since their first meeting and stayed with her mother's family in uptown Kingston. She talked about the places she'd been and said she had really enjoyed herself.

'I might go again this year, if I get some money,' she said. Sherry had now left school and started working in a hairdresser's salon. By the time they got near her house, D. could feel the girl liked him. She asked him a couple of seemingly innocent questions which he recognized for what they were by her tone of voice. She was a nice girl, pleasant and well-mannered. When he had first met her, she was a schoolgirl. And the fact that she had remembered him after all this time and still seemed keen was at least flattering.

'Tell me,' D. asked as she indicated her street for him to turn into, 'yuh have boyfriend?'

She looked at him, and paused before answering. 'I used to go out with this guy . . . But not any more.'

D. pressed on, interested to find out more.

'What happ'n, him diss yuh?'

'No.' Sherry laughed. 'He was just boring.'

Nodding, D. stopped the car a little way from the house which she said was hers. Sherry seemed in no hurry to leave him. They talked a little more, D. teasing her, asking more questions. She answered in kind, she didn't ask him anything too personal. Then she said, 'I work in Wood Green, you know where it is?'

'Yeah, man,' D. answered her.

She explained where the place was, not far from the shopping centre. It sounded like a kind of invitation.

'I gwan come look fe yuh,' D. said looking at her.

'Are you?' Sherry wanted to know if he meant it.

'Yeah, man, how yuh mean?'

She smiled.

'So, how long yuh is now?' D. asked.

'You tell me,' Sherry tested him. Slowly, D. took a good look at her then said tentatively, 'About sixteen . . .'

'I'll be seventeen in two months' time.'

'Enh! So yuh born February?' D. asked.

'Yeah.'

'What date?'

'The twelfth,' Sherry told him.

'True? Same month me born, y'know, the twenty-fifth . . .' They laughed, surprised at the coincidence. That got them a little closer. D. asked who she lived with. Sherry explained that she lived with her mother and thirteen-year-old sister. Her parents were divorced, and her father had moved out of London. She saw him regularly though. After a while, D. told her she'd better go in as her mother would surely be up soon. Sherry agreed, after making him promise to come look for her at work. He said he would, took the number and address she wrote down on a piece of paper. Then she gave him a last, meaningful smile and stepped out.

'I comin' fe yuh soon, baby girl,' D. said.

'You'd better,' Sherry told him. D. laughed and watched her until she entered the house. Then he drove off, feeling sweet. The unexpected encounter had dispelled the bad feeling about the shooting. He changed the cassette in the stereo and headed back to the main road. When he got there, D. realized he wasn't sure where he was going. For a minute he weighed up the options. Jenny would expect him back as always, but then he had hardly seen Donna during the past week. He hesitated a little, wondering about the way he felt, then decided the best thing was to go and check his little daughter. Playing back the events of the night in his mind, D. headed for Donna's house.

14

GOOD, BAD AND WORSE

ole turned right at the big pizza parlour and pushed the Mini full speed straight up the narrow street. He'd been up all night and still didn't really feel tired. Anyway, there was too much to do to waste time sleeping. Better stay busy. Right at the bottom of the street, then first left, he reached where he was going and was about to park right in front of the elegant white house with the neat hedge, when his eyes spotted the two 'bobbies' walking slowly alongside the pavement less than fifty yards up the road. Immediately he drove on. It looked like they were chatting . . . This part of Islington was usually not too busy. Still by force of habit, ever suspicious, Cole eased off the brakes and 'gas up' a bit, slipping the Mini past them unnoticed. By the time he reached the corner they had passed the house. He turned the car around and parked it across the road, a little back from the house. Cole stepped out. It was Saturday morning, early, sunny despite the winter forecast. This year, February seemed like spring for a few days at a time until in the evening the freezing wind came back to bite. After two knocks on the door a burly, light-skinned man opened it and let Cole inside.

'Butch, what's happening?'

'Yeah, al'right.'

Butch gave Cole a short grin. They presented an interesting contrast, so to speak. Cole was average, about five feet seven, slim, dark-skinned – an energetic, hi-dressing personality, sporting a top crown of short spiky dreadlocks, with shades. The man who he followed into the nicely decorated, posh living room was six foot four, probably near two hundred pounds, and wore a black baseball cap on top of a near-shaven head and a thin moustache across a closed, unexpressive face. He dropped into a deep, broad leather chair. Cole sat across from him. A large-screen TV at the window-end of the room was alive with the loud commentary of an American football game.

'Where's Simon?' Cole asked.

'Sleeping.'

He himself hadn't slept at all, but Cole couldn't believe someone could be in bed after ten on a busy morning like this. Cole took off his shades. He watched one play on the screen, a neat blocking game from the Chicago Bears which allowed their quarterback to throw off a long ball straight for a touchdown. Apart from boxing, American football was Butch's favourite sport. That was OK for Cole, but he wasn't a fanatic. Right now, he felt hungry. As he got up to go into the kitchen round the back, he said:

'Hey, I've got something to show you!'

'Yeah?' Butch answered absent-mindedly from his swivelling chair.

Cole pushed open the communicating hatch to see Butch while he made himself some breakfast.

Opening the cupboard and fridge, he threw some butter, peanut butter, cheese and bread on to a tray, while switching the kettle on. When his cup of tea was ready, Cole came back to sit across from Butch. He placed the tray on the smoked-glass and aluminium table, then from the inside pocket of his sheepskin coat, took out a cloth-wrapped object and handed it to Butch. The big man eyed the parcel, stretched his left hand and took it. Cole sat down and buttered some bread.

'Check it out now, that's quality,' he said proudly.

He watched Butch slowly unwrap the layers of cloth and expose a menacing-looking matt-black pistol. Cole was sure it would impress him. He knew Butch was something of an expert on guns, with his army experience and all that, but this thing was no rubbish. Butch checked the gun over slowly, methodically, examining it as if it were a work of art. Whether he was impressed or not, there was no way Cole could tell. It seemed no one ever managed to 'read' Butch.

'Nice . . .' he said simply, looking at Cole without smiling.

His mouth was full, but Cole opened big eyes at him, his head jerking slightly backwards.

'Nice?' he managed to articulate after swallowing. 'This is a Glock, man, state of the art.'

Butch nodded. 'Yeah; Glock 22, double-action, holds 15 of .40.'

Cole swallowed some of the tea.

'Come on, Butch, mon, you've got to admit; this is wicked . . .'

'Yeah, it's not bad, powerful . . . Where d'you get it?' Butch asked in his cockney accent.

'A customer, some white guy in south London. I just came back from there,' Cole explained with a satisfied look.

He ate some more breakfast. Meanwhile Butch quickly took the pistol apart until he had the barrel and the smaller pieces lined up on the table.

'Got to clean it, ain't yah?!' he said, looking at Cole.

Cole had to admit he hadn't thought of that.

'Even these ones can jam,' Butch said.

'Glock, no, man!' Cole exclaimed.

'I'm telling you,' Butch contested calmly.

Cole was dubious about that.

'So, what? You don't like it?' he asked amazed.

Butch was checking the gun inside out.

'Yeah . . . but I wouldn't use that.'

'No? So what are you saying then?'

Butch looked at the shorter man, straight-faced.

'If I'm going to carry a shooter, I always go for the old .45.'

'You mean the revolver? Really?'

Butch nodded and explained, shrugging.

'That's the biggest you'll get and it'll never jam on you.'

Cole listened, finished his tea. 'Yeah?'

Butch was checking a particularly brilliant play on the wide screen.

'And what'll you do when your six shots finished?' Cole asked again.

Taking his eyes off the TV Butch told him.

'Well, if you expect more guests, might as well go for the Uzi, ain't it?!'

Cole shook his head. He was always amazed how much Butch knew about weapons and fighting in general. He had never really asked him about it, he had only heard Simon mention that Butch was an ex-soldier. In the year that Cole had worked alongside Butch, he had never found out more. It had to be said that Butch wasn't always the most talkative of men, especially about himself. Inquisitive by nature, and guessing that Butch might now be in a good mood, Cole asked:

'Tell me something; you was in the army, ain't it?'

Butch held up the barrel, looked through it.

'Yeah,' he answered eventually.

'What was it like?' Cole pressed on, encouraged by the evenness in the tone of voice.

Butch paused and looked up from his task.

'You wouldn't like it.' He let out a short laugh for the first time.

To Butch, the thought of Cole enlisting in the army was a joke.

'No, I mean you didn't like it, right?'

Butch shook his head.

'There's nothing wrong with the army, you know. It's the people I didn't like . . . !'

'Yeah, I see what you mean,' Cole said. 'One of my cousins is in the army!'

'Yeah? Where?' Butch asked.

'Germany, I don't see him much.' Cole laughed, then asked: 'Where did you go?'

Butch shrugged his shoulders wearily.

'Northern Ireland, Falklands.'

Cole opened big eyes; cut in.

'You was in the Falklands?!'

'Yeah,' Butch said.

'Was it bad?'

'It was bad al'right,' Butch agreed straight-faced.

Cole would have liked to ask more; this sounded interesting, he'd never met anybody who had fought over there. He remembered watching the reports on the television, but he wanted to know Butch's feelings about the subject.

'Lots of people died down there, ain't it?'

Butch waited a little, watching the game, but he had heard the question.

'Yeah, a lot of people, for not much . . .'

Then, surpassing Cole's expectations, Butch added:

'Coldest place I've ever been to . . .'

'What about racism?' Cole asked him. 'They're racist in there, ain't they?'

Butch thought about it a little before answering that one. One thing with him that Cole and everybody else knew was that he never wasted words.

'Put it this way, so; the only time when your colour don't matter is when you go down. They don't write it on your stone . . .'

Cole thought about the answer.

Before he managed to ask anything more, Cole heard a

219

door open inside the flat, then someone clearing his throat and the click of the bathroom switch.

'Yo, Simon!' Cole called out.

'Yeah, what's hapening?' a sleepy voice answered.

Cole got up and walked to the bathroom. Simon was standing in his underpants, letting off some water.

'You oversleep, man!' Cole laughed. 'Everybody looking for you.'

'Yeah . . . I didn't go to sleep till about six,' Simon yawned.

He turned to Cole, his usually sleek, straight hair was in disorder, he had a stubble of beard and his eyes weren't fully opened yet. Stretching one hand to the side of the plastic curtain, Simon turned on the shower. He briefly told Cole that him and Butch had gone to some West End club the previous night after arriving back from Europe. They'd been away for almost a week and Simon reported the latest news briefly.

'Yeah, OK . . . I'm gonna have a shower now,' he said, stepping under the spray of water. 'And do me a favour, Cole, get this bitch out of my bed.'

Cole smiled. So that was why Simon was up so late. He pulled the door of the bathroom shut and went to the bedroom. A girl's blonde hair was half-covering her white shoulder, her arm extended as she slept.

Cole knocked loudly on the headboard, calling out, 'Oy, Simon said "get out now"!'

The girl didn't move, so Cole walked up to the window and opened the curtains. There were items of women's clothing on the floor and a handbag on one of the chairs. Standing at the head of the bed, he called again loudly.

'Hey, wake up!'

The girl stirred.

'Come on, get yourself out of here!'

Cole knew how Simon was: he'd get home with a girl

from somewhere at night, feeling nice and 'bombed out', but usually couldn't stand the sight of them by morning light. It wasn't the first time that Cole had had to shake someone out. The girl woke up, looking at Cole. She sat up in the bed hurriedly at the sight of him, the sheets gathered up against her chest.

'Who are you?'

'Yo, Simon says you better leave.'

'Get out! Where is Simon?!' She started to make a noise. Cole kissed his teeth and walked out. Opening the bathroom door, he said, 'Hey, Simon, you better tell her yourself. She's asking for you.'

From under the shower, Simon's voice came out, loud shouting.

'If she ain't out of here by the time I finish, you can have her!'

That did it. There were movements in the bedroom, and less than five minutes later she was out of the house.

Simon got ready and came into the living room, looking fresh and ready in a pair of dark-blue slacks and a green polo-neck jumper. His hair was neatly tied up in a short pony-tail. He went to the kitchen and took some juice out of the fridge.

'So what's this story then?' he asked Cole as he sat down.

'Nothing much really, there was a fight at the Satellite on Thursday night . . .'

Cole explained about the scuffle at Simon's recently opened wine bar.

'Anything serious?'

'No, nothing broken, just a commotion between two guys, one of dem drunk.'

Simon nodded, drinking his juice. Butch was into his game. He'd stayed out with Simon, but got up early, as always.

Cole remembered something.

'Oh yeah, and your Yardie friend's looking for you.'

'Is he now?' Simon asked.

'Yeah, he came last night again. He doesn't seem to take "no" for an answer.'

'It's time to have a chat . . .' Simon remarked.

He stretched, got up and opened the glass door to the garden. Outside was fresh but not in the sun, which was right above the house, bright in the clear winter sky. Simon did a few stretchings, loosened up his neck and waist, then played for a short while with the football that had been lying under the table. He was walking back in when the phone rang. Cole took the call, said a few words and put down the receiver. Simon had picked up a box from behind his record stacks. He looked at Cole.

'Martin . . .' Cole said.

'What does he want?'

'I'm not sure. I set him up as you told me on Wednesday. He's at the arcade.'

Simon sighed and got out a strip of foil paper from the box. He opened it, picked up a small amount of cocaine powder on a small blade and snorted it once. He sniffed a few more times then told Cole:

'OK, you might as well pass by there anyway. Then I wanna go to my place.'

He meant the wine bar. He'd wanted to set up something like that for years, and since it had been launched just before Christmas, the Satellite had taken off nicely, building up on the holiday ravers and becoming a regular spot for five nights a week. Simon was watching the football on the screen, following the two dozen players involved in acrobatics and physical scuffles. At twenty-five years of age he was only just beginning to feel that he was living as he should. For someone like him, always on the go, scheming, planning and scamming, life had had its highs and lows ever since he'd started out as a fourteen-year-old on the streets of Bethnal Green. Simon had done practically everything and learned how to make two out of one, getting his common sense and 'life' education at the best university there was – the street. He was the youngest of three brothers, whom their mother had raised single-handedly. The eldest had made a break early and settled in America, never coming back. The middle brother was now locked away for quite a few years after an armed robbery had gone wrong. Simon had also paid his dues the hard way, but he was smart.

For him, the main thing out there was to make your bread without getting heavy about it. With that principle in mind, he'd managed to survive off his wits and ingenuity. In his time, Simon had sold practically everything, been involved with a vast array of people, most of them hustlers like him, black youths from the estates and white guys connected to the criminal fraternities of east and north London. Only once had he spent any time inside for an 'error of judgement'. After this, he'd gotten even smarter. Jail was no place for anyone as bright as him, he had told himself.

Once, a couple of years before, Simon had done a 'big favour' for a well-connected white gangster. Thanks to that, he soon after opened a small pool room with games machines alongside the big estate at the back of New North Road. That had been his big break. By temperament, Simon had kept away from drugs at first. It wasn't 'traditional' in the world he had grown up in. At the time, it certainly wasn't respected as a business in east London, not one of the standard activities, racketeering, prostitution or gambling. But then, times were moving on. There started to be too much money floating around, too many guys with sudden spending power to ignore it. That's when Simon stepped in. First, he got some stuff and started to supply some of his yuppie friends with it. Simon loved to move in middle-class, young business-type circles, where money 'swam' and his business could operate. Then he discovered that much more money could be made from a relatively new product: crack. That thing seemed to 'breed' cash. No way was he going to play for dimes when there were dollars to be won. So, within six months, Simon had got organized. The real profit, he soon realized, was in supplying the ever-expanding market on the estates, selling to crowds of youngsters who almost always ended up being involved with drugs. There was competition, for sure, but Simon had never been daunted by that. So he had gotten himself a few 'associates' as he called them. First among them was Butch, or Robert as he was originally called. They had met in auspicious circumstances three years before. Simon had been leaving a West End gambling place when he heard some noise in an alley and found this big, drunken man being attacked by four white guys. Despite the odds, the big man didn't seem worried. He apparently damaged at least two of his assailants, then one produced a rather large blade. At that point, Simon calmly took out his gun and politely asked the men to leave, fast. He had given his new friend a lift home, finding out he lived in the East End, and they had started hanging around together in the following weeks. Robert had been out of the army for a few months. After ten years of being told what to do and where to go, he was drifting through town aimlessly. Simon had nicknamed him Butch, after a movie character, and decided he would be an essential asset.

Cole, or Colin as he was known in his younger days, had been a schoolfriend of Simon's. From the start he'd always been a pleasant, reliable sort of friend who knew the streets well and was good at organizing and managing.

Simon picked up a coat from his extensive wardrobe and led the way out. His convertible XR3 was parked in the adjacent street. They all got into the car. Cole left his Mini there until later. Simon handled the car skilfully through the early afternoon Saturday traffic. They reached the arcade in next to no time. Gary, the man who managed the place for Simon, was standing on the pavement outside, taking in the sun and watching people walking through the market.

'Simon, how's it going, man?'

'Good, how is it going here?'

'Not bad,' Gary said. 'This guy Martin's inside waiting for you.'

Simon walked inside followed by Butch, while Cole stopped to talk to a girl he knew. Most of the machines were already occupied, groups of kids, black, white, Asians, gathered around and commented excitedly on their performances. At the back, the four pool tables were unattended. A man, mid-twenties, stocky, with a beard, wearing a leather jacket and corduroys, was leaning against the wall, looking gloomy.

'Marti, what's up, man?' Simon asked, smiling.

Butch sat on the edge of the pool table, seemingly unconcerned.

'I've got problems . . .'

Simon observed the man; he truly looked like someone with a burden – bleary-eyed and beat. Martin seemed embarrassed to even look at him. Simon took a pack of cigarettes out of his pocket and lit one.

'We all do, what's yours?' he asked.

'I got busted,' Martin said in a low voice.

Simon blew out some smoke while studying the man.

'Busted, what d'you mean busted?' he said, as if speaking about it was painful in itself. Martin explained that he had been raided by the police on Thursday morning, the day after he'd picked up some stuff from Cole. According to what he told Simon, the police had broken down his door at dawn and found the drugs in his flat.

'So, how come you're out?' Simon enquired.

Martin paused before answering.

'They took me in, questioned me, then let me out.'

He knew the story sounded improbable, but it was true. Simon frowned and pulled on his cigarette. He repeated, looking straight at Martin:

'They let you out?!'

The man nodded. Simon sighed, shaking his head.

'Martin, what can I say?'

'Somebody set me up!' Martin said darkly.

'Who?'

'I don't know.'

Simon stubbed the butt on the floor then said, 'You still owe me some money, you know that?!'

'I was robbed, man, I'm telling you!' Martin tried to argue his case. He knew it was an impossible situation, especially so because by rights he should have been in jail now.

'That's nothing to do with me . . . You took some merchandise, I have to get paid. That's the rule,' Simon stated unmoved.

'Simon, man; I've got nothing, how can I pay back that much money?' Martin sounded really distressed, edgy.

'Look, man, I can't help you. I need my three grand. I'm going to give you a little time, then if you don't come to me, I'll have to come to you . . .'

Martin got agitated. Small beads of sweat popped out on his forehead as he shuffled on the spot, trying to make Simon see his side of things.

'Come on, man; give me a break . . .'

'A break?!' Simon laughed but not really amused. 'Business is business, man; you know the game.' Then he added, 'You better get busy, Butch here is the one who'll collect your debt. See you, Martin.'

Simon walked out through the games gallery; Butch

following him out after taking a cold look at Martin. Outside, Gary and Cole were talking. They stood on the pavement in the sun. Martin came out and passed them without a glance. When Simon told Cole the story, he squinted, reacting in exactly the same way: it was hard to believe!

'I think I know what happened,' said Simon vaguely. He had his own idea about the incident but didn't comment any further. Now, after the morning's activities he felt hungry.

'I'll be in there,' he told Cole, walking the few yards to the Indian restaurant two doors away. Butch followed him in. A lone waiter was sitting at a table near the kitchen reading a newspaper. Simon was a regular in the place; curries, especially curried chicken, were one of his favourite meals. He didn't do much home cooking.

'Hello!' the waiter called out.

'Hey, how you doing?!' Simon could never remember the young man's name.

He sat at the last table to the left of the door, facing it, while Butch sat opposite. Simon ordered, Butch wasn't hungry; they talked a little while waiting for the food to arrive.

Simon tucked into his meal enthusiastically. Butch was watching something on the small television set mounted high above the shelves stacked with take-away containers. While he was eating, Simon resolved to visit his mother, since he had been away for the week. The old lady, who usually worried about her youngest son even when she saw him every day, was probably frantic by now. For as long as Simon could remember, she had always been the worrying type – constantly beset by fear and dread.

Halfway through his meal, Simon looked up as he heard the door opening and closing. He was surprised to recognize the man coming towards him. Butch was watching too, of course. The man stopped by the side of Simon's table.

'Simon, I want to talk to you.'

Simon looked up, his fork suspended in mid-air, smiling.

'Hey, Chris, how you doing?'

Chris didn't seem to register, his eyes hard, focused. Simon took a sip of his drink, observing Chris's uptight attitude closely. Looking at Butch he nodded. Butch pulled himself up and brushed past Chris to go and sit in the far corner by the take-away counter. Chris sat down. He and Simon had known each other from primary school, when Chris had come over from Jamaica and his mother lived a couple of blocks away from Simon's family. They had never been close friends, but initially there was no enmity between them either. Then their paths had started to cross . . .

That morning, Chris had left his house with the firm intention of finding Simon and talking to him about things he'd been thinking about for a while.

'Long time, Chris, what's been happening?' Simon asked cheerily. He was still finishing his meal.

Chris was making no effort to seem pleasant. 'I've been working,' he answered quietly.

Simon nodded, wiping his mouth with a napkin.

'Hmmm, yeah; that's right, you're still a social worker.'

Sighing, Chris corrected Simon, looking at him without sympathy:

'Community worker, that's what I do.'

Simon pushed back his plate and tossed the napkin on the remnants of his food.

'Oh yeah, community worker,' he repeated. 'So what can I do for you, Chris?'

For the first time, Chris's face broke into a kind of smile.

'You could do a lot for me, Simon, a lot.'

'Yeah? What d'you mean?'

'I've got a problem, a big problem. Maybe you can give me some advice?'

'Some advice? You come ask me for some advice?' Simon laughed.

They had each grown up and followed a path. There was surely a lot that differentiated Chris and Simon. Yet, in the last year, they had both come to the realization that they were 'working' on opposite sides of the situation. Chris didn't let Simon's laugh put him off his stride.

'I work with these youths, as you know, and . . . I want to know if you think that I'm good enough at my job . . . I mean, you know me for years, right?'

Simon eased back in his chair, his eyes half-closed as he observed Chris in the sun-bathed restaurant.

'You want *me* to tell you if you're good at your job?'

'Tell me what you think!'

Simon frowned. 'Why you asking me that?'

There was a pause. Chris sighed as he looked to the side before focusing on the neatly dressed, self-possessed man across the table.

'This is why; I'm spending a lot of time down this club trying to help the youths, show them that it's not all bad, that there's still a lot to hope for, to work for, you know what I mean . . . ? Then a couple of guys show up juggling drugs and they give up on everything. I want to find out where I go wrong?'

It was the way Chris spoke, so controlled, unemotional, that Simon started to dislike. He felt as if Chris was patronizing him, not a nice feeling . . . He straightened up in his chair slightly.

'OK, you have a problem. Why ask me about it? I mean,' Simon shook his head, 'what's that got to do with me?'

229

Then came the punch line, Chris struck.

'Simon,' he said seriously, 'there's a couple of youths who have started selling crack around the club, I want you to put a stop to it.'

'You sure you've got the right man?' Simon asked incredulously.

'Don't play games no more, man; these guys belong to your little circle.'

Simon straightened up a little more. He looked Chris over briefly, then said, his voice a little less friendly:

'Look, man, I don't know what you're talking about.'

But Chris persisted, calm, assured.

'You don't know?! OK, but whoever it is they working for, if you see them, I don't want them at the club.'

Simon liked this less and less.

'Chris, man; you can't come distress my lunch like that with your sad stories and then start to give me orders.' He sneered, and went on: 'Tell me; how much do you make working down there? How much?' Gesturing with his right hand Simon proposed: 'One hundred and fifty pounds, two hundred pounds a week? More?'

Chris simply looked at him, unsmiling behind his glasses. Simon laughed.

'You're asking these kids to follow your good advice, to play with the system, for what? Even if it's five hundred pounds a week, you don't have a chance, man!'

Chris waited, he could see Simon wanted to say something now. Chris had known from the beginning that's what he had to expect. He knew it made no sense talking to him, but he had still wanted to try.

'You see these youths out there, they want what they see. They don't want promises, no "maybe if you work hard". That's not their style.'

'Yeah,' Chris nodded sadly, 'and you offer it to them. You show dem the way, right?'

Simon shrugged. 'They make money to look after themselves. I don't preach; I'm doing my own thing. If I have a job and a youth wants it, that's his choice. I'm in business, that's all.'

To him it was just not a problem. Simon's logic made Chris profoundly uneasy, afraid of the underlying truth of the simplistic argument.

'Business?' Chris repeated as if he was thinking about the meaning of the word. 'Yeah, I suppose it's business to you; it doesn't really matter what you sell, right?'

'You know, Chris, I remember when you first came over . . . you fought almost everybody in the class because you were new and didn't understand the way things work here. It took a little time, right?' He seemed to enjoy the memory. 'Well, you see this drug thing? It's the same thing: you've got to understand the rules of the game too. The system is set up so that it's always the same who hold power, who control the money.' Simon sounded like some expert. 'But it's all changing now; we can get money, power, because we've got this thing, that's why it's illegal, no taxes, you know what I mean?'

There was a certainty in his voice. He really believed in what he was saying.

Chris frowned.

'So, you're just running business . . . ? The rest don't concern you?!'

'Cocaine, my friend,' Simon said, 'it's just a . . . commodity.' Then he added cleverly, 'But it's not listed on the stock market.'

Chris knew he was wasting his time, yet he still asked, trying to wake up something in the man sitting across the table.

'We've got black youths out there, burning out their lives, slaves to crack, young girls selling themselves for that thing, hundreds of kids locked up in jail, kids who never had a chance to know better . . . and you're telling me about commodity?!' Then he asked, 'Would you give it to your child?'

Simon's face closed up. He threw Chris a cold look. 'Don't get personal, OK?!'

Chris shook his head. 'That shit has already gotten in your brain, man.'

Simon wasn't smiling now. He sighed loudly, annoyed.

'OK, man, you told me about your problem. It was nice seeing you. Now, I really have things to do. I'll see you . . .' Simon got up.

Slowly Chris got up too. His eyes burned deep into Simon's for a few, intense seconds. Then he turned around and left. From his corner, Butch had observed the whole scene in silence, watchful.

Simon stretched; he felt as if the unexpected encounter had spoiled his mood. Especially after an enjoyable meal! Kissing his teeth, he took some money out of his pocket and went to pay his bill, then he and Butch stepped out of the restaurant. Outside was still, sunny, mellow. Everyone was again talking about this almost mythical 'early spring', knowing full well that the freezing weather was likely to continue well into April at least . . . Simon sent Butch to fetch Cole and then climbed in his car. Together, they drove to the wine bar, which was supposed to open later on. Saturday was the main night, with two fairly popular DJs running a nice little session for the mainly 'soul' crowd. Once in a while they would play the odd reggae record, and even more rarely ragga, but on the whole it was strictly funk, rare groove type of sounds. Simon and the others spent a couple of hours at Satellite, getting everything ready for later. Cole usually managed it, though Simon was generally at hand to entertain his crowd in person.

On the way, Simon stopped at a cashpoint, drove to a little street behind Bethnal Green tube station and got out of the car, telling Butch to pick him up at an agreed time. He walked along a short pathway and stopped by the rickety wooden gate, promising himself – as he did each time he noticed it – that he would get it fixed. The door opened quickly enough after he knocked. Simon smiled to his mother as she let him in.

'Hi, Mum, everything al'right?'

She hugged him, and he wrapped his arm around her shoulder as they walked through the kitchen to the small living room.

'Simon, I haven't heard from you, I was worried.'

Simon laughed.

'I know, but you shouldn't worry. Everything is fine,' he reassured her.

She was a small woman, with sharp features behind the thick-rimmed glasses, eyes which must have been pretty years ago.

They sat on the brown cloth settee.

'I thought maybe something happened to you.'

'No, Mum, I only went for a little trip abroad.'

Patiently Simon explained that he'd spent the previous week in Europe with some friends. He made sure to mention that he had eaten and slept well, and assured his mother that he was feeling fit and well. He knew her well. The least little inkling of problems, whatever it was, and she'd start worrying and even crying at times. Then she insisted on going and making him a cup of tea, all the time giving him the latest news on the uneventful life of the neighbourhood. Simon listened, amused at the little details and anecdotes about people, some of whom he'd known as a boy but had not seen in the last decade. He drank his cup of tea, looking around the neatly arranged little room. Simon's mother had always stubbornly insisted on remaining there despite his offers to move her out of the place into a nice house. She felt comfortable here, amidst all the familiar objects accumulated over thirty years. Simon had grown up in the flat, but for him it represented nothing but memories of a childhood spent without many of the things money could have provided. He had been glad to leave his mother's flat shortly after his sixteenth birthday and move in with a girlfriend. No way did he feel sentimental about the place. But for the old lady, it was different. These two small, tatty bedrooms and living room were her universe, part of her life as a woman, a wife, a mother. Right on top of the old oak varnished shelves stood a framed picture of a smiling, handsome black man in uniform. On top of the television, a yellowed wedding picture, a small one in a silver frame, bore testimony to the passing of the years. Propping herself up from the chair with her left hand, Simon's mother got up and took the tea things back to the kitchen. In the last five years, arthritis had gradually set in, gripping the cartilages in her knees, forcing her to walk slowly and stiffly. The cold winter weather always aggravated it.

'Did you write Paul?' she asked as she sat back down.

She always asked Simon that question, and his answer always disappointed her.

'No, Mum, you know I'm not really into letter writing,' he answered lamely.

'He's your brother, you know how much he would love to get a letter from you.'

Then the old lady complained about her failing eyesight, which made it difficult for her to write.

'Me and you will go to visit him soon,' Simon assured her.

He preferred to change the subject. There was nothing useful about discussing someone who was likely to be inside for at least the next five years.

'You should go on holiday, you know, Mum,' Simon started.

'Holiday?' she repeated, looking at him.

'Yeah, it'd be good for you; get some sun, nice air by the seaside, you'd love it.'

His mother thought about it. He had mentioned it before.

Simon put his hand in his coat pocket and brought out a fat brown envelope.

'Here, I got you a little present.' He smiled, handing her the envelope.

Surprised, she turned it over, looking as if she wouldn't look inside.

'Go on, open it then,' Simon urged her, amused at her expression.

She did, slowly, her long elegant dark fingers breaking the glued edge of the flap. She had a brief look inside, turned to her son.

'Where did you get all this money?' she first asked, kind of suspicious.

Simon laughed.

'It's my money, Mum. I worked for it.'

The old lady gingerly fingered the edge of the crisp new banknotes.

'But why you give me this for?' She still didn't feel comfortable holding the envelope.

Simon put his hand upon hers and looked into her eyes smiling.

'Look, Mum, I want you to use that money and go on holiday. Go and visit the family in the West Indies. That's exactly what you need: a few weeks over there, relaxing and eating good food . . . That will do you good, you need it!'

He did his best to convince his mother that she deserved a vacation, away from the cold, the pollution, the grimness of east London. She wasn't sure he could see it. Once she stopped worrying about the origin of the money, she looked overawed at the thought of leaving her familiar surroundings for what had by now become almost a foreign land. Simon insisted, she half-agreed. He put an arm around her shoulders, kissed her on the forehead and told her he had to leave for now. As always she would have liked to keep him longer, talked to him more, but she knew he was busy. On the doorstep, Simon held her arm and promised he'd be back within a couple of days. She smiled, a timid, weak smile and told him to 'walk safely' like she always did. Simon watched her until she closed the door and walked past the rickety gate. He always had the same uneasy feeling every time he left his mother, a kind of sadness which crept all over him, seething inside him until he managed to shake it off later on contact with his peers. Checking his watch, Simon reflected that Butch should already be waiting at the nearby pub. It was Simon's 'local', although he only occasionally drank there these days. But it was nice to see some of the old faces, people he'd grown up with. The owner, a long-time veteran of the area, tall, big, red of face, yelled out at him as he entered.

'We don't want your type in here!'

Simon laughed and called out to him as he made his way towards Butch sitting near the bar.

'Tony, I thought you went on a diet?!'

Even the barmaid, shifting glasses nearby, laughed at that.

'Your mum's al'right?' Butch asked Simon as he climbed on a seat.

'Yeah, you know how mothers are: always worrying . . .'

Butch nodded; his own had been the same, until cancer finally defeated her five years previously.

Simon ordered brandy and another port for Butch.

The early crowd of a cold Saturday evening were already enjoying a carnival atmosphere. A couple of white guys on the other side of the bar acknowledged Simon with a nod and smile above the noise of music and conversations. He answered in kind. As a local boy made good, he liked to meet the old crowd from time to time. It was good for business, too. One thing Simon had learned early; there were scenes which very few black people could ever be part of, money-making schemes which had always been the prerogative of white hustlers and gangsters. Yet, as an approved long-time resident, born and bred in the borough, Simon knew that he sometimes got breaks just on account of that. Right now, with his operation running smoothly, maybe he could do some of them a favour . . .

They spent a couple of hours in the increasingly crowded pub, had a few drinks, met people, until Simon motioned to Butch – who was involved in a conversation with a buxom brunette – that it was time to move on. Within minutes, they were in the car and headed out. Simon was driving easy, not pushing the serious engine too hard, in and out of the Saturday night traffic. He drove home to freshen up and change. He dressed discreetly, sharp with not too much jewellery, just enough . . . It was after eleven when they got back on the road. Cole would have got everything rolling by now, with some good early advertising; Simon expected tonight's session to be popular. Right from the Christmas holidays, attendance had grown steadily. Satellite had become *the* place to be seen in on weekend nights. Simon had managed to bring his place to the centre of things. It had fast become a household name. The beauty was that it was also ideal for cutting deals with people he would otherwise see little of. On the whole, it was a nice business, with perks too . . . Needless to say, Simon's natural appeal amongst the ladies had grown proportionally; now it was girls galore! On reaching the place, Simon parked in his reserved spot at the side of the wine bar and they walked in, by the front door of course.

A thumping swingbeat type of rhythm greeted them as

soon as they opened the door. Satellite was already fairly full and people kept moving. Simon exchanged greetings with a dozen or so ravers lining up to enter and slipped past the two doormen. The row of tables stretching to the left of the door was almost totally occupied by attractive girls in expensive-looking clothes and their escorts. On the oval dancefloor, directly in front of the elevated podium with the turntables, a decent crowd were gesticulating, warmed up by the lively track. Simon and Butch walked down. Cole was talking to the deejay, explaining something to him. He saluted Simon and came down to meet him.

'Everything running right?'

'Warming up, just warming up . . .' Cole smiled.

'Simon, darling!'

He turned around, just in time to literally receive the short-haired spectacularly dressed girl who had run off the dancefloor to him.

'Hey, my favourite girl,' Simon lied as he did his best to escape her tight embrace. With her high heels, long split purple skirt and tiny black top she was instantly noticeable. Add to that her total lack of discretion or inhibitions, and she was hardly the kind of person Simon wished to be associated with. As a matter of fact, he couldn't even remember her name! He'd seen her around since the middle of the previous year and since he'd opened Satellite she'd become a regular, as much for the merchandise she regularly purchased, he suspected, as for the music.

Butch looked at Simon and went to sit at the back near the bar. Meanwhile, Simon managed to shake off the exuberant girl, promising he'd soon come back to her. He called out to Cole and then disappeared to the small room at the corner of the bar.

People kept coming in; neatly dressed, buoyant, calling out to friends they'd seen the previous weekend as if they hadn't seen them for years. But it was all part of the ritual;

everyone looked good, felt good and enjoyed feeling popular. Attending a weekend session at Satellite was a useful pointer to the current fashion trends. It was easy for a keen observer to notice the women watching each other, throwing casual glances around the room to assess the others' outfits. Also, it was vital that no two women should wear the same outfit. Now that would definitely be upsetting.

Glenda, the tall, brown young woman Simon had hired to see to the smooth running of the wine bar, was everywhere, with a contagious smile on her distinctive, almost Chinese, made-up face. She greeted the guests, making everyone feel welcome, kissing the girls she knew well and even a few of the men. Glenda was a singer, and was currently starting a career as a model. Above all, she was hired to relieve Simon of the 'public relations' side of the job when he didn't feel like socializing. The two deejays were taking turns to spin the records, sending out dedications, switching from funk to rare groove, house to classical soul, mixing the heat. After a while Simon reappeared and started going around talking to people, getting warm embraces, kisses and handshakes as he went. Butch didn't really dig that kind of scene. He was happy chatting to a couple of friends, sipping from a Budweiser and occasionally slipping out to the dancefloor if he really liked a record. Just after midnight, the place seemed packed, hot and swinging. Still, people kept coming, squeezing in from the cold night, happy to have made it. After his rounds and a few drinks, Simon had discreetly slipped inside the room at the back with a pretty girl by the name of Lorrie, who he'd long wanted to get acquainted with. Over the past few months he'd always seen her accompanied by a big square-headed guy, whom she said was her boyfriend. Simon usually watched her every time she came to Satellite, waiting for his chance. Tonight, though, he had looked around in vain for the guy, he was nowhere to be seen . . . So, sneakily, Simon had found his way to the table she shared with her girlfriend and after a totally meaningless conversation with them, managed to draw Lorrie away. They had a drink by the bar, Simon turning on the charm, whispering into her ear. Then he convinced her they needed a little more privacy. The sly glance he gave Butch on his way to the room clearly meant: 'Do not disturb!'

Nobody missed him, the atmosphere was too hot by then. The deejays had the dancers moving to groove after groove, keeping them busy. Even Butch had made no less than three sorties on to the floor, shaking his big frame to the beat. Now, as he sipped his fourth or fifth Budweiser, he was casting a lustful eye on a tall and slim woman, who – judging by the way she gyrated closer and closer to him – enjoyed every minute of it. It was fun all around.

From the podium where he could see the whole room, Cole was boogeying, keeping close to the deejay as if to inject him with extra energy. Busy building a spliff he didn't notice the new arrivals until they were halfway through the crowds, pushing their way in. By their clothes, as much as by the expressions on their faces, they stood out amongst the merry ravers. Two of them were tall, dark-skinned, the third one brown with a stubbly beard. Cole put down the sheets of the Rizla near one of the turntables and came down. He waited till the men had made it through the dancefloor. The one in front, wearing dark glasses, a thick patterned jumper and wide silky slacks stopped in front of Cole, looking at him. The others stood a little way back, also unsmiling.

'I wan' see yuh boss!' the man said, the scar on his left cheek hardly moving as he spoke.

Cole looked at him, nodded and glanced towards the dancefloor. Butch had already picked up on the situation. With one glance at Cole, he headed towards the back, knocked, then opened the door. Simon had the girl on his lap, one arm around her waist, a half-full glass in the other hand.

'Some of your "business contacts" are here to see you,' Butch said, stressing the words so Simon would understand.

'Can't it wait?' Simon asked, frowning.

'Not these guys . . .' Butch told him, shaking his head.

Simon sighed.

'OK. Send them in.' He whispered a few words in Lorrie's ear and squeezed her waist to let her get up. She passed Butch, straightening herself up and left. Butch walked back around the bar and signalled to Cole, who showed the man with the glasses the way. He went in, his friends close behind him, eyeing Butch on their way inside.

Cole closed the door and leaned against it, watching the man standing up in front of Simon's chair. Butch went to sit at the back on a crate of drinks, still sipping his beer. Simon didn't get up.

'Hey, Sticks, long time! What's happening?' he said with a welcoming smile.

The man above him didn't smile back.

'I been looking for yuh, man . . .' His voice wasn't exactly hostile, but not friendly either.

Simon took a sip from his drink.

'Yeah, I heard . . .'

Then he offered.

'You guys wanna drink?'

'I don't come to drink . . .' Sticks said drily.

'How about some stuff, eh?'

'I don't come to party.'

Seeing there was no easing up, Simon nodded, looking up at the stone-like features.

'Al'right, so . . . what can I do for you?'

Sticks waited a short moment then said, 'We have to talk some business. You been dissin' me, mon.'

With a look of surprise, Simon protested.

'Dissin' you? No, Sticks. How can you say that?'

'You been dealin' on my patch: that is what I'm talking about.'

Sticks was visibly intent on getting straight to the nitty gritty.

Simon looked up at him, leaning back on his chair, still holding his glass. He seemed to be considering the statement.

'What d'you mean dealing on your patch, man?'

'We run the area, you know dat. How come yuh have your own people working the estate?' He was referring to Simon's people's encroachment of the drugs trade on a particular estate.

Simon put down his glass.

'Well, Sticks,' he started, 'maybe I shoulda told you that . . . things have changed, you see; I operate that sector now.'

Sticks didn't appreciate the answer. He never really liked Simon's affected tone, his mannerisms, the way he played 'important'. Right now he was starting to dislike the man intensely.

'Yuh "operate"?' he repeated scowling. 'You got it wrong, man. I distribute, I sell to yuh and yuh supply the estate. Ah so we run it!'

Apparently Simon didn't agree with that. He got up and took a few steps and went to stand by the portable coffee machine on top of a low cabinet.

'So it used to run . . .' he replied, choosing his words. 'Let me explain something to you, Sticks. You see, I grew up in this neighbourhood. I know everybody and everybody knows me.' He stopped. 'It's true I used to buy from you, when I started out, but as I say things have changed now, I've got my own suppliers.'

'You know who yuh dealin' with?'

'It makes no difference to me who I'm dealing with,' Simon answered defiantly for the first time. 'I'm telling you, that I run the estate now, it's my patch. You understand?'

An uneasy silence hung over the room for a long minute as Sticks stared at Simon from behind his shades. Echoes of the music could be heard through the door. Linton and Pablo were watching the scene, tuned into the unhealthy atmosphere that was developing in the room. Cole was still leaning against the door, while Butch was looking at a spot somewhere down on the floor in front of him. Then suddenly Sticks's laugh exploded across the room, loudly, almost genuine sounding.

'So, yuh turn bad bwoy?' Sticks said, looking at Simon with a broad grin. 'Yuh wan' take over the business?'

Even the usually self-assured Simon didn't know what to make of it.

'Yeah, you could say that,' he said quietly.

Sticks had stopped laughing now, he looked around the room.

'I see what you mean . . . Yuh a big man now: you run drugs, you have a nice place too!' Sticks gestured towards the closed door. He took a few steps towards the centre of the room.

'Tell me somet'ing; who gwan look after you? Who you gonna trust to protect yuh, enh?'

'Don't worry about that, man . . .' Simon said, serious.

'Yuh mean yuh gwan depend 'pon dat red bwoy over there . . . an' dat freak here to protect yuh?!' Sticks pointed contemptuously at Butch then at Cole. Butch was looking at him now, Simon too, hands in his trouser pockets.

'Sure . . . I think you better leave now,' he said.

Sticks nodded, then scratched the back of his head. When he made his move, he was so fast that not even the vigilant Butch reacted fast enough.

In two quick steps, Sticks was on Simon, grabbed him

by the throat and placed himself right behind him. Butch had drawn a big black gun and was arriving in his direction but Sticks held Simon in front of him like a shield, a knife pressing against Simon's neck. Meanwhile, Cole had also been taken by surprise. Pablo had him pinned against the wall, his own Glock which he had tried to draw pushed in his ribs. Only Linton stood in the open across the room from Butch, who had his big revolver trained on him, his left hand supporting the right one police-style. Linton's arms were hanging loosely by his side. He was still very calm.

'Red bwoy, you just fucked yourself!' Sticks barked from behind Simon. Butch was watching the scene, his finger tight against the trigger. It seemed everything was up to him.

'Let him go!' he growled, his face contracted with anger.

'Yuh ah mad, man.' Sticks laughed. 'Put down de gun now.' Simon made a sound as the sharp point of Sticks's knife dug a little deeper into the flesh of his neck, right under his jaw corner. Butch didn't really know how to break the stand-off. He knew Sticks well enough to believe he was quite capable of pushing the knife right through Simon's neck.

Cole stayed very still: Pablo had also used him as a shield, just in case. Linton, still facing the black muzzle ten yards away, didn't move. Just as Sticks was ready to inflict further damage on Simon, something happened which broke the deadlock. There were two quick knocks on the door, then it opened and Glenda's face appeared in the room.

'Simon . . .' she started to say. That's all she had time for. Quick as lightning, Linton stretched out his right hand and grabbed her by the hair, pulled her against him, drew his piece from his waist and put the barrel against her temple.

'Just keep quiet,' he told her almost kindly.

There was no way Butch could have been quick enough to prevent that. He was still in the far corner, gun at the ready, now realizing that the slim chance he had a minute before was gone.

'Nice play, my yout'!' Sticks told Linton. Then he turned to Butch. 'Red bwoy!' he called out. 'Put it down . . . or yuh wan' dead first?'

It was a no-win situation. Butch could see that. This was a different type of scenario from what he was used to in the army. In fact he should have been dead already . . . but Sticks had inexplicably given him a break. Slowly, Butch lowered his revolver and rested it on the ground. Sticks then released Simon and pulled out his own gun and crossed the room towards Butch. Quickly he picked up the revolver, stood up right against the visibly uneasy big man, and looked him in the eyes.

'I wan' give you a chance,' he told him, poking him in the belly with his barrel. He came back to Simon smiling, then too fast for the man to see it come, he raised the knife he was still holding in his right hand and cut him neatly on the left cheek.

Simon cried out, brought his hand to his face and looked at the blood.

'I should kill yuh now . . .' Sticks told him without anger in his voice. 'But wha'? I give yuh a chance also.'

Slowly, he wiped the blood from his blade on Simon's shirt, then turning to his soldiers still holding their hostages he said, 'A'right: Pablo, leggo de bwoy! Yuh lead de way. Linton, keep de gal till we get out.' Sticks was taking no chances. His gun against Glenda's back, Linton told the shaking girl, 'Forward! Any noise, you lose a kidney . . .'

They went out of the room. No one noticed them as they pushed through the crowd towards the entrance of the wine bar. Pablo went out first, then Linton with the girl. As he was about to pass the two doormen, Sticks stopped, looking at the leather money belt the biggest one of them had strapped across his chest under his jacket.

'Yaow!' he called out to the man. 'Gimme dis nuh!'

The big guy wearing glasses and an earring frowned. 'What?!'

Sticks kissed his teeth, brought up his gun and stuck it under the guy's nose.

'Gimme this, bloodclat, fast!'

The other man didn't twitch: he could see Sticks was deadly serious. Quickly, still shocked, the man undid the belt and handed it to Sticks. After a last look at the two doormen, Sticks walked out. On the pavement across the road, Pablo was at the wheel of the Saab, engine running. Linton had Glenda against the car, the hand holding the gun was casually hanging down whilst he was caressing her face with his left hand. In the girl's face there was fear, deep terror.

'Yuh look like a nice girl,' Linton told her as Sticks got into the passenger seat. 'I would love to take yuh wid me, but yuh know how it go. Next time, maybe . . .'

Then he moved her aside, got into the back and left the girl on the pavement. The big car eased out and drove away. Glenda stayed there, shaking, arms crossed in front of her until Cole came out and found her. She was still unable to talk when he brought her back inside the bar. Then she burst into tears.

15

BALL GAMES

t felt like he had only just got to bed. D. stripped and pulled the quilt over his head, but soon after that, someone pulled it away again, then something slapped him on the side of the head, repeatedly. With a growl, D. turned reluctantly, half-opened his eyes and saw the culprit grinning at him. Avril looked satisfied with herself; having managed to wake up her father, she said something, bared her four front teeth at him and raised her hand to slap him some more. Despite himself, despite the tiredness he could still feel in his body, D. grabbed her and pulled her to him. Playfully, he bit her arm and tickled her belly, hoping that she would leave him alone. But no, not Avril! That only made her want to play some more. As D. tried to cover himself and resume his sleep, she'd pulled the quilt away again and yanked one of his ears. There was no way he could get any rest with her on the bed. Twice he called out.

'Donna . . . ! Donna!' Finally she came into the bedroom.

'What happ'n?'

'What happ'n?' D. repeated. 'Get this child off me nuh, man. Me cyan sleep.'

Calling Donna was probably a mistake he realized. Too late . . .

'Is me put her on the bed, to wake yuh up,' she said, standing there. D. sighed.

'I go to bed late, jus' tek her, man,' he muttered, pulling the quilt over himself again.

Donna picked up the child then started nagging him.

'I nevah tell yuh fe sleep out. Me nuh know who yuh have out dere ah keep yuh ev'ry night . . .'

She didn't leave the room until D. had kissed his teeth and literally ordered her out. Donna could be miserable when she was crossed. In the last few weeks she'd been more than miserable. True enough, D. had been busy out there, only coming home in the early hours, if he came home at all . . . He always promised he would come home early and have dinner with her and the children, but Donna only saw him a few times a week nowadays, then he was gone again for the next couple of days. She had been moaning about that, which in turn only made him stay out even more.

D. stirred and tried to get back to sleep. He had slipped into bed well after five and it couldn't be more than nine now. The previous day was Sherry's birthday, so after picking her up from work he had driven her home then out to dinner. They went to a nice restaurant, ate well and talked, enjoying the time together. Sherry had been speechless when D. had pulled out a small box from his pocket and handed it to her. It was a nice present, expensive too, and she had not expected anything. When they left the restaurant, D. drove around with her to a couple of places and finally he took her with him for his daily visit to the gambling club. Sherry wasn't used to that kind of scene, but she followed him, waiting while D. took care of business. After ensuring all was well, D. left his soldiers to take care of things and drove down to Leyton. He had taken Sherry there before. The house was empty. They listened to some music, D. rolled a couple of spliffs. Since it was her birthday, Sherry bravely took a few pulls but she was not a smoker and the strong herb had her coughing at the first attempt. D. laughed and teased her. Soon enough they retired to one of the bedrooms and enjoyed each other until dawn came to break their intimacy. By the time D. dropped Sherry home it was almost five in the morning. There was no way he could get up just yet.

D. managed to get maybe two more hours of uneven sleep, but eventually he made his way to the shower. The hard drops of warm water stung his skin, gradually washing away the sleep. He dried himself up, brushed his teeth and got dressed. As he walked into the kitchen, his cup of hot tea was waiting, but Donna walked out, apparently avoiding his conversation. D. shrugged and sat with his drink, thinking about the day ahead. It was already after twelve. Today he had planned to go to the studio where Charlie had said he would be watching over a joint Puggy and Firefly recording. It should be a good session. As Firefly's manager, Charlie had been planning to get him together with Puggy on record. Since he was also now managing the singer, things were working out fine. A couple of days earlier, he had gone into the studio with Lee and watched him lay down and mix a wicked track. All that was left now was to record the two MCs, who had been working together on some lyrics. D. finished his tea, and thought about the events of the previous day and night. He walked into the living room. As he sat down, Avril came to him and he picked her up. The little girl had started to walk only a week before. She wasn't steady on her feet yet, but usually managed a few steps before she dropped down, grinning proudly. Avril rarely left her father whenever he was home. She looked like her mother a lot, but whereas Cindy was biggish, built like Donna, Avril remained slim. She and Cindy got on fine. In fact, Donna's father adored her baby sister. Avril had also caused Cindy to love D. even more. A couple of times, he had taken the two children out for a drive, watched Cindy holding the little child against her at the back of the car. It was a good feeling, and at times like these D. felt like a bona fide family man – but he just couldn't be like that all the time. Then there was Jesse, who also was getting big, and his mother. D. realized he felt more and more like spending time at Jenny's. Whether it was because he had grown very fond of his son or because of feelings for Jenny he couldn't quite tell. Probably a combination of both. In any case, that was the cause of Donna's vexation. Not that D. had admitted to anything, he wasn't crazy. Yet, even though Donna didn't get any answers to her probing questions, she seemed to know everything. No matter how D. checked for Donna and for the little daughter, he had no intention of letting her rule his life. Right now, judging by the way she flicked over the pages of the magazine in front of her, D. reflected that the best thing to do was to go about his business. He gave Avril a few kisses on the neck, tickled her a couple of times and was about to get up when Donna's voice came across sarcastic.

'The way yuh tired, it look like yuh work too hard, man!'

There was still time to leave now, instead of getting involved in a discussion that was sure to turn into an argument. There was something in the way Donna had pronounced the word 'work', an obvious use of the double meaning of the term in Jamaican patois . . . but D. remained seated. Light-heartedly he answered:

'"X" amount ah t'ing ah gwan, yuh know . . .' Donna flicked over a few more pages; she was obviously not reading the magazine. Cindy was at school, but with Avril still too young for nursery, Donna spent most of her time at home or by Sandra, Leroy's wife. She gave D. a sideways glance and said:

'Yuh dinner still in the oven . . .'

'Hmm, I eat out yesterday,' D. answered.

Donna closed the magazine, looked at him.

'Me know . . . Yuh bettah watch out dem don't poison yuh out dere!'

The conversation was getting too specific for D.'s taste. Still he kept cool.

'Why yuh ha'fe talk dem way deh?'

'Yuh t'ink seh me nuh know weh yuh eat all de while?' Donna sneered.

D. kissed his teeth.

'Yuh love argument, enh, man!'

'No, me nuh love argument, but I want fe know wha' ah gwan?'

'Everyt'ing level, man, don't worry yuhself.' It was meant to be reassuring, but Donna didn't appreciate the answer.

'Don't worry? I don't see yuh, y'know, D.? Yuh come once in a while, early mornin', then yuh gone again. Yuh don't even look fe yuh pickney.' She paused, then, 'When yuh come back, I really did t'ink seh you'd changed. But it look like is de same t'ing yuh gone back ina.' This thing was going too far, D. reflected.

'Wha' yuh ah deal wid? Me ah run t'ings out deh, yuh t'ink seh it simple?!'

D. put down Avril and got up, went towards the window. 'Still, me look after yuh and de pickney dem, don't?' he asked. Donna looked at him; that wasn't the problem.

'Me nuh talk 'bout dat. Yuh feel seh is money alone me ah deal wid?'

'So wha' happ'n t'yuh?!' D. decided the argument was pointless.

Outside, a grey sky promised some rain later on. D. turned around.

'Yuh a diss me,' he heard Donna say.

'Diss yuh? Wha' yuh ah talk 'bout now?'

'Yuh know wha' me ah talk 'bout! Tell me somet'ing; when las' yuh tek me out?' Donna looked at him straight, waiting for the answer.

'So wait, is dat yuh ah mek so much noise about?' D. asked, half-smiling. That was a mistake.

'Yuh a laugh?!' Donna was even more upset now. 'Yuh gwan an' laugh.' She picked up Avril, who was clinging to her. The little girl could feel the tension. D. stood in the middle of the room. He didn't really think it necessary to get too deep into an argument like this one. Maybe he hadn't taken Donna out lately, that was true. Trying to calm her down he said,

'Awright, tek it easy, yuh see nex' mont', me an' yuh goin' out fe yuh birthday . . . seen?! Fe real.' Donna looked away, still holding Avril.

'Yuh see dem same girl yuh a deal wid out dere, bettah yuh stay wid dem, 'cause I'm not into no sharing business.'

Here it was, woman again! D. asked, 'So wait, yuh a kick me out now, again?'

'It's not my place to kick yuh out, yuh know me bettah dan dat,' Donna answered flatly. Then she added, looking straight at him, 'Me nuh seh yuh deh wid yuh baby mudda, yuh know?'

She cut him before he could say anything.

'No budda say nut'n. I don't want yuh fe embarrass yuhself!'

D. raised his eyebrows and shook his head.

'Yuh worry too much, man. Me an yuh cool, yuh know dat. Why yuh love talk foolishness more time?'

Donna stood there and asked him: 'Tell me somet'ing, D.; is how long yuh know me?' D. wasn't expecting that.

'How yuh mean?'

She told him.

'I firs' know yuh from I was nine, yuh come look fe me, when me t'irteen, in school . . .'

D. looked at Donna; he didn't really want to talk about those long-gone days, not now. But she did!

'Ever since then, is pure problem follow yuh, an' I always try an' help yuh, true?'

He had to admit that.

'Yeah, man . . . !'

'All dem years, anyt'ing I can do fe yuh, I do it an' I don't feel no way.' She paused. Donna's voice was calm, controlled as she asked, 'Yuh know any 'ooman who check fe yuh as much as me, from dem time deh?'

D. didn't answer right away. Thinking about it, Donna was right and he certainly wasn't going to argue about that. He kept silent, waiting for her to continue.

'So why yuh can't cool yuhself an' spend some time at home?' She pointed at Avril. 'Look at yuh child, she'll be one soon but yuh still out deh like yuh cyan settle down.' D. knew that Donna was right, all the way, but he also knew that he could never live the way she wanted him to. Not yet anyway.

'Is true, y'know,' he told her, 'but de man dem ah street still depend on me fe run t'ings. I cyan jus' sit down ah yard, I have business fe tek care of.'

'Yuh see dem t'ings yuh ina?' Donna began. 'Yuh bettah watch it. Yuh get 'way las' year already an' still yuh cyan learn.' She paused. 'Ah so yuh stay all de while, yuh push your luck, nevah believe it can run out.'

D. sighed.

'Yuh worry too much, Donna. I know it cyan go on for ever still; anytime me ready, I jus' shift and set up some business down ah Yard.'

Donna looked at him, interested. 'Ah dat yuh a plan fe do, really?'

Though he probably meant it, D. didn't want to get into details. There was a lot to be done before it could be possible.

'Hear me, now, Donna, me an yuh bona fide, believe

me, man. Gimma a lickle time an' t'ings will work out,' he told her.

Donna didn't answer, she was playing with Avril's hair absent-mindedly.

The discussion had made D. feel a little down, introspective. He knew that it was sometimes better to avoid that kind of thing. He had gotten used to taking life as it came, trusting in himself, depending on his wits and his luck to see it through to the next day. Thinking about it, he would have liked to be able to settle down in Jamaica as he had mentioned to Donna, but it wasn't possible just yet. He got up, stroked Avril's cheek and playfully ruffled Donna's hair.

He said, 'I'm going studio, soon come, seen?!'

Donna simply looked at him, didn't answer. D. got his things together and stepped out. In the car, the revival cassette he'd been listening to with Sherry the night before finished playing. It was mid-afternoon, Wednesday, not much traffic. D. eased the car along the high road, getting most of the green lights. A car horn blew three times as he drove past Dalston junction, D. smiled and waved as he recognized Paula in a white Mercedes driving the other way. Paula was a good friend, originally a higgler who had set up base in England about five years before. She operated two clothes shops and a few stalls in some east and north London markets. A fit, attractive woman in her mid-thirties, Paula had often jokingly hinted that she wouldn't mind having a 't'ing' with D. He had kept it at that, knowing that it was often more profitable to have successful women as friends than as lovers. D. made a stop at a newsagent, bought some Rizla, a soft drink and a newspaper. Back in the car, he hitched a left into Church Street then right straight down Green Lanes. Charlie had taken him to the studio at the back of Harringay once before. D. was pretty sure he'd find the place. When he reached the stadium he took a left, then, guided by his instinct more than any real recollections, he found the dead-end street bordered by neat terraced houses. He parked and walked back a little to the right number. As he reached the gate, big drops of rain started to pound on his head. D. pressed the intercom, announced himself and pushed the door when he heard the buzzing sound. The hallway leading to the stairs was bare and narrow. D. got down the stairs and knocked on the glass of the blacked-out door. Someone opened it, he walked in. The assistant engineer hailed him. D. answered and progressed through the empty connecting room with its fridge, coffee machine and chairs. The recording session was scheduled to start at 2 p.m., almost an hour earlier, but nothing seemed to have happened yet. D. passed the control room, and nodded at Lee, who was talking with the engineer. The vocal booth was empty. D. pushed open the door of the other room, the one with instruments and amplifiers; Charlie and Harry looked up as he walked in.

'Come in, blood.' Charlie smiled.

'Respeck, Don,' Harry greeted him.

D. joined them and sat on one of the amps. 'Nothing's happening yet,' Charlie explained, 'Sticks gone for Puggy.'

They talked for a while. D. wanted to know if the young MC felt ready to record. Harry told him that he'd practised his lyrics alone and with Puggy the previous day, and he was ready. Charlie remarked that the youth had no nerves at all. He didn't know anything about stage fright or nervousness, which was a definite advantage for an artist. Then a riddim track started to roll out of the studio's small but powerful boxes. It sounded heavy; an insistent bass pattern over a straightforward nineties drumbeat. Yet with the synthesizer chorus, juggling bells and talking drum sounds cleverly interspersed throughout, it was a highly addictive and danceable track. Harry was listening, head bowed, totally immersed in the music. Charlie spoke in D.'s ear, over the music.

'I went to meet dis guy yesterday, big guy in the promotion game. He's interested in setting up a major reggae festival this summer.' D. was listening. 'A tour of about fifteen artists over several towns.' It sounded interesting . . .

The door of the room opened and Sticks marched in, Puggy in tow, both looking relaxed. They greeted everyone. Charlie checked out that his artist, Puggy, was ready. He sure was; his usual dapper self, Puggy definitely seemed here to do business. As Charlie was explaining something to him, the music cut out.

'Fly,' Charlie called out, 'come check me.' Charlie explained to them that he wanted to hear the lyrics straight out, without riddim. Facing each other, Puggy and Harry started to give a rendition of both their lines. Charlie listened, nodding to the beat of the song. He made them run it twice more before he was fully satisfied. He had told them both what to expect; strict discipline and hard work.

'Music is no game, you understand?' he had pointed out from the start. 'For a poor man it's often the difference between misery and success.'

The two young musicians had remembered that. Puggy was the more boisterous one, wily, bold and even wild at times, but he definitely had talent and seemed determined to work hard at it.

As for Harry, he took it seriously too; he was never late, rather quiet when in a group, but quite forward and interesting to reason with on a one-to-one basis. Charlie had recently found that out. He had had the chance to get to know the young MC better in the last few months. For his age, Charlie realized that Harry knew quite a lot about life. He was street-wise intelligent, and also cautious. He would joke and laugh as anyone, but for a youth not yet fifteen, Charlie found him very level-headed. Charlie told the two artists about the possibility of lining up some big shows for the summer. His idea was for a contingent of Jamaican artists and another group of London-based artists to appear at a series of shows, with Puggy and Firefly headlining the British lists. Both were enthusiastic about it. Charlie said he would explain more later. He left to go and check the control room. Sticks and D. were talking. After a while Charlie came back and told the two MCs to move to the vocal booth. He and Sticks left the room for the control room. Before going in, D. called Firefly.

'My yout', I want yuh drop it jus' like how yuh do it 'pon stage. No vibes, yuh unnerstan?'

'Yes, Don, livewire!' Firefly, as a true lyrics man, always coined graphic or evocative expressions. D. laughed and left him to join the others. Through the big glass panel of the control room, they watched as the two artists put on some headphones and started warming up. Lee sent out the rhythm, 'criss' through the monitors of the room. He was operating the mixing desk while the engineer watched. That was serious business. Lee was searching for the special vibe which brought the musical best out of an artist on a particular tune. This was a science in itself. The most innovative and inspired producers were highly sought, Lee was one of them, as his string of recent hits had proved. He ran the rhythm a couple more times, then the two youths in the booth signalled that they were ready. The recording proper commenced. Puggy and Firefly did three takes together, Lee giving two or three very precise instructions at the end of each take. By the end of the third one, he nodded at the two, appreciating the tight, charged-up performance they had just given. After that, he got each one of them in turn to run their lines separately, two takes each. It sounded fine. Then, when they probably thought they had done enough, Charlie came inside the booth to his artists. 'OK, how yuh feeling?' he asked, smiling. Both Puggy and Firefly said they felt fine. Charlie looked at them.

'How did it sound to you?' he asked Puggy.

The singer scratched behind his left ear, under his 'Bears' baseball cap.

'We come out criss!' he said, looking at Charlie.

'Fly, yuh like it?'

'It sounded sharp to me,' Firefly answered after a couple of seconds.

Charlie nodded, one hand in his pocket.

'Yeah, you're right . . .' he said slowly, walking a few steps away from them, thinking about something. Puggy looked at his partner, puzzled. Charlie came back towards them.

'Which one did you like best?'

'Which one?!' Puggy repeated.

'Yeah, man; which tape you want to keep for the record?' Charlie asked, looking at both of the youths in turn.

Apparently, neither of the two could really tell; it sure was difficult to answer that!

Charlie sighed, nodding again.

'Check this out: I want you to do one more take.'

They looked at him, listening. Charlie explained.

'Your voices are warm now, right? All right, ride it neatly with just a little fresh touch. A little inspiration, you know what I'm saying.' He paused shortly. 'Forget the other takes, OK? Just punch it out with the special touch.' With that and a final confident nod, Charlie left the two and rejoined the group in the control room.

Both the young MCs took in some air and stretched for a few minutes, concentrating. As each in turn acknowledged Lee, at the ready behind the glass, the riddim track came pumping through their headphones. The talk was a short, straightforward one. When the beat faded away, smiles from the control room told the MCs that they had done well. Lee held up his hand to them, saluting the effort.

Puggy, beaming, and Firefly, harbouring a little more modest smile, went up to the control room. They were warmly congratulated by everyone.

From the desk, Lee called out, 'Wicked, man, ouno rip it!' He was already busy working on the mixing, but it would take a while.

Puggy looked at Charlie. 'Respeck, manager.' He smiled, rolling up his fist. Firefly touched him too, acknowledging the good advice.

'It was there; but you've got to bring it out,' Charlie told them. They stayed in the room talking and joking, watching Lee, the wizard, mixing, testing and remixing continuously. The engineer at his side was observing the whole process with keen attention. Charlie went to talk with Lee for a moment, then came back.

'Let's leave the mixing to the experts,' he said. 'I'm getting hungry.'

They all left the studio, Charlie driving at the front, Sticks and Puggy second and Firefly riding with D., last. By now it was night-time, a very wet Wednesday night. D. switched on his lights and reversed all the way to the intersection. He picked up on the tracks as Sticks's Saab disappeared around the corner. In the passenger seat the young MC had his two hands tucked in the pocket of his thick anorak. He seemed to be listening to the live sounds out of the car stereo. D. was really impressed by the youth's potential and style. As they were driving along, D.'s mind drifted back to the time when he was at that age himself. He had been more than keen on music, and though he hadn't been an MC himself, he had always kept close to the music circles. They were the good days in a way. D. glanced towards the youth next to him. It was hard to tell what was going through the head of a fifteen-year-old youth in days like this.

'Yuh still live by your mudda?'

'Yeah.'

'Yuh can look after her now, when yuh get big,' D. remarked.

He had heard Firefly's story about his brother, but didn't think it necessary to bring it up.

'Yuh goin' school still?' he asked, pushing the engine to beat a traffic light.

'Yeah, I'll go college next year,' the youth said.

D. nodded approvingly.

'Dat good.' He paused, then added, 'Yuh can mek money t'rough music, but knowledge is the key, seen?!'

Firefly looked at D.

'That's what my uncle says too,' he commented serious.

'Yeah? Who's your uncle?'

'Chris; he works at the youth club. He's always pushing me to study, to read books and things.'

''im right still. Yuh mus' study, man, else any man can fool yuh.'

'Yeah, but even if you get a diploma, you're not sure of getting a job.'

D. couldn't really argue with that. He put on his indicator as he saw Charlie and Sticks parking alongside a brightly lit green building.

'True, most people have to make their own jobs nowadays,' D. said, switching off the engine. They came out of the car and joined the others in the restaurant. The place had been opened for years but had only recently been taken over by a retired older man and his daughter. The cooking was excellent by all accounts and partly because it stayed open quite late, many people in the area had taken to eating there. A couple were sitting at one of the row of tables on the right. Two youths were buying take-aways at the counter. Charlie waved at the owner and led the group to a long table under a wall-mounted TV set at the back end of the room. The five sat down and went through the menu.

A young woman appeared, said hello and offered to take their orders. She smiled as she recognized Charlie. D. ordered, then Charlie. Sticks wasn't too hungry. Then it was Puggy's turn.

'I want some Yard food, seen? Yam, dumpling and some dasheen . . . Yuh don't have no dasheen? Wha' all right, banana? Banana, three fingers . . . with a curry goat.'

'How yuh nyam so much an' yuh still maaga?' Sticks joked. Everyone laughed, even the waitress. Puggy was looking at her intently. It seemed unlikely that he would pass up the chance to say something to an attractive, smooth skin, 'shiny type' black woman like her. Smiling to her suggestively, he said, 'An' when I finish, I love me an' yuh to sit down and have some dessert, y'hear?'

The waitress looked at him and gently shook her head.

'Easy, man,' Charlie laughed, 'let my yout' order.'

Firefly went for rice and peas with chicken. They had some drinks first then the food came and for a while only chewing noises and the buzz of the television overhead could be heard. One by one they finished their meals and started to relax, listening to the news bulletin on the screen. It was the same as every other evening: recession, accidents and crime. A drug bust, a major one the police claimed, had taken place earlier at a warehouse at the docks. The pictures showed the inside of a truck which had apparently been used to transport heroin through from southern Europe into Britain.

'Excess amount of drugs.' Sticks sneered as the camera stopped on a stack of neatly bound parcels. Charlie laughed.

'You notice the way they always give this big figure of "street value".'

'I wonder wha' dem ah go do wid it now?' D. asked. Cynically, Sticks suggested that the stuff would soon find its way back on the street. Charlie took a drink, looked at D.

'People believe that shit, you know. They show some-one bringing a couple of kis through the airport, or a truck now and then, and they talking like they're stopping drugs coming in.'

Sticks lit a cigarette, blew some smoke upwards.

'Stop wha'?' he laughed. 'Too much people wan' drugs, it ha'fe come t'rough.'

Charlie nodded and looked at him.

'That's right, that's why it's getting so ugly out there. Remember what I was trying to tell you last week?'

Sticks frowned. 'So wha'?'

'Check it out, everybody's into this drugs business, everybody. I'm talkin' on a big scale; you've got business people, banks, even politicians and police . . .'

Charlie explained the point he had been trying to put to Sticks the previous week.

'You've got to be careful in this game, there are some major players out there. If you come up against them, you get real problems!'

After Sticks had told Charlie and D. about his 'meeting' with Simon earlier that month, they had had a long heated discussion. Charlie insisted that Sticks should stop making moves on his own. He wanted things left as they were for the time being. After all, it had taken long enough to settle the 'other' territory problems which had almost gotten out of hand the previous year. But Sticks couldn't see that point then, and still couldn't see it now.

'Problems?' He kissed his teeth. 'Dem bwoy dere ah nuh no problem. Yuh see me?! I jus' boo-yaka business fe deal wid dat!'

D. looked at him, smiling indulgently.

'Rude bwoy, me know how yuh feel, but still; right now we ha'fe ease off ah de trigga, seen?!' Sticks still felt that Simon and his people had to be dealt with, his way.

'Don, anyhow we don't stop dis now, we gwan lose

control, more and more.' He paused, then said with conviction, 'Ah we run t'ings; any guy out dere bettah respeck dat.'

Puggy and Firefly were listening. Charlie waited until the waitress had removed their plates, then he told Sticks, 'There's only two ways you get respect; through love, or through fear.' D. seemed to agree, and Charlie continued:

'Look, man, let me tell you somet'ing about this; you see all those guys talking about don this and don that?! Well, a don is not someone who just goes around killing people, donship means you're on top, but with dignity, with a certain . . . class.'

'Ah, true; don man different from gun man, yuh know,' D. agreed.

Puggy had been listening with interest.

'Yeah, but is money we ah deal wid,' he pointed out.

'Sure it's money,' Charlie answered, 'but you don't want to spend your whole life dodging bullets on the street, right?' He paused, looked around as if to check if anybody was overhearing the conversation.

'If you start out poor, and the system only leaves drug for you to make money, the difficult step out of that is to get legit, earn a living up front.'

Charlie leaned back, his point made. Everyone seemed to ponder on that for a while.

Then D. said, 'Yuh see don?! A don is a man whe' provide a living fe man an' man. T'rough de don yuh can feed yuh family. An' if a man wan' diss yuh, is de don him ha fe deal wid.'

They talked for a few more minutes. Sticks was half-convinced by the argument, and reassured Charlie that he'd let things be for the time being. It was almost ten when they left the restaurant. Outside, as he was about to get into his car, Charlie told D.: 'A friend of mine is keeping a birthday party in south London. Let's go check it out.'

D. patted his full stomach.

'Bwoy, I was supposed to get home fe dinner.' He smiled.

'Yuh miss dat, man.' Charlie shrugged. 'So what's happening; you starting to keep times now?'

Laughing at the idea, D. explained that he had wanted to try and make Donna feel good for once.

'OK, but it's gonna be nice, exclusive guests, you know what I mean?'

D. spun the idea around in his mind.

'A'right, but me nah stay long.' They split.

Sticks dropped Firefly home, then took Puggy to Edmonton where he had an 'appointment', before going back to Charlie's house to meet them. They all climbed into the Saab, heading for the small club in Kennington where Charlie's friend was keeping the party. They would spend a couple of hours there, Charlie told D. and Sticks. He wasn't really a man to go out that much, but he would always honour a friend's request to attend a function. A host of people, mostly girls, huddled on the pavement, marking the location of the club. Sticks drove alongside slowly, looking at the girls. Then he drove through a few side streets, but couldn't find any suitable parking space. Back on the main road, he noticed the back lights of a car about to pull out. Sticks let the car out and was about to edge in, when a white Lancia shot across the road aiming for the parking space. Slamming on the brakes, Sticks swore. The other driver brazenly started to edge his car in. Sticks couldn't believe it.

'Hey, wha'ppen t'yuh,' Sticks shouted, his head outside the window. The other car had now come to a halt as the Saab was going for the space. Through the back window, they could see the back of two heads inside the Lancia. 'Something wrong with that guy,' Charlie explained. No one seemed to be coming out of the car. Sticks didn't call out again; he flicked open the security lock and got out of the car. He was already at the window of the Lancia when Charlie told D.

'I'd better go and check it out.'

His hands were still on the handle. He stopped as he watched Sticks step a little way back from the white car. From where Charlie and D. were, it seemed as if the driver of the car had his window up, refusing to answer Sticks. They saw it all happen through the windscreen of the Saab, like a movie. Sticks pointed at the man inside the car, then his right hand was holding his gun and he raised it, and smashed the heavy butt against the window. There was a loud cracking sound, the window fell to pieces and Sticks's gun hand disappeared inside the car. Recovering from his initial surprise, Charlie jumped out of the car and reached Sticks just as his hand was pressing the gun barrel into the petrified driver's face. His friend was simply sitting there, frozen eyes wide open.

'Easy, man, just let it go.' Charlie put his arm around his cousin. But Sticks was staring at his victim, his hand tightly gripping the gun, finger still covering the trigger.

'I'm talkin to you, Mikey. Give me the fucking piece, man!'

Charlie managed to get hold of the gun, and pulled Sticks away.

'Go, now!' he barked at the driver, who needed no more encouragement. He drove off – fast. In his frantic exit, he even chipped the corner of the car parked in front of him, but who cared. Once he had gotten Sticks back inside the Saab, Charlie watched him park it in the now empty space. Sticks switched off the ignition. He seemed back to normal now.

'Yuh was gonna shoot that car,' Charlie said looking at him. Sticks turned to him, serious.

'The guy diss me.'

'Yuh was gonna shoot him, right?' Charlie asked again. 'For a parking space?!'

'I was just scaring him,' Sticks declared flatly. He opened the door of the car, turned to D. and said, 'Let's check out the scene.' Then, seeing the two others were a little slow to move, he stepped out and sauntered across the road towards the club. Charlie turned towards D.

'He's starting to lose it,' he said quietly. D. waited a little before answering.

'Him just a lickle hyper . . .'

'A little hyper? This youth is getting cracked out, I'm telling you.' There was a little silence, as both men sat there considering the point.

'I gwan talk to him,' D. said.

Charlie shook his head. 'You think I'm getting worried for nothing, right?' D. said nothing. Charlie continued, 'You know what happen to Mikey . . . ? He's got power, at least that's the way he feels.'

Deep inside, D. wanted to defend Sticks, find some excuse for the youth's excessive behaviour.

'Dat yout' dere have heart, yuh know, Charlie? I have to trust him an' him nevah let me down yet.'

'Look, D., he's my cousin, remember? I know him from he was born. But right now, he's losing control. We're gonna get problems. He just can't go around starting fires everywhere. The gun and the shit . . . when they start get to you, it's over, man . . .' In the semi-darkness of the car, D. met Charlie's eyes. He nodded gravely. D. knew exactly what Charlie meant . . .

'Mek I reason wid him . . . Check him out, seen?'

Charlie shrugged.

'Sure, man.' He opened his door. 'Let's check out this place.'

16

SWEET AND SOUR

The group of uniformed boys spilled out of the school building laughing and talking, some rushing out, others strolling through the courtyard towards the gate. The grey and green tide washed over the pavement, round the corner and over the street. The longer spring evenings left a lot of time after school for leisure. Two boys, one not more than thirteen, crossed the road and shared a cigarette near the van Harry was leaning against. From behind his sunglasses he was observing his former schoolfriends as they noisily made their way out to the freedom of the streets. In order to get there on time, Harry had skipped his own late-afternoon science class. But he didn't care too much about that; some things had to take priority over mere school matters.

Throngs of pupils were still coming through the gates. Harry scanned the crowd from the other side of the van, half-hidden, then he saw her. In her neat grey uniform, wearing a striped green tie, Marcia had her school bag slung over her shoulder. She said something in the ear of the big brown girl beside her and glanced over her shoulder. They stepped up the pace towards the exit. Three boys were following them, gesticulating and laughing. One of them, a tall boy with a short haircut, was pointing at the two girls and said something that made his two friends laugh. Then they started running until they had caught up with the girls. Harry stayed behind the van and watched through the window as Marcia and her friend turned right towards the crossroads, the three boys in tow. They were now close behind them, the tall boy talking loud, his friends jeering and laughing. Marcia's friend stopped and turned around; she was as tall as the boy, but bigger. Marcia stopped too, and stood there looking serious while her friend said something which seemed to cool down the three boys somewhat. The tall one answered back and pointed at the girl, but she didn't seem intimidated. She dropped her school bag on the ground, then Marcia moved between them and said something to the boy. She seemed to be trying to stop the two from fighting. The big girl was unafraid, and was still talking aggressively, standing up right in front of the boy. His friends didn't seem to want any part of the fight; they were watching, keeping slightly back.

That was when Harry strolled across the road to them, forcing an incoming car to slow down to let him pass, and stepped up to Marcia.

'Hi, baby,' he said, with a half-smile, apparently oblivious to anyone around. Marcia's friend had just stopped cursing the boy. Slowly, Harry turned around and fixed his shaded eyes on the offender.

'What's happening?' he asked calmly. The boy frowned, froze for a few seconds. He was taller than Harry, and slightly bigger than him, with the shadow of a thin moustache stretching over his upper lip. He had recognized Harry despite the glasses and the scarf which covered his head. Though Harry had left their school, everyone knew him or knew of him now that he was making his name in the music business. The boy smiled meekly, realizing he'd picked on the wrong girl.

'Nothing, man, were just talking,' he said hopefully. His two friends said nothing. Harry nodded and turned to Marcia.

'Come on, let's go.'

Without another look, Harry started to walk away. Marcia followed. Her friend picked up her bag and came along, but not before she had thrown the boy a contemptuous look. The three headed for the crossroads, Harry answered a greeting from a friend across the road.

'I've got to come back here and sort out some people, it looks like,' he said.

Marcia laughed.

'Those guys are just stupid. Don't worry about that.'

'I could have taken care of him,' her friend, Michelle, told Harry. He laughed.

'Yeah, I bet you could beat up that boy.' They crossed over, then Michelle left them and headed towards the tall block of flats where she lived. Harry and Marcia walked slowly past the shops in the mellow afternoon.

'You left early?' Marcia asked.

'Yeah,' Harry answered without elaborating. But Marcia pressed on.

'You didn't skip a class by any chance?'

'Well, it wasn't an important one.'

Marcia stopped, looked at him. 'You promised me you'd go to all your classes.'

'I go to all my classes!' he lied. 'Only I wanted to see you . . .'

'You could have seen me later.'

Harry smiled, and gently put his hand on her arm.

'Yeah, I know . . . but I've been waiting all day.' His voice was soft. 'Anyway, it's a good thing I was there. You need a bodyguard!' Marcia couldn't help laughing. They walked on past terraced houses and through a playground full of little children. Harry wouldn't have missed walking Marcia home for the world. He'd only seen her two days earlier, but it seemed a long time ago. In the last few months, they had been going steady, meeting regularly and going out sometimes.

The previous Saturday they had been up to the West End to watch the latest Eddie Murphy movie. Eddie was

Marcia's favourite actor. They had had a good time, laughed a lot, drank soda and munched popcorn and enjoyed the film too. Harry had felt nice, free and important, strolling the busy streets with his girl. Apart from music, Marcia was all he was concerned about at the moment. She was more open with him now, trusted him, and he had surprised himself by feeling more and more for the pretty girl with the irresistible smile. The best thing was that Marcia's parents had gone on holiday three weeks before, on a long vacation that would keep them in the Caribbean sun until July. Of course he still had to deal with Winsome, Marcia's sister, who was looking after her. But since Winsome was only twenty-three herself, and had her own busy life to see to, she was much more flexible than Marcia's mother. That meant almost unlimited access to Marcia's house for Harry, and he had made the most of it.

'What you doing later?' he asked as they approached Marcia's house.

'I've got a test tomorrow, got to revise.'

'What you going to revise all evening?'

Marcia looked at him.

'Are you good at maths?' she asked. He shrugged.

'Sometimes . . . but you good. You don't need that much revision.'

Marcia stopped in front of her door and laughed.

'I revise. That's why I'm good,' she pointed out. Harry watched her as she took her keys out of her purse and unlocked the door.

'So you're not gonna see me later?'

'No . . .' Marcia held the door open, 'and I'm not going to revise if you're with me.'

'Oh, so you're not letting me in?'

Marcia paused, fixed him. He looked really disappointed, though she knew only too well that Harry could make up his face to look sad whenever it suited him.

'OK, only for a little while. When I say go, you go!'

'Sure, I'll go.' Harry smiled as he stepped in.

He sat in the living room while Marcia went to change from her school uniform. The sun was still throwing its rays across the bay windows, bathing the room in a bright, warm glow. Harry stretched on a settee, enjoying the moment, smiling to himself at the way he could relax in Marcia's house. Usually, he couldn't even show up at the front door because of her mother's strictness.

'Why do you disguise yourself to come to the school? Everybody recognizes you, y'know.' Harry looked at her and smiled.

'Why, you don't like my clothes?' he asked.

'You look like some gangster,' she declared, indicating the colourful red scarf that covered his head. He grinned.

'Rude-bwoy style!'

Marcia sat beside him.

'Well, I don't want no "rude bwoy",' she said, imitating the thick Jamaican patois accent he effected.

'Take off your glasses,' she asked. Harry complied and stared into her eyes, widening his as if in a trance.

'Stop that!' Marcia laughed, turning away. He teased her a little bit more, making horrible faces at her, and as they played, they ended up on the far corner of the settee, Marcia pressed against the leather arm, Harry's arm around her waist. They stopped, her face only inches from his, her eyes still. Marcia's hand went around his neck, up to the back of his neck and started to undo the knot that tied up the headscarf. She pulled away the piece of material, rolled it and wrapped it around his neck. Harry opened his eyes big and stuck out his tongue as the scarf squeezed his throat, playing dead. Marcia laughed.

'Ugggh, you're ugly,' she said, as he 'revived', grabbing her face gently in his two hands. She screamed and fought back and, close as they were, they both soon realized something else was between them – an urge which Marcia had been resisting those last few weeks, and which Harry had been eager to develop further.

'I'll get some drinks,' Marcia said quietly, trying to break the spell.

'I'm not thirsty.' Harry's eyes locked into hers.

'But I'm thirsty,' she insisted, unconvincingly.

Harry came closer, and said in a whisper, 'You lie . . .'

Marcia breathed deeply.

She felt Harry's hands on her waist.

'You're afraid,' he said softly.

'I'm not.' Marcia tried to sound assertive.

'Oh yes, you are . . . like Tuesday night.' Marcia stared at him, then looked away.

'I'm just being careful,' she said, after a little while.

Their eyes were doing most of the 'talking', and it wasn't the first time they had had that same conversation. On Tuesday evening, Harry hadn't left Marcia's until after twelve. Winsome worked late sometimes, and had gone to visit some friends, so the two watched television until late. Marcia wasn't in a hurry to see Harry leave, and he felt quite comfortable there too.

They had sat together on the settee for hours, talking, feeling close. In the last few weeks, with the mellow spring weather and more opportunity for close contact, both Harry and Marcia had experienced a kind of pull that drew them to each other. That night they had discussed it, but disagreed about what they should do about it. Then Winsome had come in and found them sitting side by side, quiet.

Harry brought his face closer to Marcia's, and put his lips against hers.

'I've got to be careful too,' he repeated, imitating her. She pushed him away, not too hard.

'You're making jokes?'

272

'Nah.' Harry laughed, then he fixed his face. 'Al'right, look, I'm serious, OK?'

Marcia looked at him, suspiciously. 'You think I trust you?'

'You've got to trust me,' Harry replied, sounding a little offended.

'Yeah? Winsome told me to watch out for you.'

That sounded improbable to Harry.

'What you talking about? Winsome likes me,' he countered.

Marcia had a knowing smile on her face.

'Yeah, but does she trust you?' she asked. Harry shrugged.

'So what you saying? Do you think I'm gonna leave you?' Marcia's hand was on Harry's arm, whether to hold him or restrain him it was hard to tell. She looked away.

'I don't know.'

'You know bettah than that, Marcia, man, just relax,' Harry insisted, getting a firmer hold of Marcia's waist. She stopped his arm.

'Relax?' She laughed not very heartily. 'That's when trouble starts.'

'What trouble?'

'Remember Samantha?'

'Which Samantha?' Harry frowned.

'The tall girl who was in my class last year.'

Harry knew who she was talking about.

'Well, she relaxed! She's having a baby in two months' time.'

'Oh, that girl.' Harry kissed his teeth. 'She's a fool!'

'What do you mean, she's a fool?'

'Dat girl was easy, man. She was asking for trouble,' Harry declared.

'Yeah? Well, I'm not easy. I intend to go to college . . .'

'Why you have to bring up things like that?' Harry asked dejectedly, knowing that the sweetness of the moment had gone.

Marcia laughed, poking him in the chest.

'Oh, you don't like to hear about problems?'

The game went on for a little while. Harry tried to convince Marcia that she should let him have his way. She kept pointing out the very valid reasons why it was out of the question. Then she said:

'I'm not sure you really love me, you know.'

'How can you say that, Marcia?' he said, in his most convincing tone of voice. 'You know I love you twenty-four seven, seen?!'

She looked at him, poked him again.

'Well, if you do, you'll wait.'

With that she left him there and went into the kitchen. Harry let out a deep groan of frustration. He wasn't going to give up just like that, no way.

Marcia brought back some drinks. They sat, drank and talked some more, Marcia steering the conversation to 'safer' topics. She reminded him that she needed time to revise and Harry got up to leave, as he had promised he would.

'Come for me tomorrow,' she said at the door. Harry smiled.

'If I'm not busy . . .'

The girl looked at him, raised her eyebrows.

'I might be busy next time too,' she warned him. Harry laughed, and gently pulled her to him.

'Tomorrow . . .' he said. She lifted her face up towards him and responded to his kiss. When he stepped out on to the landing, Harry felt light, tall and glowing. He smiled to himself, feeling pretty sure that Marcia liked him as much as he liked her. He could feel it now! Back on the street, he floated all the way home, inspired, making up lyrics as he went. As he turned the corner to his block, someone called out.

'Rude bwoy! Yaow!' Ricky was sitting on the stairs at the entrance of the flats across the way, waving at him. Harry went over.

'What's happening?' he asked Ricky.

'We jus' coolin' out.' The youth sitting next to him, Donovan, nodded to Harry. He'd met him at the youth club a few times, playing pool.

'Al'right,' Harry said. The two youths had a can of beer each and a small portable radio cassette was playing at the corner of the stairwell, spitting out the bass and treble of a live dancehall cassette. Ricky pointed to the machine.

'Buju – wicked! My sister bring back some cassette from Yard.' Harry listened to a piece of lyrics, it sounded exclusive.

'Listen, man, I got to get some food, I soon come,' he told Ricky.

'Al'right, go on, we'll wait for you.'

Harry left them and went for his dinner. When he got upstairs, Lorna wasn't there. He kept forgetting she'd started an evening job after her part-time work. He opened the fridge and started to look for something to eat.

Ricky and Donovan rocked to the music for a while, exclaiming loudly as the mostly new lyrics hit out of the small cassette player.

'Hey, Ricky, I want to find this bwoy,' Donovan said, scornfully stressing the last word. Ricky took a drink.

'Don't worry about that, man, you'll buck him up soon.'

'I don't want him soon, I want him now. The guy dissed me,' Donovan insisted. His face twisted up as he talked about it, and he seemed hell-bent on avenging himself for the 'dissing'. He had explained to Ricky that the guy and him had a business going and apparently Donovan didn't get all that was due to him, he felt robbed and insulted. The guilty party was a local boy, something of a hustler, boasty and loud. Not that Ricky liked the boy much himself, but he'd been trying to tell Donovan not to get too carried away with this revenge business.

'Donovan, man, just cool it,' he urged. 'You've got to have a plan, right?' Ricky turned the cassette over. 'The guy's got connections, you know wha' I mean?'

'Connections?!' Donovan shouted. 'Hey, you know who I work for. I shoot him down and feel no way.' Donovan was known to have a hot temper. He'd gotten in trouble more than once because of it.

'What, you're just going to walk up to him and shoot him?'

'You watch me. No bwoy can diss me like that, you know?' Ricky laughed and tried to reason with his friend.

'Come on, man, just work it out; find a way to rob him back. It's not a lot of money, right? Pick your time, man.'

Donovan finished his beer, crushed the empty can and tossed it into the stairwell.

'Money? It's disrespect, Ricky, man,' he insisted. 'Any guy fuck wid me, I do him in. Simple.'

It sounded simple and he seemed to mean it. Ricky drilled the subject; it was all Donovan had wanted to talk about for most of the afternoon. Ricky finished his beer.

'So what? You've got a spliff?' he asked, looking at his friend expectantly. For the first time, Donovan smiled. He wore a blue baseball cap with a big wide 'X' embroidered on it. He was seventeen with a short, round face and a gold tooth in his mouth that gleamed whenever he spoke or grinned.

'I've got better than that, man,' he said conspiratorially. Ricky frowned a little.

'I don't want to get too involved with that, man, you know what I mean?' But Donovan insisted.

'Forget the rest, rude bwoy. That's the best. Come on, let's burn . . .'

Though Ricky wanted a draw, he wasn't too hot for rock. He'd smoked the pipe a couple of times but only because he was hanging around with friends who all seemed involved with that and he didn't want to lose face. Crack scared him, but, then again, all the 'roughnecks' he knew seemed to pick up on it sooner or later. He sighed.

'I don't know, man! Not right now.' Donovan looked disappointed.

'I soon come.' He got up and climbed the stairs to the first landing, out of view. Then he took out his glass pipe and got busy. Meanwhile, Ricky waited downstairs, rocking to and fro to the music. Harry appeared on the landing opposite and came down. He looked relaxed, having satisfied his hunger. He sat with Ricky, taking in the lyrics, his face serious as he followed the ride. Donovan came back down, a grin etched across his face, his gold tooth gleaming.

'Yes, my yout'! You're chatting at the club tomorrow night?' he asked Harry.

'Yeah, I'll pass down there,' Harry said vaguely. Donovan was standing on the stairs behind Ricky, bogling to the music. Around the flats people were walking, stopping to talk with neighbours. Some children were playing football in the evening sun, and a small dog was running madly after the ball. On a cool Thursday evening such as this one, everyone wanted to be outside. The good weather had taken long to come, but after a wet spring the newly arrived month of May had brought back the sun.

'Buster was looking for you earlier,' Ricky told Harry.

'Yeah?'

'He's got an early dance in Tottenham, wants you to come down.' Harry nodded, thinking about it. He wasn't too sure he felt like checking it out. With the club on Friday, a dance with Radical on Saturday and a PA at Rocco's on Sunday it was going to be a busy weekend.

'I don't know, man. I just feel like chilling out tonight.' From behind him, Donovan intervened.

'Buster's expecting you down there, ain't it, Ricky?'

'Yeah, him and Ray came down to find you.'

Harry thought about it again; Buster was his spar, he didn't want to let him down. 'I don't want to stay out late tonight.' He remembered something. 'And I promised Chris I'd go to the black history class.'

Donovan kissed his teeth, still dancing on the stairs.

'Cho', Fly, man, let's go Tottenham,' he added. 'You can get some dollars.'

Ricky looked at Harry, waiting for him to decide.

'OK, but I'm not staying long.'

'Let's jump on a bus,' Ricky said, getting up and stretching. The evening was cool as the three left the flat and made for the high street. Donovan was still hopping along to the music from the cassette player Ricky was carrying. A bus rolled past as they reached a turning, but the bus stop was too far down the road to run for it. Two girls came out of the grocery store, one carrying a bulging plastic bag, the other with a baby in her arms.

'Hey, yuh have baby already?!' Donovan called out, smiling. The baby mother glanced at him, didn't answer and crossed over with her friend.

'I thought it was yours?' Ricky joked.

'Mine? Nah, man.' Donovan frowned. 'I used to deal wid her, but she was better looking than that.' They laughed, walked on towards the bus stop. It was just about getting dark now.

'Let's get some drinks,' Donovan said as they passed the off-licence. Ricky and Harry said they were kind of broke.

'Just cool, man, I've got some cash,' Donovan said as he stepped inside the shop.

The two others followed, the music still pumping. Inside, Donovan went to the fridge and picked up three cans, walked back to the counter and put them down. The shopkeeper, who was Asian, looked at him and said:

'I can't sell you alcohol, you're under age.'

Donovan took a ten-pound note out of his shirt pocket and put it on the counter as if he hadn't heard him.

'Tek the money, man,' he said. But the man behind the counter simply repeated what he'd said before.

'You're under age. I cannot sell you strong drinks.' Alongside, behind the sweets display, an old bearded man with a turban was watching a television atop a shelf. He paid no attention to the customers.

'Who under age? Jus' take the money, fast! I've got things to do!' Donovan was starting to lose his patience. He stared at the Asian man behind his till. Nearer to the door, Ricky and Harry just watched, slightly unsure. Apparently, the shopkeeper was determined to obey the law.

'Show me some ID, and I'll sell you the drinks.'

Donovan simply looked at him with a scornful grin.

'ID? What the fuck is wrong with you?' He scowled and held up the ten-pound note. 'This is my ID – and yuh bettah tek it if you wanna get paid.'

Ricky tried to calm him.

'The guy's an idiot. Let's move on, man.'

But for Donovan it was now a personal matter; the man was dissing him. His face was blank, his eyes fixed on the man with a deadly look. He kissed his teeth, pushed the note back into his pocket and picked up the beer.

'You don't want my money, fine.'

He started out towards the door, past Ricky and Harry. The shopkeeper moved quickly, picked up something from under the counter and ran after the boy.

'Stop!' he shouted. 'Give me those drinks!'

The older man turned to watch the play. He got up as

the first man reached the spot where Ricky and Harry were standing.

Donovan was almost at the door.

'Let's move, man,' he called out to his friends, but the shopkeeper had moved between them and the door, and had a short sword in his hand. Donovan turned and saw the man coming towards him.

'Teef!' he shouted. 'Put them back!' The youth stopped, the drinks in his left hand, then moved forward.

'Give me those drinks.'

He raised the sword, either to intimidate or strike the black youth. The old man came from behind the counter, calling out to him, saying something in their language. Ricky was about to bumrush the sword from the man. But he didn't have time. Donovan pulled a small silver handgun out from underneath his shirt.

'What you wanna do wid dat?' he asked coldly. But the shopkeeper stood his ground.

'Put back the drinks,' he repeated. There was a dry crack and he staggered back, dropped the sword, and tried to hold on to the counter to stop himself from falling. A dark wet patch had appeared on the left side of his shirt. The old man ran to him, shouting. Donovan stood there for a few seconds, watching as the man dropped to the floor. He looked at Ricky and Harry, both frozen.

'Come on, let's go,' he shouted. Ricky, still holding the cassette player, recovered from the shock first. He pulled Harry's sleeve and started moving.

'Come on, man – fast!' Harry couldn't take his eyes off the man bleeding on the floor. Ricky pulled him again, harder, and he started running. Donovan pushed the gun in his pocket and ran out of the door – straight into a tall, fat, white man trying to come in. Donovan's baseball cap dropped to the floor and he ran on, pushing the man out of the way. Ricky and Harry sprinted down the road after him.

They left the high street and took to the back alleys and ran until their lungs ached, finally dropping, out of breath, hearts pumping, by the side of the canal.

On the board, the large map of Africa and the Middle East shone under the glare of the neon lighting. There was no noise in the room. Only the occasional scratching of the marker pen on the large, white sheet of paper whenever the man half-seated on the table stopped talking. His thin, dark fingers crossed over his lap, he slowly looked around at the little group sitting in front of him; they were waiting with eager anticipation for the final part of the story. The man cleared his throat.

'So, Hannibal left Carthage, with his army and his elephants and marched them up all the way across these mountains . . .' The tall man went to the map and pointed: '. . . and into Italy. He conquered the whole southern region of the country and stayed there for almost twenty years.' Walking back to the table, the man's dark eyes shone with malice for a brief moment. He smiled. 'That's why a lot of Italians still look very dark, even to this day . . .'

There were a few laughs amongst the listeners. Passing his hand over his grizzly beard, Piper breathed in and concluded.

'This African general, Hannibal, is considered to be one of the greatest military leaders of all time. He was at least the equal of Julius Caesar, and Napoleon. Yet you won't hear much about him at school . . .' Piper glanced around his audience; even Chris, seated amongst the youths as every Thursday, seemed captivated.

'Well, that is all we have for today's class,' he said. 'Try to research some more about it, always research more by yourself . . .'

Piper stood up as the class came alive again.

'Are there any more questions about this or anything else?' he asked. Above the humming of hushed voices which had started, a feminine one rose up from the back.

'Yeah! What about . . . ?'

Piper tried, but couldn't hear the question.

'Excuse me!' he called, raising his hand to call for the others' attention. 'Could you repeat that, please,' he said, always polite.

The young girl at the back of the class was standing up.

'You said we would discuss the point someone talked about last week, about Muslims . . .'

'Ah, yes . . .' Piper smiled at her. The previous Thursday a youth had raised the debate about the black Muslims he had seen in the area; the lively discussion which followed had to be cut short because of lack of time. Piper was aware of the interest a number of youngsters had expressed in the subject.

'We need a class on this subject, specifically,' he told the girl. Looking at the whole class, he announced in his usual even voice, 'Thursday after next is a lesson the rise of Islam in the sixth century . . . BC!' Piper paused. 'Half of that lesson will be a class discussion.' There was silence, then he added: 'For those who wish to research for the lesson, I will ask you one question . . .'

The students sat up knowing that the question would be worth hearing. Piper had a way of teaching black history, which always mixed study and games.

'By today's standards, what would the founders of Judaism, Islam and Christianity – and even Buddhism – be classified as? Try and research that,' Piper said as he went to the board to take up the map. A few of the youths left their seats and walked towards him. There were always questions left unanswered. Chris was getting up too, when a door at the back of the class flew open, slamming noisily against a chair. Everybody stopped and turned towards it.

Chris frowned and watched as the white man in shirt, tie and jacket walked in.

'Excuse me,' the man, who was in his late forties with greyish hair, came towards him. Quickly, like in the movies, he flashed out a warrant card, declared his name and rank and flashed the badge back into his pocket. He glanced around the room. Meanwhile, another younger plain-clothes officer and three uniformed officers had entered the room and stood gazing at the youths. Chris looked the first policeman straight in the face.

'Look, you can't just bust in like that. You got a warrant? What's your business here?' He refused to be stepped on. Piper stood by the blackboard, watching the intrusion. The youths were watching too, hostile.

'We're looking for three of your lads. A shopkeeper just got shot down the road,' the policeman announced importantly.

'You won't find them here. No one has left this room for the last two hours,' Chris told him firmly. Then he asked, 'What do you mean three of my lads?'

The policeman had a false smile.

'Well, you're the chief around 'ere, ain't you? You're supposed to keep that sort of thing from happening.' Whether it was the sardonic tone of the voice, that plastic smile, or the insulting stupidity of the statement, Chris couldn't tell, but he was beginning to feel angry. To top it all, the younger plain-clothes officer, tall and blond with a boyish look, butted in.

'Yes, sir. We're looking for three West Indians, about sixteen, seventeen . . .' he said, chewing hard on his gum. 'One of them lost a red baseball cap at the scene . . . Any ideas?'

Chris threw him a scornful look, then turned to the other officer glancing around the room suspiciously.

'What did you say happened?' Chris asked calmly.

'We have an Asian off-licence owner in a critical state, got shot at close range.' Then, as if he thought he had been too polite, he added sarcastically, 'You West Indian people are pretty violent, ain't you?'

Chris couldn't believe it, he sighed heavily, shaking his head.

'Why don't you call us what you usually do when you're with your friends? Do you call us West Indians then?'

Chris hadn't heard him move, but Piper was now standing a little way behind him, unexpressive, listening. His voice cut in before anyone else could say anything.

'We are not from the West, and we're not Indians. Columbus made a mistake,' he declared neutrally.

There was a short silence as the policeman and his friends let the words sink in. Then some of the teenagers started to laugh, enjoying the policeman's inability to respond to the facts. Chris relaxed a little and smiled at the green-eyed policeman standing before him. The man had a last brief look around.

'Al'right, let's go.' Then to Chris, 'We'll call on you again, if we need your help.'

'I don't think so,' Chris told him as he left.

Once the police had gone, the youths started chatting amongst themselves about the incident. Chris turned around. Piper was still there, thin and calm. He smiled at him. They stayed in the room for a while, talking while the youths left. After he closed up the centre, Chris went home. He told Myrtle the news as he sat down to dinner. He thought about calling Lorna, but the evening passed and time got the better of him. Soon, he slipped into bed and into a deep sleep.

17

SPRINGTIME SUNDAY

Only a small amount of milk remained at the bottom of the long plastic dish. The small grey and white cat sniffed at it; it wasn't worth it. Turning away, he left the kitchen and entered the living room, pausing near the door to watch the man asleep in the chair. Slowly, the cat approached him, then leapt up effortlessly and landed on his lap. Seeing there was still no reaction, the cat lifted its right paw and started to claw lightly on the thick strings of his vest – pulling, letting go, then pulling again. A sharp claw pulled at the man's skin, and he stirred and made a noise. The cat stopped, watched him, then started again, bolder this time. Soon, the sleeping man shifted his head and started to open his eyes. He sighed heavily, rubbed one hand over his face and straightened up in the chair, stroking the cat. He looked around the room, and saw that the TV screen was blank and the stereo was still on.

'What happen to you?' Sticks yawned, fixing the cat. The animal looked up at him, head tilted, and headed out of the room. Sticks got up and stretched. The rising sun was filling the bay window, big and welcoming. Sticks opened the window, took a deep breath and went out to the bathroom, scratching his head. Splashing cold water on his face freed his mind from the lingering sleepiness. In the same way, the cold hard gush of the hosepipe at five in the morning back in Jamaica never failed to get him fresh for the day ahead. He dried his face with his rag, and came back to the living room but couldn't find his shirt.

Remembering, he went down to the bedroom and picked it up from the hanger on the wardrobe handle. Spread across the bed, the sheet half-covering her, Mona was deep asleep. Sticks glanced at her and decided against waking her up. They had been out all the night before, came home a little after four and she had gone to bed a little tipsy. Sticks had meant to join her but first he had listened to some music, then watched a video . . .

The next thing he knew the cat had been waking him up. Closing the bedroom door, Sticks put on his shirt and found his shoes beside the coat stand. The cat was in the kitchen, sitting near the milk dish, waiting. Sticks smiled as he went for some juice in the fridge; there was none, but he picked up the carton of milk and poured some out for the cat. Straightaway the animal started to lap it up. Sticks left the kitchen, picked up his keys from the living-room table, checked his pockets and left the flat. Outside was nice, still cool, but it felt like there was a warm day ahead. The Saab gleamed in the early morning, and inside it smelt of tobacco, leather and perfume. Sticks sprayed some air freshener around inside, rolled down the electric window and started the engine. Reliable as always, the car rolled, first time. He adjusted his glasses, turned up the stereo and drove away. Apart from a few people walking their dogs or out buying their Sunday papers the streets were empty. The clock on the dashboard said 8.07. Sticks drove on until he got to a junction. Turning right would take him home. Left led to Soni's. He'd left the previous morning saying he'd be back, but then, as always, he had been busy. He pondered what to do for a short while and then decided to head back to Holloway. Soni would probably still be asleep. Ten minutes later, Sticks parked alongside a row of shops across from her house. Locking the doors, he tapped the roof of the car. He liked the Saab, it drove smoothly, never broke down and could give some serious speed when required, too. A couple of times Charlie had suggested that he should sell it and get something else. But Charlie was always worrying too much. He walked inside a newsagent and picked up a newspaper and a carton of juice. The Indian shopkeeper picked up the money and handed him back the change. Sticks was already glancing at the paper. A big picture of the new heavyweight champion was spread on the front page.

'Did you see the boxing last night?' the shopkeeper asked smiling.

'Yeah, wicked fight,' Sticks replied. He'd seen the fight on satellite television with a friend before he went out. They talked boxing for a couple of minutes, then he crossed over to Soni's house. Inside, everything was quiet. Soni was in bed, and opened one eye when he entered the bedroom, then made a muted protest as he flashed open one of the curtains.

'Wha' happen?' Sticks said, tossing the newspaper at her. She made a noise and turned over to escape the brightness, but he came and sat on the bed, started to pull her ear and pinch her neck. Soni turned towards him.

'What time is it?' she asked. Then as she remembered, 'You said you was coming back.'

'Yeah, certain t'ings happ'n,' Sticks explained.

Soni stretched on her back. Sticks pushed his right hand under the sheet and started to rub her stomach. She opened both eyes fully and looked at him.

'Go away,' she said, but didn't mean it.

Sticks smiled, still rubbing her gently.

'Dat good fe yuh, man,' he said.

'What do you know about that?' she asked, visibly doubtful.

'How yuh mean, me ah docta yuh no know?' Soni picked up one of the pillows and hit him on the head with it. He grabbed her arm and started to bite her shoulder playfully, making her scream. After a little while, Sticks got up, picked up the juice from the side table.

'Yuh bettah start eat properly, y'hear?' he said as he went to the bathroom. He switched on the shower, adjusted the taps for water temperature, came back into the bedroom and started undressing. Soni was pregnant – at least that's what she reckoned. She hadn't been to the doctor for confirmation yet, but all the signs were there. She had told Sticks about it a week earlier, watching for his reaction. He seemed rather pleased about it and had shown her a lot of consideration in the last few days, bought her an enormous amount of fresh fruit, and even made her cornmeal porridge twice! But then he had always treated Soni good; they had their fights, and Sticks was ignorant at times, but on the whole they suited each other. Soni was no angel either, she could be stubborn when she wanted. Maybe now, with a baby on the way, something different would develop. In his shorts, Sticks came back from the kitchen to pour some juice for Soni. He took a couple of swallows himself and headed for the shower. When he came back, steaming, rubbing himself over with the towel, Soni had opened the windows and was changing the bedsheet. She stopped and looked at him.

'You're the one who needs to eat more. Look at you,' she remarked with a concerned look. Sticks had never been fat, on the contrary, but she was right. He didn't seem to have much weight on him.

'Wha' yuh ah seh? Yuh like fat man?' he joked.

He went to get some clothes to put on. Soni shook her head.

'You're not eating, you know that?'

Sticks kissed his teeth, mumbling.

'Me eat, man . . .'

'I'm gonna make you some breakfast,' Soni declared.

Sticks dressed and followed her to the kitchen, picking up his paper on the way.

'I don't really feel too hungry, y'know,' he said. But Soni just sent him back to the living room and got cooking. A short while later, she brought him a tray. Soni stood over him, watching, so he put aside the paper and drank some of the tea, took a piece of bread and bit into it. She switched on the TV and sat beside him while he ate. Breakfast over, Soni went to the bathroom while Sticks continued reading his newspaper. He couldn't find his lighter, so he knocked on the bathroom door to ask her, but Soni didn't know where it was either. He found it in the clothes basket, inside his trouser pocket. When he had finished with the pipe, he put on a stage show video that a friend had lent him earlier in the week. He absorbed himself in the warm atmosphere of the show, and didn't notice Soni until she came to sit right against him. He stayed there for a time, commenting on the show, relaxed. With her head against Sticks's shoulder, Soni asked: 'Yuh going out today?'

'Why,' he said, his eyes on the screen.

'I wanna go see my sister,'

Sticks said, 'Hmmm,' absent-mindedly, but Soni insisted.

'Will you take me down there?'

He turned to her. Many times he'd promised Soni that he would go with her to visit her sister who lived about twenty miles outside London. Somehow, he never actually got around to doing it. He thought about it, then said, 'Al'right. Me an' yuh drive down there.'

But Soni knew him only too well.

'Don't just say that and then change your mind. You sure?' she asked. Sticks turned away from the show on the screen again.

'So wha', yuh nuh hear me seh so?'

'Yeah, but I know you. You always agree, then you disappear and leave me.'

Sticks laughed, shook his head.

'Nah, man, yuh cyan seh dat.'

'You do,' Soni insisted. 'Like last week I waited for you all evening to go to my friend's house, and you never came back until two days later . . .'

'Al'right.' Sticks held up his hand, trying to avoid the recriminations.

'Hear dis. Yuh see today, we gwan to yuh sistah's. An' yuh see after dat, yuh come wid me, do some runnins, and even all tonight, when yuh tired an' yuh wan' go home, yuh cyan go. I will keep yuh wid me so yuh cyan cuss again . . . talk 'bout me always leave yuh.'

Soni laughed, wondering if he meant it. In any case, it sounded genuine enough. Despite his mischievous smile. A little later, they were getting ready to go out. Soni watched as Sticks put away his pipe; he noticed her look.

'Dat done fe yuh, y'know,' he said casually.

She didn't answer but turned and put on her shoes. In the past few months she'd been using the stuff a lot, too much probably. She'd lost her job too, because of her repeated lateness and frequent absences, though she hadn't told Sticks that was why. Soni's little daughter stayed by her mother most of the time. Though she had not really thought about it up to now, her pregnancy meant changes and Soni could see the wisdom of what Sticks was saying. They left at midday, and Sticks held up the keys. 'Yuh drive, man,' he told Soni.

She threw him a sideways glance, and went round to the passenger side, patting her stomach.

'You're my chauffeur now, open the door,' she said in a mock-posh tone of voice.

*

At about the same time, D. was trying to get through to Jamaica for the umpteenth time. There had been problems on the international exchange all morning, and the only time he had got through the number he had called was engaged. He put down the phone after another unsuccessful try. He wasn't really watching the television, it was just on, the sound turned off. On the radio, a station was playing some back-to-back revival selection, ideal for a really sunny, laid-back Sunday afternoon. D. was relaxing, listening to the music and following a train of thought. He'd woken up a few hours earlier after a series of dreams which had disturbed his sleep. Even after he had showered and eaten breakfast, he still felt a kind of eerie light-headedness. By now, D. was used to that. It happened at least once every few months. One time, during his stay with Thomas in Jamaica, the dreams had been almost 'real'. D. had woken up, his throat dry in the middle of the warm night, and had to go out to the veranda in the dark, to escape their spell-like grip.

The previous evening, he had gone to south London to visit Sammy. They had a nice time talking, had a drink and enjoyed a fine dinner which Sammy's wife had cooked. D. had come to Donna's at about two in the morning and gone straight to bed. He had been in bed when Donna had gone out to Leroy's house for dinner with the children, then he had slept a few more hours and since then he had been sitting there, meditating. It had been one of those long weeks when too much takes place for comfort. Last Sunday night a fight had broken out at the gambling club between two good friends – at least they had been until then. D., who happened to be there at the time, had to personally intervene to stop them settling their score right there and then. All week a kind of tense vibe had hung over the place. They both had reputations to live up to, and in most cases like that the murmurs, su-su, of the rest of the crowd only edged them on. By Friday D. had arranged to meet them both in private. They talked, there was some shouting, and much 'flexing', but in the end they both agreed that the initial bone of contention was 'foolishness'. Everything was cool now . . .

Then, in the middle of the week, D. had met a long-time friend of his who had just flown in. They talked and D. learned certain things which troubled his peace of mind. He needed to know more, which was why he was trying so hard to get the overseas phone connection. That wasn't all. Firefly was on the run. Charlie had heard about the incident soon after it took place on Thursday night, and no one had seen Fly since. D. had found out that a shopkeeper had been shot by one of three black youths, and one of the three was said to be Firefly. He couldn't imagine the young MC doing the shooting. The main thing was to try and find him, D. thought, still hoping Charlie would get a call. While he thought all this over, the phone rang.

'Yeah, hmmm-hmm. So how it go las' night?'

It was Pablo calling, as he was supposed to do. Everything was OK, nothing to report. D. arranged to meet him later at the place. He replaced the receiver. He thought about calling Jenny, but remembered she wouldn't be in. She was supposed to spend the weekend by Carol, her sister. D. realized he hadn't seen her or Jesse since Thursday. Maybe he could pick her up later? He got up and went to the kitchen, opened the oven, looked at his dinner inside, and closed it again. Then he went to the patio window, opened it and stepped into the garden. In the sun, D. looked around the small square of grass. There hadn't been any decent weather until this month, so D. hadn't really used the garden. Last Wednesday, as the almost hot afternoon was coming to an end, D. had sat on the ledge after his dinner and lit up a spliff. The wood fence around the garden was nearly seven feet tall, high enough to keep him from sight. As the evening breeze came down, he had been reminded of what he missed.

D. knew he would only ever really feel good if he could enjoy it back home. Nothing could buy that atmosphere – and as he sat there, watching the sun burn red over the fences, he realized that returning home would have to be his goal. Anyway, for the time being, much was left to do.

He had absent-mindedly started to play with the small plastic ball which Cindy had left there. D. rolled it under his right foot, lifted it up with the point of his toe and bounced it a couple of times. It had been a long time since his last touch of the real thing. He balanced the small ball on one foot, then the other, sent it upwards and killed it neatly on his extended thigh. D. recalled the times he used to play football practically every day. In those days, as a boy, he had nothing better to do. He promised himself that he would organize a football game soon.

D. walked back into the living room and crashed down on the settee. He felt restless, 'haunted' as they say, but he didn't quite know why. He thought about the dreams again, and switched channels with the remote control, but his mind couldn't settle on the TV. For all the Christian upbringing his grandmother, then his mother, had forced upon him, D. had grown up only too aware of the interplay between the living and the spirit world. He knew those dreams always ended up meaning something.

An old Western was starting on TV. D. forced himself to check it out and relaxed, concentrating on following the plot. Later on, he thought, he would go for Jenny . . .

The cake had been cut, the dancing competition was over. Holding their ice-cream, the children ran out of the room to go and play in the front yard. Glancing through the window, Carol made sure the gate was locked, then came back to sit down. Charmaine was finishing her ice-cream. She had arrived a few hours earlier, bringing Marcus to Venetta's birthday party. Jesse and his mother had been here since Friday night. Together with half a dozen other children, Venetta's friends, they were a good little group – running and shouting, taking the opportunity to release their excess energy. The three women were starting to relax now that the noisy youngsters had left the room. Early on, they had dinner together, a delicious traditional Sunday meal prepared by Carol. Jenny had insisted that she helped, but that was denied by her sister, who took all the credit for the meal. Charmaine laughed, enjoying the kind of harmless argument those two always had whenever they met. To avenge herself, Jenny teased Carol by threatening to reveal a secret piece of news. With all the excitement of the birthday celebration, they had all forgotten about that – everyone except Charmaine, that is. Charmaine was too 'nosy' not to find out.

'So what's this news you were talking about?' she asked Jenny mischievously. Carol looked at her, then at Jenny, squinting threateningly. Jenny laughed at the sight of her sister's face.

'Oh, come on, Cal, you can tell Charmaine. She's like family,' she insisted. Carol sighed, smiling.

'It's no big thing, but this gyal here gets excited over nothing,' she said, shaping up as if to throw the dessert spoon she was holding at her sister. Jenny turned to Charmaine, and paused, then revealed:

'She's thinking of having a baby . . .'

'What?!' came Charmaine's incredulous reaction. Jenny laughed.

'That's exactly what I said!'

'What's the matter with that?' Carol asked, looking at the two.

'Oh, nothing . . .' Charmaine assured her, cautious. There was a sly grin on her face. But Jenny wanted to put her point across.

'Hmmm, I wonder what happened to the girl who gave us that big lecture last time about women having too many children?' she said sarcastically, eyes on Charmaine.

'I only have two,' Carol pointed out. 'Anyway, I only said I was thinking about it.'

Charmaine looked at her.

'So, I thought you said you weren't having a relationship?'

'Enh!' Jenny agreed, casting a suggestive glance at her sister, who lay back in her chair.

'Well, yes, but you know how people change their minds sometimes.'

'Yes, we know . . .' Jenny agreed, sardonically.

'What does he say about that?' Charmaine asked.

There was a pause before she answered.

'He doesn't know about it yet.'

'Ugh-ungh!' Jenny exclaimed.

'You're not going to tell him?!' Charmaine asked, alarmed.

'Of course I'm going to tell him,' Carol said. 'Anyway, it's only an idea. The way you two are going on, it's like I'm having it already.'

The 'him' referred to was Carol's boyfriend of just over a year. He didn't live with her, but apparently they had a satisfactory arrangement, and both seemed to like the way things were. He was in the same line of work as Carol, but on the probation side.

'So what about your job?' Charmaine asked.

'I can keep the job, but that's what really got me thinking about that,' Carol replied, thoughtful. She explained that having worked for so long as a social worker, she often felt discouraged about what she was doing. Sometimes, she said, she doubted whether it was wise to refrain from having more children just for her career's sake.

'I don't even know if I want to stay in this line of work,' she admitted.

Charmaine was surprised. 'You're earning all right, aren't you?'

'I'm not complaining about the money. It's just the work itself; it's depressing at times.'

That was something Charmaine wanted to know more about. She had started college part-time and was thinking of studying full-time the next year to become a social worker herself.

'So you don't think it's interesting work?' she asked.

Carol took a sip. 'Yeah, it's interesting, but after a while it makes you feel . . . helpless.'

Charmaine wanted her to explain further. Jenny was listening too.

'It's just not getting any better. There's more and more problems and you end up feeling like you can't really make a difference.'

'So what yuh gonna do?' Jenny asked her.

Carol shrugged. 'I don't know. That's why I'm thinking about this baby.'

'It sound serious,' Jenny remarked.

'Are you going to get married?' Charmaine asked, half-joking.

'No thank you,' Carol said.

'I am married to the kids' father – for all the good it does me.' Then she added, 'We're al'right as we are, I don't want to spoil that . . .'

'So what if he doesn't want a baby?' Jenny asked her sister.

Carol laughed.

'We'll negotiate,' she said, grinning.

Marcus ran in, holding one of his shoes.

'Mum, somebody kicked me,' he told Charmaine.

'Who kicked you, darling?' Carol asked him compassionately.

Charmaine laughed. 'Don't bother with him, he's a troublemaker.'

She put the shoe back on and sent him back out to play.

'So what about you?' Carol asked, switching the focus.

'What do you mean?'

'When you having your next one?'

Charmaine was coy about it. 'Oh, I'm not sure.'

'But you're thinking!' Jenny butted in.

Charmaine didn't protest too hard.

'Well . . . yeah, I can't have just one. Plus, it wouldn't be good for Marcus to grow up as a single child.'

Then Jesse walked in, looked at the three women, stopped by the tray on the table, and turned to his mother.

'Al'right, take a piece then,' she said.

The little boy picked up some cake and walked back out without a word. Carol laughed. 'Ah so him stay?' she asked. Jenny had to admit that the boy had his ways, but he wasn't bad or mischievous like some. Cleverly, she steered the conversation around to a different topic. After Carol had brought some more drinks, she put on a video then one by one the children started to drift in. The evening was winding down, easy. Some of Venetta's friends went home. Tired by all the excitement, Marcus had fallen asleep on the settee. Jesse was sat on Jenny's lap watching television. Charmaine got up to answer the door.

D. walked in, looked at the little boy first, then called out, 'Yaow, Carol, wha' yuh ah seh?!'

'How yuh do, Missa D.?' Carol answered from the kitchen, clowning.

Charmaine sat back and D. dropped himself down on the other side of Marcus.

'So wha'ppen?' He looked at Jenny.

'Nothing.'

D. stretched out his hand and immediately Jesse slid down off his mother's lap and ran to his father. Carol came back in as D. was asking him about the birthday party. As usual, she got into a reasoning with D. That was how she was, especially with D., whom she always enjoyed talking to. The two of them would discuss almost any topic and still end up both satisfied, even though they rarely agreed on anything. Jesse lasted almost another hour before he drifted off to sleep, then both he and Marcus were carried up to the bedroom. Then Carol pronounced that she could beat D. at Ludo 'any time'. It sounded like a challenge, and sure enough D. couldn't resist taking it up. A lively game of Ludo ensued. At the onset, D. left the three women behind, spinning a series of sixes which put him well ahead – then his luck ran out, and three of his pieces were kicked out; hard times. They all got quite passionate about the game. Finally, neither Carol nor D. could win, and Charmaine beat them both. There was another game, then another. D. looked at his watch, amazed to see it was twelve o'clock.

'Wait, me have certain people fe check, y'know?'

'You're just afraid I'm gonna beat you now,' Carol teased.

D. didn't pay her no mind. He badly wanted to win at least that last one and did, declaring himself champion. He got up, teasing Carol. She was the only person who hadn't won a game. D. agreed to drop Charmaine home as well. Carol told her sister that she might as well leave Jesse – she was off work and would keep him until the next day. She loved the little boy as her own. That was OK with Jenny – it meant she wouldn't have to get up too early. Marcus still asleep on D.'s shoulder, he said goodbye and left. Outside it was a sweet, warm, summer-lit moonlit night, when no one seemed to want to stay inside. D. drove to Camden and dropped Charmaine and Marcus off. Jenny studied him closely the rest of the journey.

'You look tired,' she said finally.

'Hmmm, I couldn't sleep good last night.'

She smiled.

'Oh, you have worries?'

The way Jenny had said it, D. couldn't really be sure what she meant. He shook his head, serious.

'Just some vibes,' he said.

Jenny didn't ask any more about it. D. was funny when it came to certain things. She knew that now. Sometimes, he wouldn't answer any questions at all. Those times, he was best left alone. They got home, and D. went to the bedroom and changed. Jenny watched him for a little while then asked:

'Are you going anywhere nice?'

D. finished buttoning up his shirt. He asked, 'Why?'

'Nothing, just asking,' Jenny answered, smiling. As he was checking his face and hair in the mirror, she came behind him and adjusted the back of his shirt collar. He could see Jenny's eyes reflected in the mirror.

'You nah work tomorrow?' he asked.

'Yes.'

'Ohhhh,' he said, turning around.

Jenny didn't move out of the way, she stood there eyeing him.

'But I can start late?'

D. stood her stare for a few seconds. His face straight, he said: 'Come now.' Jenny's eyebrows raised up.

'Really?' she asked.

With the same movements of his eyebrows, imitating her, D. smiled.

'Fe real!'

'I won't be long,' Jenny shouted as she disappeared inside the bathroom.

D. went to the living room, switched on the TV and tried the number in Jamaica again. Still no luck with it. The line was out of order, they said. Jenny reappeared, looking elegant in a two-piece white leather suit and booties. D. gave her an admiring glance.

'I bettah have some bodyguard t'night,' he joked. They stepped out into the street, got in the car and D. headed for Finsbury Park. When he got there, everything was going smoothly. Pablo was keeping things under control. D. went down for a while, talked briefly with a few friends, showed the radiant Jenny around then decided he could safely go about his business. On his way out, he came across Costa standing outside, smoking the end of a spliff. He greeted D. 'How it go, my yout'?'

'Nice yuh know, Don!'

Jenny was waiting as D. stopped. Costa wasn't working tonight.

'Wha' ah gwan?' D. asked curious.

Costa shrugged.

'Nut'n – ah just check out de action.'

Costa wasn't a great talker, but he was a serious, reliable soldier who had proved himself valuable. The previous week, when there had been tension at the club, D. had noticed his resolve and cool disposition in handling the situation.

'Tune in, man! I wan' mek some circles,' D. said to him.

Costa came along. First D. decided to pass by a club which had an early session on Sunday night. He had remembered Sticks talking about it earlier in the week. He hadn't seen his 'lieutenant' for a few days, everybody was busy. After that they could all go and check Rocco's, where a set from New York was guesting. That should·be a ram session! When they arrived at the club, D. saw a good amount of ravers hanging outside, so downstairs had to be pretty hot. He parked on the street adjacent to the high road, they got out and walked back up. Sticks's car was parked half on the pavement just before the junction. They walked down the steps into a cloud of sweaty smoke. The music was pumping, soulish, for the moment. Costa made a way through, and D. and Jenny walked through to a part where the ceiling of the club was shaped like some arches. There they found Soni sitting with a tall glass in her hand, talking with another girl. She told D. he would find Sticks near the set, and he was there all right – D. could see his tall frame leaning against the wall. The crowd looked quite thick around him. After a while, he spotted D. looking at him, acknowledged him with a raised arm and made his way over.

'Yes, D.!' he exclaimed as he emerged from the multitude. He said he'd arrived a little earlier and met a few people. He told D. what he needed to know. While Costa went to get a round of drinks, Jenny mingled with Soni and her friends. She'd met Soni before, briefly, a couple of times at dances. The atmosphere in the relatively small club was stuffy and the music wasn't to D.'s taste. He and Sticks went up the stairs and out on to the pavement, where a sizeable crowd was hanging out.

'What happ'n to Linton?' D. asked.

Sticks laughed, drew from his spliff.

'Linton deh ah country from last week. Him have a t'ing over dere. I talk to him yesterday.'

Three girls passed them, going down to the club. One smiled at D.

'Who dat?'

'One gal from west, she comes to The Spot regular.' The Spot was D.'s gambling place. He had renamed it after taking it over. D. borrowed Sticks's lighter and lit up his smoke. Soni came up the stairs.

'It's too hot down there,' she said. She went to sit on the low wall in front of the pub next door.

'What about Fly, anything?' D. asked. Sticks shook his head.

'Nobody's seen him.'

'Put more people on this. I wan' know whe' him is.' D. thought he was probably still hiding somewhere, knowing that the police were still looking for him as well as the others. He was still hoping the young MC would call Charlie.

'Is not him shoot de guy still,' Sticks remarked.

'Yeah, but yuh know how it go, man. If dem hol' him dem will charge him same way.'

It was getting up to three o'clock, the official closing time, and groups of people had started coming up from the club now, wet from the heat.

'Mek we go check Rocco's,' D. said.

He knew the session there would be hot too. From what he had heard about the visiting sound, they was supposed to 'tek life'. Jenny soon came up, wiping her brow with a handkerchief. Sticks signalled to Costa, who was talking to a man further up the road. They all went to the cars, D. in front with his arm around Jenny's shoulders, Sticks and Soni walking a little way behind. Costa brought up the rear, finishing his beer. Noisily the other ravers were also leaving, laughing and calling out to each other. D. and Jenny were almost by Sticks's car, they slowed down. Fifty yards down the road a dark car was parked under some trees. It started to pull away from the kerb, lights off.

'Me have a yout' ah run a cassette from the session at Rocco's yuh know?' Sticks called out to D.

D. turned around, Jenny stopped. It was Costa who first realized what was happening. The dark car was coming down, fast, too fast, and still without lights. The soldier froze as he watched it picking up speed as it came towards them in the middle of the road.

Jenny was in front, D. next to her with his back to the

road and the car was almost level with them now. Sticks had his keys out and was opening the driver's door of the Saab, with Soni by his side.

When the powerful full-beam lights of the oncoming car suddenly came on, dazzling them, Costa reacted instinctively. Tossing away his bottle, he dashed past Sticks and Soni to D. Sticks was facing the road now, watching the bright lights coming up.

Costa shouted, but what he said was lost in the roar of the engine. He slammed into D., arms outstretched, pushing him away from the front of the Saab and into the space between it and the next parked car. Jenny stumbled and fell as the soldier brought D. to the ground.

Sticks realized something was wrong and went to take cover, then saw that Soni hadn't moved. She was stood there against the Saab, blinded by the light, one hand over her eyes. Sticks grabbed her arm as the car passed them.

A loud bang echoed in the night all around them.

D. got back up in time to see the car race away across the junction, narrowly missing traffic coming through from the other direction – and then saw Sticks leaning back against his car. As he looked, Sticks slowly slid down the side of the car.

D. tried to hold him up. He knelt down, supporting the youth. The whole right side of Sticks's white linen shirt was wet with blood. Soni was still standing against the car, silent, shaking, her eyes wide open. Blood ran down the left side of her face on to her neck. Costa stood watching D. as he laid Sticks on the road.

Jenny had got back up too. She was limping from where she had hit the pavement. After what seemed to all of them like a long time, she was the first to speak.

'Oh my God.'

She went to Soni, put her arms around her, and carefully sat the girl down on the pavement. People were walking up the road to find out what had happened. A light came on in the top window of a house opposite. Two young guys who had been at the club looked down at Sticks lying on the ground.

D. was looking down into his friend's face, calling his name, but Sticks's eyes were closed, and it looked like he had been hit bad. Pellets had penetrated his whole right side, cutting him to shreds from the shoulder downwards.

More people started to gather. D. didn't notice them. He cradled Sticks's head in his arms and stared at the youth's face – he looked peaceful, almost as if he was sleeping.

Once again Costa was a step ahead of everyone else. He recovered quickly.

'Don, yuh cyan 'tan yah,' he called out. D. didn't look up at him, he just knelt there in the warm night, staring into Sticks's still face. Jenny was still holding Soni; it was hard to tell if she'd been hit. The blood on her face could have been Sticks's. They heard the sound of police sirens.

'D., we ha'fe lef him, police soon come,' Costa insisted, shaking D.'s shoulder. D. looked up at him blankly.

'Come, den we'll carry ah hospital,' the soldier said sombrely. D. looked at Sticks again then gently took his arm from under the youth's head. He started to get up, then leaned over, took Sticks's gun from the waist of his pants and pushed it discreetly into his own pocket. The noise of the sirens was getting louder. Jenny came up to him as he got up, her eyes full of tears, her face drawn.

'D., we ha'fe go, now!' Costa called out.

Jenny understood what the soldier was saying and put her hand on D.'s arm. Wiping tears from her cheeks, she told him: 'Go, I'll stay wid him.'

D. looked at his woman, then at the body on the ground. Jenny pushed him away and he followed Costa, running the rest of the way down the street to the car. Costa took the keys from him and quickly reversed the car to the end of the street. As they pulled away, D. saw flashing blue lights illuminate the crowd surrounding the Saab. Costa put his foot down, then had to pull over to the left to make way for two more police cars racing to the scene of the crime.

PAUSE

The light from the flame was gently dancing on the wall. The candle had burned down while the sleeping woman was slouched on the table, her head resting on her arms, dreaming of some other time, some other place.

Outside it was still raining hard. From time to time, a series of lightning flashes lit up the room.

The woman moaned and stirred slightly. Her eyes flicked open then closed again before she finally woke up fully. Slowly, she raised herself from the table and leaned back in her chair, rubbing the back of her neck. For a moment she was held captive by her dreams then the dancing flame in front of her caught her eyes. Everything came back to her. The cake was there, untouched. Five small candles stood unlit around the big one, which had burned through half its length.

Lorna stared at the flame for a while, images spinning in her head. Almost against her will, she leaned forward and, through her dry lips, managed to blow out the flame. In the dark, silent room, she got up and glanced at the time displayed on the front of the video recorder: sixteen minutes after three. Wearily, she took a few steps and let herself down on to the sofa. She stretched and rubbed her eyes. She had meant to stay awake, hoping that she would soon hear the familiar sound of the key opening the front door . . . waiting up for her son to come home, tonight of all nights . . .

But again she had slept and again she had woken up

306

alone in the silence. Nine days and nine nights of hope and despair, spent praying that Harry would come back safe.

She had hoped so much that he would come home tonight, on his birthday, and end her torment. She had rushed home from work, cooked, set the table and put out the cake with the candles on it, and dressed up. Then she had waited, and waited . . .

Every time the phone had rung she had practically jumped out of her skin. Along with the fear, the dread of hearing the voice of a police officer at the other end of the line, there was the hope, the almost painful hope that Harry would call her name down the line, and blow life back into her tortured soul. But there was only one call, from a friend, who Lorna hardly had the heart to speak to. Sleep brought relief, but cruel reality returned with her first moments of wakefulness. Tonight she had looked back over the life of her younger son, dwelling for as long as she could bear on the blissful days after she had given him birth fifteen years ago. How she had loved him, that tiny baby with the deep dark eyes. Lorna wasn't exactly a regular churchgoer, but she had faith and she always prayed in her own way. After Harry had been gone for three days she had dropped to her knees, with tears streaming down her face, and asked God why He would allow her to be hurt again. Deep inside herself, she refused to believe that she could lose Harry so soon after she had lost Tyrone . . .

Eyes wide open in the darkness, Lorna tried once again to think positive. Today, surely, she would hear from her son. And no matter how much trouble he was in, as long as he was safe she would cope. Being the youngest of the family, Harry had always been a little wild. He had got into fights at school, often neglected his work and had to be disciplined quite often, but most boys his age went through that – and everything had been more or less under control until Tyrone had died. Lorna took a deep breath and forced herself to stop thinking. There was no point in going over the whole story once more, as she had done almost every night since Harry had gone. Tyrone was dead, and nothing could change that. Harry was all that she had left to live for, and Lorna clung to his memory with all the strength of a mother. He would come back today, she told herself firmly. The video clock told her she only had about three more hours before daylight came and another grim working day began. Lorna closed her eyes.